# TWISTED ROADS

# TWISTED ROADS

## TRAVIS ERWIN

For information contact; Barbadum Books

www.BarbadumBooks.com

Cover Art and Design by LoudMouth Visual Works

Cover Model Jostlynn Plums

ISBN: 978-1-934606-49-0

Second Edition: April 2017

10 9 8 7 6 5 4 3 2

# DEDICATED TO

... the musicians, singers, and songwriters out traversing the twisted roads in pursuit of their dreams.

# 1



Lucas Cahill had never spent a great deal of time pondering death. Being an eternal optimist, he refused to dwell on the finality of life — any life. Way he saw it, death was nothing more than a change, and unlike some, Lucas did not fear change. Actually, he embraced change, hoped for change, even encouraged change when need be. Then again, he was only thirty-four. Maybe when he was older and the idea of death felt more tangible, maybe then, he would come to fear the inevitability of its arrival.

Flat on his back, he stared up at the moth, struggling in one of the many spiderwebs gathered in the wood rafters of his garage, and wondered if the insect realized change was at hand. Others might find the scene morose, but spiders had to eat too.

The circle of life. One thing giving way to another.

You could call it death, or you could call it change. Either way, it was inevitable. Laying there beneath the flickering fluorescent light in the backseat of the Cadillac convertible, Lucas chose to remain positive. He'd spent most of the night thinking about her. About what tomorrow might bring. The moth provided a welcome distraction.

Maybe he could write a song, use the spiderweb and the moth as a metaphor. His Martin guitar sat propped up in the front seat of the convertible, the neck reachable from where he lay, but Lucas remained in the same position he'd been in for the better part of an hour: reclined, with his arms folded across his chest. The front seat had more room, but hoping for musical inspiration, Lucas stretched out in the backseat as he had every night for a week now. So far that hope, like most of his others, had been denied.

After doing most of the restoration himself, he'd sent the car's seats off to Amarillo for the upholstery work. Last week he bolted them back in place, and he'd spent hours out here with his Martin D-28 every night since. The sun would be up in an hour or so, meaning once again, Hank's ghost had failed to appear. Of course, this wasn't the actual car Hank Williams took his last breath in. Same make, model, and color—but that particular '52 Caddy was on display in a museum in Montgomery, Alabama, whereas Lucas Cahill's garage sat in the small town of Grand, Texas.

At six-three, Lucas was taller than Hank Williams, so his feet stuck up on the side door when he stretched out.

Up above, the moth fluttered a few more times and finally escaped the spiderweb.

There went his metaphor, at least for the song he had in mind. He'd written a shithouse full of songs about her these last sixteen years. Some with metaphors, others nothing but the stark truth. Both were simply about loving what he couldn't have.

He'd yet to sing any of them for her. That would change soon—maybe today.

The hinge on the back gate creaked, and the crickets stopped chirping. Lucas didn't need to sit up to know the identity of his visitor. Sometimes she snuck up on him, but not today.

"Morning, Abby."

"Saw the light from my kitchen, so I brought you some

coffee."

He sat up. Last thing he wanted was Abby handing him the cup while he was inside the Caddy. The seats were black leather with baby blue piping, and he didn't want to chance a single blemish.

Abby DeWitt was dressed in her work clothes—a knee-length black skirt and white button-up shirt. As usual, one button too many had been left undone. Later, if he swung by the Whirlwind Café before opening up the Oasis, she would have her ample cleavage hidden, but Abby never failed to let the girls breathe when she visited Lucas. He owned the bar smack across the street from her employer, but as both neighbors and classmates, he and Abby had always swam in the same fishbowl.

Getting out of the Cadillac, he reached for the offered mug, letting his eyes linger on Abby's pale skin, mostly because that's what she expected.

"So, is it ready to drive?" Abby ran her hand over the car's bold curves. "I'm eager for that ride you've been promising me all these years."

He took a sip. "Good coffee, Abby. Nobody serves it up hot and steamy like you." He enjoyed the game they played, even though their banter was more than a game for her.

"The seats look nice. Can I sit in it?"

Lucas nodded and opened the passenger door. "Watch out for my guitar."

She winked. "I'm not interested in the front seat. I want to try out the backseat." Abby reclined exactly there with her knees up and her legs parted, giving Lucas an unimpeded view of her purple panties.

He took another sip of coffee. Abby DeWitt had been flashing him since ninth grade, so this wasn't anything he hadn't seen before. Someday he would give her that ride, though not the one she wanted.

He pointed at his watch. "You're gonna be late opening up if you don't hurry. Big day. Y'all might be busy."

Abby sat up, not a bit fazed he'd once again ignored her overt attempt to gain his attention. "You think that skank will show?"

He pretended to ponder the question, even though he already knew the answer. Draining the last of the coffee, he said, "Yeah, she'll be here. And both of our places will be full of people gossiping all about her."

"Oh, I hope so." Abby stepped away from the Caddy. "We need some excitement around here." She winked and brushed the dark, wavy curls away from Lucas's eyes. "And since you won't provide me any, I'll have to settle for the return of Angela Ross."

Abby took the empty mug and strolled toward the garage door. Lucas waited until just before she stepped out into the purple predawn light before calling to her. "Hey, Abby!"

She turned.

He flashed a dimpled grin. "The purple ones are my favorite.


Angela Ross lifted her foot from the gas pedal. The duct tape covering the inch-wide gap above the passenger window flapped in the wind, but for the first time in over a thousand miles, the noise didn't slap at her nerves. A couple miles of barren highway and few hundred acres of flat rangeland were all that separated Angela from Grand, Texas.

The sight of the town, rising up from the flat horizon, churned her stomach.

From this distance, and in the silhouetted light of dawn, Grand conjured thoughts of an oversized grave site. A dingy, off-white grain elevator loomed over the northern end of the settlement like a tombstone while the trees and smaller buildings resembled a mound of freshly dug earth.

The dull beige water tower came into focus as she neared. Painted in an arc over a growling cougar were the years of the football team's six state titles, none of which had occurred in the sixteen years since she fled. That kind of dry spell might have finally gotten Coach Harvester fired, or at least Angela hoped. It was September, that time of year when the current Cougar squad was the talk of the town, and last thing Angela wanted to hear was people extolling the genius of longtime coach, Waylon Harvester.

His hold on this town had been nearly as firm as his hands on her ass, but whereas the citizens of Grand showed unwavering patience for the man's off-the-field transgressions, they wouldn't share the same tolerance for losing teams.

The city limit sign came into view: **Grand, Texas Pop. 1972.**

"God help me." The highway led her right down Main Street.

The town had changed in her absence. A flashing caution replaced the single streetlight that once upon a time directed traffic in and out of the grain elevator. Yellow, waist-high weeds surrounded the concrete structure. Her father had died beneath an avalanche of grain within those very walls. Passing the structure, she nodded with revengeful satisfaction at its obvious abandonment.

Plywood windows and faded, weather-beaten signs adorned most of the business fronts along Main. The canopy above the old gas station's pumps had collapsed, and the glass had been knocked out of all but one of the garage doors. Frozen in time, the rusted sign listed regular unleaded for eighty-eight cents a gallon.

The decay reinforced her belief that nothing thrived in

a town like this, although the stench of manure drifting through the vents made it clear the feedlot south of town still housed thousands of cattle ready for slaughter, and both the Whirlwind Café and the Oasis appeared operational. People had to eat, she supposed, and no one survived such desolation without the solace of booze.

Despite seventeen straight hours at the wheel and the eleven hundred miles of pavement behind her, Angela itched to keep going, to drive straight through Grand and never look back.

But she couldn't do that. Not before the miserable task that brought her back was over. Not before she righted her wrongs. Not before she claimed what was hers.

# 2

Shelly Sampson scrutinized herself in the small compact mirror. One gray hair stood out among all the perfectly arranged black. Checking to make sure no one was watching, she plucked the offensive strand before snapping the case shut.

She felt foolish sitting in this parking lot by herself, but her only other choice was to enter the café without her friends, and that meant engaging Abby DeWitt in conversation. Today promised to be stressful enough without playing nice and listening to endless babble about Lucas or whatever stale town gossip the waitress had happened to overhear. Gabby Abby was too low on Grand's social hierarchy to know the newest or latest word on anything, and Shelly needed firsthand knowledge, not secondhand reports of last week's news.

The clock on the dashboard read seven minutes past eight. Both Charlene and Misty were late. It wasn't like Misty, but then again, this damn funeral had everything fouled up.

The three high school friends had met for lunch at the Whirlwind Café every Monday for better than a decade, but Elizabeth Ross's death screwed up their routine, forcing them to have breakfast instead. She wished they had scheduled the crazy old woman's services for the afternoon. Shelly hated changing her plans.

Checking her watch for the umpteenth time, she decided to go inside. She couldn't sit out here all day, not by herself. Someone would see her and wonder why she didn't go on in, and Shelly didn't like giving folks call to start wondering about her motivations.

The wind tugged at her hair as she started across the gravel parking lot, and her high heels dug into the small rocks. It was a struggle to look decent in this environment, but smiling at her reflection in the diner's glass door, Shelly took pride in the fact she did a better job than most.

The cowbell tied to the front door clanged with her entrance. The aroma of bacon grease and coffee filled the air. The group of old men along the worn, horrendously yellow counter turned and nodded hellos before returning to their stories of the good ol' days. Nothing had changed in this place since it opened. Shelly couldn't even say when that was; it had been here all her life.

"Morning, Shell." Abby waved as she waddled out from behind the register. "You're awful early this morning."

Abby wouldn't walk like a penguin if she'd stop wearing her skirts too tight. Shelly gave the waitress an obligatory hug but was careful to avoid her left shoulder where a grease stain darkened the white material. "The funeral is at eleven, so we decided to come early for a bite."

"Yeah, me and Lucas talked about that this morning over coffee. He likes it when I take him a mug before I open up."

Shelly didn't respond. She never did when Abby tittered on about Lucas, though Shelly often teased him about his chubby girlfriend, but only because Shelly knew she was the only woman Lucas had eyes for.

"I sure would like to be in that church to see what happens, but Frank wants me to stay and keep the place open.

Don't know why. The whole town will be there." The waitress smacked her gum. "Think she'll show?"

"Who?" Shelly played dumb, hoping to avoid another round of talk about Angela Ross.

"Angela. Who else?"

"Don't know. Don't care. I have better things to wonder about than Angela Ross."

"Damn! It's too dang early for this shit." Charlene's slow Texas drawl filled the room the instant she banged through the door. The wind had whipped her red hair into a tangled mess, but she didn't even seem to notice.

Abby blew a bubble. "What do you think, Charlene? Angela gonna show?"

Charlene shot Shelly a look before addressing the other woman. "How about traipsing your butt back to the kitchen and getting me some coffee? I need my caffeine."

The waitress shuffled away, looking dejected.

Shelly smiled a thank you as the two friends moved to their regular booth near the window.

"Gossiping with Gabby Abby? You desperate for conversation or what?" Charlene withdrew a pick from her purse and stabbed at the brassy, dyed snarls on her head. An inch of duller red roots hung close to her scalp.

Shelly rolled her eyes. "If you'd been here on time, I wouldn't have had to. But since neither you nor Misty were here, she threw her arms around me the second I hit the door."

"She's damn sure clingy. Been that way since high school. That's why she can't keep a man." The redhead lit a cigarette.

A thin furl of smoked drifted upward. Shelly did not point out her friend's five divorces over the last fifteen years.

"Here's your coffee." Abby placed a black mug on the table. White porcelain showed along the cup's chipped rim. "What y'all think? She gonna show or not?"

"Nope"—Charlene flicked ashes onto the floor—"That whore wouldn't dare show her face in this town again."

Shelly spied Misty's minivan turning into the parking lot. The last of their trio got out and hurried inside.

The waitress leaned down close to the table. "I heard she died of AIDS."

Shelly clinched her jaws. She couldn't stand to listen to any more talk about Angela. "Abby, we've all heard the rumors—she died of AIDS; she's a prostitute in Dallas; so-and-so saw her stripping in Vegas. I couldn't care less what became of that tramp. But I do know if she gave two hoots about her grandmother, she would've come back long before now."

"Well, Lucas thinks she'll be here," the waitress sniped before retreating.

The cowbell on the door clanged with Misty's arrival. Shelly hoped the conversation would now turn away from Angela Ross. Misty never wanted to engage in town gossip.

"You're late." Charlene stood to allow their friend to scoot into the booth.

"I know, I know. I tried to get here on time, but I had to get my girls off to school, and then my dad called just as I headed out the door." The late arriver fanned at the cloud of smoke hanging above their booth.

Charlene snapped her fingers and gestured for Abby to return. "Let's order. I'm hungry enough to eat the ass-end of a dead skunk."

The trio had been friends since high school, and while Shelly considered herself the unspoken leader of the group, she rarely challenged Charlene's crudeness out of fear of her friend's willingness to say whatever popped into her mind.

Shelly managed to get through the meal without further mention of Angela, and if she could survive this funeral without her rival showing, maybe, just maybe, the ghosts of the past would vanish once and for all.

They'd just finished their breakfast when Abby brought the bill and placed the slip on the edge of the table. Charlene picked up the paper, looked at the total, and set it back down. "Can you cover me, Shell? I left my purse at home."

Shelly pulled out her credit card.

Charlene's unemployment checks were coming to an end, and without a steady income or an impending groom, her friend was likely to be short for some time to come. Misty never had much money, either, but she possessed too much pride to ask for charity, so Shelly handed the card and ticket to Abby.

"I don't have any cash, so I'll take care of both of y'alls and one of you can get mine next time." That next time would never come, but Shelly didn't mind. If Angela did show, Shelly wanted her friends to remember who took care of them—who had been there for them all these years.

Signing the receipt, she made certain to add in an ample tip for Abby. Not necessarily for the service, but Shelly didn't want anyone to say, or think, she was cheap or hurting for money. The Sampson name carried a certain reputation, a reputation she'd worked hard to cultivate.

Jake and his dad weren't the only farmers in the family, but Shelly considered her crop way more important than any of theirs. You could survive a year or two of poor harvest, but in a town like Grand, you had to protect your reputation at all cost.

# 3

Angela stood between the rows of wooden pews and stared at the mauve metallic casket. The sweet, pungent scent of cut flowers permeated the air. A prism of color from the stained glass windows sparkled against the burgundy carpet.

Slowly, she covered the distance to the open coffin until she could almost touch the body. The sight of her grandmother's face squeezed the oxygen from Angela's lungs. She leaned her trembling body against the pulpit for support as tears of sorrow and regret blurred her vision.

Blinking, she focused on the lifeless form. Relief enveloped her like a soft veil. This was not the troubled face she had expected—had feared.

Elizabeth Ross lived in a perpetual state of emotional pain for many years, and her features had always been pinched and tight from the strain, but the ever-present lines of worry were now gone. The tense muscles that once accentuated her jawline had relaxed. With the weight of the town's suspicion lifted, Angela spied a hint of her granny's once youthful beauty. If only she could remove the burden of guilt from her own slender shoulders.

Reaching out, her fingertips caressed Elizabeth's cheek. She whispered, "I'm sorry. I should've explained why I had to leave." She leaned her forehead against the cool edge of the casket. "I never meant to hurt you when I ran out of this town."

Moisture spilled from her eyes. "I left you here, in this place. Alone." Angela's body shook. "I'm sorry."

A hand gripped her shoulder, jolting Angela from grief to anger. Twisting around to confront the intruder who dared invade her pain, she melted at the sight of the weathered old man.

"Oh, L.J." She wrapped her arms around his scarecrow frame.

Angela clung to him until her tears dampened his flannel shirt, until her sobs ceased. He smelled of tobacco and booze. Just as he always had.

Minutes passed before she finally raised her chin and looked at her grandmother again. The task was easier this time.

"Don't feel bad for leaving." L.J.'s gravel voice cut the silence. "She was glad you did."

Angela turned toward him. "She was?"

He nodded. "Claimed she should've left back when she had the chance."

"What chance?"

L.J. didn't answer. His face took on a distant look. Physically, he'd always appeared old to her eyes, but in the past his spirit seemed spry and mischievous, which had lent a youthful spirit to him. Now, he looked every bit of his seventy plus years, as if all of Elizabeth's burdens had settled upon his back.

"I don't know why anybody stays in this town." Bitterness crept into her voice.

He stared with one brow cocked. "I left once. Didn't change a thing. No matter how many miles I put between me and this place, I never managed to forget where I came from. Or who I left behind." His dull gray eyes bored into her.

Squirming beneath the insinuation as well as his steady

gaze, she pointed at her grandmother to redirect the conversation. "She looks happier now."

The old man rubbed the salt-and-pepper stubble on his chin. "I reckon she is. For Elizabeth, dying was easier than living."

Angela melted at the sadness in his rough voice. "You always did love her." She reached for his hand. "I'm sorry. This has to be just as hard for you."

"I did love her." His Adam's apple bobbed below his whiskered chin. "But that was never enough for either of us." He turned and focused on the stained glass windows for a heartbeat before proceeding back up the aisle.

"Why didn't she ever contact me?" Angela said.

He stopped just shy of the exit. "How could she? She never knew where you went."

The church doors clicked shut behind him.

Angela stared across the empty sanctuary. If her grandma never knew where she went, how on earth had the lawyer handling the estate found her so fast?


Shelly convinced Charlene and Misty to leave their vehicles at the Whirlwind so the three of them could drive over to the church together.

"Is Jake coming?" Misty asked from the backseat.

Coming from anyone else, Shelly would've taken the question as a snide jab, but Misty was too naïve, too forgiving to purposely bring up past transgression. "No, they started the corn harvest today. What about Mark?" Shelly deflected the conversation away from her husband. She tried not to speak about Jake too much, even with her friends. Let the entire town keep on thinking of them as the perfect couple—homecoming queen and king. So what if that was sixteen years ago?

"No, Mark couldn't get off work," Misty said.

"Jesus!" Charlene pointed at the church parking lot as they rounded the corner. "I didn't know there were this many cars in Grand."

The crowd forced Shelly to park along the street a full block and a half away. She shook her head as the trio hurried down the sidewalk, past Opal Jenkins gorgeous snowball bush, past the Potter's shameful, dandelion-infested yard, and past Tate Kincaide's house, which badly needed a fresh coat of paint. Of course, the old fool spent half of his Social Security check on lottery tickets, so chances were he couldn't afford even a gallon of paint.

"This is ridiculous," Shelly said. "People in this town are too nosy. No one would be at this funeral if they weren't afraid they might miss something."

Charlene snorted. "I sure as hell wouldn't have drug my ass out of bed otherwise."

"That's an awful thing to say." Misty glanced around nervously. "And watch your language, before somebody tells my dad we were out here cussing."

Shelly nodded and smiled as they passed a knot of elderly women huddled in a gossip circle, but Misty's warning only incited Charlene.

"Crap on a crutch, Misty." Charlene rolled her eyes. "Preachers' daughters are supposed to be wild. You're thirty-four years old and still worried what Daddy will say." A devilish grin spread across her face. "Besides, I only said 'ass,' not something bad like 'GODDAMN!'" She raised her voice loud enough for the offensive word to turn heads.

"Stop. Y'all are giving me a headache." Shelly rubbed her temples.

"Ain't us giving you the headache," Charlene said.

Shelly glared. "What's that supposed to mean?"

The redhead stopped to light another cigarette. "Means

you're touchier than a sore-assed bear because there's a chance Angela will show."

"And why would that bother me?" Shelly tried to sound unconcerned, but the raw nerves churning in her gut made the words sound feeble.

"Give it a rest," Charlene puffed. "We all remember what that tramp did. But Jake married you. You won, Shell."

Won? Won what? Jake? Yeah, she'd taken the prize—a third rate husband with no ambition, a marriage without romance, and a life devoid of excitement.

Charlene exhaled a cloud of smoke before adding, "Besides, you're getting all worked up for nothing." Charlene took up her march again, her three-inch heels clicking against the pavement. "That bitch will never show her face around here."

Misty cleared her throat as they reached the steps of the church. "She's already here."

"What?" The other two spoke in unison.

"She drove in early this morning. My dad called and told me. That's why I was late to breakfast."

Shelly felt the color drain from her face. This could not be happening.

"And you're just now telling us?" Charlene grimaced and flicked a butt into the bushes. "What the hell's wrong with you?"

"I didn't think it was important."

"Oh, hell no! Why would it be? The one slut that fucked over all three of us sashays back to town every frigging week." Charlene waved her arms like a revivalist seeking salvation.

Misty frowned. "We shouldn't call her a slut. And please don't cuss. At least not so loud."

Shelly narrowed her eyes. "What should we call her?"

"Yeah, what do you call a skank who screws your husband?"

Misty cringed. "Me and Mark weren't married then. It was high school. We were all kids."

Shelly shook her head in disbelief. Misty gave everyone the benefit of the doubt, but there was no doubting Angela's actions.

"And what about my nose? She damn sure broke it." Charlene pointed at the bump, still visible after a decade and a half.

"But you started the fight." Misty fidgeted with her hands.

"And how are you going to defend Angela trying to break up Shelly and Jake?"

"I'm not defending anyone, but—"

Shelly put her hand up to stop the conversation. She leaned in close to her friends so only they could hear before speaking. "Either you stand beside us, or you stand against us, Misty. There's no room for 'buts,' and there's no room for Angela Ross."

# 4

Through the thin walls of the children's Sunday school room, the murmur of voices in the sanctuary reminded Angela of a swarm of bees—no, flies. Bees were too good for that group. Bees fed on the nectar of flowers, whereas the citizens of Grand thrived on filth and garbage.

The preacher claimed family members always waited in this room, but Angela wondered if he simply wanted to keep her hidden. Given the trouble she'd caused his daughter, he could've told her to wait out by the dumpster, and she wouldn't have blamed him.

Of all her past mistakes, Angela regretted betraying Misty the most. She should have listened to her friend's advice back then—but no, she had to prove her independence. The worst part was Mark never even interested her. Then again, neither had most of the others.

Angela wanted to shake her mental anguish, but her every sense and emotion shackled her to the past. Being in this room did not help. Crayoned artwork of Jonah and the whale adorned the bulletin board. A collection of papier-mâché creations emitted a pasty smell. Hundreds of tiny handprints occupied one wall under the words, *Jesus Loves Me.*

All of it linked Angela to her childhood.

As a young girl, she'd sat at one of these half-sized desks and colored pictures and created all sorts of crafts. She'd even dipped her hand in paint and plastered her palm to the joy wall. Then, her mom up and left, taking every bit of her father's joy with her. Angela hadn't understood what it all meant, not at first. But as her father sank deeper into despair, he went away from her, then he left her for good. Intentional or not, his death marked the end of her childhood.

Angela stared at the wall. Somewhere in that mosaic of greens, reds, and blues was a tiny imprint of her hand. What she wouldn't give to go back to that day and start over. Her father was dead, and nobody knew where her mother had gone. Now, her granny was gone too. She squinted to fight back another deluge of tears.

"The preacher said I'd find you in here." L.J. stood in the doorway. An ill-fitting navy suit hung from his shoulders.

Twice now he'd shown up when she started crying. But even in her youth, he'd always been there in times of need.

Angela motioned him in. "Have a seat."

"Kinda figured you might want some company, and I sure didn't want to perch out there with all those old hens."

Angela forced a grin, but L.J. never saw it. He sat down and leaned forward, resting his forearms atop his knees. His bony frame rose and fell with each breath. She'd lost the last member of her family, and he'd lost the woman he loved. He deserved better, even if she did not.

The preacher stuck his head in the room. "It's time."

Shelly stared ahead in stony silence, despite Charlene's constant yammering. The ramifications of Angela's reappearance consumed her. The past should remain buried, but Angela's arrival represented a shovel. With her return, the townspeople could not help but dig into their memories, and Shelly feared what would resurface.

"Here they come." Charlene nudged her friends with her elbows.

Shelly bit her lip and stared at the procession. She heard the air being sucked out of the room as everyone spotted Angela.

"What the hell is L.J. doing with her? He ain't family."

Two old ladies turned and frowned, but Charlene didn't notice. She leaned forward as if the entire scene was a play put on for her entertainment.

Angela walked to the pew on the first row and sat without so much as a sideways glance at the crowd. Shelly had hoped the years would have been unkind to her rival, but as with everything else about the day, disappointment reigned. Angela looked as good, or better, than the day she disappeared. Her bright blond hair just touched the top of her shoulders, and her black dress did nothing to hide her still-lithe figure.

Preacher Malloy spoke about death as a new beginning and not an end. He rattled on about Mrs. Ross's commitment to God and the church, but Shelly paid little attention to the sermon. She had far more dire things to worry over than Crazy Lady Ross's place in the afterlife.

# 5

Angela concentrated on the preacher's words while feeling the singe of the townspeople's burning stares at the back of her neck. Aware she'd been holding her breath, she inhaled and listened to the eulogy.

"Death is not the end as we know it, but the beginning." The minister gripped the sides of the pulpit and scanned the faces.

His eyes locked on Angela's before continuing. "Our life is merely a vessel to transport us to the great reward. Our every decision and activity should reflect that goal. Elizabeth Eleanor Ross lived in such a manner. She believed in a better tomorrow. She believed in our Lord as her savior. She believed in her place in heaven." His volume increased with each sentence.

Angela met his stare, but she couldn't read the intent behind the words. Was he trying to say the future would be better—or that a sinner like her would never visit heaven?

The vice of righteousness squeezed the air from her lungs, and the town's critical eyes pushed from behind while the preacher's gaze bore down from the front.

Defiance and resentment swelled within her. These hypocrites would not intimidate her. Their high-and-mighty attitudes had exiled her once, but she refused to let them bully her again. When she left this time, the departure would be under her own terms—with no regrets and for damn sure, no tears.

Angela quit listening to the preacher. She did not need him to verify her grandmother's place in heaven. Besides, no one in Grand had ever uttered a good word about the Ross family after her grandpa's untimely death. Rumor placed the blame on Elizabeth's shoulders, and the family had been looked down upon ever since.

The story claimed Elizabeth and her husband, Ansel, got into a fight at the annual Fourth of July celebration. According to legend, she looked her husband in the eye and boldly told him out loud to drop dead and die. The declaration must have seemed harmless enough that night, but when Ansel collapsed in the middle of church service the very next morning, everything changed.

A hardworking, seemingly fit farmer, gone at thirty-six. Nobody believed the official listed cause. Heart attack. Everyone whispered she'd poisoned him, or hexed him—cast an evil spell.

The incident happened years before Angela's birth, and her grandmother refused to speak of it, but the kids at school relished telling the story they'd heard from their parents. The tale forever labeled Elizabeth Ross as crazy, as a witch, a murderer. And as a result, Elizabeth Ross spent the rest of her days cowering from the town's scrutiny, afraid to do anything that might raise the town's collective brows.

Reared under the fearful eye of her grandmother, Angela went another direction. She'd done her very best to shock the town's morals at every opportunity, and what a job she had done.

Gripped by memories, she did not realize the preacher had wrapped up his eulogy until L.J. stood to greet the line of mourners—or, more fittingly, curiosity seekers.

A plump woman with rosy jowls and a vaguely familiar face shook his hand and stepped close to Angela, bearing an eager expression.

The idea of cordially thanking these hypocrites sickened her, but she wasn't about to give them the show they desired by turning her back and walking out.

"Sorry about your grandmother. She was a sweet lady."

Angela bit her lip. This woman did not know the first thing about Elizabeth Ross. Except for L.J., none of these people did.

She received condolences from what seemed like the whole town, and to her surprise detected genuine sympathy from a few. Maybe she'd been wrong. Maybe more people cared than she wanted to admit. Maybe Grand had changed these last sixteen years.

The maybes vanished the instant she looked at the next person in line.

Contempt, not compassion, flickered openly on Shelly's perfectly made-up face. Not everyone had forgotten—or forgiven.

Angela nodded at her former classmate. "Thanks for coming."

Shelly leaned in close to whisper, "I didn't come for you." She stepped back, smiled sweetly, and raised her voice. "It was so nice to see you again." Syrup dripped from the words.

"Well, look who the cat dug up."

Angela knew the source of the slow drawl before she turned her head. Some voices you never forget. Besides, Charlene never had strayed far from Shelly.

"Wow! Look at your nose. That thing never went away, huh?" Angela feigned surprise. "I still feel horrible about that."

"Yeah, I bet. When are you leaving?"

Angela gave her credit. Charlene didn't beat around the bush, nor did she care who heard her thoughts.

"Leave? Haven't you heard? I decided to move back for good."

"Don't get cute. No one wants you here."

"Thanks for your concern, but you better hurry, Shelly might get away."

The redhead opened her mouth but rolled her eyes and walked away without spitting out a reply. Angela greeted another handful of people before finally finding herself face-to-face with the last person in line. Misty stood blinking her big, brown doe eyes. Silence separated the two one-time friends until L.J. followed the other mourners out of the sanctuary, leaving them alone.

"I'm real sorry about your grandmother." Misty dabbed at her lashes with a soggy tissue.

"Don't be. She's better off."

"Was she in pain?"

"Yeah. Her entire adult life." Angela stifled the anger she possessed for this town and its unwavering scrutiny. Misty wasn't to blame for any of that.

Misty frowned. "She still attended church regular."

"She hid it well." Angela offered no further explanation.

She sensed the other woman wanted to say more but struggled to find the words. Misty stared at her shoe tops.

"Thanks for coming. It's good to see you again." Angela also wanted to say more, but this didn't seem like the time or place.

"You too. Is there anything I can do? I know this must be hard." An expression of genuine empathy graced Misty's face.

"I don't think so. It's all kind of surreal right now." This time Angela looked down. "I would like to see you again before I leave. There are some things I need to say."

Misty sighed, as if acknowledging the need to clear old hurts from her memory as well.

"I should be here a few days before I leave again," Angela explained.

"Okay. I'll drop by later. You at your grandmother's?"

Angela nodded. She didn't want to stay there alongside the ghosts of her mistakes, but with little cash, she had no choice.

"Okay, see you then." Misty gave her a motherly pat as she walked away.

Alone with the coffin, her regrets, and the promise of more emotional turmoil, Angela bowed her head and sobbed.

It was too early to jack off. Wasn't even lunchtime yet, but Jake Sampson knew there was no other way to get rid of the hard-on he'd had since sunup.

Sometimes it seemed like he'd spent half his life in this tractor, pulling both this damn grain cart and, in turn, his pecker. It didn't matter that he was thirty-fucking-four. The routine was the same as it had been back when he was a sixteen-year-old kid with a handful of hard dick and a head full of stupid ideas.

Hurry up and wait. And don't fuck up.

He'd learned as a teenager how to keep one eye on the combine and one on the *Penthouse* positioned just right against the steering wheel. Back in high school, he'd rub one out three or four times a day, but these days he had to pace himself, despite the fact his dick was preconditioned to always be at-the-ready. Screw those little blue pills; the rumble of a John Deere 4850 and rattle of a grain cart was better than any damn pill, especially with the chance of Angela Ross returning to Grand.

By now she was either here, or she wasn't. The town would be talking about her either way. Either she was a bitch for skipping her grandmother's funeral, or a greedy slut for coming back now after breaking her granny's heart—Angela wouldn't be able to win either way. But Jake didn't give a shit about any of that. He just hoped those firm, luscious tits hadn't started to sag or that sweet ass hadn't started to spread, like Shelly's.

Thinking about Angela made his already hard dick stiffer than the broom handle up Shelly's ass. Yeah, if he got the chance, he'd relive prom night and give Angela a proper welcome back to town. Shelly would lose her fucking mind if she caught them again, but a man has needs, and she sure as hell wasn't fulfilling them.

Jake watched his dad turn the bright red combine on a dime at the end of the field and continue to cut the yellow corn stalks without missing a beat. Of course, Jake would rather be running the combine, but hell no, his old man refused to relinquish that duty again. Catch one damn pivot sprinkler, and a decade later his dad was still bitching.

Jake was sick of working for his dad. Sick of farming. Sick of this damn tractor and this damn land where there was never enough rain and too much fucking wind, dirt, rolling thistle, and blowing stalks. An hour into the day and already he could taste the soil stuck to his teeth, feel the grit in his eyes.

The auger on the combine started to extend, so Jake cut across the land and lined up the grain cart underneath the auger to catch the grain. His dad glared at him from the cab of the combine, and Jake simply stared back. Why couldn't the old man fucking die already?

Things would be different when all of this belonged to him.

Jake shook his head.

No, it wouldn't—it would be exactly the same, except

he'd be the one running the combine, and one of his boys would be here in this 4850 hiding his stash of porn and wishing he was anyplace else.

*Just another day.* That's what Lucas kept telling himself, but he still didn't believe it. Today was the day he'd waited for all these years.

He'd tried to get some sleep after staying up all night, but he never managed to shut his mind down enough for that to happen. Still, he didn't feel tired or sleep deprived. Matter of fact, after his hot shower, he felt pretty damn good. Excited by the possibilities, he buttoned up his shirt and reached for his favorite cap. He'd been letting his hair grow out a bit, so several wavy strands stuck out along the sides.

Shelly claimed she liked the waves that showed up when his hair got longer, but Lucas had always hated them. Not that it mattered—he almost always wore a ball cap. Shelly didn't like that, either, and she particularly didn't like this one with its threadbare bill, though the fact it read *Cowboy Junkies* bothered her the most. Damn few of his customers at the Oasis even knew who the Cowboy Junkies were. So far more often than he wanted, Lucas found himself explaining they were a Canadian band. Used to be, he'd elaborate by saying the band was named for a Townes Van Zandt song, but one person too many had said, "Townes who?" and Lucas simply could not forgive ignorance when it came to the greatest songwriter to ever call Texas home.

"I don't care if you like their music. It sounds trashy to me," Shelly would say. "Like you're proud to be some pot-smoking pen rider from the feedlot. Like, most of that stuff you listen to, nobody has ever heard of that band.

People already wonder why you gave up being a lawyer to run a bar, so why make them think you're some kind of druggie as well?"

Lucas had heard that speech a hundred times or more, but he took his music seriously. He'd never apologize for considering most mainstream music soulless. He gravitated to songs with real emotion behind them, songs that spoke to your heart and mind. But he understood few people even bothered to listen to the lyrics as long as they could remember the chorus and bang out the rhythm on their steering wheel.

He fielded requests to add the latest Nashville pop hit to the jukebox with a smile. Of course, he never relented, not even when Shelly asked. His place was the only joint in town to buy booze, so Lucas could afford to maintain his standards without losing customers. Too bad he hadn't always been that adamant in regard to all his passions. If so, he wouldn't have spent last night staring up at spiderwebs while hoping today brought about the change he craved.

If things worked out the way he hoped, Lucas wouldn't be wearing this cap nearly so often. Shelly liked his hair unbound, free. She'd told him so a thousand times. He always fired back with the same thing, "I'd like you the same way. Unbound. Free."

She pretended to be taken aback—shocked even, when he boldly voiced his desire. But that reaction was part of the game, not unlike his role when Abby hung it out there for him to see. Though there was one difference: Shelly wanted to be free as much he wanted it for her, for himself. But in a town like Grand, with a queenly reputation like Shelly's, freedom was anything but free.

Kristofferson had it right when it came to freedom: just another word for nothing left to lose. Lucas only hoped he wouldn't be singing the blues like Bobby McGee when all was said and done.

Normally, he opened the Oasis by two-thirty or three each afternoon, but here it was, a quarter till four, and he was just now leaving the house.

His old pickup complained and belched black exhaust when he fired it up. With every new vibration and odd clank from the engine, Lucas cranked the stereo just a little bit higher, but sooner or later, the truck was going to give up the ghost. His dad had bought her new back in '78 as a fill-in for the Cadillac after his mom wrapped it around a telephone pole. Now that he'd restored the Caddy to its former glory, Lucas could drive the convertible if need be, but he hated the idea of parking it at the bar for one of his drunken customers to back into.

Lucas made the short three-block drive to the Oasis before Robert Earl Keen finished singing about the Corpus Christi Bay. Pulling up next to the building, he parked but kept the engine running long enough to listen to his favorite part about throwing stuff into the sea. Lucas wasn't the least bit surprised to see the two old men waiting on him. They were sitting there, biding their time in a pickup truck in even worse shape than his own. When he finally turned off the truck and got out, they followed suit.

"You're late." Chester spit a wad of chewing tobacco onto the dusty ground. "Me and L.J. thought we might hafta send out a search posse."

Lucas pulled a ring of keys from his pocket and unlocked the door. "Neither one of you will have trouble making up for lost time."

On their way in, the two old codgers flipped on the lights. Not that the dingy, cigarette-stained bulbs provided much illumination. As always, Lucas turned on the jukebox before assuming his post behind the bar.

The actual bar was a beautifully grained plank of oak, though Lucas did not take care of the wood as he should. The length of it ran along the far wall, and Chester and L.J.

assumed their normal positions at the two stools next to the cash register. More days than not, they were the lone customers until the pen riders out at the feedlot got off work.

Lucas pulled two beers from the cooler beneath the counter line and set them in front of the pair. "How was the funeral?"

"Don't ask me." Chester took a long swig. "I don't like churches. This is my house of worship"—he patted the bar—"Our Lady of Eternal Alcohol." His bloated belly bobbed with laughter. Neither Lucas nor L.J. cracked a smile.

"'Bout like any other," L.J. said after a significant delay.

Lucas waited to hear more, but L.J. never had been a conversationalist. "How was Angela?"

L.J. cocked his head. "How'd you know she was back?"

"News travels fast around here."

Chester nodded. "That's damn sure a fact. Why, the other day I heard somebody accuse me of being an alcoholic. Can you believe that? I told 'em, 'Hell, alcoholics go to meetings. I'm just a damned old drunk.'" He threw back his head and laughed again.

Lucas wanted to hear about the funeral, but he also knew how tight L.J. held onto his words, especially when pressed. By feigning disinterest, Lucas hoped the subject would come back up.

After unstacking the chairs from the tabletops, he ventured into the walk-in cooler behind the bar and brought out a couple of cases of beer to refill the stock. Next, he emptied the ashtrays and swept off the small, seldom-used dance floor. Guy Clark sang about desperadoes and trains from the jukebox, and still, L.J. said nothing.

"Kinda late for spring cleaning." Chester tossed his empty bottle into the trash can.

"Somebody has to clean up after you guys." Lucas

handed him a second beer. "Ready for another, L.J.?"

"I don't think so."

Both Lucas and Chester turned to face the old-timer.

"What the hell is the matter with you?" Chester looked disgusted. "I've been haulin' your ass to this bar every day for thirty some-odd years, and you've never turned down a beer."

"Don't feel much like drinking." The skinny old man stood. "Think I'll walk on home." L.J. disappeared out the door before either could respond.

Chester stuffed a wad of tobacco in his cheek. "Damn woman is still in his head."

"Who? What woman?" L.J.'s departure unsettled Lucas. Not only was he worried about the old man, but now how was he going to find out about the funeral, and Angela, and Shelly?

"Who?" Chester shook his head. "For a damn college boy, you sure are dense. Ain't you learned a damn thing listening to him every night? He's only been infatuated with that Ross woman since Nixon held office."

Lucas tried to conjure a mental picture of L.J. and the Ross woman as a couple, but he'd only seen the lady once in the past decade, so the image proved as elusive to grasp as the wind.

"Didn't you ever wonder why he did all that work for her? Mowed her lawn, painted her house." Chester guzzled the cold Coors. "Hell, he even did her grocery shopping."

"I thought she paid him."

"He did it because he wanted to. Because he loved her."

"He loved her?"

Chester shook his head. "Dense and deaf. I already said he did."

"But he was here every night. If he loved her so much, he should've been with her. He should have married her."

"He asked God knows how many times. Even bought a ring. She never said yes. Beats me why anybody wants to get hitched anyway."

This revelation further unnerved Lucas. True love was supposed to win out. The idea he could go the rest of his life without getting to hold Shelly in his arms again was not one he could accept.

"You gonna stand there with your mouth hung open, or you gonna fetch me another?" Chester chunked the second empty into the trash where it landed with a clink atop the first bottle.

"You think L.J. is alright by himself? He's gotta be tore up."

"He'll be fine. Damn funeral has him thinking today, but he'll come around by tomorrow. He's gotten used to not having her over the years."

Lucas had never gotten used to not having Shelly and hoped he never would. Twisting the top off another beer, he handed it to Chester. "L.J. say anything about the funeral to you?"

"Like what?"

"About Angela?" Lucas avoided eye contact.

"Just that she showed up this morning."

"What about Shelly?"

Chester stopped mid-drink. "Damn, boy, you're ate up with it."

"Ate up with what?"

"The dumbass. She's married. Time you got over it."

# 6

Dusk bathed the living room in pools of violet shadows. Angela sat up and rubbed her swollen, red-rimmed eyes. Physically spent from the long drive and emotionally drained from her homecoming, she'd collapsed onto the couch and cried herself to sleep the moment she entered the old home. Now the sun dipped below the horizon and the resulting dimness matched her mood.

Rising to her feet, she moved around the room. The scent of mothballs and mentholatum permeated the house. The floor creaked underneath as she struggled against the urge to weep again. Everywhere she turned, sights and smells kindled recollections of the past. The place appeared untouched since her departure. White lace curtains still dangled in the windows. The collection of commemorative plates hung on the walls. The same floral print furniture filled the sitting room, as if she'd been gone only a day or two, instead of sixteen years.

Part of her was glad nothing had changed. She would have felt like an intruder had the house undergone a major metamorphosis. Nevertheless, the realization her grandmother's life had remained stagnant pained Angela.

She paused at the foot of the stairs. Pictures lined the

paneling all the way up to the bedrooms, a gold frame holding a black and white of her grandparents on their wedding day, followed by images of Angela's father as a toddler, then her own parents' wedding. The wall served as both a visual timeline and withering family tree.

Halfway up, Angela stopped to stare at the proof of her entry into the world. Her dad grinned down at her tiny pink face, her mother's face awash with maternal pride.

Angela bit her lip. She, and possibly her mother, were the only people still alive.

Reaching, Angela grabbed a loose photo tucked into the corner of a frame. It was a small picture taken on her first day of school. Angela stared at the image. She sat atop her father's shoulders, a pair of pigtails the color of a newborn chick hung on both sides of her face.

That day was one of her earliest and fondest memories. Perched high in the air, she felt like a princess as her family marched the four blocks to the schoolhouse. At that time, she'd still had a mommy and a daddy who loved her. Riding on his shoulders was like riding a carriage of love and stability. Back then it seemed as if nothing could ever go wrong.

Even as she stood outside Stephen F. Austin Elementary School, afraid to go in, things had worked out. She first met Misty on that sidewalk. They walked in together, beginning a decade-long friendship that remained the truest and best of Angela's life. Until she screwed it up.

The old adage, "You can never go home again," finally made sense to Angela.

Even if she wanted to stay, the townspeople would never allow it. Shelly and Charlene's words at the funeral proved as much. They'd barely tolerated her when she dwelled here as one of them, and she'd transformed into an outsider the instant she hiked over to the highway and stuck her thumb in the air.

Angela took the photo with her and moved upstairs to her old room.

She was ill-prepared for what she found. Her old clothes still hung in the closet. Her posters still lined the wall. The crumpled sheets on the bed appeared to be in the exact position she left them. Her heart thumped at the sight of the slip of paper on the dresser. She did not need to pick up the hastily scribbled words to recall the message: *I'm leaving and I won't be back.*

That one sentence contained years of anger and resentment.

Had her grandma moved forward, not dwelled on the negative, life could have been easier for both of them. The chance for happiness was there, but Elizabeth never reached out.

Angela closed the door to her room. The heavy thoughts of the day had taken their toll, and now she wanted to forget the past and relax.

Alcohol was the best mind eraser she knew of, but chances of finding a stiff drink in her grandmother's house were slim. Her search of the cabinets and pantry reinforced the memories of Elizabeth Ross's abstinence. Angela gave thought to walking down the street to L.J.'s house. He would have booze on hand, but no doubt he was busy waging his own emotional war.

Using the saltshaker, she propped the photo of her family up in the middle of the table. Angela gave up her quest for liquor and opened the refrigerator, ready to settle for iced tea, milk, or whatever her grandmother might have on hand.

"There is a God." She spotted an old bottle of cooking sherry behind a jar of sweet pickles and an ancient, discolored box of baking soda. She unscrewed the cap, took a small sip, and shuddered. Bitter, but she'd already swallowed a lot of bitterness in her thirty-four years. What was a little more?

A knock at the door interrupted her mission to get drunk. Her first inclination was to ignore the visitor and drink alone, but when she peeked through the curtains, Misty stood beneath the glare of the porch light, clutching a foil-wrapped bundle. Angela opened the door.

"Hi."

Misty smiled. "I know it's late but—"

Angela cut the apology short. "I don't even know what time it is."

"Just after nine." Misty handed her the mound of warm foil. "Thought you might be hungry, so I brought you a plate."

Angela carried the covered dish back to the kitchen. Until now, she hadn't thought about eating, but the mention of food made her stomach growl. The memory of a greasy cheeseburger at a truck stop somewhere in Oklahoma came to mind. Sometime yesterday afternoon.

Misty followed. "It's not much—leftover pot roast, green beans, and mashed potatoes."

"Sounds great. Thanks." Angela pulled out a glass and sat at the table with her dinner and the bottle.

"You might want to heat it up." Misty eyed the sherry.

"It's warm enough." Angela pointed to the sherry. "I'd offer you some, but it's pretty bad stuff. Supposed to be for cooking, but it was all I could find here in the house."

"That's okay. I don't drink much. Haven't had a margarita since Charlene's last bachelorette party."

"I don't know how you survive this town sober. I've been here less than a day and already resorted to cooking sherry."

Misty smiled. "Oh, it's not that bad. Maybe a little boring, but I can't imagine living anywhere else. This is home."

Angela bit her lip. Not wishing to offend with her opinion of Grand, she changed the subject. "So, how have you been? I guess you're married." She pointed at the small diamond on Misty's left hand. "Do you have kids?"

"I married Mark. You remember Mark. We have three little girls."

Staring down at the table, Angela lowered her voice. "I do remember Mark." She didn't know what else to say. She regretted having slept with Mark, but regrets never helped anyone. "I always pictured you with girls."

Would Misty be better served to hear an apology, or were old wounds better left to die? Deciding she would rest easier once she said something, Angela cleared her throat. "I'm sorry for what I did. That whole thing with Mark and me. I never should have . . . "

"That was a long time ago. We all made mistakes. We were kids," Misty's voice quivered.

"I made more than most."

"At least you know, and it's kind of you to say you're sorry. You didn't have to after all these years, but it does mean a lot." Misty dabbed at her eyes.

The compassion and forgiveness of her old friend forced Angela to fight back tears of her own. "I appreciate you being here," she whispered. Choking back emotion, she poured a glass of sherry to soothe the ache in her heart.

Misty reached for the picture on the table. "I can't believe we were ever this little."

Angela nodded. "Doesn't even seem like that was me."

"I don't remember your mom, but you look like her." She held the photo up to compare the two faces.

Angela could see Misty meant no malice from her statement, but she didn't want to discuss her mom, nor did she want to be compared to the woman. "It's weird being back."

"I'm just glad you're okay. I worried maybe you were dead or something."

The vile liquid elicited another shudder from Angela. Or maybe it was the macabre statement from Misty. "Dead? That sounds kind of harsh."

Misty looked down at her hands. "We heard a lot of stories about you over the years. I didn't know what to believe, but I always hoped you were okay."

Angela hated to imagine the horrific gossip the people of Grand had concocted. The tales would be far from flattering, but then again, the actual details of her life were not exactly fairy-tale material. Besides, someone from Grand had known enough to know she lived in Chicago. L.J. claimed that somebody wasn't Elizabeth, but who else cared enough to keep track?

"So, tell me one of these stories."

"They're not important. You know how people are around here. They like to gossip, especially when they don't know the facts."

"Come on, I could use a laugh, and who knows? The stories might be right."

Angela didn't actually want to hear what the townspeople said about her, but doing so might be the only way to discover who'd kept track of her.

"Let's see if I can remember one." Misty's forehead wrinkled in concentration.

Angela watched her friend try to sort through the collection of rumors and come out with one not overly offensive.

"Umm . . . We heard you went to Dallas when you left here."

"Dallas, huh?" she said. "And how was it I died?"

Misty blushed. "Maybe I will have a sip of that." She pointed at the sherry. "Do you have another glass?"

Angela poured one for her friend. "You don't have to sugarcoat it. I know what my reputation around here was. Still is, I suppose."

"Somebody said you were a prostitute in Dallas. Of course, I heard the same thing about Albuquerque, Oklahoma City, and San Antonio." She took a small sip and cringed. "This stuff is awful."

"What about Chicago? You ever hear anything about me in Chicago?"

Misty shook her head. "I don't think so, but there for a while every time somebody went away, they came back with a new story about you."

"That's funny, because Chicago is the only place I ever sold my body."

Misty's eyes widened in disbelief.

"I'm kidding." Angela waved her hand. "So, what other fine careers have the good people of Grand credited me with?"

"Well, I heard you were making movies in LA."

"A movie star." Angela smiled. "That's not so bad."

"They weren't those kinds of movies. They said you caught AIDS and died." Misty appeared ready to cry.

Angela laughed, but without any real joy. "Never thought anyone would see those flicks, but between all those pornos and the street walking, I was bound to catch something."

Misty's mouth gaped open. Tears flooded her eyes.

"I'm kidding again." Angela had forgotten how naive and gullible her friend was. "You can rest easy. I've never been a prostitute or made a porno, and far as I know, I don't have any terminal diseases. I've lived in Chicago the last nine years. Before that I was in Vegas."

"Oh, yeah." Misty nodded. "I almost forgot the one about you being a stripper in Las Vegas. I don't know where you found the time to do all that stuff." She grinned, joining in on the joke. A pair of dimples showed among a smattering of freckles.

Angela's smile faded. The truth slapped her in the face.

A week ago, she considered the past to be safely buried, but she'd never been more wrong. Someone in Grand knew she lived in Chicago, and now she knew someone from Grand had spotted her dancing in Vegas.

Only one person could link her to both places. And he was dead.

# 7

Stars twinkled overhead while the porch swing creaked a steady cadence. A cricket chirped a tune off in the distance, and occasionally the hum of a car traveling down the highway could be heard. Angela savored the dark, tranquil night. She'd forgotten how quiet nights away from the city were. In Chicago a car alarm, or horn, or siren always echoed off the concrete, steel, and glass to disturb the peace. And the glare of a million lights erased most of the stars twinkling in the sky.

The bottle of sherry sat between her feet, but she'd given up drinking the foul liquid. Not that it mattered—she was unlikely to forget the past tonight, regardless of how much alcohol she consumed.

When she left, Angela's sole objective was to disappear. Discovering she'd failed so miserably was equal parts sobering and disturbing. Not once at LiveWireZ did she recognize a familiar face, yet someone spotted her. Then again, Washington, Lincoln, and Jefferson were the only faces she cared about those days. She took no pride from her stint at the strip club, but little regret either. She did what was necessary to survive, and considering things she'd done back in Texas, dancing topless seemed tame by comparison. In hindsight, it seemed like desperation.

Angela swayed to the steady rhythm of the swing as her mind swung back to Vegas. She danced at the posh cabaret for six months before Kenneth Hodgemann stepped into her life. He was in town for some type of law convention, but Angela didn't learn that until later. She'd been only vaguely aware of his group of drunken men until he offered two grand for a private dance in his room. An extravagant amount to pay, even in a city filled with instant winners and high rollers, so she assumed he wanted more than a dance. Instinct told her to stay away, but something about him intrigued her, so later that night she found herself standing in the doorway of his suite at Caesar's.

Until then, Angela thought she knew all about men and what drove them. Kenneth dispelled that myth within ten minutes. For the first time in her life, she found a man interested in something other than invading her panties. Ironically, his interest lay in the very things she'd fled.

Her accent drove him crazy. At first she thought only her voice intrigued him, but later she learned Kenneth had a strange fetish for all things Texan. He collected a wide array of things she regarded as junk. Boots, barbed wire, spurs, and everything else he could find from the Lone Star State. Years later, she learned half of the people working for him were native Texans. He denied it, but she suspected he hired them solely for their slow drawls.

When the convention ended, he went back to Chicago, and Angela figured she'd seen the last of the debonair lawyer, but two weeks later she came out for her set to find him smiling up at her from pervert row. For a time, they carried on a strange courtship through frequent trips and lengthy calls. Eventually she shared his bed. She took care of his emotional and physical needs, he cared for her financially.

Kenneth moved her to Chicago, set her up in a downtown high-rise, and lavished her with expensive gifts and an extensive expense account. Truth be told, she'd loved the thought of having someone to love more than she ever loved Kenneth, but the memories made her teary-eyed just the same.

"One of these days I gotta oil that old swing." L.J.'s voice drifted out of the darkness.

She squinted until his scarecrow frame became distinguishable among the shadows. "You always wander around at night scaring the bejesus out of innocent daydreamers?" She scooted over as he walked up.

"Usually I'm over at the Oasis 'bout now, but tonight I took a walk." The swing complained when he sat beside her. "I walked out to the cemetery. To say my good-byes."

Angela swallowed the lump in her throat. A train rumbled in the distance. When the boxcar's rattle faded she turned toward him. "I can't believe she's gone. I have no one left."

L.J. put his arm across her shoulders. "You still got me."

She nodded. "Are you sure she never knew I was in Chicago?"

"Yep."

"She never looked for me?"

He shook his head. "She figured you'd let her know when you wanted found. Like I told you this morning, she was glad you escaped, though it hurt her you never said goodbye."

"Was she happy for me, or happy I'd no longer tarnish the family name?"

L.J. shrugged. "Both, I reckon, but I think there at the end she saw the foolishness in worrying what others thought. Came too late to make much difference, but she would've liked to know you were okay."

The sounds of night filled the silence as the two sat. A myriad of questions swirled in Angela's mind.

"Did you ever hear any rumors about me in Chicago?"

"I never listened to those folks blowing smoke."

"Someone knew enough to find me. To let me know about the funeral and the will."

"I wondered about that. Thought maybe you'd been keeping track of us." He pulled out a package of rolling papers and a pouch of tobacco. "Mind if I smoke?" He deftly rolled the cigarette with one hand.

"No, go ahead." She watched him closely. As a little girl, she'd considered this talent to be akin to a magic trick.

His match flared. "You going back?"

"Back where?"

"Chicago." He exhaled a cloud of gray smoke.

"There's nothing there for me anymore."

"No husband or young'uns?"

She shook her head. "I had somebody, but he died in a car wreck. We didn't exactly have a normal relationship."

L.J. chuckled. "I know the feeling."

"He was married to somebody else." Angela blurted. "And he was twenty years older than me."

"Life's funny that way," L.J. said. "Would be nice if we got paired up with somebody we could have, but doesn't always work out that way."

He stood and started across the yard. "Don't drink too much of that stuff." He pointed at the bottle on the ground. "It'll ruin you."

He disappeared into the darkness as he crossed the street. A light came on in his trailer home several houses down. His was the only residence on the block with wheels underneath it, yet Angela viewed him as the most stable man in town.

Shelly stared into the night. The darkness depressed her. The kitchen window never offered much of a view, even by daylight, but at least then she could gaze across the miles of plowed fields and imagine life beyond the horizon. After sunset, blackness surrounded her and she could only see the reality of her existence.

"Is dad home yet?"

"Do you see him?" Shelly twisted around to scowl at her youngest son, Austin. "Time for you to get in bed."

"It's not even ten."

"Close enough."

"But—"

"Don't argue with me. I'm not in the mood."

Folding his arms across his chest, he puffed up with indignation. A strand of wavy blond hair hung low on his forehead. Austin looked exactly like his father.

"Taylor gets to stay up until ten-thirty. That's not fair."

"He's fifteen. You're twelve. Keep it up and you'll find yourself in bed at nine tomorrow."

Austin sulked out of the room. Shelly wished he would act more like his older brother, but he'd inherited too many of his father's bad habits for that to happen.

She paced around the kitchen. Jake should've been home by now. Normally she enjoyed the days he worked late, favoring his absence over another evening watching him vegetate on the couch and guzzle beer. Tonight, however, she wanted him home. To know where he was. To know he was nowhere near Angela Ross.

Jake Sampson jammed the pickup in gear and headed for the house. His back and shoulders ached from the long day, but he would feel better after he got a six pack and some food in his belly.

The lonely stretch of county road between the farm and his house was deserted. A fly scrambled against the driver's window searching for freedom. Jake knew what it felt like to be trapped. He rolled down the window, but the rush of air forced the insect to the other side of the cab. He knew how that felt too.

Rolling up the glass, he switched on the radio, only to turn it off after the first chorus. The same old songs over and over. The same old everything over and over.

Wake up next to the same wife, go to the farm, listen to his dad harp about the same stupid shit. Go home and get ready to do it all over again. Only the amount of beers he downed between dinner and bed remained a mystery.

Approaching town, Jake looked for the porch light at his house. He liked the fact their brick three-bedroom sat on the edge of Grand instead of being hemmed in. Nosy old Mrs. Schumacher neighbored the one side while empty plowed fields adjoined the other. Of course, his dad actually owned the property, but that bothered Shelly far more than it did him.

Pulling into the driveway, he was surprised by the lack of light. Shelly usually waited up. Then again, it was nearly eleven, and she liked to hit bed soon as the news ended.

When the garage door went up, he saw she'd parked smack dab in the middle again, leaving no room for his pickup. A two-car garage meant nothing to her. He'd griped about this very thing dozens of times, but the woman couldn't park any better than she could drive.

Inside, he tossed his keys on the foyer table and hung his sweat-stained Longhorns' cap on the coat closet doorknob. Rubbing his aching shoulder muscles, he headed for the kitchen and a cold bottle of brew.

"Where have you been?"

"Jesus!" He jumped at the sound of his wife's voice. "What the hell are you doing hiding in the dark?"

"Where have you been?" Her voice held an accusatory tone.

"The queen of England invited me for tea and crumpets, so I hopped on a plane and flew to Paris."

"Don't be a smartass. I want to know where you've been. And Paris is in France, not England."

"Whatever." He walked on through the living room. With Shelly in this mood he'd need a twelve pack of Shiner just to put up with her.

"Don't walk away from me. I want to know—"

"Dad! Dad! Guess what?" Austin ran into the kitchen, interrupting their argument. "Brendan broke his arm in practice so coach is moving me to middle linebacker."

"Sweet!" He reached out and slapped his son's hand in a high-five salute. "Carrying on the Sampson tradition. Grandpa, then me, and now you."

"Austin, get in bed right this instant." Shelly's right foot tapped the floor. "I need to talk to your father."

The boy looked to his dad for help.

Jake winked and nodded. "Go on. You can tell me about it at breakfast." He twisted the cap off the beer and guzzled the dark lager after his son disappeared across the living room and down the hall. He nodded in his wife's direction. "What's got you all pissy?"

"I want to know where you've been."

"Working. Where the hell do you think I've been? I told you we were starting corn harvest today." Jake flopped down on one of the kitchen chairs and tugged at his cowboy boots.

Shelly scowled.

"Can you help me with these?" Jake held up one foot.

She ignored his request and sat on the opposite side of the table. "Did you go into town today?"

"Yeah, right. You know how Dad is once we start." Jake was relieved to see the fire extinguished from his wife's eyes. He didn't feel up to yet another all-night fight. With a grunt and a steady pull, he finally extracted his right foot.

"She's back." Her voice quivered.

"Who?" Jake took another drink and reached for the left boot.

Shelly rubbed her temples like a baker kneading dough. "Angela."

Jake swallowed hard and bit his lip to conceal his grin. The hunt was on.

# 8

Shelly pulled into the Whirlwind's lot and parked next to a rusted-out flatbed. The blue heeler sunning atop the spare tire opened one eye at the disturbance.

"Go back to sleep, Highway." The dog's tail thumped the metal bed at the mention of its name.

Inside, Shelly nodded and smiled at the dozen or so farmers and ranchers gathered at the lunch counter before joining Misty at their regular table. As usual, Charlene was late and nowhere to be seen.

"Pathetic." Shelly flopped down across from her friend.

Misty glanced around the room. "What's pathetic?"

Shelly spread her arms wide to encompass the restaurant, Grand, the entire world. "It's bad enough I know the name of every single person in here, but do I have to know the names of their stupid dogs too?!"

"There are worse things," Misty said.

"You're right about that"—Shelly stared at her friend—"It's much worse to have my best friend slap me in the face by hanging out with my worst enemy."

Misty blushed. "I—"

"Don't try to lie. Leann Grayson already told me your minivan was parked in front of that whore's house three different nights this week."

"Angela's not the horrible person you think. She's been

in Grand a week and hasn't caused a bit of trouble. She's changed."

"People don't change. Once a home wrecker, always a home wrecker."

"You're wrong." Misty eyes went damp with unshed tears. "Angela isn't like she was back in high school. Besides, she's leaving just as soon as the estate is settled. She meets the attorney this morning."

Shelly shook her head. "The world's not a Disney movie, Misty. Everything doesn't end happily ever after."

"Damn, y'all look like you just lost your best friend." Charlene plopped down next to Misty in the booth.

"Not so sure I haven't." Shelly nodded at Misty. "Go ahead, tell her who you've been visiting."

Misty held her chin high. "Angela."

"What the hell for?"

"She needed someone to talk to. She's been through a lot. And despite what y'all think, she's not out to get anyone." Misty picked up the menu and studied the selections, even though the choices hadn't changed in twenty years.

Charlene displayed a toothy grin. "Well?" She yanked the laminated sheet from her friend's hand. "Give us the dirt."

Misty snatched back the menu. "Let's order."

"Come on. Where's she been all these years? Was she a hooker? Pornstar?"

Misty kept her attention glued to the menu.

"Oh, so that's how it's going to be." Charlene rolled her eyes. "Go ahead, act like Mother Teresa and leave us in the dark, but you ought to be ashamed, holding out on your best friends."

"Only thing I'm ashamed of is how you're acting." Misty waved to get the Abby's attention.

Full of disgust, Shelly shook her head. "Tell me one

thing, how can you be so forgiving? How can you look at her and not worry she'll leave town with your husband in tow? Do you want to raise three little girls all by yourself?"

Misty's eyes moistened all over again. "I have faith in Mark, and Angela is part of the reason. What they did hurt me, but it happened a long time ago and without that experience, Mark might always wonder what he was missing. I know he loves me."

"That doesn't excuse the fact Angela screwed your boyfriend. Y'all were supposed to be friends—*best* friends." Shelly refused to let Misty forgive.

"Put yourself in her shoes. How would you feel if your mother abandoned you? And your father died in an accident, but everyone claimed he killed himself because his wife left?" Misty's voice rose like her father's did when delivering a stirring sermon. "Elizabeth Ross never showed Angela any affection. No one did. Except boys."

"Okay, both of y'all shut-up." Charlene slapped the table. "All this talk about that whore is ruining my appetite."

Gabby Abby appeared and took their orders, but Shelly declined food. Anger, resentment, and jealousy filled her belly. She continued to glare at both Misty—who'd fallen silent—and Charlene, who kept up attempts to lighten the mood by talking non-stop about nothing.

"Talk to Loverboy?" Charlene used the smoking tip of her cigarette to point out the window and across the street to the Oasis. The bar's parking lot was empty at this noon hour.

"Don't start in on me again about Lucas," Shelly said.

"I didn't say anything about him being madly in love with you." She batted her fake eyelashes like a lovesick schoolgirl. "I just asked if you'd talked to him."

"No, I have not."

Since Angela's return, Shelly had made it a point to avoid Lucas. She missed their frequent texts and weekly phone conversations. At times, his wit and flirtatious taunts were all she had to look forward to in the otherwise tedious routine, but it felt dangerous to even talk to him with all the reminders of the past fresh in everyone's mind.

"That explains it." Charlene hoisted the greasy cheeseburger Abby had just dropped off at the table.

Misty picked at her salad, still holding onto her silence.

"Explains what?" The smell of Charlene's fries made Shelly's stomach growl, and a measly glass of iced tea did little to appease the pains. She should have ordered.

"Normally, when I show up at the Oasis with a new guy you hear about it before he's up and out of my house the next morning."

"Don't tell me." Both Misty and Shelly spoke at once.

"Yep. I've found my one true love. His name is Jimmy."

Shelly rolled her eyes and said, "One true love number thirty-two. I don't even want to know where you found this one."

"This one's different."

Misty cracked a smile. "So was the last one."

Lucas tried to focus his attention on the bank ledger, but it was hard with L.J. scrutinizing his every move. The old man had studied Lucas all afternoon, and frankly it was starting to get under his skin. Then again, the codger had acted peculiar all week.

Since Elizabeth's funeral, he'd made a habit of drinking one, maybe two beers, then leaving. Just when that seemed the new norm, L.J. up and stayed until closing yesterday, but drank only black coffee. Chester was convinced his buddy had lost his mind, and Lucas had started to agree.

"You ever talk to your mother?"

Startled by the question, Lucas looked up to be certain the inquiry was directed at him. L.J.'s pale gray eyes waited for an answer.

"Not often. Christmas and Mother's Day. And she usually calls on my birthday. That's about it."

Lucas stared at the column of numbers, but his attempts to add the expenditures were futile. He seldom allowed memories of his mom to invade his mind, but once he gave in, she took complete control.

Molly Cahill had packed up and left her son and husband the day after Lucas's tenth birthday. For the first couple of years, he ventured north to stay with her a week at Christmas and a month during the summer, but he quit going after she remarried. He could've continued, but Lucas never felt welcome, and it struck him as traitorous to stay in a house with his mom and any man other than his dad. Not that it mattered. Hank Cahill never saw a sober day after his wife's departure—nor many before, for that matter.

In the last two decades, Lucas had seen her only once, and in truth, he made that trip for his college roommate's wedding. It was pure coincidence they both lived in the same city. He'd inherited her jet black hair and wavy texture, but far as he could tell, that was all she'd ever given him. According to his dad, she never even wanted kids.

"What's a feller got to do to get a drink around here?" Chester slid his empty down the length of the bar.

Lucas extracted another beer from the cooler. "Why the sudden interest in my mom?"

L.J. smiled and sipped his coffee. "Just making conversation."

The absurdity of the statement caused Chester to twist around on his stool and address his suddenly reformed drinking partner. "Since when do you give two shits about conversation? You ain't said ten words all week, and now you want to parley about a woman that hightailed it out of town twenty-some-odd years ago. Only good thing to come out of Hank's death was we never had to hear him pine away for her anymore."

Lucas might have taken offense to the callous description of his parents had the statements not been true. To this day, he could not understand why his father mourned her departure so when all the couple ever did was fight. Lucas's earliest memories were of himself sitting in his room, talking to stuffed animals and trying to ignore the shouts from the other side of the house. Maybe that's where his lifelong aversion to confrontation stemmed.

"Okay, I'll change the subject." Again, L.J. flashed a bizarre smile. "Ever consider hiring a waitress to help out in here?"

"Doesn't take much to keep a bunch of drunks happy."

"Why the hell would you ask that?" Chester shook his head. "You best start boozing it up again 'cause you ain't making a damn bit of sense. Musta hit your head when you fell off the wagon."

Sunlight streamed through the door before L.J. had the chance to respond. The golden ray bounced off the Jack Daniels mirror behind the bar, temporarily illuminating the room.

"God, this place reeks." Charlene's wretched voice scraped the air.

"You could always go someplace else." Lucas held up his hand to block the glare until the door closed, returning the dimness. He'd hoped Shelly might be with the redhead, but no such luck.

"I would, if this wasn't the only shit hole in town."

"I love it when you talk so eloquently."

"Don't be a smartass, Lucas. Where's Jimmy?" She flopped down on a stool and extracted a pack of smokes from the depths of the cleavage exposed by her neon-orange tank top.

"Jimmy who?" Lucas pulled out the ingredients to mix Charlene's drink of choice while Bruce Robison appropriately sang "Desperately" from the jukebox.

"The guy from the feedlot that I was with Saturday night. I need a screwdriver."

"I know what you need." He mixed the Minute Maid and vodka. "And I don't have the time or memory to keep up with all your men." He handed the cocktail to her. "Three bucks."

"What do you mean, 'all my men'?" She drained half the drink in a single swallow.

Lucas rolled his eyes. "We both know damn good and well half the guys in this town would still be boys without your, shall we say, hospitality."

Charlene smiled and finished off the beverage with a second swig. Her eyes drifted below Lucas's waistline. "Yeah, and you would be one of them." She inhaled a long slow drag. "Jimmy will pay when he gets here."

"You're not getting another until he shows."

Lucas turned away from his unwanted customer. His experience with Charlene qualified as the second biggest mistake of his life, and she relished bringing their encounter up every chance she got. Especially when she got drunk, which was every time she came in the Oasis. Maybe someday he could set her straight that she was not his first, but that would have to wait.

He never would've slept with her in the first place had he been thinking clearly, but those weeks right after senior prom amounted to the worst of his life. And they'd started out so promising. He still remembered the whole ordeal in perfect detail.

He'd stayed away from the big dance. Several girls made it clear they would accept if he asked, Abby included. But he only wanted to take Shelly, and a week before the event it looked as if he might get the chance when Jake broke up with her and asked Angela out. But Shelly believed everyone would pity her if she showed up with Lucas, because they were "friends." No siree, she wasn't about to take a mercy date.

Lucas worked hard to convince Shelly his intentions were genuine, but she refused to listen. In the end, she went solo and he stayed home. An hour into the dance, she showed up on his porch, traumatized by the sight of Jake and Angela making out on the dance floor. In the ensuing hours, Lucas and Shelly shared a bottle of rum from his father's liquor cabinet while discussing their thoughts and dreams. Eventually, they shared their bodies. The night remained the best of his life.

Foolishly, he'd thought the two of them would continue on forever in each other's arms—he'd been mistaken. Not a week later, Shelly was once again Jake's girlfriend, and Lucas resorted to sleeping with her best friend, Charlene, out of jealousy and spite. Of course, he'd replayed the incident a million times in his head and knew exactly where he went wrong. He'd spent the last sixteen years plotting ways to fix his mistake.

Another jolt of sunlight cleared Lucas's mind as a group of pen riders from the cattle yard stomped through the door. The unmistakable smell of cow shit filled the air.

"Pour me another. Jimmy's here." Charlene threw her arms around a scrawny cowboy clearly a decade her junior.

"That boy don't stand a chance," Chester said. "She'll have him at the altar before he knows what hit him."

The feedlot workers were hard drinkers, and Monday Night Football always brought in extra patrons, so the better part of the evening passed before Lucas got another chance to visit with his two best customers. L.J., however, continued to watch his every move.

Hours later, when the football game ended and most of the clientele had staggered home, including Charlene and her latest victim, Lucas leaned down next to the old-timers. A thick cloud of smoke billowed near the ceiling and the sour smell of beer and sweat hung in the air. Chester hummed along as Jerry Jeff sang about being down on his luck in London.

"Busy night," L.J. said.

"Always is for Monday Night Football." Lucas rocked his head from side-to-side to ease the tense muscles in his neck and shoulders. "I could use a warm shower and a soft bed."

"If you had a waitress . . . "

"Okay, L.J. What's this waitress stuff?" Lucas folded his arms across his chest. "Why do I suddenly need help?"

"'Bout time you asked." The old man leaned forward. "Angela needs a job, you see."

"Angela?"

"Yep. Seems somebody led her to believe she'd collect a large inheritance if she came back for the funeral, and she used what little money she had getting here."

Chester stopped humming. "I shoulda knowed that Ross woman had a bundle of money hoarded away." Tobacco juice stained the corners of his upturned mouth.

"Elizabeth didn't have much money, but someone made it seem as if she did," L.J. said. "Now Angela is stuck here. Spent her last dollars making the trip."

Not liking where the conversation was headed, Lucas spoke up. "I'd love to help, but—"

"Good," L.J. interrupted. "She only needs to work until she saves up enough to leave, or finds a reason to stay."

Lucas met L.J.'s gaze. "I'll ask around for her."

The old man grinned, leaned back on his stool, and rubbed his stubbled chin. "Your mom still live up near Chicago?"

Lucas nodded.

"That's where Angela's been living. Hell of a coincidence." L.J. smiled.

Lucas swallowed hard.

L.J. knew.

Or maybe he was fishing. Either way, it didn't matter. The old-timer could arrive at the fact via snow sled, and it wouldn't change Lucas's position. He couldn't afford to have the old man discussing his theory in public. Because if Shelly got wind of it . . .

"Send her in. I'll see what I can do."

L.J. nodded. "Figured you'd come around." He stood and headed out the door. His skinny frame disappeared into the dark night without so much as a backward glance.

# 9

Angela's second Tuesday in Grand marked the first official day of autumn, and her optimism had disappeared along with summer. Yesterday she'd driven up to Amarillo to meet with Bradley Vanover, Attorney at Law, with the hope she could soon leave Texas for good. That hope rotted like fruit left on the vine. Actually, there was no vine, no fruit, no anything.

Vanover misled her from the start. She should've questioned him more when he called her in Chicago. In hindsight, the conversation seemed sketchy. He never promised cash, but did proclaim Mrs. Ross left a sizable estate.

Angela guessed the family home and four-hundred acres south of town could be considered sizable, but the last thing she wanted was to set up residence in Grand. And the acreage? A farmer she would never be.

From her time with Kenneth, she knew plenty about lawyers, and her visit to Mr. Vanover's office left her with two observations. At best, Bradley was a second-rate attorney and a third-rate liar. He'd ducked her questions, but not without revealing the fact there were answers.

Skilled attorneys did not make that mistake.

Deeds and the necessary paperwork could have been signed via the mail. Maybe getting her back to Grand was her grandmother's idea of a joke. Perhaps Elizabeth was smiling down from heaven right now. Angela wanted to rage against society, to feel sorry for herself. But those tactics had never worked in the past, and what she needed now was a plan. Pouring a cup of coffee, she went out on the porch to ponder her dilemma in the steady sway and creak of the old wooden swing.

The lack of ready cash effectively stranded her in Grand. She might have the funds to get back to Chicago, if the car managed to run that long, but she had even less going for her in the Windy City than in Grand. At least here she didn't have rent to pay.

Her original idea had been to start over somewhere new once she received the inheritance, and that's what she would still do. Only now it would take time—time she did not want to spend in this shit hole.

She could sell the house and land, but that could take months. She might be able to rent the house, but to who? Some cowboy from the feedlot? Her grandmother would spin in her grave. Elizabeth Ross had always considered them hobos with jobs, lecturing Angela about their nomadic ways. "Stay away from them, they're no good. Here today, gone tomorrow," she'd say. Angela longed for that description to fit her.

Taking a page from her past, she could gather her things and simply leave, but where would she go, and what would she do when she got there?

She never considered those problems when she left the first time, but at eighteen she'd been both reckless and stupid. She'd also possessed a youthful spirit and a sense of adventure to guide her. Both were long gone, buried along with her hopes and dreams.

Many of those goals had been formulated when she was a little girl sitting in this very swing. If she rocked long enough, maybe she could recapture that youthful zeal. A mockingbird took up a plagiarized song as the sun transformed the gray predawn sky into a clear blue vastness.

The irony of her situation forced Angela to concede she'd wasted her time up until now. All these years later and here she was, back in Grand, looking for a way out. She knew what had to be done, but she hated the thought. She needed a job. Hard work and determination were the only things that would set her free at his point.

Before she left again, Angela would give L.J. whatever he wanted from the house. There were bound to be things of sentimental value to him. Then anything Misty needed, she could have. The rest Angela would after she acquired the necessary funds. That way if she ever had a daughter of her own, she would have something to leave her.

Until recently, Angela never doubted she would one day become a mother. She used to name her future children and visualize what they might look like. Lately, when those thoughts arose she forced them away, abandoning her dreams the same way her mother had abandoned her.

"How's a man supposed to sleep with that damn swing a squawking?"

Angela looked up to see L.J. walking toward her. Steam rose from the mug clutched in his hand. "I didn't mean to wake you. I didn't realize I was making that much noise."

"You're not." He sat down beside her. "Was pulling your leg. Never been much of a sleeper myself. Figure I'll get all the rest I need once I'm dead."

The two rocked in steady silence as the world woke around them. Three houses down, a teenager came out and started a pickup. He revved the engine for a minute or two before taking off in a swirl of black exhaust.

"Get a handle yet on what you're gonna to do?" L.J. pulled out the makings for a smoke.

Angela sighed. "Don't have much choice. I'll put the house up for sale and get a job in the meanwhile."

"Not much available here in Grand."

She nodded, having already suspected as much. "Amarillo's only thirty miles. Surely I can find something there."

"Maybe, but will that"—he pointed at her beat-up car—"make the trip twice a day?"

She shrugged. "It'll have to."

"They need a waitress over at the Oasis."

"I don't know." She appreciated his suggestion, but she could think of far more appealing places to work.

Misty pulled up at the curb as L.J. stood and stretched. "Stop in tonight and talk to Lucas anyway. Me and Chester will be there. We'll put in a word for you." He walked across the yard, giving Misty a nod as he passed.

"I didn't mean to run off your company." Misty said.

"Don't worry about it. He was just telling me about a job over at the Oasis." Angela finished off her coffee. "Come on inside. I'll pour you a cup, and I need a refill."

"I didn't know Lucas was looking for help."

"Lucas who?" She reached for the sugar canister.

"Cahill. Lucas Cahill. Don't you remember him? He graduated with us." Misty sat at the kitchen table.

"Lucas? The valedictorian? I thought he got a scholarship or something." She refilled her cup and poured a second for her friend.

"He did. Went off to Tech, and then law school. When his dad died, he came back to run the bar. Been here ever since. Misty sipped from her mug. "Don't get me wrong. Lucas is a nice guy, but you don't want to hang out at the Oasis every night."

Angela's hopes dipped. If the smartest guy in town had failed to escape this place, how could she expect to get away?

Nothing about today motivated Lucas to climb out of

bed. His long-awaited, best-hatched plan to bring Shelly and him together had gone completely awry. And damned if he could see an out.

He'd plotted himself right into a hole for which there was no escape. Shelly would be hurt, disappointed, and outright angry if he hired Angela. But if he refused, and L.J. started discussing his theory in public . . .

Shelly would never forgive him if she found out he'd orchestrated her rival's return.

Lucas sat up in bed and reached for his guitar. His fingers absent mindedly plucked out Robert Earl Keen's "I'll Go Downtown" while his mind sought answers.

He had no choice but to hire Angela. And, in truth, it was the right thing to do. He knew that. But Lucas also knew Shelly would not take the news well. Especially if she heard about his new employee secondhand. Gossip traveled fast in Grand.

He finished the chorus, set the Martin aside, and reached for the phone to dial her number. Time to swallow his medicine. Listening to the unanswered rings, he imagined the lecture he'd hear until he realized she wasn't going to pick up. He shouldn't be surprised. She hadn't answered any of his calls or returned the dozen or so texts he'd sent the past week. He took both as positive signs.

From past experiences, Lucas knew she avoided him when she and Jake were having problems. Not that they didn't always have problems, but Shelly went to great lengths to portray their marriage as perfect. Sometimes Jake would run his mouth to one of his buddies and the town would whisper all was not well in Perfectville. Or Jake and Shelly would have a public disagreement, and she would tighten the couple's perimeter and shut Lucas out for a while. Lucas longed for the day when one of the embargoes led to his taking Jake's place.

His unwavering devotion to a married woman was

not healthy, or even practical, but Lucas could not simply wish away his desire. He'd tried to run from his feelings, which only made his yearning worse.

When he enrolled at Texas Tech, Lucas never planned to return. His dad never would've missed him, and it was too painful to see Shelly shackled to another. Lucas joined a fraternity. He dated. He submersed himself in both his studies and songwriting. Over time, the challenges of law school, the parties, the bevy of coeds that hung out at the frat house, and the miles that separated him from the memories dulled the pain, yet he never felt satisfied.

Those first few years at college, he dated dozens of women, searching for one to steal his heart the way Shelly had. Some were prettier, some were smarter, and most treated him better than she ever had, but none gripped his soul. He turned to music. Played the open mics and put together a decent little band that picked up some fair gigs, but he gave all that up once he got accepted into law school. Lucas put his focus into graduating and passing the bar. Accomplishing those goals, he landed a job dealing with mineral rights at a firm over in Midland that specialized in oil and gas. Lucas hated every damn minute of those seven months.

Then, he returned to Grand for his father's funeral. After the divorce, Hank Cahill held a vile contempt for all lawyers and judges. He believed them to be the most evil people on the face of the earth, able to destroy lives with the single stroke of a pen — or the whack of a mallet.

Part of Lucas's decision to enter law school was based on his desire not to be compared to his dad. He wanted to prove to the world he was nothing like the drunken, bitter old man, but as they laid his father in the ground, that motivation crumbled.

And then there was Shelly.

One look at her reignited his old desire.

Far enough into his career to know he despised the confrontation that went along with his chosen profession, Lucas e-mailed in his resignation and stayed in Grand. He began playing the guitar and writing again, but still he told himself the stay was temporary.

Nine years later, he was still here and not one damn bit closer to having Shelly. Oh, they talked often, but it wasn't enough. He wanted to hold her in his arms, to whisper goodnight in her ear, to wake up beside her.

Shelly wanted those things too. He was confident of that. But she was too selfless—too pure of heart—to leave Jake and file for divorce simply because she was unhappy. She had her boys to consider, and their wellbeing meant too much to risk an affair. But if Jake ever stepped over the line . . . gave her a reason . . .

Lucas let his thoughts trail off. Jake would screw up again. He was a stick of testosterone-filled dynamite. And Angela was quite the flame. With her working at the bar, Lucas would have ample opportunity to stoke the fire and ensure an explosion.

Shelly leaned against the washing machine with the phone propped between her ear and shoulder. "What do you mean, she's going to stay awhile?" Panic made her voice sound shaky.

"There are some issues with the estate, so she has to stay a few months. Problem is she needs a job. That's why I called you," Misty explained. "I heard the co-op needed office help. I figured you would know if they were still looking for someone."

Shelly clenched her jaws. She wanted to die. It was bad enough Angela had to be in town for a while. And worse that Misty was trying to land her a job at the one place Jake visited on a regular basis. The last thing Shelly needed was her husband and that tramp thrust together.

"I think they already hired someone." Shelly tried to make the lie sound believable.

"Well, I'll tell her to call anyway."

Shelly pulled out the damp contents of the washer and stuffed them into the dryer. She made a mental note to call Mrs. Blathchild and point out the disadvantages of having a known tramp work alongside her husband. Especially one that looked like Angela.

"What's this I hear about Lucas hiring a waitress?" Misty asked.

"Lucas?"

"Yeah. This morning L.J. was just leaving Angela's when I stopped. He said Lucas wanted to hire a waitress."

Shelly dumped another load in the washer, closed the lid, and shifted the cordless to her other ear. "That old drunk is probably confused."

"Could be," Misty admitted. "Is your party on Thursday or Friday?"

"Thursday. Seven o'clock."

"We'll be there, but we can't stay late, it being on a school night. You should've had Lucas move it to Friday this year. Tell Jake hi and give him a hug for me. It's been awhile since I've seen him."

Shelly hung up. "Just perfect." Her voice echoed off the walls of the laundry room. Why did Elizabeth Ross have to die right before her birthday? This whole thing with Angela was going to ruin her party. Life wasn't fair. Her birthday bash was two days away, and instead of her being the focal point of conversation, everybody was focused on Angela.

Even though Jake could pop in for lunch at any time, Shelly decided to finally return Lucas's calls. He always made her feel better, and she needed to clear up this waitress rumor. Lucas threw her a big party every September twenty-fourth. It would be wrong to move it even by a day. Birthdays were meant to be celebrated on the actual day. You couldn't just move them for convenience, as they did for some third-rate holiday like Presidents' Day. Dang near everybody in town under the age of fifty attended her party each year. The event was Grand's premier social gathering.

The singsong chime of the doorbell rang throughout the house. She peaked out of the kitchen curtains on the way to the door. Lucas's old pickup sat out front.

Shelly shook her head. She wanted to talk to Lucas, not have him standing on her front porch. It didn't look proper for a single man to visit a married woman in the middle of the day. Nosy old Mrs. Shumacher was probably at her picture window right now, craning her neck for a better view.

Well, Shelly would just deny her neighbor a chance to gossip by keeping Lucas outside in full view. She checked her hair and makeup in the hall mirror before opening the door.

"Hello, stranger." Lucas grinned. A faint set of dimples framed his smile. God, how she loved that smile.

"I've been meaning to call, but . . . " She didn't have a ready lie to finish her explanation, but Lucas shrugged his shoulders, as if to say he understood.

"Can I come in? I need to talk to you."

"Actually, I was about to come outside and water my roses." She brushed past him.

Turning on the hose, she stared over at the neighbor's house. The face in the window disappeared when Shelly waved. She smiled.

"So, tell me about this rumor going around. Why do you suddenly need a waitress?"

Lucas grimaced. "I don't really need one."

She detected a hesitation in his voice. "So, it's not true?"

He shook his head. "People in this town talk too damn much. Look, I wanted you to hear it from me first, but I'm gonna hire Angela and, before you get mad—"

"Who said I was mad?" She turned her back. The hose dangled in her hand. Water and mud splashed on her feet. Tears flooded her eyes.

"I know when you're upset." Lucas placed his hand on her shoulder. "The longer she has to hunt for a job, the longer she'll be in town."

"But I don't want her here at all."

"I know you don't." He took the hose from her hand, tossed it to the ground, and spun her around to face him. He clasped her hands between his. "I want to help you."

"Then why are you helping her?" She sobbed.

He embraced her with his lean, strong arms. "Look at it this way. I can keep an eye on her six nights a week. And before you know it she'll be gone and our life will be the way it should be."

*Our life?* She decided to ignore the *our.* "Promise?"

She stared up into his eyes. He always had a way to make her feel better.

"I'll make sure of it. One way or another."

For one brief moment, she believed him, but then the face reappeared in the window next door and erased her optimism. She pulled away from Lucas. Shelly hated to think how it must look, her standing in the middle of the yard crying in the arms of a man who was not her husband.

Regardless of Angela's whereabouts, Shelly would never feel at ease. Her secret would always be lurking beneath the surface of her tranquility. And in a place like Grand, it was an everyday struggle to keep such a truth buried.

# 10

Angela stormed out of the co-op. Damn this town and damn its judgmental, narrow-minded people. The opportunity had seemed perfect when Misty mentioned it, but that didn't matter now. The manager's nervous twitches gave away the fact the job was still very much available, just not for her.

Determined not to let one roadblock stop her, Angela got in her car and contemplated her next move. L.J.'s tip about the Oasis came to mind, but she really didn't want to work in the bar knowing it would not be long before some drunken idiot expected her to be the same old free-spirited gal from high school. And when she rejected their advances . . .

She didn't even want to think what would happen. L.J. would be there, so she would have at least one ally, but she didn't remember enough about Lucas to know where he would stand. He might even be the one to bring up her past. Or expect her to . . .

Maybe that's why he wanted to hire her. He didn't owe her any favors. They barely knew each other, even though they grew up in the same place. He'd always been kind of a loner back then.

At least she'd never slept with him.

Not that it mattered. The Pope could run the Oasis for

all Angela cared. She didn't plan to work there, and if there was no chance of a job in Grand, then she would make the daily commute to Amarillo just like lots of other people. She stuck her key in and twisted. A sickening metallic grind responded. She turned the ignition again, only to hear the same depressing sound.

With a sigh, she got out and popped the hood without any idea what to look for. Greasy black tubes and rusted metal filled the space. Nothing looked obviously broken.

"Car trouble?" The co-op manager walked up behind her and stared down at the engine.

Angela fought the urge to call the man an idiot for stating the obvious. "Appears so. It makes a grinding noise when I try to start it."

He rolled up his sleeves and leaned down closer. "Give her a try, and let me listen."

She cranked the car three more times with the same result.

"Might as well forget it." He came around to the driver's door shaking his head. "I ain't no expert on these foreign jobs, but sounds like the starter to me."

"What does that mean?"

"Means you ain't going nowhere until you get a new one."

"Are they expensive?"

"Can be. Especially for a foreign job like this." He kicked the tire. "You know anybody works on cars?"

She shook her head. "Is there still a mechanic in town?"

"Ain't no real garage anymore, but there's a few old boys that work on cars on the side. Come back inside, and I'll get you a number. Might be tough getting parts though."

"That's okay. I bet L.J. knows somebody. Do you mind giving me a ride back into town?"

The man cringed. "I . . . uh . . . " Avoiding her eyes, he

said, "I would . . . but I'm waiting on an old boy to show up. You're welcome to use the phone though."

"That's so kind, but I'd hate for you to be seen alone with me. That's how rumors get started, you know. It's only half a mile back to town, but what the hell, people around here expect me to be walking the streets." She took a few steps before turning back around. "Look, I'm sorry. I'm sure you're just trying to stay out of trouble."

He nodded and shrugged almost apologetically.

"Hope it's not too big an inconvenience for me to leave my car here until I figure something out."

He ran his fingers through his comb-over. "Suppose you don't have a choice, but my wife sure ain't gonna like it when she gets wind of it." He turned around and went back inside.

The co-op sat to the east of town, but mad as she was, Angela covered the distance to L.J.'s in quick time.

Before arriving on his doorstep, she reached two conclusions, one, she did not have the money to fix her car, and two, she had no choice but to take the job at the Oasis. At least until she saved enough to pay for the repairs so she could find work elsewhere.


Lucas left Shelly's with new determination. She took the news of him hiring Angela better than expected. Now he simply had to find a way to get Jake and Angela together so nature could run its course.

With a good hour left before time to open the bar, he headed over to the café. A Whirlwind burger sounded a lot better to his stomach than another nuked Salisbury steak or a heat lamp chimichanga from Gulp and Go.

The lunch crowd had already drifted back to work by the time he arrived. Three old farmers sat at the counter, nursing steaming cups of coffee and swapping lies about the supposed good old days. Abby flashed Lucas a smile as he sat on a stool midway down the line.

"Hey Lucas, settle a bet," one of the coffee drinkers said.

"I'll try. What do you got?"

"Give us an honest opinion. A slice of pie is riding on this." The codger in overalls leaned closer. "You're down by six in the fourth with a minute left. No time-outs. Who do you want under center, Aikman, Montana, or Elway?"

Lucas shrugged. "Y'all might want to ask someone else. I'm not much of a football fan."

"There ain't nobody else here but Abby and Frank back in the kitchen, and he's a Cowboy fan to the bone. He'll say Aikman for sure. We need an unbiased answer."

"Okay, Elway."

"Pay up, boys." Mr. Overalls clapped his hands together.

"Ah, hell. I knew we shoulda waited on someone else. You can't expect a lawyer to come up with a common-sense answer to a straight-up question."

Lucas grinned at the sore loser's comment. Only in Grand could you get labeled as something you hadn't been in a decade. Fact was, he didn't know, or even care, who the best quarterback was. He simply went with the favorite team of the only man in the group who frequented the Oasis.

Abby leaned down a little too close for his comfort. "What can I get you?"

He scooted back from the counter. "Cheeseburger, no onions. Double order of fries, and a Dr. Pepper."

"Don't you get tired of eating Frank's greasy cheeseburgers, Lucas? Or those gawd-awful things Rene fries up at Gulp and Go? Let me cook you dinner tomorrow night. That way you can eat a decent meal the one night you don't have to work. A man shouldn't buy his gas and his dinner at the same place."

"'Least the convenience store sells 'em separate," Overall Man piped in. "With Frank's cooking, the gas comes automatic with the food."

All three farmers laughed when Frank called, "Watch it!" from his post at the grill.

Lucas was glad for the diversion. It was getting harder and harder for him to think up reasons not to let Abby cook him dinner. Anymore, they were about the only two single adults in town.

"I'm not a bad cook," Abby said with more than a hint of desperation to her voice.

Lucas felt a tinge of guilt as he always did when Abby got her feelings hurt. It didn't happen often, and he could have long ago sat her down and made it clear the two of them were never going to be more than friends, but something told him she would take that conversation badly. Perhaps it was a cowardly way of thinking, but wounding her pride every now and again seemed better than flat out breaking her heart.

The meat on the grill sizzled, and the fries popped in their grease bath, and still Abby didn't come back over to talk. Lucas watched her fold silverware into paper napkins as she stared out beyond the plate glass windows in the direction of his bar. At least Abby had it better than he did while working. The Oasis didn't have a single window.

Lucas sipped his soda and listened to the farmers complain about bind weed, Democrats, and the lack of rain.

After a few minutes, Abby headed his way, but her expression made it clear not all had been forgiven. "So, it's true? You hired Angela?"

He sipped his drink before answering. "Not yet, but I guess I will. If she's even interested."

The waitress's forehead wrinkled. "You know, I can

wait tables if you need help over there."

Lucas shook his head. "I don't really need help. I'm doing L.J. a favor more than anything. For all I know, Angela doesn't even want the job."

"Oh, she wants it." Abby folded her arms across her chest and pushed her lips out into a pout.

"What makes you say that?"

"Because she's standing over there by your front door." Abby pointed across the street.

Lucas twisted around on his stool and stared over at his building. Two gravel parking lots and a street separated the establishments, yet Lucas instantly recognized Angela. Her curvy figure and long blonde locks distinguished her from any other woman in Grand.

"Order up!" The cook slapped the silver bell and set Lucas's burger on the counter.

"Keep that warm for me. I better run across the street and talk to her before I eat."

Lucas kept his focus on Angela as he walked toward the bar, but she was staring off across the highway in the direction of the old grain elevator. An eighteen-wheeler roared through town, not slowing the least bit for Main's blinking caution.

The semi broke Angela's gaze, and for the first time, she looked up and spotted Lucas headed her way. She watched his approach through narrowed eyes.

His stomach tightened with every step. He didn't know why, but he couldn't shake the nervous feeling in his gut.

"Lucas?" The word came out more of a question than a greeting.

He extended his hand. "How are you, Angela? It's been a long time."

Her fingers felt clammy in his grip, but she was every bit as beautiful today as she was five years ago when he spotted her in the hallway of his college roommate's Chicago law office. Lucas could certainly see why the senior partner of that firm chose her as his mistress, but he wondered how she wound up in Chicago in the first place. He'd asked his buddy what he knew about her, but the guy was too worried about his nuptials the next day to care about the boss's girlfriend.

She snatched her hand back. "L.J. says you need a waitress." Her voice lacked enthusiasm.

"Only pays minimum wage, plus tips."

"When can I start?"

Her abruptness made him question his decision to hire her. Paying her salary wasn't going to strain his finances, but if her surly attitude drove customers away . . .

He grinned. "I didn't say I'd hire you yet."

She frowned and folded her arms across her chest. "Fine. Don't." Even with the scowl she was flat-out pretty.

"You have any experience?"

Angela snorted. "You've lived in this town your whole life. You know damn good and well I've had lots of experience."

He put up his hands. "I didn't mean—"

"Save the explanation. I can do the job. You want a reference, call L.J. Now, are you going to hire me, or not?"

He squinted at her, then nodded. "Come back at four. It'll be slow until the feedlot workers get off, so I'll have time to get you set up and show you how things work."

His stomach growled, so Lucas turned his back and headed for the Whirlwind and his waiting hamburger. If she wasn't going to bother with politeness, why should he?

# 11

Lucas sat alone at the Oasis, trying to decide if the rock in his gut resulted from the greasy Whirlwind burger or his frosty encounter with Angela. Confrontation and tension always left him distraught. Lucas knew he'd have a good-sized bleeding ulcer by now had he continued his law career. Not that it mattered. Quitting and moving back to Grand landed him in this current situation. He should've listened to his musical mentor, Cody, a long time ago and hit the road with his guitar, let the wind blow him someplace new every few days. Lucas wasn't the greatest guitar player or best singer the world had ever heard, but he was good enough to make a wanderer's living.

Instead he'd tied himself here, to this town, to this bar.

Surveying his surroundings, he noted the general decomposition of the place. Water stains bloomed on the yellowed plasterboard ceiling even though it hadn't rained a drop in months. Cigarette butts littered the floor, reminding him of a field of smelly, cancer-inducing wildflowers. And the bar itself felt sticky, as if the fifty-year-old wood had started to emit sap again. When he first came back to run his dad's business, everyone claimed the place would grow on him. They'd been correct. The Oasis had turned into an ambition-eating fungus.

He couldn't expect Shelly to celebrate her birthday in this kind of dive. Tomorrow, when the bar was closed, he would clean from top to bottom.

"Sitting here with all your friends?" Chester called out as he and L.J came through the door.

"They ran out the back when they seen y'all coming." Lucas reached into the cooler to retrieve Chester a beer.

"Who you kidding? Me and L.J. are the only friends you got. And truth be told, we only come for the beer." Chester laughed. "'Least I do. Don't know why this teetotaler comes anymore." The drunkard took up residence on his favorite stool.

Lucas returned the grin, though the statement contained enough truth to sting. Most people in Grand seemed to like him well enough, but there was nobody outside of Shelly he could confide in, and even with her there were limits to what he could reveal. He still talked to Cody on the phone, but only about music, and even those conversations ended in frustration. Cody never failed to bust his balls about being in love with Shelly, and Lucas had let his friend listen to far too many songs he'd written to try and deny the accusation.

"What's your poison, L.J.?" he asked, even though Lucas already knew the answer. L.J.'s latest drinking habits had turned him into a bartending barista.

"Coffee, if it's ready." The old man surveyed the room. "Where's your helper?"

"She'll be in later, but I hope she comes back in a better mood than she left. Didn't seem too enthusiastic about the job. Got the impression she feels the same way about me." Lucas handed the two men their drinks.

"Already told ya', don't nobody like you but us drunks." White foam fell off Chester's moustache when he laughed.

"Ain't you she doesn't like," L.J. said.

"Who is it then?"

L.J. shook his head. "Would you like to be caged in, surrounded by nothing but bad memories?"

Lucas shrugged. "I have my share of memories, but—"

"Then you ought to understand." L.J. pointed north across the highway. "Her father died in that grain elevator over yonder. Her mother ran off with Butch Jordan, leaving her to live with Elizabeth. I loved that woman, but she never done right by that girl."

"My family wasn't perfect either," Lucas interjected.

L.J. nodded. "Exactly."

Irritated, Lucas shook his head. "Exactly? What the hell does that mean?"

"Nothing." The old man dug out the makings for a smoke.

As the minutes ticked by, Lucas's aggravation grew, and he didn't even know why. He kept a nervous vigil on the door in anticipation of Angela's arrival.

"You're watching that door closer than you do the cash register. Get me another and take a deep breath," Chester said through a tobacco-stained grin.

Lucas shook his head, gathered up the empty bottle, and retrieved another beer. The two of them were acting smug, as if they knew something he didn't. He had his back to the door when the sunlight spilled in. He didn't need to turn to know it was Angela. He just had a feeling. It wasn't lost on him that Lucinda Williams was on the jukebox singing "Drunken Angel."

"Here's your beer. Now that I'm getting some help around here, maybe I'll get more done than play nursemaid." Lucas turned his attention from Chester and L.J. and focused on Angela. Slowly, she made her way toward the bar. Her eyes were fixed upon her shoe tops. Earlier today, she'd broadcast an air of confidence, almost defiance, and Lucas remembered her being self-assured in the past. Now she looked scared and lost.

"Hey, Angela. Glad you're here. These two have given me nothing but trouble all afternoon." Lucas pointed at the only customers in the joint.

She almost grinned.

Maybe L.J. was right. The anger she'd displayed earlier seemed to have evaporated. Lucas took a deep breath and led her behind the bar. He showed her around, where to find everything she would need, and then got her set up on his laptop to take the four-hour class required by the state to serve booze.

The evening progressed smoothly. Angela finished her certification and jumped right in to help keep tables clean and beers opened. She mixed a few drinks, but the Oasis wasn't exactly known for cosmopolitans and appletinis, so the learning curve wasn't too steep. Several of the cowboys complimented Lucas on his choice of waitresses, and he noticed the tips they left her were far more generous than they ever gave him.

By eleven, Lucas decided he should've hired help years ago. Business boomed for a Tuesday. He hadn't considered how many non-regulars would stop in for a quick beer to satisfy their curiosity by getting a good look at Angela. He wondered if she felt like the prodigal son, or if she'd gotten used to the attention over the years.

Angela had a good rapport with the feedlot guys but was quiet and distant with the town's long-time residents. Despite his best efforts to win her over, Lucas remained in the latter category.

"You're doing great. Easiest night I've had in years." Lucas helped her open bottles of beer for the table of pen riders.

"That's what you pay me for." Angela picked up the tray and walked away.

He looked up into the smiling faces of Chester and L.J. "What's so damn funny?"

"You," they both said.

Lucas went down to the other end of the bar to escape the old men. It was obvious they were up to something, but he couldn't decide what.

"Well, goddamn! It is true." Charlene's voice filled the air while her skinny body and shaggy red head filled the doorway. Her latest boyfriend clung to her arm.

They staggered over to a table and flopped down, both obviously soused even though they'd just arrived.

"Hey, you! Barmaid!" Charlene snapped her fingers and waved at Angela, who was busy at the other table. "How about some service over here?"

Lucas came around the bar just as Angela started toward Charlene's table. He held up his hand to indicate he would take care of them while addressing Charlene. "Don't come in here starting trouble." Lucas kept his eyes on the cowboy to make sure the idiot didn't feel compelled to defend his girlfriend.

"You started the trouble when you hired that whore." Charlene pointed across the room.

Lucas smiled despite the situation. "Charlene, you of all people have no—"

"Don't go there." She held the palm of her hand up to his face and cast a worried look at her companion, who thus far seemed content to stay quiet. "Matter of fact, we're leaving." She pushed back her chair and stood.

"But I ain't even had one beer," her date protested.

"You drank half a bottle of whiskey at my house. Now let's go." She latched onto his arm and pulled him to his feet. "I'll make it up to you." She sauntered toward the door, grabbing a handful of his ass on the way out.

Lucas snuck a peek at Angela who'd watched the entire scene from a few feet away. She stood motionless, her face devoid of emotion.

Going to her, he took the tray from her hand. "You

okay?"

She snatched the tray back. "I'm fine. Why wouldn't I be? I don't need you or anybody else to save me. I can handle my own problems." She stomped away.

The dressing-down left Lucas scratching his head. From the corner of his eye, he spied Chester and L.J. grinning like shit-eating possums. The old-timers were bound to offer advice he didn't want to hear, so Lucas scooped up the Gibson he kept behind the bar and marched off to the walk-in cooler. It was chilly inside, but at least he could take a breather and relax without Angela's attitude or L.J. and Chester's smiling at him like a couple of dumbasses.

Sitting on a case of Coors Light, he pulled the Hummingbird out of the case and began strumming the familiar chords of a song he'd been writing for months now. The guitar had seen more years than he had and with it in his hands, Lucas felt older, wiser, and more in control of the world around him.

The cooler wasn't totally soundproof, but only someone working behind the bar could hear. Nevertheless, Lucas only mouthed the words. Sometimes he played and sang a few old classics for L.J. and Chester when no one else was around, but no one in Grand had ever heard him sing anything he'd written.

He finished the part of the song he was happy with and tried a few combinations to keep it going, but nothing seemed right. So he abandoned his songwriting attempts and did his best to pick out Townes Van Zandt's "Lungs." Even though the Gibson once belonged to Townes, Lucas simply couldn't pick as well as his guitar hero. Still, it never failed to make him feel better to pick this guitar. He preferred it to the Martin he kept at home, but this guitar lived at the bar. It's where his dad always kept it after acquiring it from Townes himself, and Lucas couldn't imagine it ever leaving.

Had anyone asked, he would say he didn't believe in ghosts, but holding this guitar was the only time he ever thought of his dad as anything but a bitter old drunk. Of course, the Cadillac made him think of his mom, and she was still living, so most likely Lucas was guilty of romanticizing objects rather than believing in ghosts.

Angela snuck a glance at the bar while she wiped tables. Lucas leaned next to the cash register, chatting with L.J. and Chester. Everyone else had gone. The night had turned out better than she feared. Other than Charlene and a handful of gawkers, no one seemed to care about her past, though something about Lucas unnerved her.

Up until she ridiculed him for defending her, he'd acted friendly enough—almost too friendly. And he fidgeted like a child asking for candy before suppertime whenever he talked to her, but those habits didn't seem reason enough not to trust him. And she did appreciate his chivalry in standing up to Charlene. So why the unease?

Lucas had given her a job and ran Charlene off. Maybe he was simply a do-gooder like Misty. She made up her mind to apologize once L.J. and Chester left. Lucas had not said more than ten words since disappearing into the cooler. She'd heard him playing that guitar in there, and while that struck her odd, the world was full of people who did strange things. If they were going to work together, she needed to set things right.

Half an hour later, she'd cleaned the tables, emptied the ashtrays, swept enough cigarette butts off the floor to fill a cancer ward, and still, the trio of men had not moved a muscle. The clock above the bar read ten minutes until two. L.J. and Chester would surely leave soon.

"Damn, Lucas." Chester leaned against the bar for support and looked around. "Another week and she might get this place looking respectable." He spoke slowly with slurred words.

"This place will never look respectable with a mangy dog like you camped out all night long," Lucas shot back.

Chester pulled a wad of keys from the hip pocket of his Wrangler's. "Wanna ride?" He addressed Angela.

She watched him sway like a light pole in a hurricane. "No, you and L.J. go ahead. I'll walk. I want to talk to Lucas a minute."

"We can wait." Chester sat back down. "It's awful dark out there for a pretty lady like yourself to be taking a midnight stroll."

Angela smiled. "I'll be fine. This isn't Chicago. Nothing bad ever happens in Grand." She helped the drunk to his feet. "Maybe you should let L.J. drive."

Chester laughed. "Hell, he ain't even got a license. Come on, old man. Let's go." He slapped his skinny buddy on the back.

L.J. nodded for a good-bye and followed his friend outside.

Angela waited until the door closed behind them. "Can he drive?"

Lucas shrugged. "He's been going home like that long as I can remember. Nobody else is out this late, and it's only a few blocks. And like you said, nothing bad ever happens in Grand."

"Nothing good either," she added with sarcasm.

Emptying the register, he placed the cash in a large blue bank bag. "You could've taken off with them if you wanted."

"I wanted to talk to you." She picked at the coral nail polish on her thumbnail. "I wanted to apologize and say thank you for the job."

He zipped the money pouch before turning his back.

"I shouldn't have snapped at you for defending me either. I just . . . well, I've been taking care of myself for so long, and . . . I don't like to depend on other people too much. I've made that mistake before."

"Fair enough," he said. "I won't infringe on your independence again." He reached above the rows of liquor bottles and turned off the TV up in the corner, all the while avoiding eye contact with her.

"You're closed tomorrow, right?"

"Yep, every Wednesday."

Still, he wouldn't look her way. "Okay, guess I'll see you Thursday." She gathered her purse from beneath the counter and followed him to the door.

He flipped the light switch and locked up. "Yeah, Thursday." He smiled. "We'll be busy with the big birthday party. Should be an interesting night."

Climbing in his battered pickup, Lucas drove off leaving her alone in the empty parking lot to wonder whose birthday it was, and why it would be so interesting.

# 12

Lucas groped for the phone through the clutter on his night stand. "Hello," he croaked, his throat raspy from sleep.

"Lucas, I know you were asleep, but I need you do me a big favor."

"Shelly?" He shook his head to clear the drowsiness.

"I'm in Amarillo, God only knows where Jake is, and I refuse to call his mom, but the school called my cell, and somebody needs to pick up Austin. He hit his head and the nurse thinks he should go home and rest. I told them to let him walk, but the nurse won't release him without a ride."

"Yeah okay, but what time is it?" Lucas had played his guitar and worked on writing songs deep into the night. The last thing he wanted to do was get out of bed now.

"A little after ten."

He grimaced but swung his feet to the floor. "Call the school. Tell them I'll be there in a few."

"You're a life saver."

After he hung up, Lucas stood and stretched. He was stiff from the work he'd done yesterday at the Oasis, and he really didn't want to drive over to the school, but he could expect to be doing these kinds of things full time soon enough. Not for the first time, he gave thought to how Taylor and Austin would deal with their parents' divorce. Lucas hoped they wouldn't have a difficult time accepting him. Maybe he and Shelly would have a kid of their own. He'd always wanted children.

Dressing, he wondered what kind of father he would make. Hopefully, better than his own.

Actually, Lucas had to admit Hank Cahill was the type of father most teenage boys longed for. He'd never expected much of anything from Lucas, never preached, or yelled, and he allowed Lucas to come and go as he pleased. Hank didn't even mind if Lucas drank from the stash of booze at the house. He never concerned himself with anything his son did. The only thing his dad took an active interest in was alcohol, which was exactly why Lucas's mother left town.

Lucas resented his mother for leaving more than he did his father for being a drunk. At least his father only abandoned him mentally, not physically. Gathering his truck keys, he forced his mother from his mind. His feelings toward her were irrelevant. Soon enough he would be with the only woman that mattered to him.


Thursday morning dawned with Angela in better spirits than any time since she left Chicago. Her one night at the Oasis had erased most of her fears, and she'd earned nearly seventy dollars in tips. At that rate, she'd have enough money to move in a month or two. Things were definitely looking up.

The big birthday party was her last misgiving. If ever there was going to be trouble, Angela knew it would be tonight. She thought about calling Lucas and asking off when Misty told her the bash was for Shelly, but Angela refused to ask for more favors. Besides, she'd survived worse ordeals in her life. And Misty promised to be there, so did L.J. and Chester. That gave Angela three allies at the very least.

And Lucas had stood up for her with Charlene—but he wasn't likely to do it again, not after the way she'd reacted.

Actually, she felt more at ease about working for her former schoolmate after talking to L.J. and Misty. They both vouched for his character, and once L.J. revealed a few things about Lucas's past, Angela found herself sympathizing with her new boss.

Both of their mothers had ditched them, though Angela did not buy into L.J.'s notion they experienced a similar loss of fathers. Lucas's might have been an alcoholic, but she would take a drunk dad over a dead one any day. The eeriest parallels between her and Lucas were the events that brought them back to Grand. Both had returned as the result of a death, but unlike Lucas, she didn't plan to linger.

Neither L.J. nor Misty offered an answer for why Lucas stayed and abandoned his career after going to the trouble of earning a degree, though L.J. acted as if he knew more than he was sharing. Actually, neither of her friends wanted to talk about Lucas's past, but they both seemed eager to point out the fact that he was single, and as Misty said at least a dozen times, good-looking.


"Think. Think." Jake slapped his forehead with one hand and steered with the other.

He'd been racking his brain all morning trying to figure out a good present to buy Shelly. He'd gotten his ass in a crack before by not taking her birthday serious enough. No way in hell would he make that mistake again. Even if he didn't give two shits, she did, and Shelly would make his life miserable if he screwed it up. Her birthday meant more to her than Christmas, Valentine's Day, and their anniversary put together because unlike the other occasions, she didn't have to share the limelight.

Jake knew better than anyone how much Shelly thrived on being the center of attention, and when she wasn't, somebody paid—usually him. Last year, he set her off when he forgot to tell her happy birthday before leaving for the farm. For the next month, she pissed and moaned how he took her for granted. That's why he needed a show-stopper of a present.

He'd already hit up Charlene for suggestions, but she could only come up with jewelry, and he didn't want to spend a fortune. Besides, the only jewelry you could buy in Grand were cheap imitations, and Shelly wouldn't be caught dead wearing imitation anything. And he sure as hell didn't want to spend his afternoon driving up to Amarillo and back for a gift.

Jake headed over to the town square where there were a couple of shops and an antique store. If he didn't come up with something there, she'd be shit out of luck. He could always tell her his gift was on order and hadn't come in, then pick something up the next time he was in Amarillo. That story wouldn't keep him out of trouble, but Shelly would wait until they left the Oasis before pitching a bitch fit.

Driving over to the square gave him another chance to swing by the old Ross place. He'd driven by half a dozen times since Friday without so much as a glimpse. Supposedly, she worked at the bar, so he would see her tonight, but he wanted one look without his wife around.

Angela had to still be hot. Otherwise, Shelly would've gone on and on about how bad she looked, and his wife had been damn quiet regarding that subject. Too bad that was all she'd been quiet about. He was sick to death of her bitching about everything from firewood to his muddy boots.

He turned the corner, and there she was. Angela-fucking-Ross. Jake felt the blood rush to his dick and his heart accelerate. He couldn't believe his luck. There she sat on the porch swing staring blankly ahead. His eyes burned a hole in her as he drove past, and he swore he could smell the sweet scent of perfume as he drove past. She didn't seem to notice, even though he circled the block twice more.

On the third trip, Jake knew he had to stop. She was even hotter than he remembered. He needed to hear her talk. He wanted her voice in his head, so it would be her voice urging him on the next time he jacked off or fucked Shelly from behind and pretended she was somebody else.

As he idled up to the house, Angela glanced up, noticing the truck for the first time.

"Long time, no see." Jake hollered across the yard.

She leaned forward and squinted before responding. "Not long enough."

"Come over here and give a proper hello to an old friend." He tried to sound inviting so she would catch his drift.

"Will do. Next time I see one."

"That's no way to be." He opened the door and stepped outside. "You're breakin' my heart." He clutched his chest trying to look sincere. "We had some good times together."

She rose to her feet and finally offered him a full shot at her well-defined body. He liked the way her tits bounced as she stomped toward him. Boldly staring as she approached, he focused on her heaving chest. "Oh yeah, I remember the good times."

"I sure as hell don't." Angela crossed her arms, cutting out his view.

"Sure. Don't you remember prom? I gave you the best night of your life."

"All I remember about prom is some guy with a needle dick laying on top of me. If you say that was you, who am I to argue?"

"Look at you, a comedienne now. You and I both know why you came back. You wanted one more go around with Jake's snake, didn't you?" His eyes devoured her shapely body.

"You don't have a damn thing I need, or want. I'm not interested in any of you small-town losers. I'm used to real men now."

Jake smiled, glad to see she was still fiery. Their little game made him hard as a steel fence post. "Bet you do know a thing or two about men. Why don't you show me what you've learned?"

She turned and headed back toward the porch. Her ass was still damn nice too.

"Oh, come on. Don't act all uppity. It's not like you haven't already given it up to every man in this town. We both know what you are."

She stopped and turned back around. "What am I?"

"Willing and able."

Her cheeks flushed.

"You'll change your mind before long. I give it less than a week and you'll be begging for a piece of ol' Jake." He grabbed his crotch. "You know you want it."

"Looks to me like you're the one wanting something."

Angela hurried back toward the porch.

"Hell, I already had all I wanted!" he called after her. Actually, nothing was farther from the truth. He wanted her the way a junkie wants a fix, but he wasn't about to let her know that. Women like her only wanted what they couldn't have.

Jake watched her tight little ass disappear into the

house before getting back inside his truck. He hadn't felt this much adrenaline since he spotted that ten-point buck on the first day of deer season. Only this time, his sights were set on Angela.

One way or another, he would have her again. Another taste of her would be worth the risk. He'd cheated on Shelly before without getting caught, and if she found out this time, so be it. He would deal with that problem if it happened.

Putting the pickup in drive, he pulled up to the stop sign at the end of the block, still imagining Angela's body underneath his, writhing, sweating, moving in unison. A car horn shook him from his daydream and withered the image of them together. Jake was surprised to discover the beat-up truck that had pulled right up beside him.

Lucas Cahill's head hung halfway out the window, a shit-eating grin spread across his face. "She still looks good, huh?"

"Who?" Jake wasn't about to admit a damn thing only to have whatever he said repeated to Shelly. He wasn't stupid. He knew the two of them still talked. He'd tried to put a stop to it, but he couldn't afford to press too much, and Shelly was too damn worried about her precious reputation to actually have an affair. Not to mention Jake wanted something to hold over his wife's head in case he ever got caught with his pants down.

"Angela. I saw you two talking. What did she say?"

Jake shrugged. "Not much."

"That's funny," Lucas said. "The other night at the bar, you were all she talked about."

"Really?" Jake remained cautious.

Lucas held his hands up. "Don't get me to gossiping. All I'm gonna say is you must have left a lasting impression with her back in school."

"Don't jack with me."

"I'm just telling you what she said." Lucas started to roll up his window, then stopped. "You might want to go home and check on Austin. I just left your house, and he has a nasty knot on the back of his head."

"Austin? What the hell—" Jake's question was cut off the by the rattle of Lucas's pickup speeding away.

Jake shook his head and threw a U-turn in the middle of the street. Shelly would have to wait on her damn present. Right now, he wanted to know why his son wasn't in school and what the hell Lucas Cahill was doing at his house. Shelly had questions to answer, and Jake didn't give a shit what day of the year it was.

13

Angela scooted the wilted lettuce around the bowl with her fork. She should've known better than to order a grilled chicken salad in a place that specialized in grease-induced heartburn. The Whirlwind Café had never been a haven for healthy eaters, but it almost seemed as if they'd gone out of their way to serve a bad meal. Pushing the dish to the edge of the table, she tried to rekindle the optimism she'd felt this morning, when her life seemed headed in the right direction—before idiots from the past began showing up everywhere she turned.

Jake's audacity was not only aggravating, but stressful. His interest spelled nothing but trouble, and he was too stupid to accept he didn't stand a chance. He would make more ridiculous propositions. Sixteen years ago, his swagger and cocky attitude made him seem like a man among boys. Now those attributes had the reverse effect. Far as Angela could tell, the paunch above his belt and the thinness of his hair were the only things about him to change.

She could handle Jake if he tried again. In her days at LiveWirez, she'd dealt with plenty of misguided fools, but Shelly would be another matter. Once she found out her husband had wandering eyes, she would blame Angela.

"Something wrong with your salad?"

Angela stared at ghost-of-the-past number two. If she'd

known Abby DeWitt worked here, she never would've come in, regardless of her hunger. "It's fine. I don't eat much."

Abby picked up the uneaten lunch. "Watching your figure, huh? Afraid Lucas will fire you if you gain a pound, since it seems he won't hire a waitress, unless she's skin and bones." She stomped off to the kitchen.

The attitude from Gabby Abby was more comical than Jake still thinking of himself as Mr. Studly. As a teenager, Abby earned the reputation of being everyone's friend to their face, and spreading gossip behind their backs. She'd apparently grown some. Least now she was honest about displaying her true opinion.

Abby stayed away but a few minutes. "Here's your bill, and just so you know, we don't take checks, 'least not from out-of-towners."

"I have cash. People leave really good tips for us skin-and-bone waitresses."

Abby flinched and turned red. "I don't know why Lucas hired you. He's gotten along for years without help." She scooped the money off the table.

Suddenly, it dawned on Angela. The waitress was jealous. Nobody in their right mind wanted to work at a shabby place like the Oasis, so her envy had to stem with Lucas.

Angela stepped outside and shivered. Thick, gray clouds had drifted across the sun, and the wind had picked up and shifted to the north. She'd forgotten how hard it blew here. Chicago might have the Windy City name, but the title didn't hold in comparison to the blustery Texas Panhandle.

The winds in Chicago had been cold and damp blowing off the lake. Like a bullet, it hit hard and fast before ricocheting off the buildings. The stiff gusts started at the lake and ended in the tangle of buildings, houses, and people of the city.

The gale force here was much different. It went on evermore, with no starting or stopping point. The squall seemed to barrel down from the very edge of the earth and continue on forever. The wind here grabbed hold of you and did not let go, as if it could gather you in and roll you along, like a tumbleweed.

She'd despised this wind as a child but now viewed it as a sign. Shivering, Angela wished the breeze could carry her straight out of town. Instead, she trudged across the street to the Oasis.

Paint fumes permeated the air outside the entrance and her mouth dropped when she entered. The place looked totally different than it had thirty-six hours ago. Perched three-quarters of the way up a stepladder, Lucas was hanging a huge banner. *The Happy Birthday, Shelly* sign stretched all the way across the room.

"Am I in the right place?"

Lucas jumped at the sound of her voice. "You always sneak up on people?"

"The door was open." She ran her hand down the freshly sanded and stained bar. "You've been busy. Doesn't look like the same place."

"Thanks." He stepped down and carried the ladder back to the cooler.

Angela meandered around the room, checking out the rest of his handiwork. The place had been filthy, now it seemed almost too tidy for a small-town dive. The walls were covered with fresh paint, the floor had been swept and waxed, and somehow he'd coaxed an extra amount of brightness from the fluorescent lights. Nowhere could she see so much as a speck of fly crap.

He reappeared and began meticulously arranging the chairs. "You're early. Chester and L.J. won't be here for another half hour or so."

"I saw your truck from the café, so I decided to come on over. Abby wanted me out of there, and I thought you might need a hand getting the place ready for the big birthday party. But I see you managed without me."

He shrugged and continued to shift the tables and chairs as if his life depended on their precise placement. "You're not the only self-sufficient person in this town."

She smiled at his jab. His defiant indifference somehow made him more likable. "So, why did you suddenly decide to hire a waitress?"

He stopped what he was doing. "Why do you ask?"

"Abby made it very clear you've never needed help before, so she can't understand why you hired me."

He stepped back, surveyed one of the tables, then scooted it two inches to the right. "She's just jealous I didn't hire her."

"I kind of figured." Angela pointed to one of the tables. "Move that one three more inches to the left."

"You think so?" He stepped back and surveyed the alignment with one eye closed.

"No. Stop being so anal. The place looks great."

He took a deep breath and smiled, revealing a faint set of dimples. "Thanks. I've about killed myself. How about I pour us a couple of cokes and we take a break?"

"Okay," Angela said, taking a seat at the bar. "But only if you answer my question. Why did you hire me?"

Lucas looked her in the eye. "Because L.J. asked me to."

"That's it? You didn't really need a waitress?"

"I probably did," he said, filling two glasses with ice. "But I've managed to go alone this long, so hiring help wasn't anything I'd considered until he asked."

Taking the offered glass, she liked the fact he was being honest, but while he was in the mood to speak the truth, she had a few more questions. "Were you worried about my reputation?"

"It's a bar."

"What does that mean?"

He shrugged. "It means nobody gives a shit about reputations, long as the beer is cold and the whiskey does the trick."

"That's a load of bullshit." She set her coke on the bar. "Half this town hates me because they think I'm gonna screw their man, and the other half hopes I will screw them. All the booze in the world isn't going to change that."

Lucas smiled.

"You think that's funny?"

"I think it's true," he said. "Though your numbers are skewed. After all, a good portion of the folks are too damn old to care about you one way or another, some are too young to know the stories, and Buddy Hibbs is gay, so I doubt he's hoping you seduce him, nor is his partner overly concerned with your reputation."

Pleased he hadn't tried to deny what they both knew was the truth, she nodded and said, "I have to confess. Back in the day I actually tried to seduce Buddy Hibbs. 'Least now I know why he ran like a scared rabbit."

Lucas tilted his head back and laughed.

She liked the sound.

When he looked at her again, he said, "Buddy Hibbs? Really?"

Angela shrugged. "What can I say? I wasn't all that choosy in those days."

"Well, shit, you really know how to give a guy a complex."

Angela studied Lucas. It struck her they were at a pivotal point in their conversation, in how they would interact from this point forward. She could play the part—pretend to be the slutty vixen so many considered her to be, or she could tell the truth about her motivation to sleep with Buddy Hibbs and most of the others. But did she really want to give that much of herself to Lucas, who after all was just her boss? Sure, they'd gone to school together, but she didn't know him? Not really. Not now. And not back then. So, she chose a safer, less personal version of the truth.

"Hate to break it to you, Lucas, but I don't remember much about you from school. I know you were always there, and I remember you giving the speech at graduation, but as far as who you dated, who your best friend was, why we never ended up in a backseat together" — she took a sip of her drink — "that I can't tell you."

"So what you're saying is I was insignificant."

Angela smiled. "Take the lawyer out of the office, but you still can pick 'em out of a crowd. Insignificant is your word, not mine. Fancy vocabulary aside, I mean you were not on my radar. Which might be my best decision ever, because if I'd slept with you, I wouldn't be here now. Last thing I want is intimate knowledge of my boss, and without this job I'd be in a hell of a mess."

"Aha!" Lucas pointed a finger in dramatic fashion. "Ladies and gentlemen of the jury, I offer proof that now the tables have turned, and it is this witness on the stand that is, to borrow the phrase, serving up a load of bullshit." He stood and paced around the bar like a TV lawyer. "Tossing aside the ridicule of my eloquent vernacular, the witness clearly used the word *decision*, which by its very definition applies a choice was made. And if said witness made a choice, one can only presume she did, in fact, notice one Lucas Cahill."

She clapped at the end of his performance. "Yep, a lawyer to the bone, and an egotistical one at that. Though, now I wonder why you're here slopping drinks rather than railing poetically in some courtroom."

"You and everybody else," Lucas said, but a shadow

blocked the open door before he could say more.

"Can we close this damn blowhole?" Chester stepped inside with L.J. right behind him.

"Go ahead, "Lucas said. "But don't blame me if we all die from the fumes."

"Whew," Chester let out a low whistle. "This place is purtier than a Parisian whorehouse."

"Sorry, I'm fresh out of whores, French or otherwise, but I'm clean up to my ears in foolish old drunks and their reformed sidekicks." Lucas grinned.

His comment formed a lump in Angela's throat. Perhaps it was pathetic to consider such a statement flattering, but Lucas's words affected her just the same. He might've still made the statement if he considered her a whore, but he would have hesitated, or at least glanced guiltily her direction. Not doing so convinced her Lucas really didn't care about her reputation. Working here for him wasn't going to be so bad after all.

"Damn, what's taking you so long? Figured you'd be in a hell of a hurry to go see Lucas."

Shelly whirled to face her husband. "Shut up about Lucas. If you would turn on your damn cell I wouldn't have had to call him."

Jake shook his head. "How many times do I have to tell you, service is spotty at best out on the farm. And hurry the hell up. It's after seven already. Everybody's going to be drunk before we get there."

"It's a bar, not a frat party. There'll be plenty of beer left, and I'm sure it won't take you long to catch up. It never does." She studied her face in the mirror. "It isn't proper for the guest of honor to show up early. I'm supposed to make an entrance after everyone else arrives." She patted the underside of her chin.

"You ain't the Queen of England. Nobody gives a shit what time you get there."

She grabbed her handbag. "Let's go." She could never explain to Jake why she needed to be the last to arrive. He would never understand she wanted everyone to have their small talk over and done with so she would be the focal point of conversation. This was her birthday, not some ordinary gathering.

The parking lot was full by the time they pulled down Main. Shelly nodded with satisfaction. Elizabeth Ross's funeral wasn't the only attraction in town.

Jake parked in the café lot and launched into another speech about being late. "Told you we should've left earlier. I hate parking over here. It's too friggin' cold to be walking."

"Walking isn't going to kill you. Might even work off some of that gut." She poked a finger into his midsection. "Besides, it's not that cold. It's only September. What are you going to do when December rolls around?"

He patted his stomach. "This is muscle, not fat."

"Whatever." Shelly stopped and faced her husband before they stepped inside. "Look, I know you think you have to get drunk and act like Mr. Macho, but just this once, don't do or say anything stupid. Okay?"

Jake opened his mouth to reply, but his wife brushed passed him before he could get the words out. He followed her in, but she trotted straight over to Charlene, who was latched on to some wannabe-cowboy's elbow. No wonder she hadn't called him lately. She was always on the prowl for fresh meat, but at least she didn't complain about his stomach.

He eyed the scrawny kid. That Stetson on his head didn't make him a cowboy, or a man. Charlene would use up a young punk like him in no time. Eventually she'd need a man with staying power. When that happened, she would tell Shelly something needed fixing at her house. And like a dutiful friend, Shelly would send Jake over to make the repair. Just once, he'd like to tell his wife what really went on at Charlene's when he went to unclog the pipes.

Turning his attention to the bar, he spotted Angela. Shelly couldn't fault him for ordering a beer, so he strolled over to the cash register. "Hey good lookin', how about a cold one?" Jake looked over his shoulder to make certain Shelly wasn't within earshot. "Or a hot one?"

Chester and L.J. were the only customers at the bar, so he wasn't worried about anyone relaying his words to his wife. Nobody paid attention to those two old drunks, and everybody else was gathered around the table kissing Shelly's ass.

Angela bristled at the sound of Jake's voice. She'd been chatting with Chester and L.J., and hadn't noticed him arrive. Without looking up, she was willing to bet Shelly wasn't nearby. Otherwise, he wouldn't be so bold. So much for getting through the night without trouble.

Ignoring Jake, she continued her conversation with the pair at the bar. Lucas had made it clear he would handle the birthday party if she took care of Chester and L.J., so Jake could wait.

Chester glanced down at Jake and then asked, "You gonna get him a beer?"

"Nope."

"He might go away if you do." L.J. offered.

"Here." Angela pulled a beer from the cooler and handed it to Chester. "You give it to him."

Chester slid the bottle down the bar like a seasoned bartender in an old western. She refused to so much as glance his way, but she could see him out of the corner of her eye. He stood there for another couple heartbeats and then finally walked away.

"What the hell was that all about?" Chester asked.

"He's a cocky jackass that mistakenly thinks his reputation impresses me."

"Keep an eye on him. The Sampsons think they're entitled to anything they want," L.J. said.

"Since when did you become an expert on Jake Sampson?" Chester guzzled his beer.

"He's just like his daddy."

"Jake ain't near as tough as ol' Bud. Hell, I betcha Shelly makes him toe the line at home," Chester laughed. "That's why he's gotta act like Billy Bad-Ass everywhere else."

"I don't trust him," L.J. flatly stated.

Angela agreed, but she didn't want to discuss Jake, so she drifted to the other end of the bar. Problem was, that put her in closer proximity to the partygoers.

Shelly, her back ramrod straight, perched at the end of the longest table, sipping a margarita with Charlene to her right and Abby DeWitt on the left. Misty and a couple of other girls Angela remembered from school filled out the rest the space. The men, with the exception of Charlene's boyfriend, had all migrated to the pool table. She kept a tight grip on the poor fellow's hand, as if he might make a break for the door. Angela wouldn't have blamed him.

When Lucas wasn't fetching drinks from the bar, he hovered around Shelly like a bee over the only flower for miles. It all began to make sense—why he had gone to so much trouble cleaning the place. He was enamored with Shelly. And just when Angela thought he might be a nice, normal guy.

Placing another full tray of mixed drinks on the table, he cheerfully asked, "You ready to open presents?"

Angela shook her head at such a pathetic display. How could anybody so damned smart buy into Shelly's *Look at me, I'm little Miss Perfect* routine? But Lucas wasn't alone.

Shelly opened one present after another. How could such a self-centered, ungracious person have so many friends? And frankly, she wasn't even that pretty anymore.

As kids, Angela disliked Shelly for these very reasons, and now all that old resentment resurfaced. To get away from the scene, she walked back over to the two old-timers. She had no time for jealousy. Those kinds of petty feelings were for high school girls.

"What's Lucas's deal?" She handed Chester another beer to replace the one he'd just drained.

"What deal?" He twisted the cap off and flung it in the direction of the trash can.

"He's making a fool of himself over there. Acting like some love-starved teenager."

Chester leaned back on his stool to look around L.J. "He always acts like that around her. Gal has some sort of magic spell over him. Ain't that right, L.J.?"

"I don't know if I'd call it magic, but he's sure ate up with her. He needs to snap out of it. Loving a woman too much is a damn shitty road to travel," L.J. commented with sadness in his voice.

Angela understood he was talking about himself as much as Lucas.

"Maybe you can snap him out of it," Chester addressed Angela through a crooked smile.

She put her hands up. "Not me. That's not my job."

"Could be," L.J. said. "If you decided it was."

"Uh-uh." She shook her head. Lucas is my boss. Nothing more." Angela folded her arms and cocked her head to study the scene over at the party table. "Granted, someone should save him, but not me. He's only my boss."

L.J. raised one brow. "You said that already."

Angela stared at Shelly. "I don't know what everyone sees in her."

Chester nudged L.J. with his elbow. "She sure is gettin'

riled up about a feller that's just her boss."

"Don't start with me. Lucas Cahill can be infatuated with whomever he wants. Doesn't affect me one way or the other."

"Whatever you say." Chester nodded.

Angela turned her back on the would-be matchmakers before they said anything else. Lucas might be a nice guy, but any man that had a thing for Shelly had serious problems, as well as bad taste. Angela had enough of her own issues without trying to save somebody else.

Her opinion of Lucas dropped lower as the night wore on. They'd had a nice conversation this afternoon, but he hadn't said two words to her since Shelly's arrival, and he'd been just as rude and distant with L.J. and Chester. Lucas needed to learn how to treat his friends. He was in for a surprise the next time he tried to buddy up with her. He wasn't going to have his cake and eat it too, not at her expense. From now on, Lucas Cahill was merely her employer.

"You look like you're mad at the world."

Angela looked up at the sound of Misty's voice. At least there was one person not completely blinded by Shelly's "brilliance."

"Not mad. Just facing reality. How's the party?"

"Okay, but me and Mark are leaving. Shelly and Charlene are starting to get tipsy, and I don't like when they get drunk. I'm glad you got this job and all, but I miss us getting together."

"Yeah, me too. Maybe we can have lunch sometime."

She waved to Misty and her husband as they headed for the exit. Mark gave her a barely noticeable nod as they walked out. Until then, he'd avoided eye contact all night, but Angela didn't hold his aloofness against him. Matter of fact, aside from a few sideways glances and no doubt whispered comments, the partygoers had all steered clear of her, even though most of them were former classmates. Jake was the lone exception. He'd only spoken the once, but his constant stares made the hair on the back of her neck stand up.

Only Misty had left, but Shelly felt interest shifting away from her. She still held Lucas and Charlene's undivided attention, but she'd lost the others' focus. To make matters worse, her guests were starting to talk about Angela.

Lucas touched her shoulder. "How about a birthday dance?"

The Oasis did not have the best of dance floors, but Shelly agreed. Lucas was a good two-stepper and Jake would be jealous. Later tonight, he would make some snide remark about Lucas being light on his feet and launch into his usual speech about it not being right for her to have a male friend.

"What do you think?" Abby asked when Shelly sat back down.

"What do I think about what?"

"You don't even want to know," Charlene chimed in.

"About Angela. Think she's had plastic surgery? I mean, by all rights she should have that rode-hard-put-up-wet look by now. I say she's had plenty of work done to still look like that."

Charlene rolled her eyes as Shelly felt a burning inside her. Not only were they talking about Angela, they were saying she looked great.

"I say once a whore, always a whore," Charlene offered.

Several eyebrows raised. It was the pot calling the kettle black for Charlene to call anyone a whore. Her sexual escapades were common knowledge to everyone in attendance, yet not a soul commented. The redhead knew secrets that would embarrass every single person at the table, and she wasn't afraid to speak her mind, so no one dared risk her wrath.

Shelly didn't want to discuss Angela, but if she let her true feelings be known, someone might pick up on her bitterness and jealousy. Somehow she needed to make Angela look bad without sounding petty. She took a big swig of her margarita for inspiration and tried to think of a way to accomplish her goal. The now-empty glass in front of her offered no solution. Maybe another drink would help her think. She looked for Lucas to order another round.

He was nowhere to be found. "Where's Lucas?" She asked Charlene.

The redhead pointed to the cooler door.

Lucas's absence inspired Shelly. "Hey, barmaid," she shouted, putting a strong emphasis on the word *maid*. "We need service over here." She snapped her fingers.

Every eye in the bar turned to Angela. Even Chester and L.J. put down their drinks and twisted around on their stools. As much as she hated to, Angela had to go over to the table. Shelly was calling her out. Only the setting and the lack of six-guns distinguished this scene from an Old West gunfight. Angela hoped the expression on her face did not reveal the turmoil in her gut. She wanted to choose her words wisely—to stay in control and not be goaded into something she'd later regret.

Nearing the table, Angela strived to appear indifferent. "What can I get for y'all?"

Shelly's mouth opened and closed like a hungry baby bird's, yet not a sound escaped. Angela could tell her rival had expected a different reaction, and now the stunned birthday girl didn't know how to react. She bowed her head and mumbled an order for a pitcher of frozen margaritas. Angela suppressed a victorious grin and returned to the bar.

Chester watched her pour the tequila into the blender. "You should've told her to kiss your ass. She's trying to impress her friends."

"I know, that's why I didn't. I'll beat her at her own game."

"I'd tell her to kiss my ass anyway. It's people like her that make this town a shitty place to live, thinking they're all high and mighty. Their shit stinks just like mine." Chester took another pull from the bottle in front of him.

Angela smiled. She could not agree more. She had expected and dreaded this very attitude, but now that it was here, she felt at ease. Problems were always easier to deal with out in the open. Besides, she could outwit these people. Shelly was too predictable, too sure of herself. Life had gone the spoiled woman's way far too long.

Lucas stared at the guitar in his hand. He'd planned to bust it out tonight, and sing *Happy Birthday* and maybe one of the songs he'd written as well. But that idea seemed stupid now. Pathetic even.

Lucas was no fool. He knew damn near everyone on the other side of the cooler door was aware how he felt about Shelly. He'd never been all that good at keeping it a secret or disguising his true feelings. The crowd gathered around Shelly would simply view his performance as a shameless attempt to woo their friend. Some would pity him, others scoff. Jake had been drinking enough that the act would piss him off and possible provoke him to do something stupid. But Lucas didn't care about any of the partiers except one. And if things turned ugly, or Jake made a scene, Shelly would blame Lucas.

He set the guitar down. If only he could give her a private show—let her listen to any number of the songs he'd written, mostly about her.

Lucas opened the cooler door just in time to hear Shelly call out, "Hey, barmaid!" He watched Angela nonchalantly stroll over and take Shelly's order. She wasn't exactly smiling, but she wasn't scowling like Shelly either.

He stepped out as Angela made her way toward the bar. He was all at once surprised, disappointed, and strangely proud of his new employee. The defiant spitfire he remembered from their school days never would've allowed Shelly to openly call her out like that. She would have marched over, grabbed Jake by the hand, and led him off to temptation. 'Least that's how the legend was told these days.

Angela supposedly slept with the boyfriend of any girl who dared cross her, and given her reputation in school, not a single hormonal boy ever refused. Back then, Lucas often regretted he didn't have a steady gal to get on her bad side.

He sat down beside Shelly just as Angela delivered a margarita.

Shelly took one drink before making a horrible retching sound and spitting her drink back into the glass. "Yuck! This is the foulest margarita I've ever tasted! Lucas, I know it's hard to find good help these days, but couldn't you hire someone smart enough to mix a drink?" She spoke loud enough for all to hear.

"Yeah, this stuff tastes like shit!" Charlene joined in. "Of course, her family has a history of poisoning people."

Angela visibly stiffened at the not-so-subtle reference to her grandmother. She stood expressionless behind the bar, clearly hurt by Charlene's statement.

Lucas stood. "I'll make some more."

"No." Shelly grabbed his arm. "She screwed them up. Let her fix them." She continued to speak loud, although the bar had again gone silent except for the jukebox.

Not wanting to cross Shelly, he nodded at Angela to go ahead. Lucas longed to bail her out, to get up and make the drinks himself. It wasn't like Shelly to be this coldhearted. But he struggled to go against Shelly, especially with her fingers curled around his arm.

This was not part of his plan. He hated to see Shelly degrading Angela. What Lucas wanted was to see Jake in trouble, but when he looked over at his rival, he noticed Jake was too drunk to do anything other than sit and stare at Angela with his mouth hung open.

Angela finished the new batch of drinks and started their direction with the tray held high in one hand. She stepped between Shelly and Charlene to deliver the drinks, but then chaos erupted. The tray and glasses landed on Charlene with a heavy thud.

"You stupid bitch!" Charlene's hand shot to her nose.

It took Lucas a few seconds to realize what happened. Apparently, L.J. had bumped Angela on his way by to the restroom. Now he was staggering around as if drunk while explaining how he'd tripped. The longer he talked, the worse his speech slurred, but Lucas knew good and well the old man had not had a drop of alcohol in over a week. Charlene continued to screech like a demented cat.

L.J. continued his garbled apology. The old codger was angling for an Oscar. Lucas bit back a smile until he looked at Shelly and discovered most of the liquid from the pitcher had found its way onto her. Hatred illuminated her eyes as she sat motionless, staring into space. Margarita dripped from her hair, and her normally refined features had transfigured into something dark and sinister, almost ugly. Brows pinched together to form a hostile V and her thin, straight lips were held in a tight, straight line. When Lucas's eyes met hers, she looked away.

"Lucas Cahill!" Charlene screamed. "Are you going to

fire that whore for this, or you gonna just sit there looking stupid?"

Lucas turned from Shelly and faced Charlene, who was rubbing the fast rising knot on the bridge of her nose. No doubt Shelly, too, wanted him to fire Angela. But even if he wanted to, he couldn't, not with L.J. already in a cantankerous mood. All the old man had to do was state his theory about Angela's return, and Lucas would really be in trouble.

"Looked like an accident to me. I'd say L.J. is to blame if anybody is, and I can't exactly fire him." Lucas chuckled. No one else did.

"I ain't staying anyplace where she's welcome." Charlene pointed at Angela. "I'll never step foot in this dive again."

"Well, that breaks my heart." Lucas clutched his chest.

"Fuck you, Lucas!" Charlene stepped toward the door. "You coming, Shelly?"

All eyes turned to Shelly. Lucas wished she would say something. Her stillness and lack of physical reaction worried him.

Finally, she nodded. "Yes. I need to go home," she whispered. Attempting to stand, she immediately stumbled and fell back into the chair.

Lucas rushed to catch her, realizing she was far drunker than he first thought. "Shelly, let me drive you home. Neither you or Jake has any business behind the wheel." He didn't give a damn about Jake, but if something happened to Shelly . . .

"You've done your part," Charlene snapped. "Hiring that whore was quite enough."

# 14

Angela tried to focus on her work instead of the hubbub near the door, but her eyes flicked that direction just the same. Jake winked when he caught her looking, Charlene screamed about suing, and Shelly stood there still dripping margarita on the floor.

Lucas looked absolutely panic-stricken. Angela didn't even try to hide her smile.

As the partygoers exited, she spoke to the pair at the bar. "Thanks, but you didn't have to do that."

"Don't go thanking me. It was an accident." L.J. stood. "Now that the path is clear, I better hit the head." He retreated to the bathroom without the slightest hint of a stagger.

Chester shook his head. "Don't let that old goat fool you. He knew exactly what he was doing."

"It was sweet for him to defend my honor like that."

"He didn't do it for you." Chester lifted his beer. "Well, it mighta been partly for you, but mostly your grandma. He wasn't about to sit here and let Charlene run her down by bringing up Ansel's death."

Angela nodded. "I know he loved her. She loved him too. That's what makes the whole thing so sad."

"You be careful." Chester changed the tone of the conversation. "Don't be fooled into thinking that's the end of it. Those two will blame you, not L.J. They ain't the type to let a thing like that slide."

L.J. and Lucas's arrival cut short their discussion. The four were the only ones left in the bar. Everyone else trickled out after Charlene left with Shelly in tow.

"Sorry, Lucas, it was a—" L.J. lowered his head.

"You don't have to explain. Let's just leave it at that." Lucas didn't blame L.J. for what he'd done. Charlene had it coming. Her comment crossed the line, and the incident would've been funny had Shelly not been drenched.

The four stared at one another for several long minutes until Chester broke the silence. "This damn somber mood is ruining my perfectly good drunk. I'm cutting out before y'all sober me up." He stood when nobody reacted. L.J. followed suit and followed Chester out the door.

Lucas was relieved when the pair left. He wanted to be alone. Turning around, he faced Angela. "You can go, too, if you want. Doubt anyone else comes in."

"I'll stay," Angela answered tersely. "The more hours I work, the faster I escape this town."

Her harsh tone struck Lucas. Every time he started to feel sorry for her, that attitude showed up and chased away his regret. What did she have to be upset about? No one dumped a tray of margaritas on her head. The love of her life hadn't just walked out the door without saying a word.

"Take the rest of the night off, I'll leave you on the clock. Go home and relax. You'll get paid."

"I'm outta here then. It's not like I want to stay."

Lucas watched her gather her things from beneath the bar and hurry toward the door. Obviously, she blamed him. He knew how she felt—Lucas blamed himself for starting this whole mess. He hollered across the room in a last-ditch effort to show he accepted the responsibility.

"See ya' tomorrow! It has to get better . . . ," he trailed off when she disappeared outside without so much as a backward glance.

He shook his head. *Let her be mad.*

To avoid being compared to his dad, Lucas rarely drank whiskey. Tonight would be an exception. Pulling out a bottle, he poured a shot. The bourbon burned all the way down. He barely noticed, as the doubt burning a hole in his soul was far more painful. For the first time, he gave thought to the notion his plan might not succeed. The set-up had been too easy. He should've known the execution would be a struggle. Something like this happened every time he got close.

Downing another shot, Lucas's mind drifted back. Not a day went by without him thinking of their prom night. The memory of their first kiss carried him to this day — nothing compared to that moment. Lucas yearned to feel not only her soft lips again, but also that sense of hope and promise.

Rarely did he think about the rest of that night so as not to tarnish his memory with thoughts of sex, or maybe he chose to forget because the rest of their encounter was far from spectacular. As two drunken, inexperienced teenagers, they were not capable of earth-shattering sex. None of that mattered. That first kiss was magical, and that's what he clung to.

He'd mistakenly believed that night to be the beginning for him and Shelly. Instead, it proved to be the end. The next day, she reconciled with Jake. A month later, they all graduated, and two weeks after that, Shelly became Mrs. Jake Sampson.

Lucas tried to talk her out if it. He tried to discuss the night they spent together, but all Shelly would say was it had been a mistake. She pleaded with Lucas to understand, but that was something he'd never managed to accomplish.

He left for college and stayed away from Grand until his father's death eight long years later. By then, Lucas could see Shelly no longer loved Jake, but with two little boys, she was hopelessly stuck in the loveless marriage.

Carrying the bottle over to the jukebox, he punched up his favorite Mike McClure song and sang along to "Haunt Me No More" while wondering how many more years it would take to convince himself, and Shelly, their one night together was anything but a mistake.

Jake took one look at Shelly passed out in bed and knew what he had to do. Watching Angela parade around the bar with her tight little ass poured in those jeans had left him hungry. And since his wife was down for the count and basically worthless, he had to satisfy his needs elsewhere. Angela didn't know what she wanted yet, so that left Charlene. Long as he didn't start his truck, Shelly would never know he was gone. And no one stayed up in this town later than the news, so the nosy old bats wouldn't see him. The walk to Charlene's would be chilly, but she could warm him when he got there.

Grabbing his coat and the last bottle of beer from the fridge, he headed out into the darkness. If he got his ass in gear, he could be at her place in less than ten minutes.

Taking a swig of beer, he paused at the corner of Angela's street. She was the one he really wanted to see anyway, and if the lights were off, he could still go on to Charlene's. It would only be a block out of the way.

Jake started down the street but turned around after only a few feet. It was already late, and he would have to smooth talk Angela into bed. On the other hand, Charlene wouldn't take much convincing. Pop in, have his fun, and be back home in an hour. Satisfy his urges and get some sleep, without any extra bullshit. Besides, in the dark he could pretend it was Angela beneath him.

Sucking in his stomach and swelling up his chest, he knocked. Charlene had never complained about his physical appearance, but he didn't want to give her the ammunition to start.

She opened the door and pulled him inside. "What the hell are you doing here? I've told you never to show up unless Shelly sends you."

"Damn, you look like shit." Jake studied her face. Her nose had swollen to twice its normal size in the hour since he'd seen her. Both eyes had developed black circles around them, making her look like the bastard child of a prizefighter and a raccoon.

"Screw you, Jake! It's not like it's my fault. What are you doing here? Does Shelly know?"

"Hell no, she doesn't even know I'm gone, but you know what I'm here for." Jake grabbed her around the waist. "She's passed out. What she doesn't know won't hurt her."

Struggling out of his grasp, Charlene pointed a long red nail at him. "Someone else might have. It's too risky. What if Jimmy saw you?"

"I ain't scared of that little shit-kickin' punk." He reached for her hand. "I came because I've missed you and that hard-working tongue of yours." Jake flicked his tongue suggestively back and forth.

He wasn't about to tell the redhead that seeing Angela got him all hot and bothered, not when he could tell Charlene was warming up to the idea of some loving.

"I'll leave if that's what you want." He knew she didn't by the way her eyes traveled up and down his body.

"Stay, but you're going to do some fancy tongue work of your own."

He smiled. Charlene spoke her mind, told him exactly what she wanted. And he could do the same. That's what made these visits worthwhile. She looked rough tonight, but he could turn out the lights and pretend otherwise.

"Wait in the bedroom. I'll be there in a sec." Charlene pinched his ass as he slid by.

Less than an hour later, Jake put on his coat and headed out the door for the trek home, but satisfying his needs hadn't quenched his sexual hunger the way he'd hoped.

Now it was painfully clear—only Angela Ross could do that.

# 15

Shelly blinked and opened her eyes as the patch of sunlight streaked through the mini-blinds and splashed across her face. Oblivious to the world, she laid there a few minutes before the memory of last night washed over her. In a wave of panic, she realized today was Friday. She'd overslept. The boys were supposed to be at school.

By now the entire town would be gossiping. Word would spread she'd drank too much. Then talk would shift to the fact her children were not in class. By this afternoon, everyone in Grand would consider her an unfit mother and an alcoholic. The pounding between her ears told her to stay in bed, but the fear in her heart screamed, *Get up, get the boys out the door for everyone to see.*

Turning to wake Jake, she discovered his side of the bed empty. Furthermore, by the look of the sheets, he hadn't slept there at all. The drunken fool must have passed out in the recliner and never crawled to bed. She sat up. Like every other crisis, she would have to take care of everything. Her skull throbbed. Her body urged her to lie back down, get more sleep, but she had to get the kids up and to class. It was only ten. She could divert some of the gossip if they showed up late.

Shelly swung her feet to the floor, struggled through the nausea, and shuffled down the hall only to find Taylor's room empty. She opened Austin's door. Again, an empty bed.

A survey of the living room and the garage left Shelly bewildered and amazed. Jake's truck was gone, so apparently he'd gotten up and taken the boys. Dialing his cell, she wanted to make certain he hadn't done something stupid, like take them to the farm to help him feed cattle.

"Speak," he answered in his usual cocky way.

"Did you take the boys to school this morning?"

"No, they flew. How the hell you think they got there?"

"Don't be a smartass, Jake. I didn't know you were capable of such a feat on your own."

"What the hell's that supposed to mean?"

"It means you don't do a damn thing around here even when I ask, so it's pretty remarkable you did this without being told."

"Somebody had to do it. God knows you were too drunk to do anything."

"One damn morning! One time I sleep in and you act like it's an everyday occurrence! You weren't exactly sober either." She grabbed her pounding head and leaned against the kitchen sink. "At least I made it to bed. You didn't even accomplish that." Fighting with Jake was not doing her hangover any good.

"I couldn't go to sleep. When I went to bed, you were sprawled across the mattress, moaning and groaning. I stayed up all night watching TV, then I took the kids to school."

"About time you did something useful."

"Don't bitch to me because you woke up pissy and guilty about forgetting your sons."

"Kiss my ass." She hung up and vomited into the sink.

Rinsing her mouth, she remembered how L.J. and Angela played her like a fool. She'd grossly underestimated her rival. Angela had not taken her bait. Instead, she'd set a trap of her own. Shelly did not care who bumped her. All the blame rested on that whore's shoulders. Shelly would get revenge—she would disgrace Angela, make everyone in Grand hate her the way they used to. The garbage disposal took care of the mess in the sink. If only a flick of a switch could do the same elsewhere.

The mere idea of shaming Angela improved Shelly's outlook. The fiasco at the party mortified her, but at least she'd tempered her reaction. Yelling and screaming like Charlene only brought more attention, more embarrassment. Staying calm and quiet was the right thing. No one knew how humiliated she'd felt. At least Shelly hoped not.

Shelly had wanted to find a clever response to being doused with margaritas, but even this morning she could not think of one. Standing in her kitchen, she felt as helpless now as she had standing alone in the middle of the high school gym.

The night still ranked as Shelly's all-time worst, but not for the reasons anyone imagined.

When Jake ditched her for that tramp, Shelly thought he would be sorry. She thought he would beg forgiveness. As fate turned out, she was the one forced to ditch her chance at happiness and scramble to protect her name and future.

Just like last night, that slut made a fool out of her. Everyone in the gym saw Angela stick her tongue halfway down Jake's throat. All eyes turned to Shelly. They waited to see her reaction. Unlike last night, she'd been unable to hold her composure. In a moment of weakness, she showed her fear and her insecurities by fleeing the scene.

But she, too, could play the game. If Jake could take Angela and kiss her in public, Shelly could do the same with Lucas. Only she decided to take her revenge one step farther—the hell with getting even, she would get ahead. She would show Jake who was in control.

Until that night, she'd ignored how Lucas Cahill looked at her. She did the same thing now to both avoid enticing Lucas and to pacify Jake's jealousy. That night, however, she didn't give a rat's ass about Jake's insecurities.

Shelly followed her plan to a tee. Until their lips met. The tenderness of that first kiss changed her motivation. Wants and desires replaced the drive for vengeance. She'd always viewed Lucas as a nice guy, but too quiet, too distant, too much of a loner, unworthy of her affection. She wanted her boyfriend to be somebody everyone looked up to, respected, even feared. In high school that was Jake Sampson, but with her eyes closed and their lips pressed together, Lucas seemed like another person—like the right person.

Sometime during their embrace, reality hit her. It wasn't the actual experience that turned her heart cold. Matter of fact, their encounter was better than any of her and Jake's previous experiences, and most of them since. No, it was the thought of her ruined reputation that ended Shelly's enthusiasm. Of course, she didn't completely come to that realization until later that night when she was home alone.

She worried what her friends would think if they discovered what she and Lucas had done. She didn't want to be thought of as a whore, but less than a week after breaking up with Jake, she'd had sex with someone else. Not to mention it was Lucas Cahill. Some of the girls whispered he was cute and mysterious, but Lucas wasn't prom king material like Jake. Even under normal conditions, her popularity would take a hit dating him.

Her eyelids never closed that night. The worries compounded as she stared up at the dark ceiling. And after all these years, she still did not know if it was fear or woman's intuition that led to her suspicions, but by morning Shelly had convinced herself of the worst.

Grand, Texas was no place for any woman to have a child out of wedlock, much less a high school girl. Her name would not be worth a thing if her premonitions proved correct and someone discovered Jake was not the father. Not only would she be a slut, she would be a two-timing slut.

Shelly lay awake until morning, searching for an answer to a problem she wasn't even sure existed. But with each passing minute, she became more certain. Shelly needed to find a way to blame Jake, but they had not fooled around in weeks. Up with the sun, she knew what had to be done to protect her future. Shelly swallowed her pride and begged Jake to take her back.

Several weeks later, her worst fears came true when the home pregnancy test displayed a positive. She told everyone their makeup session caused it and as expected, Jake's ego never allowed his mind to suspect his sperm had not "scored the winning touchdown," as he put it. Of course, she had no way of knowing for sure herself.

Their parents expected them to get married, so they did just that. June fourteenth, two weeks and a day after graduation, they walked down the aisle, breaking Lucas's heart as well as her own.

He left town that same week even though his first semester of college was two and a half months away. Lucas never even knew she was pregnant, and by the time he came back, she had two sons. Not a single person in Grand ever questioned the truth, but in her heart, Shelly knew. She had no proof, but when she looked into her oldest son's eyes, she saw Lucas.

Taylor's dark hair and features favored his biological dad. The physical similarities had become great enough that she worried someone might make the connection. When Taylor wanted to join the school band, she sided with Jake, who said only dorks marched in the band, and refused to let him simply because Lucas played the guitar. Each passing day her fear increased that something would tie her son to his true dad and reveal her lifelong lie.

Jake and Lucas would be devastated, Taylor would be emotionally scarred for life, and the whole town would turn on her. Her very existence depended on keeping the past hidden.

The townspeople had watched Taylor grow up. They'd witnessed his slow transformation into a younger version of Lucas. That made them less likely to see the resemblance, but for a newcomer like Angela, the likeness would be more noticeable.

That was yet another reason Shelly feared and loathed Angela. Shelly blamed the harlot for all her own disappointments. Her life could have turned out differently.

Without Angela, Shelly never would have run from the prom to Lucas's house. She wouldn't have gotten pregnant. She wouldn't be trapped in a lousy marriage. She would have had a chance to experience a lifetime of genuine love and compassion, the way she did that night in Lucas's arms.

# 16

"I'm closed. Come back at four." Perched atop the ladder, Lucas didn't bother to turn around, but he did regret not locking the front door since this was the second person to wander in.

The door closed again, giving Lucas the idea he was alone again until she spoke.

"Four? I'd rather come right now."

Lucas closed his eyes. He didn't want to deal with Abby DeWitt.

Not right now.

"I know you're hungry. For some hot, juicy—"

"Hang on," he cut her off. "Let me take this down." He untied the **Happy Birthday, Shelly** banner and watched it flutter to the floor while hoping like hell Abby was holding a Whirlwind cheeseburger and not simply hiking up her skirt again.

He snuck a peek before beginning his descent and was relieved to see she was indeed holding a grease-stained sack. Of course, she'd undone several buttons on her shirt. Her always impressive cleavage was even more so from his vantage point on the ladder, but Lucas simply didn't have it in him to make a witty pun today, so he stepped down onto the floor without comment.

Abby set the food sack on a ladder rung and pointed at the fallen sign. "Quite the party last night. I hear Shelly is spitting mad at Angela. Probably at you, too, for hiring her. Some women are like that." She sidled next to Lucas. "Easy to offend. Not to mention hard to get."

Lucas felt Abby's hand touch his chest. No doubt she could feel his heart hammering, but he refused to look at her. Instead, he stared at the birthday banner and realized it wasn't the only leftover debris from last night.

"I'm not one of those kind of women," Abby said as she slid her hand down to his stomach. She didn't stop there. "Don't you get tired of chasing things that are hard, Lucas?" Her hand cupped him. "Let me go after what's hard."

"Abby, don't."

She smiled. "See, I already found something hard."

"Abby."

"Shh. Forget Shelly. I can make you much happier."

"Damn it, Abby." He grabbed her hand.

Their eyes locked, and for a few seconds she gazed at him with wide, startled eyes, then tears pooled in the brown depth. "I'm sorry. I thought, maybe . . . " She turned and started to go.

"Abby, wait." He grabbed her shoulders and turned slowly around. The desperation, the hurt, the yearning on her face was more than he could bear. He kissed her, long and slow, and she wrapped her arms around him and kissed him back.

Lucas instantly regretted his decision. He'd kissed her for all the wrong reasons, and now he lacked the courage to break her heart twice in thirty seconds, so he merely smiled when they separated.

Abby bit her bottom lip and flashed him a grin.

"Frank is going to think you skipped out on him."

"I don't care about Frank." Abby lifted the front of Lucas's shirt. Her fingers toyed with the button on his jeans.

"We can't do this, Abby." He stared hard at her, hoping she understood by this he meant any and every thing.

She smiled a wicked smile. "I'm not worried about any-one walking in on me showing you just how happy I can make you." Again, she caressed him through his jeans.

He took a deep breath. Maintaining his conviction would be a hell of a lot easier if his body wasn't so eager to betray him. "I can't, Abby. I have to get this mess cleaned up, and you need to get back to the café."

"You worry too much," Abby whispered.

He backed away from her. "You're right. But a worried man is never at his best."

Her eyes settled on his groin. "You felt up to the chal-lenge to me." When he didn't return her smile she said, "Fine, I'll leave you for now. But later. You're all mine." At the door, she turned and blew him a kiss.

"Well, fuck." Lucas took off his Cowboy Junkies cap and ran his fingers through his hair. He'd done a lot of stupid shit lately, but kissing Abby DeWitt ranked right up there. He wondered if by "later" she meant when she got off work, or when he did. It only mattered in determin-ing how many hours he had left until he made her cry yet again. There was no other out.

She loved him. He didn't love her.

Maybe it wasn't love, but lust. Maybe she didn't want all of him but only certain parts. Maybe she didn't want honor and trust, but rather sweat and thrust. Lucas smiled and abandoned the ladder, cheeseburger, and the task of cleaning up in favor of a note pad and his guitar from be-hind the bar.

He snapped open the case and began picking out a tune, pausing to write down a few lines…

*Maybe it's not love, but lust*

*I don't need your honor, your trust.*
*Cause forever, it ain't the only thing*
*No, there are other songs to sing*

He shrugged. He'd written worse lines and it was nice to be working from a different point of view. The last eight or nine songs he'd started were unfinished, just languishing in the recesses of his mind waiting to be completed. They were all about Shelly in some fashion, and try as he might, he couldn't tie any of them together. Then again, not a damn thing in his life tied together anymore.

He sang the lines several times, toying around with the chord progression until he found something that might work as a chorus. He thought of Abby standing there the way she always did and began working on an opening.

*She had that look in her eye, I couldn't deny.*
*That need on her lips, swagger to her hips.*
*Send her away, or invite her to stay*
*The choice ain't ever easy, when the promise is sleazy*

He shook his head. That was shit. Scratching out the last two lines he started over.

*She had that look in her eye, I couldn't deny.*
*That need on her lips, and swagger to her hips.*
*So keep your 'til death do us part,*
*Cause I've had my last broken heart*

Lucas shook his head. The lyrics were not nearly as bad as the line of thought that made him actually ponder what it would be like to relent, to succumb to Abby's wanton ways there for a few moments. Sure, he could have some fun—fleeting fun—with Abby, but he could take his guitar up to Amarillo and play open mic night most any Wednesday and find the same kind of fun. Without creating a shit storm of other problems. Without breaking Abby's heart. Without complicating his life way more than he already had.

Abby was nice, and he enjoyed their banter, but her sex-kitten routine was nothing more than a charade to gain his attention. She didn't act that way toward others or when there were people around. Truthfully, he and Abby were not all that different. In love with the wrong person. In love with someone they couldn't have. Of course, unlike Abby, Lucas had a history with the object of his desire, a real tangible history.

The door opened again before he could close the guitar case. He feared it was Abby back too soon to fulfill her, *"Later you are all mine,"* promise. Turning around he was happy to see  Angela instead.

"Afternoon," he said.

She didn't respond at first, didn't even look away from the Happy Birthday banner to glance his direction, but then with a shake of her head, she walked passed him and around to the back of the bar.

"Any more big parties tonight, or are Friday nights in Grand wild enough without soirées in honor of homecoming queens past?"

Lucas ignored the sarcasm in her voice and said, "Actually, they crown a new homecoming queen tonight, so we'll be dead until the game is over. Might just be me, you, Chester, L.J., and a few feedlot cowboys until then."

"Good." Angela grabbed a plastic tub and filled it with hot water.

He set his notebook inside the case with the guitar. "What do you got against homecoming queens anyway?"

Angela grabbed a rag and the bucket and walked by him while saying, "Be faster to list what I don't have against them."

She squatted down and began scrubbing the sticky remnants of last night's margarita spill. Lucas couldn't help noticing the contour of her snug-fitting jeans and he'd already noted the thin fabric of her tight-fitting tank top. Watching her body move, Lucas again thought about hitting the next open mic night because either every damn woman he came in contact with had lost her mind, or his body was telling him it had been far too long.

Angela knew he was watching her. And she knew what he was thinking. Men had been thinking those same thoughts about her since she was fourteen, especially when she dressed like this. She scrubbed a little harder, not for his benefit, but her own. Manipulating men required a certain attitude, a particular mind-set, and she was rusty.

"You know," he said, still watching. "I have a mop in the closet."

"Who needs a mop?" She flicked her hair, shot him a seductive look over her right shoulder, and scrubbed with even more vigor.

"Okay. What gives?"

Damn. She'd gotten carried away and been too obvious. Settling back into the work, she ignored Lucas and concentrated on finishing the job rather than gaining his attention.

But she knew Lucas was still watching her, waiting for an answer. She could sense his eyes upon her. Still she ignored him and his question.

Finally, he walked closer, grabbed a sack sitting on the ladder, and said, "You been talking to Abby DeWitt?"

That threw Angela. She frowned at him.

"That's more like it," he said. "Now, tell me again this town sucks and you don't need any help from anybody, so I can be sure the world is back spinning on its axis."

"Is that sarcasm?"

"Nope. Truth." He took a bite of his hamburger and

went back to the bar where he closed his guitar case and stowed it beneath.

He wanted truth? Okay, she would give it to him. "Hey, what about this sign? What me to fold it up and stick it under the bar, or do you wrap it in silk and stow it in bubble wrap in anticipation of the homecoming queen's next birthday?"

He grinned and met her stare. "Throw it away. I buy a new one every year. I can't be honoring a queen with reused party favors."

Angela did as she was told, almost with a newfound admiration for her boss. At least he didn't deny his infatuation. Angela had no respect for liars.

Chester and L.J. showed up soon after. A few stragglers came and went here and there, but Lucas was right. They were far from busy, which meant the pair of old codgers had more than ample opportunity to tease her. They'd mistaken the motivation behind her new attire and flirty work demeanor. They thought she was not only trying to impress Lucas, but perhaps make him jealous by flirting with every customer she could. Nothing could be farther from the truth, but Angela liked both men too much to set them straight and burst their bubble.

Interested indifference.

That was the term Rosalie used. Rosalie had been her best friend in Vegas. She'd been the one to get Angela a job a LiveWireZ, the one to teach her how to maximize her earnings.

Interested indifference.

"Make 'em think you're interested, but not too interested. Make 'em think they gotta work for your attention. Make 'em think you could be interested, if only they impressed you somehow. Men are lazy, so most will try to impress you by giving you a ten when a one would do. That's when you smile the smile. The smile that says, close but no cigar. That smile will make them give you a twenty, maybe even a hundred if it's inviting enough."

Angela missed Rosalie and the Spanish lilt of her voice. They'd kept in touch for the first few years after Angela moved to Chicago, but then Rosalie moved to LA and bounced around from place to place and from man to man, and somewhere along the way, they lost contact.

Angela had been thinking about Rosalie all night. Mostly because it was her old friend's techniques she was now using to enhance her tips, but also because Angela would need to go somewhere when she left Grand. She wondered if Rosalie was still in LA, if she had found both a place and the means to settle down. If she ever had a dark-haired little girl, like she dreamed.

That's what Angela missed most about Rosalie. The hours they lay in the dark, sharing their dreams. Their apartment had been so tiny, their voices easily carried across the small hallway separating their rooms. Deep into the night they talked until one of them drifted to asleep. More often than not, it was Rosalie that nodded off, but Angela never begrudged that about her friend.

Angela wasn't naïve enough to think she could revisit those days. Even if she found Rosalie. Time had moved on. There were too many years gone, too many dashed dreams to ever lie about, voicing a bunch of what-ifs. But Angela liked the idea of moving to a place where she had at least one friend.

Angela was doing quite well executing Operation Interested Indifference right up until Cody Cantu walked in the front door. She hadn't seen him in years and he had no clue to the impact he'd had on her life, but Cody was the one person from Grand she sometimes thought about. He was also one of the first people she asked Misty about, only to learn he still performed, but mostly just here in Texas. He lived down near Dallas with either his third or fourth wife. Misty couldn't remember. Cody never glanced her direction as he walked to the bar.

Lucas smiled and checked his watch. "Game over already?"

"Was over before it started. Kind of like your music career."

"And your first two marriages," Lucas fired back.

Cody held up a hand that Lucas high-fived. "How the hell you been? You don't call, you don't write. You don't send me any new songs."

Angela moved closer, as if drawn by some invisible force. Like a moth to the flame.

"I already told you, I'm not sending you any more songs," Lucas answered. "Besides, I haven't written any. 'Least not any good ones."

Cody laughed. "That's because you're still trying to write them about her."

Lucas grimaced before noticing Angela standing there. "Cody, you remember Angela."

Cody spun around and broke into a wide grin. "She lives!" He raised his hands like an evangelical preacher and let his eyes travel the length of her body before adding, "Lives . . . hell, she flourishes."

"Hello, Cody."

He stood and covered the distance between them in two easy strides. Embracing her in a hug, he said, "You in town for homecoming too?"

"No, I . . . "

"She can't stand the sight homecoming queens," Lucas interjected.

Angela felt her cheeks blush, so she turned away, oddly embarrassed by her embarrassment. She blamed that fact on Cody. He had been two years ahead of both her and Lucas, but everyone in Grand knew and liked Cody Cantu. At least they did up until he went AWOL.

Cody returned to his barstool and began chatting with Lucas. Angela moved back behind the bar close enough to listen but far enough not to get dragged back into their conversation.

For a while, Cody had been considered the town's great hope for stardom, given his musical talents and natural good looks. Angela and Misty had driven to several rodeos scattered around the Texas Panhandle simply to hear him perform at the dances afterward. But then he got Denise Loudermilk pregnant, and everyone whispered what a shame it was. The prevailing thought was he'd have to give up his music and settle down into a regular job here in Grand, or up in Amarillo.

But Cody rejected that idea.

Barely a week after Denise delivered their son, Cody up and left for Nashville. He never hit it big, but he did play and sing backup for a few famous acts. He sent money back to Denise and gifts for the boy, but far as Angela knew, he never came back to town. At least not before she split herself. People used to whisper and gossip how terrible it was for him to abandon Denise and the baby, but back then Angela admired his guts—his courage. The day she left, Angela had been thinking about Cody when she walked out to the highway and stuck her thumb in the air.

Lucas and Cody continued to talk about music and bands and songs and other stuff Angela had little knowledge of. She didn't recall the two of them being friends back then, but they appeared to be the best of buds now.

Like Lucas, Cody's hair was a bit too long, but the dark waves sticking out from beneath Lucas's ball cap added a certain charm, a boy-next-door kind of mischievousness that Angela might have found endearing under other circumstances, whereas Cody wore his hair wild and free. He also had two-day-old stubble on his face and a silver ring in each ear and was anything but boy-next-door material. He was sex-up-against-the-wall material, just like he'd always been.

Angela handed Chester another beer and refilled L.J.'s coffee mug. Mercifully, neither one gave her a hard time about Lucas. Maybe they feared their great matchmaking efforts were in danger, given Cody Cantu's presence. Angela could never convince them otherwise—that she wasn't interested in either man. Lucas for all the obvious reasons in regard to the town and his blind devotion to Shelly, and Cody because he was exactly the kind of free-wheeling, good-time, goodbye man she could not afford to get involved with.

She watched them talk. Truth was, both men put her on edge. Made her feel defensive, on guard. With Lucas, it was the contradictions that unnerved her. One moment he seemed intelligently introspective yet keenly aware. But then he'd come across as naïve, even foolish. And through it all, his dark eyes carried an almost guilty quality. The combination rattled Angela and left her confused, as if she should shake some sense into him, or embrace him in a hug and whisper everything will be okay.

Cody, on the other hand, exuded nothing but confidence. He carried himself as if he could have anything he wanted, simply by asking. It bothered Angela because she couldn't be certain he wasn't right.

Angela made three trips around the bar, taking orders and delivering drinks. The place was busier now that the game was over, and most of the customers were long-time locals. The combination made her antsy and eager to escape, but there was no place to hide.

Cody watched her pour milk for a Colorado bulldog. "Sorry to hear about your grandmother," he said. "But you escaped once. Don't get sucked back in like some people I know." Cody turned and stared straight at Lucas. "Grand, Texas ain't nothing but an ambition-sucking, dream-stealing, wide spot in the road."

Angela agreed, but since she was stuck here and didn't want Cody Cantu thinking he was too smart, she said, "So what are you doing here then?"

"Came to see my kid play ball, but you won't catch me laying my head down in this town ever again."

Lucas snorted. "That's because you're afraid what Denise might cut off once you close your eyes."

"That ain't no shit." Cody slapped the bar and stood. "That is why I need to get on the road."

Angela smiled. "For the record, I'll be leaving soon. And just so you know, I was rooting for you when you left for Nashville. You gave me the courage to leave as quick as I could."

He shook his head. "Nashville sucked. Ate me up, but this town would've done the same."

"Don't let him bullshit you, Angela. This town could never hold Cody Cantu. No town ever has. He leaves a wake of ex-wives and forlorn band members everywhere he goes."

Cody ignored Lucas and faced Angela. "He's right. I've screwed up plenty, but hiding out in some rundown dive bar in bum-fucked Egypt is worse. So, do me a favor Angela, when you leave again, take dipshit there with you."

"Rundown dive? Hell, I just painted the joint," Lucas called to his exiting friend.

Cody walked to the door before stopping and turning around. "Hey, Lucas! Remember when I told you to stop writing songs about women?" He paused, but Lucas didn't respond, so Cody added, "I was wrong. Write a song about her." He pointed at Angela before adding, "And I'll record it for my next release."

17

The folks that wandered in after the big football game drifted away not long after Cody's departure. Angela heard them complaining about the team's winless start to the season, the lack of coaching, the blind refs, and even the piss-poor choice of songs the band played at halftime. But it wasn't until last call, when it was down to the four of them—herself, Lucas, L.J. and Chester—that she mustered the courage to ask about Coach Harvester.

"Gone," Chester said, taking a swig of his beer. "Eight, maybe nine years now."

Lucas shook his head. "It's been longer than that. He'd already left by the time I came back."

"Left, but still alive," Chester pointed out.

"He's dead?" Angela wasn't sure how that revelation made her feel.

L.J. had been watching her intently since she first asked and, without his saying so, she realized he knew.

"Yep." Chester raised his hand up to his head and fashioned his fingers into a makeshift gun. "Blew his own brains out."

Angela looked to Lucas, who nodded and said, "He left here to take a job at a bigger school downstate. Won a title, too, but then he got caught with a student. A female student. Three or four more came forward and accused him of everything but rape. Never went to trial, but guess he was guilty."

"Damn right he was guilty," L.J. said. "Never did like the son of a bitch, but he proved himself a coward. That bullet was better than he deserved." He stood. "Come on, Chester. Let's get out of here. I don't like to get mad this close to bedtime."

Angela held steadfast to the bar until the pair left. She was afraid to let go.

Lucas walked the two old men to the door and immediately began stacking chairs on tables. "You want to sweep?"

He turned around when she didn't answer. Angela made no attempt to hide the tears streaming down her face.

Lucas crossed the room. "Angela?"

She stared at him, still unwilling to trust her voice.

He came around behind the bar, his face framed with worry.

"I could have stopped it," she said.

"Stopped what?"

Angela had never told anyone, not since the day her grandmother demanded she keep her mouth shut. But her grandmother was gone and so was that bastard Harvester. And Angela knew she could not keep it bottled up inside her one moment longer.

She gritted her teeth and stared into Lucas's eyes before finally speaking. "Harvester."

Lucas frowned for a half a second, but his face softened as the meaning of her words dawned on him. He started to reach for her, hesitated, then grabbed hold of her hand. "Come sit. I'll fix you a drink." He guided her around the bar to one of the small two-chair tables before going to the jukebox and turning down the volume. "Glass of water?

Or something stronger?"

"Bourbon, on the rocks. Better make it a double."

Lucas filled two glasses with Maker's Mark and carried them over to the table.

Angela took a long, slow drink and set it down. Staring up at the ceiling, she took a deep breath, and started telling her story. "Maybe I wasn't his first, but he was mine. Bad thing is I liked the attention in the beginning. I was fourteen, about to turn fifteen, and it was just me and my grandma. L.J was around, but I viewed him as an old man, so his opinion didn't mean much to me. Harvester started out pretending he cared about me. He told me stories about my dad. They went to school together. He told me he felt obligated to look out for me since they'd been friends."

She picked up the glass and finished off the whiskey, letting it warm her throat and chest. She was grateful when Lucas didn't speak, didn't interrupt her thoughts.

"I went to him crying. I don't even remember about what, but I think Charlene was involved. We never did get along."

Lucas nodded. "I'm with you there."

"I told my grandma, but not that first time." Angela shook her head. "I don't know. Maybe I thought I was something, fucking a man twenty years older than me. I did the same thing later. That's how I got to Chicago. So maybe my grandma was right. Maybe it was what I asked for." She picked up the glass again, though nothing but ice remained.

Lucas arched a brow. "Another?"

She nodded and closed her eyes. The jukebox played softly in the background, and suddenly Angela thought how nice it would be to simply go to sleep.

But then Lucas was back with the bottle of bourbon. He poured enough to cover the ice in her glass, but did not refill his own. "My dad was a bourbon man," he said. "I live in his house, sleep in his room, run the bar he loved, but I never really feel his presence except when I play his old guitar or drink bourbon whiskey. He drank Jim Beam."

"I think about my dad far too much," Angela said. "Wish I knew exactly what happened in that grain elevator. I wish I knew if he left me on purpose, or at least remembered what kind of man he was. I don't even know if he drank. My grandma didn't. That didn't make her any easier to live with."

They sat there in silence except for the music turned low.

After a few minutes, Angela said, "She blamed me. Not at first. But when I told her it had been going on for a while, she said no one would believe me. And even if they did, they'd say it was my fault."

She took another drink. "Harvester said the same things. He was right, even about my grandmother."

Lucas sighed. "That sucks. No other word for it, but karma is a bitch. He got his punishment."

Angela shook her head. "I don't believe in karma. You can't convince me people get what they deserve, not in this life anyway. Was it karma that allowed him to move on? To ruin those other girls' lives? Was karma to blame for him picking me? For my mom ditching me and my dad? Or was it me? I was just a little fucking girl, but maybe I did something to drive them away."

She met Lucas's stare until he shook his head. "No. Sometimes shit just happens for no reason, with no one to blame. Maybe that's why they say karma is a bitch."

Angela laughed. "A bitch? The world is full of bitches, but not all of them screw you over at every chance. No, if karma truly exists, I'd bet anything she was once homecoming queen."

Lucas shook his head, but smiled as he did so. "Funny,

I always pegged Lady Luck as more of the homecoming queen type and karma as a cynical heartbreaker."

Pouring herself another drink from the bottle on the table, Angela said, "Next, you're going to tell me Mother Nature is a cold-hearted woman and Miss Fortune is a gold digging whore."

"You got a point. Maybe I should write a song about all the evil women who control our fates."

Angela sipped her whiskey before saying, "Would be a damn shitty song, but go ahead."

They fell back into silence for several long minutes before Angela felt like speaking again. "When I left here, I went to Vegas and danced in a club. We had a dancer named Karma and another that went by Miss Fortune. Both were coke addicts. No Lady Luck or Mother Nature though. Nobody wants to think of their mom while at a strip joint, and the other was too obvious, even for Vegas."

The whiskey had done the trick—warmed her soul and loosened her tongue. She watched Lucas closely to gauge his reaction to her confession, but he never so much as lifted an eyebrow. Perhaps he already knew the truth of her past. Perhaps he was the one that spotted her dancing on that stage.

"And what name did you use?"

She was still trying to wrap her whiskey-shrouded brain around the theory that Lucas had been the one to discover her in Vegas, so his question took her by surprise. She stared across the table. He didn't strike her as the gossipy type to run back to Grand eager for fifteen minutes of fame, and if he'd seen her dance, he wouldn't need to ask her stage name. Unless, of course, he forgot, or was trying to play off his knowledge.

She decided to answer his question with one of her own. "You ever been to Vegas?"

Lucas shook his head. "I'm not much of a gambler."

"What about strip clubs?"

He shrugged. "I've been to a few. Back in college. But frankly, they play real shitty music, so I'm not much of a fan."

She nodded. "Angel. I hated it. Not because it was just my real name minus the last A, but because every DJ said the same stupid things about being heavenly, or a divine diva, or some other ridiculous pun. I never meant to become a topless dancer. Even now it seems more like a bad dream than a real part of my past. But I survived. A lot of the girls didn't. Doubt I would have either if not for Rosalie."

"Rosalie." Lucas closed his eyes and began tapping out a rhythm on the tabletop.

Angela shot him a befuddled look.

He stopped tapping the table and said, "Rosalie? Bob Seger?" When she didn't respond, Lucas stood. "Okay, so I'm a shitty drummer, but surely you know the song. Maybe Thin Lizzy's version?" He retrieved his guitar from under the bar.

Angela admired the way his fingers deftly moved to create music, but she still didn't recognize the song until he started to softly sing the words. "That's her song," she said. "Rosalie always started her first set with that song."

Lucas grinned. "In that case, I take back my earlier statement. Apparently, they don't always play shitty music."

With a shrug Angela said, "I like the way you play it better. It's softer, more fitting than the fast guitar and hard rock. Play some more."

He shook his head. "I don't really know the song very well. I did good to get that much out, but I know another Rosalie song that's closer to what I play."

Lucas closed his eyes and began strumming the strings. He sang the love story of a girl named Rosalie and a guitar player, but their relationship didn't last. The haunting way Lucas sang it made Angela feel sad for them both, and for Lucas. He was good—real good. And yet here he was in a dive bar in Grand, Texas, serenading her. Not until the end of the song did she realize Rosalie was actually the name of a guitar.

"What are you doing here, Lucas? You should be out there playing under a spotlight."

He shook his head, but before he could answer, the front door opened and the lights went out. A rush of cold air swirled around the room as Lucas said, "What the–"

"Oh, Luuuu . . . cusssss." A woman's voice sang out.

"Oh, shit."

Angela heard his whispered curse, but apparently the woman at the door did not.

"Youuu can run Luuu . . . cusssss, but youuu can't hide. You are all mine, and I am here to collect."

The lights came back on and there stood Abby De-Witt—in all her naked glory.

# 18

"Maybe she's not coming." Shelly spoke with a false hope she did not feel. She tried to refrain from staring at Charlene's hideously bruised face, but both eyes were ringed by nasty shades of purple and gray despite the makeup plastered on her face. The knot on her nose glowed an ugly shade of magenta.

"She'll be here. She always is," Charlene answered. "Misty never misses an opportunity to preach."

Shelly knew both counts were correct. While she and Charlene missed an occasional Monday at the café, Misty never had. Why would she? She and Mark didn't have money for vacations, so she never ventured away from Grand. These weekly meetings were Misty's sole break from the monotonous routine of being a housewife and a mother.

Sometimes Shelly felt sorry for her friend, staying home to take care of Mark and the girls all the time. Shelly lived the same unsatisfied life for the most part, but unlike her friend, she snatched bits of freedom wherever she could—the whispered phone conversations with Lucas, the daily daydreams of one day escaping the tedium of Grand, the occasional all-day shopping spree to Amarillo. A new wardrobe had a way of making Shelly believe the future still held hope. On the other hand, Shelly didn't think Misty had bought a single new item for herself in the five years since the birth of her youngest. She claimed her girls needed new things more than she did. Shelly did not believe that. Misty had worn the same four or five Wal-Mart rack dresses to church for years.

Charlene was also right about their friend loving to preach. Misty came by it honestly, but that didn't make the habit any less annoying. She constantly urged them to be nicer and less judgmental. Rarely did she participate when they gossiped. Her daddy's sermons must have soaked in over the years.

Neither Charlene nor Shelly had talked to their friend since the birthday party disaster, but the events of that night had to be common knowledge by now. And like a naïve fool, Misty would believe the entire incident truly was an accident.

Shelly broke the silence. "Did you talk to that boyfriend of yours yet?"

Charlene nodded as she lit a cigarette. "Yeah, he came over last night."

"Is he going to do it?"

"He couldn't say no." A mischievous smile covered the redhead's face. She blew two smoke rings upward in the direction of the café's dingy, grease-stained ceiling tiles. "I had him in a compromising situation. Told him if he didn't do what I wanted, he wasn't getting what he wanted."

"Oh, you are evil." Shelly giggled.

"I know, but don't say anything. Here comes little Miss Innocent. We don't want her spoiling Angela's surprise."

"Hey, y'all. Sorry I'm late." Misty slid into the booth.

"No problem," Charlene said. "It gave us time to talk about you."

"Ha-ha, funny." Misty batted her eyes and displayed a forced smile. "So, what did y'all do this weekend?"

Shelly looked at Misty through narrowed eyes. Was

she trying to bait them? But Misty never played games. If something bothered her, or she had something to say, you knew it. She wasn't like Charlene, who would just blurt it out, but you knew nonetheless.

"Not much, I guess," Shelly finally answered looking back and forth between Charlene and Misty. "Just hung around the house."

"We missed you at church." Misty turned her head. "How about you, Charlene? How was your weekend?"

Slapping her hand on the table, Charlene hollered, "Come on, Misty! Cut the act! Look at me. You know damn good and well what I've been doing this weekend—healing! Where the hell is that damn ashtray I asked for? Abby, if you don't get your ass over here pronto, I'm gonna flick ashes on the goddamn floor!"

Misty blanched. "Sorry for trying to make conversation. I didn't mean to make you mad."

"Don't give me that shit. I'm sure you spent all weekend talking about me. You and that bitch." She crushed the smoking tip of her cigarette out on the tabletop.

The anger in Charlene's words scared even Shelly. She nudged Charlene's foot under the table when the other diners began to stare. "Misty doesn't gossip. She probably hasn't heard yet."

"Like hell." Abby still had not materialized, so Charlene flicked the butt across the room.

Misty lowered her head. "I heard, but not from Angela. I heard at church. If y'all would've came to the services—"

"Don't even start that shit." Charlene held her palm up. "I ain't in the mood to hear your preachin'."

The conversation died when Abby came to take their orders. The waitress lingered a moment at the table as if she wanted to join in, but drifted away when no one spoke other than to order. She didn't even complain about the ashes smeared on the table top.

"What did that whore have to say? I know you've talked to her since Thursday."

Misty cringed at Charlene's harshness. "For your information, she never said a word. And please don't call her
that."

"The guilty never do speak," Shelly said.

"I heard it was L.J.'s—"

"Bullshit!" Charlene screamed. "That slut has been out
to disfigure me for years."

"I'm telling you, Angela's changed. If y'all would only
give her a chance, you'd see what kind of person she's become."

"Look at me!" Charlene thrust her face within inches of
Misty's. "Do you see what that whore did to me? I don't
need you telling me what kind of person she is or how
she's changed. I can look in the mirror to see she's still a
two-bit slut."

Shelly sunk down in the booth. "Calm down, Charlene.
Everyone's staring."

"Let 'em. I don't give a damn! I'm not calming down
until Misty chooses. Either she's friends with me, or she's
friends with that cunt. It can't be both."

"But it was an accident. How can I blame Angela?"

"Forget it. You've made your choice. Hell, maybe you
can both sleep with Mark at once this time." Charlene el-
bowed Misty in an effort to escape the booth. "Lord knows
the poor bastard deserves some excitement in his life."

Tears filled Misty's eyes as she stood. "How could you
say that? We're supposed to be friends."

"Please, Charlene, just sit down and listen." Shelly tried
to intervene.

"Hell no! I've heard enough. Far as I'm concerned,
Misty and Angela can rot in hell together. I never liked her
sweet-and-innocent act anyway. Come on, Shell, let's go."

Shelly considered herself the leader of the group, but

she wasn't about to assert her position with Charlene in this mood. So for the second time in a matter of days, she stood and allowed herself to be led away from confrontation. Shelly stopped near the door and looked back. Tears streamed down Misty's face, and her brokenhearted expression made it clear things would never be the same for the three of them.

Just before the door closed behind her, Shelly heard Abby say, "Charlene is right. That whore ruins everything."

# 19

Angela set out on foot for the Oasis as she had every day for nearly a week. This afternoon was pleasant and warm, and she told herself that was the source of her good mood, but halfway there, she admitted she actually enjoyed her new job. And while she still cringed at the reality of her predicament—being stuck in Grand, Texas, the last place on earth she wanted to be trapped—Angela begrudgingly conceded even that fact was not nearly as bad as she'd feared.

Rounding the street corner, she was glad to see Lucas's old truck parked beside the building. She'd left a good half hour earlier than normal and a full hour earlier than he'd told her to come in, but she had nothing else to do, and something told her he would already be at the bar. If not, she would've had to either stand out front or go across the street and wait for him inside the Whirlwind. Given that she'd already seen far more of Abby DeWitt than she ever expected, Angela didn't relish that idea. However, she couldn't help smiling, thinking about Lucas and his flushed cheeks after Abby had shucked her clothes right there in the middle of the Oasis.

That was after he'd gone out into the night to catch Abby, who had taken in Angela, the guitar in Lucas's hands, the whiskey glasses on the table, and assumed the two of them were having some sort of intimate moment.

"Go back inside and sing to your skinny little whore!" Abby had shouted loud enough for Angela to hear through the open door. A few minutes later, she screeched, "Go to hell!" and then Lucas came back inside, closing the door behind him.

Angela hadn't poked nearly as much fun at him as she'd wanted, because despite the fact the whole thing amused her, it also contained a certain element of sadness.

Today, Lucas looked up when she walked inside. He made no mention of the fact she was so early, but instead gave a wave as he took a crunching bite of something greasy. At least Angela figured it was greasy, judging by the stains on the paper wrapper.

Only the slightest whiff of new paint still hung in the air, despite the fact Lucas had painted the joint less than a week ago. The stench of cigarette smoke, stale beer, and even more unfortunately, cow shit had all but erased the scent of his hard work. Given that better than half of the place's business came from the feedlot cowboys, she supposed that mixture was inevitable, but how Lucas could happily eat away among the aroma baffled her.

"How's the Pied Piper of Promiscuity today?"

Lucas grinned and crunched another bite.

"What are you eating anyway?"

"Chimichanga," he said.

"It looks horrible."

He shrugged. "Tastes horrible too. But I was hungry, and it beats a spit burger."

Angela smiled. "What's a poor bachelor to do when he breaks the heart of the waitress at the only joint in town?"

"Don't start," he said, but did so with another dimpled grin.

"Bet you could summon her now if you got out your guitar and started playing."

He rolled his eyes.

"Let's see. Last time you were playing a song about a man and the guitar he did wrong, and she came streaking in. So you better choose your song wisely. Didn't Jimmy Buffet have a song about a cheeseburger? Maybe she'll bring one when she tells you to go to hell this time."

They both laughed, but his nervous chuckle gave away that he still felt bad about the whole ordeal.

Angela felt obligated to cheer him up. "Don't worry. Abby will forgive you once I save up enough money to split town. If she's been flashing her goods at you this long, she's not likely to give up because the town whore came back and disrupted her plans."

"'Skinny little whore'," he said. "You gotta get the verbiage correct."

"The 'skinny' and 'little' are better adjectives that most people around here use for me. Guess Meatloaf had it right," Angela said. "Two out of three ain't bad."

"For a gal who spent so much time listening to nothing but bad music, you sure seem to know a lot of songs."

"And for a single guy, you sure have lots of lady trouble."

"Me? Lady trouble? No, what I got is a waitress problem. A naked one that wants to carve my heart out and feed it to me instead of the bacon cheeseburgers I love. And a smartass one who shows up to work an hour early just to harass me."

"Don't forget about the homecoming queen."

"Yeah, well the homecoming queen might as well be a waitress, too, because she's serving me up a big old piece of avoidance pie."

Angela grinned.

"What's so damn funny now?"

"You could've had pie, but no, you made her cry."

"Why do I get the feeling you're going to start calling

me Georgie Porgie now?"

"Could be worse," Angela giggled. "You could've slept with Abby before you broke her heart. In that case, I'd have to call you Humpty Dumpty."

Lucas shook his head and said, "Thanks a lot, Mother Goose."

Afternoon gave way to evening. Chester and L.J. occupied their usual seats at the bar. The feedlot cowboys filtered in after work and a fair number of others wandered in to watch Dallas play Washington on "Monday Night Football." Chairs had been scooted around to face the TV above the bar, so Angela had to maneuver around a labyrinth to deliver beers. But the tips had been good so the added trouble was worthwhile.

L.J. and Chester were the only ones not paying attention to the game. They sat at the bar watching her and Lucas with the usual smirks plastered to their faces.

She was the only female in the joint. Not that she minded. Men were far better tippers. Just after halftime, Angela slipped off to the restroom to count her wad of tips. She couldn't believe it. Over three hours left until closing, and already she'd earned nearly a hundred dollars. If the Cowboys played on TV every night, she could escape this town in a matter of weeks.

Stuffing the money back in her pocket, Angela left the bathroom to check on her customers. A hand reached out and grabbed her waist.

"Whoa! Hold up there, sweetie. Where's the fire?" A scrawny cowboy clung to her.

"Let go, Asshole!" Angela wrenched herself free.

"Okay, okay. But bring me another beer."

Back at the register, she leaned down between L.J. and Chester and whispered, "What's that guy's story?" She pointed out the idiot harassing her.

"Hell if I know. 'Cept he hangs out with Charlene.

Why?" Chester rubbed his bloated belly.

"Just wondering."

"You can do better," L.J. said.

"That's not why I wanted to know. Y'all aren't half as smart as you think. I'm not interested in every single man that walks through the door."

"We know." Chester took a drink and sat the bottle back down. "You're only interested in the one that unlocks it."

"No, I'm . . . That's it. I'm not talking to either of you ever again." Angela walked away before they spotted her grin.

For some damn reason, the three people in this town she called friends were hell-bent on fixing her up with Lucas. They were all under the same mistaken notion she wanted to linger in this one-horse settlement.

"Hey, honey! You gonna bring me that beer or what?" The cowboy shouted over the cheers as Dallas kicked another field goal to pull within ten.

"Patience!" She called back in hopes a carefree attitude would keep the drunk within certain bounds. This time Angela made certain to keep the table between her and the idiot.

"Hey baby, how about you blowing off that head?" The cowboy leaned back in his chair.

"Don't worry. Your breath will melt the foam," she retaliated.

"I wasn't talking about the beer."

"Well in that case, your breath for sure already melted your shot."

Laughter erupted from the other guys within earshot of the conversation. She'd dealt with plenty of horny drunks in her day, but this guy made her nervous. Most of the time, the offender would take the punishment and laugh with the others. Put in their place, most men stopped trying to act so damned cute. This fool had a different look about him. He didn't appear ready to quit.

"Oh hell, come on." He grabbed her wrist when she reached for the five on the table. "I hear you used to screw every man in this town. Why be picky now?"

"Let go of me." Angela flailed her free arm wildly in an effort to escape.

"I've been told you can suck the chrome off a trailer hitch."

Before anyone else could say a word, Lucas leapt over the bar and grabbed the back of the offensive cowboy's shirt. In one swift motion, he jerked the wide-eyed loud-mouth to his feet and propelled him against the wall. His left forearm pressed against the man's jugular.

"Let him go," one of the other pen riders challenged. "He was just having some fun. You want to take us all on?" He pointed a fat sausage-like finger at Lucas.

Lucas reached over with his free hand and pulled a pool cue from the rack. "If anyone so much as takes a step, I'll crack this over their fucking head."

As a group, the men took half a step back out of range.

"Apologize." Lucas increased the pressure on the captured man's throat. The cowboy gagged from lack of air.

"Don't do it, Jimmy!" one of the crowd called out as the cowboy simply sneered.

"Fine." Lucas drug the guilty party to the front of the bar where he kicked open the door and shoved the young punk outside. "The rest of y'all get out too." He pointed the pool cue at the group of feedlot workers. "None of you are welcome here until he comes in and apologizes. You'll learn to treat her with the respect she deserves." Lucas's jaw flexed as he spoke.

Casting evil looks, the men filed out the open door.

Lucas looked like a different man when angry. Angela had never noticed the sharp angle of his jawline. The way the muscles in his neck flexed made it clear he was more than willing to swing that pool cue if need be. She'd never had anyone defend her honor so forcibly. Matter of fact, no one had ever defended her honor, period.

"If any of you try to come back before he apologizes, I'll call the sheriff!" Lucas hollered as they helped the injured guy off the ground.

He slammed the door and turned back to Angela. "You okay?"

Angela nodded.

He reached out and touched her elbow. "I know you can take care of yourself, but I also believe in taking care of friends."

Angela muttered her thanks and turned away. She practically ran to the women's room. The last thing she wanted was for someone to see her cry. She'd spent her entire life ensuring no one knew how fragile her emotions really were.

Tears flowed freely once she reached the restroom. Confusion reigned over her. Just when she thought she hated this place, something happened to make her feel like she belonged. She had friends here, but no future, nothing to strive for. She wanted stability. She wanted a family, someone to hold onto for the rest of her life. Friends were one thing, but she needed someone to be her everything.

A soft knock sounded on the door. "You okay in there?" Lucas's voice drifted through the wood.

"Yeah. I'll be out in a minute." Angela concealed the sadness in her voice.

"Take as long as you need."

She remained in the restroom, trying to get a grip on her emotions, but old memories and dreams stampeded across her mind. The mother she never knew, her father's death, the whispers he killed himself. The guilt she'd done something wrong to make him not want to carry on, her grandmother's demands to be perfect, her own desire to show the world nothing affected her. Why had one stupid, skinny cowboy brought it all to a head?

Try as she might to compose herself, all of life's hurts and disappointments flowed steady down her flushed cheeks. Maybe she would be better off emotionally to take the little money she'd already earned and leave town. Misty would give her a ride to the bus station up in Amarillo. She could buy a one-way ticket away from the past, away from the memories, away from the hurt. But that strategy had never worked before. At no time in her life had she ever been able to put the pain and regret behind her—not on stage in Vegas, not in Kenneth's arms, not in the high rise penthouse in Chicago, and not here in the bathroom of this smelly, rundown bar.

Angela remained in the tiny room until the noise faded to the murmur of only a few. Emotion held her prisoner.

Finally, the noise vanished except for the tinkling of glass. She could not spend the night in the bathroom, and Lucas would be the only person left to peer into the gaping window of her soul. Slowly, she pushed open the door. His face was the first thing she saw.

Deep lines etched his forehead. "You okay?"

"Yeah, I'm fine. Sorry."

"Don't be. You don't have a thing to be sorry about." He frowned. "I bet anything Charlene put him up to that."

Angela nodded, having come to the same conclusion in her self-imposed seclusion.

"Let's get out of here." He placed a hand on her shoulder. "I'll finish up tomorrow."

Again, she only nodded. Somehow she did not trust her voice.

"And I'm giving you a ride home," Lucas said. "You don't need to be walking. Not tonight."

# 20

Lucas was tired and wanted to go to bed, but he needed to set things right with Abby first. He'd given her all weekend to calm down. 'Least that's what he tried to tell himself. What he'd really done was avoid a conversation he didn't want to have. But here he was now, in the shadows of predawn, sitting on the small concrete pad that served as her porch. He'd brewed a pot of coffee just to bring her a cup. Keeping watch from his garage, he'd spotted her bedroom light flicker on nearly a half hour ago, but there'd been no sign of life inside since. The coffee would be cold before long, if it wasn't already, but surely she'd be showered and ready to leave for work soon.

She'd always showed up at his place earlier than this when she brought him a steaming mug, but maybe she'd gotten up extra early just to do so. The fact she'd been going to extra trouble all these years just to see him several mornings a week only added to his guilt.

The truth. Complete and unveiled. That's what he had to deliver this morning. No more playing games. Letting her flirt and flash. Or flirting back simply for fun. No more leaving things unsaid. Of course, he needed to do the same with Shelly, but Lucas was a hell of a lot more afraid of how she would react than Abby. He hated that Abby was mad, hurt, brokenhearted, but they were never going to be more than friends, regardless. With Shelly, he wanted so much more.

The kitchen light came on, bathing the yard in a strip of rectangular light. Lucas stood, knocked softly, and waited.

She came to the door for several long seconds while merely staring at him through the glass. Just when he'd decided she wasn't going to, Abby opened the door.

She didn't speak, so he said, "I brought you coffee."

"Why?"

"So we can talk."

She rolled her eyes. "You sing for that whore, and all I get is talk."

Abby turned and walked back inside, but left the door open, so Lucas stepped inside. "I understand why you're upset, but don't blame Angela. And don't be so quick to label her. She has nothing to do with the fact we're never going to be what you want us to be."

Spinning around, Abby jabbed a finger into his chest. "Don't you dare lecture me about her. I saw the two of you. My God, Lucas, I've brought you coffee for years. I've made a fool of myself, just trying to win a piece of your heart." She jabbed him again and again. "I'm not stupid. I know how you feel about Shelly, but I always hoped you'd wake up and face the fact some dreams never come true." She stopped poking him as tears streamed down her cheeks. "I was never even jealous of the way you felt about Shelly. But I really did believe you were different. That your love for her was about more than looks. Then you go off and hire that tramp. That fucking skinny tramp. I could've helped you. All you had to do was ask."

Abby sank into a nearby chair.

"I hired her as a favor to L.J."

"Did you sing to her for L.J.?"

"I wasn't really singing to her. We were talking and a song came up, but she was confused, so I pulled out my guitar and played it. There is nothing going on between me and Angela."

Abby stared down at her hands. "Sometimes I stand outside your garage and listen to you play just so I can hear your voice, but the second I step inside, you always stop."

"Abby—"

"But you fucking sang for her. And she's never done anything for you. For anyone in this town. Not even her grandmother. Angela Ross is a destroyer. She was before she left town, and she picked right up where she left off."

Lucas shook his head. "Listen to me. I was playing a cover. When you come over, I'm always writing my own stuff. I don't let anybody hear or read what I'm working on. Nobody. And this isn't about Angela. I screwed up. Me." He poked himself in the chest. "I led you on. It's my fault. I should've been honest with you a long time ago. I like you, Abby. I enjoy your company and yes, even flirting with you, but I never meant any of it to become real. But I am a man, so when you came to the Oasis . . . "

He ran his fingers through his hair. "Damn it, Abby, I was horny, and yes, there for a few minutes I was more than ready, but trust me when I say all that would do is ruin our friendship. Us having sex is not going to lead to us being a couple. Not now, not last week, not a year from now. That's my fault. Not yours. Not Angela's."

She stared up at him with red-rimmed eyes, and for a second it seemed as if she was going to accept his words, but then the lines around her eyes bunched and her arms folded across her chest. "Say what you want, but ours isn't the only relationship she's destroyed. Misty and your precious Shelly aren't even speaking anymore. All because of that conniving slut."

"Damn it, Abby. Stop blaming someone else. I'm the asshole here."

She nodded. "Oh, you're an asshole all right, but she's not innocent either. I get it. You don't care what a woman is, was, or will be, long as she's a size four. Fine, but don't think you're going to come crawling in my bed after that bitch sucks you and this town dry, and Shelly is home snuggled up next to Jake."

"Fine, Abby. Have it your way. I'm an asshole, Shelly is married, and Angela is leaving. You have all the facts, so there's nothing left for me to say." Lucas turned and walked out. He didn't stop, not even when Abby called his name.

Angela awoke Tuesday morning and was surprised to discover Lucas was the first thing she thought about. He'd defended her honor so forcefully, so willingly, so emotionally. It had taken her aback. She wasn't used to people caring about her with such passion. He'd risked his own livelihood, and hers as well, but the lost tips didn't seem so important in the face of his actions.

Walking out on the porch, she marveled how well the day matched her outlook. The ever-blowing wind had taken the day off, and the sun bathed the ground in golden light while the cool crispness of fall caressed her skin.

Looking across the street at L.J.'s trailer, she realized the Oasis was the only place she ever saw him anymore. It didn't seem right for him to be alone over there all the time. He deserved companionship.

Going inside, she continued to puzzle over Lucas. Nothing about her boss made sense. Maybe L.J could offer some insight. A visit with the old-timer would serve a dual purpose, and she was in far too good of a mood to sit idly at home by her lonesome. Picking up the phone, she dialed his number.

After a little persuasion, she convinced him to accompany her on a walk through town. It would do both of them good to get outside and breathe fresh air. Preferring to keep as low a profile as possible, she hadn't really ventured out much since her return, but today she felt alive, ready to explore.

Thirty minutes later, she joined L.J. outside. "Thanks for coming with me," she said.

"No, thank you. I need to get out of there once in a while." He pointed back at his place.

They exchanged idle chitchat as they ambled through the streets of Grand. On Main, they passed JoAnn's Beauty Parlor, closed down now, but Angela remembered the smell of hairspray and perms from childhood visits. A movie rental place had apparently moved into the building once occupied by Grand hardware, but it, too, was now shuttered and closed. L.J. pointed out places and things he thought she might be interested in. She asked questions as they moved past the meager business district and turned down Ash Street. Who lives there now? Whatever happened to so and so? Do you remember when? Half an hour into their stroll, Angela decided to change the direction of the conversation.

"Think my dad did it on purpose?"

L.J. glanced over the treetops at the towering concrete structure. "Not a chance in hell. He's not the only man to die in a grain elevator. Hell, he's not the only one to die at that elevator. Chunky Green's boy died a few years before your dad."

"Did everyone say he committed suicide too?"

"No." L.J. frowned. "Your dad's foreman over there said it almost looked like he jumped. And then some other idiot started telling people your dad told him he was going to kill himself. You know how this town is. Boredom sets in and everyone wants a story to tell. It was no secret he was tore up when your mom took off like that. But I'm telling you, your dad wouldn't have quit like that. He wouldn't have left you. He used to come into the Oasis now and again. You were all he talked about, even after you mom left."

"Has anyone heard from her?" Angela feared the answer. She had no desire to see the woman who'd abandoned her.

L.J. shook his head. "She had problems long before you came along. They weren't your father's and they shouldn't be yours either."

Twisting a strand of her long blonde hair, Angela paused beneath a large, crooked-limbed elm and toed a crack in the concrete where the tree roots had pushed from below. "Tell me about Lucas."

L.J. glanced at her. A thin smile emerged on his weathered face. "I shoulda known we'd get around to him." Taking a dramatic sigh, he went on. "What do you want to know?"

"I'm confused. Misty's told me some and so have you, but I still can't figure him out. I know he's never been married or even had a steady girlfriend. Misty told me he left for college, became a lawyer, and only came back to run the bar when his dad died. Anyone can see he has a thing for Shelly, but that's all I know. Are they having an affair?"

L.J. closed one eye. "That's kind of a personal question about someone who's only your boss."

Angela grinned back. "Okay, so I said I don't care what he does. I changed my mind. You and Chester can have your fun at my expense, but I need to know—is he?"

"No. 'Least ways not anywhere but his mind."

The two walked on for several minutes without speaking until L.J. took up where he left off. "Lucas ain't the cheating kind. He's above having an affair. I know him well enough to say that. He hates Jake, but he wants more than a stolen moment or two. He wants her for himself. I suspect he's hoping they'll get divorced. I guess he's willing to wait."

"But why?" Angela wondered out loud. "What's so special about her?"

L.J. shrugged. "Wish I could answer that. -He doesn't talk about her around Chester and me anymore, but I can tell you it's nothing new. He's felt this way for as long as I can recall. Was there something between them when y'all were kids?"

"Not that I remember. Shelly always belonged to Jake."

*Except for that one night at prom.* But Angela was too ashamed to confess that sin, so she said, "To tell the truth, I don't remember much about Lucas, except he kept to himself and made the best grades in the class."

Silence again surrounded them. They passed a chain link fence where two Schnauzers yipped at them the entire length. An old woman peeked out from a geranium-lined porch. Several houses held pawprint-shaped signs that read *A Cougar Lives Here* and displayed a jersey number.

"He must have some strong feelings for you," L.J. finally said.

Stopping, she was surprised how L.J.'s words made her heart accelerate.

"It took a lot for him to do that last night."

She studied a chalk drawing on the sidewalk. "I know."

"I don't think you do." He paused. "Lucas is a hell of a guy—smart, funny, loyal. Hell, he has more good points than anybody I know, but boldness ain't one of 'em. I've sat at that barstool for years and watched one person after another take advantage of him. That boy runs from conflict like a nun from sex." L.J. chuckled at his own joke. "Only one other time have I seen him get riled enough to toss someone out on their butt."

"Who did he throw out then?" Angela asked, not seeing the point of L.J.'s story.

"Jake." L.J. gave a sideways look before adding, "He was drunk, running Shelly down. Lucas gathered him right up and planted him on the front step just like he did that cowboy last night."

Angela smiled at the mental image of Jake being dumped on his butt.

"But I think that fella last night got it worse. Puts you in with some pretty serious company." The old man started walking again.

She shook her head. "Why would he care about me?"

L.J. pulled out his rolling paper. "Why wouldn't he?"

Angela shrugged. She had to get used to the idea that everybody here did not hate her—to the idea people actually cared for her. "Do you think he would ever leave Grand?"

"Not so long as he thinks he's got a chance with Shelly."

"What about the Oasis? It was his dad's place, right?"

L.J. stopped to roll a smoke. "He doesn't care about the bar. You saw how he let it go to pot. He only spruced it up for her."

Angela didn't respond. Between his story and her preoccupied mind, she hadn't noticed they were back in front of their houses until he said good-bye. She stood out in the street alone for several minutes considering the old man's words before finally turning toward the house.

Lucas had been nothing but nice to her. He'd hired her when he didn't have to. And he could've taken Shelly's side and fired her. Now she could help him. From her years in Chicago, Angela knew what it felt like to love someone who was married—who could never fully return your love.

Lucas deserved better. He deserved better than Shelly

Sampson. He deserved a chance to escape this dead-end town, to use his talents and play music under a spotlight before an audience. Angela sat down on the porch and smiled. He deserved someone who could love him back. And, damn it, so did she.

Lucas tried to grab some sleep, but after a few hours he gave up and reached for his guitar. As he lay in bed, his mind had shifted from Abby, to Shelly and Misty, to the idea Angela had somehow caused a rift between them. He supposed Shelly was upset Misty had not held the past against Angela. Regardless of the reason, he was to blame, not Angela. Same as the conflict between him and Abby.

He strummed Steve Earle's "More Than I Can Do" as he came to the realization his every action only compounded the problems he created by trying to manipulate the fates of those around him. Last night's incident served as just another example.

He tried to convince himself he would have acted the same regardless of who the cowboy propositioned. Deep down, he knew the truth. His reaction had been fueled by a desire to protect Angela. The real question was why he felt that compulsion.

Publicly, he could explain. She was his employee; therefore, it was his duty to shield her at the Oasis. Privately, he told himself his reaction resulted from guilt—shame and remorse for the fact he orchestrated her return to Grand. That played a part, but in his gut Lucas knew his motivation went beyond that to a strong desire to show Angela he wasn't a bad guy at heart.

He felt a strange connection with her, like somehow they were partners in crime. Of course, she had no knowledge of how closely they were linked. He felt bad, not only for his involvement in her current situation, but for everything that had happened in her past. Despite the stories, Lucas could see Angela meant no harm. She simply wanted to make her way in life.

His plan had seemed so easy back when he formulated it, before he realized his scheme affected Angela. Before he cared. Now, regardless of what he did, his actions would have a lasting effect. The only solution was to abandon his scheme to get Jake and Angela together. To stop manipulating the lives of those around him.

At least then he would be the only one to get hurt.

# 21

Shelly stood in the kitchen, staring out at the plowed field behind her house. Wind gusts picked up the soil and sent it whirling her direction. The tiny grains clicked against the windowpane. The solitude of life here in Grand had eroded many of her dreams. She didn't enjoy being alone. Normally, she would call one of her friends when these feelings hit, but she couldn't call Misty after Monday's incident, and Charlene had gone into Amarillo to check on her unemployment.

Charlene's desperation had reached new heights, otherwise she would never stoop so low as to date the riffraff from the feedlot. But single men were scarce, and her only real requirement was a man with a steady job. Already she called this guy, Jimmy something or other, the next one.

Shelly could not believe Charlene's gall. She'd been married and divorced so often no one noticed anymore. For that, Shelly envied her friend. The whole town would gasp if she up and divorced Jake, even though she'd entertained the idea for years. But it was hard to say whose side the residents would take. People liked them both, but only because they did not live with Jake. They still viewed him as the glorious middle linebacker that twice led the team to state titles. And his family had practically settled the area, whereas her parents had come and gone like a springtime rainstorm—welcome at the time, but soon forgotten.

Life would definitely be easier and a whole lot more pleasurable if she divorced Jake. Of course, she would never stay single. She hated to be alone far too much to live by herself, but next time she would choose a man who shared some of her interests. Somebody who would go shopping with her, sit and have a decent conversation, or at least be willing to watch a movie that did not involve shoot-outs, topless women, or a single car chase.

Shifting her gaze away from the field, Shelly stared down at the chicken breast thawing in the sink. She needed to start peeling potatoes. The boys would be home from school soon, followed shortly by Jake. The ringing of the telephone saved her just as she pulled out the paring knife.

"Hello."

"Your boyfriend is out of line," Charlene blurted.

"What are you talking about?" Shelly sat in the kitchen chair.

"I'm talking about your little boy toy, Lucas. He ruined the whole damn thing."

"Don't start in about Lucas again."

"Oh, you're gonna be pissed, too, when I tell you what happened."

"About what?" Shelly asked again.

"Let me light a cigarette, and I'll tell you the whole damn story."

Shelly listened to the click of the lighter and her friend draw in a several puffs.

"On the way back from Amarillo, I swung by the feedlot to see Jimmy and find out how things went last night."

"What did he say?" Shelly interrupted, excited to hear.

"Let me finish. Anyway, the little bastard tried to hide and his buddies told me he quit, but I knew they were lying because I seen his pickup. So, I marched from building to building until I found the little prick hiding behind some feed sacks. I told him to get his scrawny little ass out to my car so we could talk."

"No, you didn't."

"Yes, I did. The smell out there could gag a maggot."

"Why was he hiding?"

"Embarrassed, I guess." Charlene heaved a big sigh before relaying last night's events at the Oasis.

The tale of Lucas's aggression left Shelly speechless. She recalled the time he tossed Jake out of the Oasis. Neither one would ever admit what happened, but Shelly found out from Ruby Riggins, whose brother had seen the whole thing.

Charlene wrapped up the story. "So, when are you going to tell him to fire that bitch?"

"I don't know if he'll listen."

"Don't give me that crap. He'd rob Fort Knox with a butter knife if you asked. All you gotta do is give the word and Lucas will do it. Tell him to can her ass."

"I . . . don't know," Shelly stammered.

"Well, I do," Charlene answered. "Listen, I got to go. Jimmy's coming over when he gets off from work, and I need to get ready. But it's in your hands now. That job is the only thing keeping her here. Hell, give in and let Lucas have what he's always wanted if that's what it takes. A little strange might do you some good too. He's not a bad lay."

Shelly stared at the phone after she hung up. She considered dialing the Oasis. It would be interesting to hear Lucas's version of the story, but she wanted to talk to him without that slut around.

She couldn't wait for the day when that tramp was gone from the Oasis, from the town, from the entire state of Texas. She looked forward to the day she could rest easy. To the time when putting up with Jake would again be her biggest problem.

Too bad she couldn't get rid of her husband and that whore all at once.

Shelly's mouth dropped open. Why hadn't she thought of that? Here she'd worried about Angela coming back to town and making a move on Jake the way she did at prom, but now that Shelly thought about it, that very thing would solve all her problems. The townspeople would view Angela as a homewrecker and Jake as a fool for abandoning his family, both of which would pave the way for Shelly to pursue the life she actually deserved.

# 22

Lucas was grateful when time came to head for the Oasis. His heart was being yanked two directions and he didn't know which way to go. Love and affection for Shelly tugged one way, while compassion for Angela pulled the other—a tug of war, with his happiness stuck in the middle. He longed for an easy way out, but there didn't appear to be such a thing.

These feelings for Angela had taken him off guard. Were they based solely on guilt and a sense of responsibility, or was there more to them than that? Lucas told himself he simply didn't want to cause more injustice in her life, an easier argument to make before last night. But things changed when he bounced that cowboy.

Lucas found it increasingly difficult to deny his motives went beyond merely looking out for her. He was genuinely attracted. Not for the obvious physical attributes, although he couldn't deny his appreciation for the way she filled out a pair of jeans, but for how she carried herself—for the way she stood strong in the face of a lifetime of adversity, the set of her chin that seemed to say *I will carry on despite what anyone else thinks*. Angela had invaded his mind, and he didn't know how to push her out.

He'd tried and failed to catch some sleep after the early

morning debacle with Abby. Then he'd tried to lose himself in song. He played the guitar until his fingertips hurt, and he worked on a few lyrics going through his head, but nothing stuck. Finally, he gave up and took a shower, hoping to refresh his mind and body, but afterward when he looked in the mirror, Lucas was greeted by red-rimmed eyes with dark circles underneath. He took one look and decided there was no point in shaving the two-day stubble, so he simply threw his Cowboy Junkies cap over his wet hair and called it good.

Firing up his old pickup, he felt jittery and anxious. About what, he couldn't exactly lay his finger on. Maybe he would do a few shots before work today just to calm his nerves. But he would have to down them before Chester and L.J. arrived to prevent the duo's commentary on his sudden need for a stiff drink.

Making the short drive, he wondered if all alcoholics got started this way. That thought terrified him. He didn't want to turn into Chester, L.J., or God forbid, his dad.

As the Oasis came into view, he decided to forego the drink. No matter the situation, he would face his problems with a level head. Good thing he felt that way, because Chester's truck already occupied the parking space nearest the front door.

There would be no time alone. No time for a drink.

Lucas pulled into his usual space and got out with his mind still clouded by doubt and fatigue.

Chester called out, "You're starting to make a habit out of this opening late. We need to buy you a watch?"

"Y'all are early," Lucas answered while sorting for the proper key to unlock the bar.

"A watch and razor, I reckon," Chester said. "You're looking a mite scruffy there, Lucas."

"I don't know," Angela chimed in. "I think a man looks sexy with a bit of stubble."

"Whoa! 'Sexy,' she said." Both Chester and L.J. laughed, but Lucas ignored the codgers.

He hadn't noticed Angela with the two old men, but as his eyes settled upon her, he couldn't help but stare. She was beautiful.

Gorgeous, actually.

He'd thought her pretty before, but stunning was the only way to describe her appearance now.

Her long, shimmering blonde hair hung in layered curls in just such a way to frame her flawless face. The ankle-length skirt and pink sweater seemed a bit too nice for waitressing at the Oasis. Though her eyes, not the clothes, captured Lucas's attention. A touch more makeup outlined her lashes, but even that wasn't the major difference. Angela met his stare and brazenly matched it. Her eyes sparkled. There, in the gravel parking lot, suddenly one side of his emotional tug of war pulled a lot harder.

Unlocking the front door, he flipped on the lights and stepped aside to let the others enter. Of course, Chester and L.J. flashed him knowing smirks as they passed.

Once inside, he fired up the jukebox, popped open a beer, and started a pot of coffee for L.J. while Angela went about her business prepping the tables for the night. Lucas focused on her as she glided about the room. She stood out like the moon on a cloudless night. She caught him watching and flashed a smile. As usual, Chester and L.J. took in the entire scene from their perch at the bar.

"What do you think of the hitchhiker we picked up?" Chester broke the silence.

"I think she must've been hard up to get in the truck with you two." Lucas avoided the real question.

"L.J., can you believe he's gonna talk about his two best customers that way?" Chester swiveled on the stool to address Angela. "Hope he treats his help better than that."

She smiled, making it obvious she knew what the two

were up to. "He treats me just fine."

The way she said "just fine" made Lucas's heart dance a true Texas waltz.

"Good to hear," L.J. said. "Especially since he is only your boss."

Chester's fat belly bobbed with mirth. Lucas frowned and looked at Angela, who blushed and shot the two would-be comedians a stern look before joining Lucas behind the bar. The skin on her neck and cheeks matched the neon Budweiser sign above the jukebox.

"Don't let 'em get to you. They think they're cute," Lucas said to ease her embarrassment.

"I won't." She reached out and brushed her fingertips on his forearm. "I know cute, and they're definitely not it."

The combination of her words and touch affected Lucas in ways he didn't want to think about. He opened his mouth to speak, but the words clung to his throat like gum to the bottom of a table. Without saying a word, he grabbed a box of whiskey tucked under the bar and headed for the cooler, never considering how strange his actions appeared. Inside, and away from the others, he opened the box and grabbed a bottle. The first drink lifted his spirits, the second kicked him in the balls.

All his life, Lucas had vowed not to become a drunk. Not to be like his dad. Now here he was, doing exactly that. With a heave, he tossed the bottle against the far wall where it shattered, sending shards of glass and whiskey through the air. He refused to look for answers at the bottom of a bottle.

Angela appeared at the cooler door. "You okay? I heard glass."

"Yeah, just had a little accident," he said, stepping toward the door.

Blocking the exit, she studied his features. "Something bothering you?"

"No. Dropped a bottle."

Her eyes narrowed as she continued to scrutinize him. "I'll get the broom."

Lucas didn't argue. The glass could stay there forever, far as he was concerned, but if she wanted to clean it up, he wouldn't stop her. Leaning against the counter, he rubbed the stubble along his jaw line.

"Pretty nice to have someone clean up your mess," L.J. said.

"I suppose." Lucas shrugged.

"Boy, you're the biggest damn fool I know."

Lucas straightened at L.J.'s harsh tone. He'd grown to expect some good-natured ribbing from time to time, but the old man's voice made it clear this was no joke.

"For fifty years I was just as big a fool." L.J. stared at the ceiling. "I spent too much time loving a woman who couldn't, or wouldn't, love me in return. At least not publicly. I was convinced we'd be together one day. Until the day she died, I believed that lie."

Unaccustomed to L.J. being so candid about his personal life, Lucas leaned in to listen.

Sadness filled the raspy voice as L.J.'s eyes took on a far-off look. "I was stupid. Elizabeth told me so herself the morning she died. We both knew her time was about up." L.J. swallowed hard. "She called me over to her house that morning. Said she wanted to tell me something. I expected her to tell me she loved me and say goodbye. Know what she told me?"

Lucas shook his head, not sure if L.J. wanted an answer. Chester continued to nurse the bottle in his hand. Apparently, he'd already heard this story.

"'Sorry.' All she could say was sorry. Being an idiot, I asked her what for. Her response showed me for the fool I am."

Lucas said nothing.

"She apologized for the way she'd treated me all those years. Told me she never married me because of the way it would've looked. That wasn't news to me. For years, she turned me down, claiming the rumors she killed old Ansel would resurface. Don't know how many times I told her they never went away, but she always used that same old excuse." He rubbed the scraggly whiskers on his chin.

Lucas looked over at Chester, who appeared unconcerned about his buddy. Lucas, on the other hand, was worried. He'd never seen L.J. so forlorn.

"Two hours before she died, Elizabeth confessed all of that was a lie. There on her deathbed, after fifty years of tormenting my heart, she told me . . . "

Lucas held his breath as the old man paused. The pain etched on L.J.'s face unnerved Lucas. He looked as if he could join Elizabeth at any moment.

"She told me she was ashamed to be seen with me in public. Her refusal had nothing to do with the rumors." The words came out in a throaty whisper.

Lucas barely made out the last sentence.

L.J. leaned over and grabbed the amber bottle in front of Chester. "She told me she'd always loved me, but her reputation was bad enough without marrying a drunk." He took a long, slow pull from the beer. "Me. A drunk. Can you believe anyone would call me a drunk?" L.J. emitted a sick, hollow laugh before looking Lucas in the eye. "Boy, don't fool yourself the way I did."

Lucas didn't know what to say. His situation was different, no matter what L.J. thought. He wasn't a drunk, would never be a drunk. And Shelly would never lie to him. They were too close for that.

"What's ironic," L.J. said. "I only drank this stuff because of her. Now that she's gone, getting drunk don't do a damn thing for me." He handed the bottle back to his longtime drinking partner. "I got angry until it hit me—I'd already spent too many years allowing Elizabeth to cause me pain. I still love her to this day. Loved her too many years not to. But I was a fool. Lived my whole life for the future. Ignoring today. Ignoring things right in front of my damn nose."

Lucas frowned. "But—"

"Don't 'but' me. It's plain to see you're up to your elbows in some scheme using Angela, but I'm telling you that Sampson gal ain't everything you think she is. Neither is that girl back there cleaning up your mess. She could clean up your life if you'd open your eyes. I've been down the road you're traveling, and let me tell you, it's one shitty trip."

Angela reappeared from the cooler before L.J. said more. Not that it mattered. Lucas didn't want to hear the rest. It was different with him and Shelly. Only Jake prevented them from being together.

Angela emptied the dustpan in the trash and joined them up at the bar where the four spent the night huddled around, swapping stories. They grew quiet at the sad ones, laughed at the funny ones, and not once did any of them comment how quiet it was without the feedlot cowboys.

Lucas realized early on that Angela was flirting. Not like she did with the customers, but boldly flirting—touching his arm, letting her fingers linger against his skin while staring into his eyes, smiling coyly as she twirled her long hair around her finger. As the hours passed, he couldn't help succumbing to her charm. He even began to return the attention. Through it all, L.J. watched, saying with his intense gray eyes what Lucas refused to acknowledge.

Later that night, alone in bed, the guilt hit him. Bothered by the fact Angela had caused him to forget about Shelly, he felt like an adulterer. Angela was nice enough, and she was damn sure sexy as hell. But she wasn't the one he'd been in love with for twenty some-odd years.

# 23

Shelly watched her boys come up the driveway. A backpack hung from Taylor's lean frame while Austin walked carefree without the burden of books. No doubt her youngest son had homework, too, but for him, school assignments were secondary to good times. The boys came through the door.

"Do your homework and stay inside," she yelled from the kitchen. "We're going to eat early and go to church tonight."

"Do we have to?" Austin whined.

"Yes, and I don't want any lip about it."

Like always, Taylor simply went to his room and did as instructed. Austin stayed in the living room, stalling for time. When he thought she wasn't looking, he turned on the TV.

"Austin, I'm not telling you again. Get in your room and finish your homework right now. Otherwise, you'll be standing up at church!"

She stuck her head around the corner and watched him sulk down the hall. He frustrated her. Getting him to do anything was a fight. She turned her attention back to dinner just as Jake emerged from the garage, covered in dust.

"Go take a shower and get ready. We're going to

church."

"I'm not." Her husband flopped down in a kitchen chair. "All I'm gonna do is eat and sit my ass in the recliner."

Shelly placed her hands on her hips. "We're all going to church. As a family. We didn't go Sunday, and it won't look good if we miss tonight too."

"I don't give a shit how it'll look. I'm tired."

"I don't want to go either." Austin slid into the kitchen on his socked feet.

"I've told you three times already. Go do your homework and get ready. We are *all* going!" Shelly stared directly at Jake until he lowered his eyes.

"Humor your mom and do as she says," he said to his son.

Shelly shot her spouse a look of disdain but didn't respond. Ten minutes later, she placed the food on the table and called the family.

"This is good, Mom," Taylor broke the silence a short while later.

"I don't like these potatoes. They have onions in them," Austin complained.

"And these pork chops are tougher than an armadillo's ass cheek." Jake agreed with Austin that dinner was far from perfect.

"Don't eat. I don't care. That leaves more for Taylor and me."

Not another word was uttered as the family finished up and left. Jake pulled into the church parking lot and easily found a spot. Only half as many people attended the Wednesday service. The family trudged inside in silence.

Shelly gasped upon entering the sanctuary. There beside Misty, in Shelly's normal spot, sat Angela.

Sitting down abruptly at a pew near the back, Shelly said, "Let's sit here."

"Why do we have to sit way back here?" Austin complained.

"Because I said so. Now be quiet. I don't want to hear another peep out of you."

Even after the sermon started, she continued to stare at the pew where she was supposed to sit. None of the preacher's words found their way to her ears.

September had been a horrible month, full of dark clouds from the past and margarita monsoons. By getting out of Angela and Jake's way and letting nature solve both problems, Shelly had been hoping to find solid footing among the mud here on the first day of October. But Misty's betrayal threatened to engulf Shelly. Feeling as if she were drowning, she couldn't wait to escape the confines of the church. To get away from the hideous sight of her former friend sitting side-by-side with that tramp.

Finally, the choir struck up the last hymn and the preacher started down the aisle. Shelly stepped out behind him as he passed. She wanted in front of the throng that would gather to shake his hand at the door, to escape before anyone had a chance to mention that whore. And she sure didn't want to be placed in another social situation with Angela.

A quick hello and handshake with the preacher at the outer doors and she stepped into the freedom of the outside world. Taylor stood by her side, but the rest of her family was nowhere in sight.

"Where's your dad and brother?"

Taylor shrugged. "Dad stopped to talk to somebody."

Shelly shifted her weight from foot to foot. With every passing second, she became more convinced Jake was doing this intentionally. When he finally appeared, she shot him a look to let him know she was pissed before heading for her SUV.

"Can I walk home with Trevor?" Austin ran up behind

her.

"No. You can get in the car and be quiet. I'm tired of arguing with you today," Shelly snapped at her son.

"Dad?" Austin whined.

"Come on, Shell, let him walk. Just because you're in a shitty mood ain't no reason to punish him."

Shelly flashed her husband a look. She was about to berate him for again undermining her authority when she thought better of it.

"Okay, Austin, walk. Taylor, go with him and make sure he comes straight home." Shelly wanted Jake alone anyway. She could express her displeasure more effectively without the boys around. He barely closed his door before she unleashed.

"I don't appreciate you always taking up for Austin when I'm disciplining him!"

"Calm the hell down. You're too hard on him. He wanted to walk home, not get a tattoo."

"I'm hard on him because he acts just like you!"

"He acts like little boys should."

"Taylor doesn't act like that."

Jake shrugged. "That's his problem."

"What's that supposed to mean?" Shelly demanded. "Just because he doesn't act like a whiny, selfish slob, Taylor has a problem?"

Jake stared at her and shook his head. "Come on, Shell, you're going nuts. This whole thing with Angela is sending you off the deep end."

"This has nothing to do with Angela. You're trying to turn this around so you won't have to admit you play favorites with Austin."

"You're full of shit! You've been this way ever since she came back. And the only thing I'll admit is I can relate to Austin easier."

Shelly stared at him, but kept her mouth shut. She

would never admit it, but he was right. She was upset over the Angela situation. That tramp's return brought all this out of her—anxiety, jealousy, fear.

Jake treated the boys the same. But she treated them differently. Especially now with the worry that Angela's return would expose her secret.

He may be right, but she wasn't about to let him off the hook. She glared at her husband. "I don't want to hear another word about Angela. Just because she's your old girlfriend doesn't mean we have to discuss her. And I better not catch you so much as looking her direction."

"God, do we have to start with that again? One little date, and I've heard about it all my life. Let it go."

Shelly stifled a smirk. The harder she pushed, the quicker he would go over the edge and do something stupid—something she could use against him, something to sway public opinion. Jake never had liked to be told what not to do. "I'm warning you. Stay away from her."

His forehead creased. "Just shut the hell up already."

"I mean it, Jake. Don't you so much as look at her. Don't think about her. Don't utter a single damn word to her, or about her. Or I'll—"

"You'll what?" His upper lip shook.

Shelly suppressed a smile. Jake was so easy to control. "Just do it and see what happens."

Jake pulled into their drive and flung open his door. Grabbing his jacket, he stomped down the driveway, away from the house.

"Where are you going?" Shelly hollered after him.

"For a walk." He didn't turn around. "I'm not sticking around to listen to you bitch." Hurrying down the street, Jake shook his head. Shelly had gotten crazier by the day, maybe by the hour. How dare she tell him what he could say, or do, or think? He had half an idea to march over to Angela's right now and show his wife what he thought of her threats, but he needed to relieve some tension, not create more. Heading for Charlene's, he planned on doing just that.

Rounding the street corner, he spied the old pickup at the curb long before he reached Charlene's. "Damn it." That little punk shit-kicker had beat him to the saddle. Jake's luck kept getting worse.

He wasn't about to go home, and the Oasis was closed on Wednesdays, so that left him only one option: walk to Angela's.

That tight ass of hers had looked damn fine beneath that dress. He'd pretended to care about Denny Wright's winter wheat plans just to hold back and watch her walk out of church. Now all he could think about was watching her step out of that dress.

To hell with Shelly and her threats.

Rounding the next corner, Jake cursed again. Misty's van sat in the driveway. This simply was not his day. Walking past the house, Jake made a promise to himself. The next time he came by here he would stop, regardless of who was around. It was time for Angela to stop fooling herself. One way or another, he'd prove they both wanted the same thing.

# 24

Closing her eyes, Shelly dipped her shoulders below the bubbles. On Saturdays, the boys ventured to the farm with Jake, so she pampered herself. Shelly deserved one day a week to satisfy her needs, but this morning she could not unwind and enjoy the bath in the serenity of the empty house. The warm water soothed her tense muscles, but not her troubled mind.

She hadn't been able to relax for weeks, not since that troublemaking tramp sashayed back into town. Before Angela's arrival, Shelly slept in on Saturdays and rose sometime mid-morning to soak in the tub until Lucas called, at which point they would talk for hours about movies, places they hoped to go someday, or the interesting things that had occurred down at the Oasis. It wasn't so much the subjects she enjoyed, as much as talking to a man who actually listened.

This morning she couldn't even look forward to that. Lucas had acted peculiar ever since Angela went to work at the Oasis, and Shelly had heard from several sources that Lucas and the whore had gotten to be quite friendly with each other. Abby DeWitt swore they had stayed at the bar long past closing every night this week.

Shelly didn't believe the stories. Lucas was probably nice to Angela. He was that kind of guy, but he also had way better taste. And how would Abby know what went on at two in the morning? Nevertheless, Shelly didn't want Angela working at the bar anymore. She didn't want Lucas keeping Angela from Jake. Matter of fact, she wanted Lucas kept away from the harlot.

Easing out of the tub, she toweled off.

Once Angela got fired, Shelly could turn her attention to getting Jake and his little prom slut together. No doubt Jake would stray given the chance. He was no angel. Any decent-looking woman could lead him down the path of temptation. She took for granted that Angela would be interested. A hard-up desperate whore like her would take any man she could get her hands on.

Shelly planned to give Jake and Angela just enough rope to hang themselves. Affairs were hard to hide in a town as small as Grand, and it would be better if the town discovered their indiscretions. If she were the last to know. Once the rumors took off and the entire town was whispering, Shelly would pick an opportune time and break down publicly. A few tears and sobs would be enough to swing public opinion.

To get what she wanted from her father, Shelly had perfected the ability to cry on demand as a teenager, but it'd been years since she deployed the trick. Studying her reflection in the bathroom mirror, she conjured up every sad thought compressed in her brain until salty tears streamed down her cheeks. Wiping the streaks from her face, she smiled with the knowledge she still possessed the necessary skills.

*Home wrecker.*

*Slut.*

*Two-timing bitch.*

Shelly could almost hear the town's comments now. And what would Misty say when her long-lost friend ran off with Jake? Shelly could barely wait for that apology.

Dressing, she found it difficult to suppress her anticipation. Lucas slept in until close to noon, but she couldn't wait that long. At ten minutes after eleven, she picked up the phone and dialed his number.

Lucas stared at the ringing telephone. Normally, he eagerly awaited his Saturday morning conversations with Shelly, but today he dreaded the prospect. With each ring, his heart skipped a beat until the noise finally stopped. Shelly would wait ten minutes and call again. Whether he wanted to or not, Lucas would have to answer, or she would come looking for him, and in a town like Grand, there was no way to hide.

On a normal weekend, he would still be sacked out, but this was no normal day. Apprehension had prevented him from sleeping yet again. The eastern sky had begun to lighten before he ever got in bed, and then he'd tossed and turned. Sometime around seven, he finally gave up the fight, got dressed, and went to tinker on the Cadillac, despite the fact there was very little work left to do on the car.

Lucas picked up the phone to call Shelly back because its ringing again was the one thing he could be certain of. But he couldn't bring himself to dial her number. Just as he couldn't accept the fact he'd officially fallen for Angela. Even though he knew it was true, because last night, she was who he thought of while finishing the song he'd been writing for months. But why?

Why couldn't he shake his attraction?

Why did she have to be so alluring?

Nowhere in his plans had he considered falling for Angela Ross.

Her draw on his heart had to be the temporary result

of working too close together, the side effect of his guilt, the physical response of his body demanding affection. Or perhaps it was fate's punishment for his deception.

It didn't matter. Angela was leaving soon.

Besides, Shelly was the woman he'd always wanted. This other thing had to be some bit of fleeting lust.

The jumble of thoughts stacked up in his mind like cord wood beside a lumberjack.

By now the entire town had to know about him defending Angela. News like that traveled fast in Grand. What if Shelly read into his motives and sensed his attraction to Angela? What if she discovered they stayed at the bar talking until nearly four the past two mornings? Or heard he drove her home every night? But above all of that, his greatest worry was that his devotion to Shelly might not be as strong as before.

Angela had invaded the space in his heart he'd held in reserve for Shelly. He'd grown accustomed to loving her, and he was not prepared to abandon those feelings.

Lucas jumped when the telephone rang. The sound pierced his brain like a bullet from a firing squad. Even expected, it hurt. Reaching for the receiver, he prepared for the worst.

"Hello?"

"Morning, sleepyhead." Her voice sang out like a cardinal at daybreak. "Did I wake you?"

"No, I've been up awhile," Lucas said, his mouth dry.

"You sound tired. Are you okay?"

He let out a long sigh. Her chipper mood made it clear she had no idea he and Angela had been spending lots of time together. That, or she didn't care. Lucas shook his head. Shelly would care; she would be livid to discover he'd befriended her rival.

"So, how's business down at the Oasis?"

*Here it comes*, Lucas thought. "It's there." Maybe vagueness would persuade her to change the subject.

"Heard y'all had a little trouble the other night," Shelly pressed.

"Not really. Just an idiot drunk."

"Oh, I didn't know L.J. was involved," Shelly quipped.

Lucas started to defend his friend, but bit his tongue. Last thing he wanted was to get her started on the birthday party. "Just one of the cowboys from the feedlot blowing off a little steam. Didn't amount to much."

"You're being modest. Way I heard the story, you were a regular knight in shining armor." Her voice took on a sugary sweetness. "Sure was nice of you to defend poor little Angela's honor like that."

"I didn't want any trouble in the bar was all." Lucas backpedaled from her not-so-subtle accusations.

"He must have done something bad. It's not every day you toss citizens from the club and banish them until they come back and apologize," Shelly pushed.

Lucas's head swirled. She knew too many details.

"Had nothing to do with Angela," he lied. "Those cowboys were trying to buffalo me and I had to set them in their place."

"Well, you won't have to protect her anymore."

"Why is that?"

"Because I want you to fire her."

Shelly continued to talk, but Lucas's mind raced too fast to actually listen. Her demand caught him off guard. He needed time to think of a reason to keep Angela. No way could he tell her the truth.

"What about Jake? If I let her go, she might go to work for the co-op. You don't want that to happen."

"You shouldn't be burdened by my troubles. I know the Oasis isn't a gold mine."

"Business has actually picked up," Lucas answered in a panic. "Some men come in just to see her."

"I bet they do." Scorn laced Shelly's words.

"And Angela takes care of Chester and L.J. so I don't have to baby-sit those two every night."

His reasons weren't total lies, and maybe the explanation would be enough, if only he could change the subject.

"So, how's Misty and Charlene? You haven't mentioned them lately."

"You'll have to ask Angela about Misty. They're best of friends, so it seems. But Charlene wants you to fire Angela too."

*Another reason to keep her*, Lucas thought to himself.

"Well?" Shelly chimed in after several long, silent seconds.

"Well . . . what?" Lucas played dumb.

"When are you going to fire her?"

"I'm not!" He spoke too fast, too loud.

Again, silence filled the phone line. He couldn't believe what he'd said. Especially in that tone. He'd never told Shelly no, much less raised his voice. He half expected her to hang up, but with each passing second, he felt more sure she would remain on the line.

"Shelly?" Maybe she'd fainted and was passed out on the floor. "You still there?"

"Why not?"

The lack of anger surprised him. She sounded defeated. The sadness in her voice caused Lucas pain, as though another piece of his heart had broken.

"Because of you," he answered with sudden inspiration.

"Me?"

"Yes. I know you don't like her here in town, and if I fire her, she'll only be here longer. Each day she has a job is one less day she spends here." The statement was true, but the thought caused him torment as well. "I know you're trying to be nice and save me some money."

"No, I—"

"But I won't hear of it," Lucas interrupted, not giving Shelly the opportunity to finish her statement. "I don't get a chance to do anything for you very often, so I'm going to make up for it now. I'm not taking no for an answer. I want to do this . . . for you."

Lucas paused just long enough to catch his breath and gather his thoughts. "I'm supposed to meet a liquor distributor at noon, so I got to go, but I'll call you when I get the chance later."

"But I wanted—"

Lucas pretended not to hear and hung up. At least he would have time to think before he talked to her again. He hated to guess how Shelly was feeling right now. Shocked, he imagined. He only hoped she wouldn't be too mad once she recovered. She might come looking for him. Considering that, he needed to head on over to the Oasis. That way if Shelly drove by either place, she wouldn't know he'd lied.

He started out the door and suddenly remembered he'd promised Angela last night that he'd pick her up on his way to work, and sure as he went to the bar now, someone would see his truck and come into the bar. They would assume he'd opened early, and once he had customers he wouldn't be able to leave and go get Angela. Maybe he could go ahead and swing by and get her now. But what if she wasn't ready? His truck would sit out in front of her house that much longer, increasing the chance someone would report the news to Shelly. He would call first.

He found the number in the phone book easy enough.

"Hello."

Lucas nearly hung up at the sound of her voice. For some stupid reason, he felt nervous as a teenager calling a girl for the first time.

"Hello?" Angela said again. This time more a question

than a greeting.

"Howdy, this is Lucas."

Howdy? What the hell did he say that for? Why did he analyze everything he said?

"Hi, Lucas. I thought you were Misty. Normally, she's the only one who calls."

"No, I'm not Misty."

God, the intelligent thoughts just kept spewing from his mouth. Of course he wasn't Misty.

"Is there something I can do for you, or did you call just to chat?" Angela asked.

"I wanted to let you know I have to go to the bar early. Something came up and I need to go in now. I'm not sure I can get free to come pick you up later. So, if you want to come in late I won't mind. That way you can catch a ride with L.J. and Chester. I'll still pay you for all day, even if you're late," he quickly added, remembering the last time he offered to shorten her workday.

"No, thank you," she laughed. "One ride with those two was enough. Chester can't see straight in the first place, and he spent all his time looking at L.J. or me telling some old story. I thought he would kill us for sure."

"Um . . . well."

"I'm ready though. I can ride in with you now if you don't mind. I'm not doing anything. Maybe I can help you with whatever it is you need to do. And you don't have to pay me any extra," she added.

"Great! I'll be there in a few." That's exactly what he'd hoped she would say.

Lucas hung up feeling like a schoolboy, and a giddy schoolboy at that. As if he'd just asked the homecoming queen out on a date and she'd accepted.

He smiled. Angela would have a fit if she knew he'd compared her to homecoming queen.

# 25

Angela gazed out of the passenger side window. From this angle in her driveway, she could see a faint grey light on the eastern horizon. Another day was dawning—Monday, October sixth. She'd been back in Grand three weeks, been working for Lucas two. So much had happened in that short time that in some ways it seemed a lifetime ago when she loaded her car up and left Chicago behind. But then again, it sort of felt like she'd just gotten here, like things were just beginning anew for her. She had Lucas to thank for that.

She looked over at him. He smiled back. "What time is it?" she asked.

He consulted his watch. "Almost six."

"I have to get inside. I told Misty I would go with her to the café at eight thirty, and I need a couple of hours of beauty rest."

"Don't go in yet." Lucas reached for her hand, but she pulled away and opened the door.

She should've said good night earlier, but Angela savored his company, and she kept thinking he was going to kiss her. She'd made it obvious she wouldn't mind if he did, and it seemed clear he wanted to. Yet Lucas held back.

They'd stayed at the Oasis hours after closing every night for over a week now. However, tonight they'd extended their conversation an extra two hours in her driveway.

Lucas leaned across the seat and caught the door before she could push it shut. "Go if you must," he said, "but don't believe for a second you need beauty rest."

Smiling, she shut the door and padded across the lawn, not daring to look back, although he'd yet to start his truck. She half hoped to reach the porch and find him right behind her, but as she unlocked the door, the truck engine cranked behind her.

Each minute she spent with Lucas made her want to spend ten more. They'd laughed together and swapped stories of people they knew and places they'd been. He'd listened as she told him more about Las Vegas and even Chicago. She told him the details of her life without holding back. For some reason, she believed he could handle the truth and even understand her reasons for leaving Grand in the first place. He nodded and listened without appearing judgmental or even disappointed.

In their hours of conversation, Angela had been surprised to discover they shared many of the same goals—a stable family, someone to say good night to, a few kids running around the house. Only Lucas believed all of that could be found here in Grand while she could not envision finding any semblance of happiness in this place, at least not in the long term. But her outlook had improved for the short while.

Angela regretted not getting to know him better back when they were kids. Maybe her soulmate had been right here in Grand all along. She especially liked when he talked about music, when passion lit up his dark eyes. Only his hang-up with Shelly prevented total harmony between them. That self-centered, socialite-wannabe was all that anchored him to this windy, desolate hellhole. Angela recognized that much. She'd brought Shelly's name up only once in all their hours of talking. The look of shame that flickered in Lucas's eyes and his quick dismissal let Angela know all she needed to, and forced her to abandon the subject.

The more she got to know Lucas, the more his infatuation confused her. A witty, fun-loving guy like him had nothing in common with that stuck-up, self-serving attention seeker.

Maybe Misty could explain the attraction. After all, she and Shelly used to be friends. Angela felt bad about that. She didn't like Shelly or Charlene, but it bothered her to know she'd brought about the end of Misty's long-time friendships. Angela suspected it would've happened eventually even without her influence. Misty was too good-hearted for a pair like them.

She'd told Angela all about last week's incident at the Whirlwind Café. That's why she couldn't turn down Misty's invitation, and Angela could understand the need to go. Misty had gone to the Whirlwind every Monday her entire adult life. Pride refused to let her former friends' petty actions stop her now. Angela would do the exact same thing if she were in Misty's shoes. However, she would not have made the concession and switched from the normal lunch to breakfast. But then again, Misty was more congenial than most.

Shelly looked over at the Oasis as Charlene turned into the Whirlwind's lot. She missed Lucas and hated the fact he now spent so much time with Angela.

"What the hell is she doing here?" Charlene pointed to Misty's clunker of a mini-van in the café's parking lot.

Shelly shrugged. "I don't know." She hadn't wanted to come at all today, but Charlene persisted. She even insisted on picking her up and driving. Now there was going to be another embarrassing confrontation. No way would Charlene simply ignore Misty.

"She best not be in our booth. It'll be a cold day in hell before I sit with her again." Charlene jammed the car in park.

Shelly slipped out of the vehicle, dreading the thought of what awaited inside.

"Well, kiss my ass! Look at that!"

Shelly lifted her gaze away from the tops of her shoes long enough to look where Charlene pointed. She stopped and took a step backward. No way could she go inside, not with Misty and Angela boldly sitting there next to the window.

"I didn't think she had the balls," Charlene laughed. "I can't believe she brought her here, can you?"

"I . . . We can't go in."

"The hell we can't. We have to, otherwise they win. This is going to be fun." Charlene grabbed Shelly's arm and dragged her inside.

Once again, Shelly found her friend leading her, only this time *into* trouble and not away. Before entering the Whirlwind, she gazed up into the low-hanging gray clouds and mouthed a silent prayer. All she wanted was to get through the day without another embarrassing encounter.

Shelly hoped to sit as far away from Angela and Misty as possible—but not Charlene. She plopped down at the table right beside their booth. Four feet of bacon-scented and tension-filled air was all that separated the four rivals. Shelly was grateful when Charlene chose the chair facing them as that allowed her to turn her back on the situation. At least Angela and Misty could not see the nervousness on her face.

But Shelly could see Abby, standing behind the counter, grinning in obvious anticipation.

Hatred flickered in Charlene's eyes as she stared beyond Shelly's shoulder. The brazen redhead would hold her tongue only so long. Again, Shelly wished they'd skipped today's meal, or at least waited until their normal lunchtime. But Charlene had a one o'clock appointment up in Amarillo.

A broad smile plastered across her face, Abby appeared to take their order.

"Well, look who's here. What can I get you?" Abby spoke too loud, as if she wanted to make Angela and Misty take notice.

Like they hadn't already.

"Just coffee for me." Shelly refused to look at Abby. She didn't want anyone to see the tension and fear in her eyes.

"Coffee, black." Charlene lit a cigarette and took a long drag while the waitress waited. She blew a cloud of smoke in the direction of the enemies. "And some eggs."

"Scrambled or fried?" Abby pulled out a pencil.

"Give me whore eggs. Or as we call them around here, the Angela Ross Special." Charlene raised her voice.

Shelly cringed.

Through furrowed brows Abby said, "Whore eggs?"

"You know, over easy. Like that slut." Charlene pointed her finger.

Shelly hunkered down in anticipation of a response.

None came, though she heard Misty whisper something.

When Gabby Abby ventured off to the kitchen, Shelly whispered, "Please, Charlene. Don't make a scene."

"I don't give a damn what anyone thinks, and you shouldn't either. Hell, we both know we're better than any of these people. Their opinions don't make a shit to me. Watch this.

"Misty! Misty! Oh, come on. Don't tell me you've gone

deaf."

"What do you want, Charlene?"

Shelly turned around. She didn't want to, but she had to see if Misty's face showed the same defiance as her voice.

"Tsk, tsk Misty. All that hostility is going to turn your hair gray. Mark might not like you anymore if that happens. Hell, he's liable to run off and screw your little friend there. Oh, wait, that already happened."

Misty's face flushed scarlet. She started to respond, but Angela reached across the table and grabbed a hold of her hand. Shelly watched, transfixed as Angela turned to speak instead.

"Y'all should be ashamed. You've let your hatred for me fall on to Misty." Angela held onto Misty's hand. "She doesn't deserve it. She's been nothing but a friend to both of you. She told me the things you said to her last week, and you know what? She still never said a bad thing about either of you. No, she blamed herself even though I'm at fault. Me and your own narrow-minded, blind hatred."

Angela's words angered Shelly. Not because they were untrue. What angered her was the fact Angela spoke them so calmly. Where was the angry, belligerent Angela? The one who could be easily provoked? Shelly was used to being the voice of reason. Her reputation was built upon it.

"Oh, aren't you the caring one?" Shelly rolled her eyes. "You sure as hell weren't this loving to Misty back when you fucked Mark, now were you?"

"You're right, I wasn't." Angela met Shelly's hateful stare. "Of course, back then I screwed lots of people I now regret. Some because it hurt people I care about." She looked at Misty. "Others because I wonder what the hell I was thinking." She stared hard at Shelly.

"Cut the act, Angela!" Shelly slammed her hand down on the table. The saltshaker bounced to the floor. "We all know what you are! Stop the charade. You don't care about anything but yourself. You've always been nothing but a troublemaking whore, and we all know that's why you're here now!"

Shelly's outburst forced Misty to stand. "Come on, Angela, this was a mistake. Let's go."

Angela stood and followed Misty several steps before turning back toward the table. Leaning down close to Shelly's face, Angela placed her hands on the table and stared intently at Shelly, completely ignoring the now silent Charlene.

"You know, you're right." Angela lowered her voice to a whisper, but never lifted her gaze from Shelly. "I'm not nearly as strong as you are, Shelly. Just take Jake for example," she said, as if they were two old friends.

Shelly grew nervous by both Angela's relentless stare and proximity. Clearly eavesdropping, Abby stepped closer.

"Well, since y'all do know me so well I might as well be honest," Angela said, now mimicking Charlene's slow Texas drawl. "I enjoy a man that can please me, if you know what I mean." She slapped Shelly on the back. "After prom night, I knew Jake wasn't the man for that job. Of the hundreds—no, thousands—of men I've slept with, he was by far the worst. And that teeny, tiny prick." She waggled her pinky.

Shelly's mouth fell open. She started to speak, but Angela cut her off.

"Yep, you surely are a better woman than me to live such an unsatisfied life all these years. That's why I had to turn him down the other day when he offered a piece of ol' Jake's snake. Since it was your birthday and all, I figured I'd let him save up what little stamina he has for you. Besides, Lucas is lots more fun. Well, I hate to run girls. You know how we whores are, too many men and not enough time."

Shelly and Charlene sat in numbed silence after Angela's departure. For once, even Charlene had nothing to say.

"Here." Abby plopped Charlene's plate down so hard the eggs slid off onto the table. The look on the waitress's face told Shelly the exchange had gone every bit as bad as she feared. Angela had hunkered down whispering her filth, so no one except Abby and themselves heard her confession or slutty boasts. Shelly couldn't stand the fact she'd lost. Now even Gabby Abby would have worthwhile gossip to spread.

"Please, let's go. I really don't feel like being here," Shelly whispered, barely loud enough for Charlene to hear.

The redhead shrugged. "Might as well. I don't even like these damned things." She poked the runny eggs with a fork. "I try not to eat anything that just fell out of a chicken's ass."

The two walked to Charlene's car in shocked silence. The gray clouds of earlier had turned a sinister shade of charcoal and a drizzle fell from the sky. The atmosphere added to the already miserable day. Once again, Angela had shown her up.

That was more painful than the revelation about her husband. He'd always denied he slept with Angela, but in the back of Shelly's mind, she knew that to be a lie. After all, the slut screwed every other man in town, so why not Jake?

To make matters worse, the whore seemed genuine when she claimed to have shot down a proposition from Jake. If that harlot wasn't interested in him, Shelly had nowhere left to turn.

"I should've hit her." Charlene spoke for the first time since they left the café.

"Huh?" Shelly had been engrossed in her own thoughts.

"I should've punched her in the fucking face. No, I should have stabbed her with my fork. Would've served the bitch right."

Shelly didn't respond. Charlene's *wouldas* and *shouldas* meant nothing. Besides, Angela had already left Charlene's nose disfigured twice. Matter of fact, that tramp had always come out on top in confrontations with either of them.

"Don't just sit there. Say something," Charlene barked.

Shelly glanced over at her only ally, but quickly looked back out the passenger window. Tears welled up in her eyes, and the last thing she wanted was for Charlene to see her cry. She refused to let anyone know Angela's words had hurt. Somehow she needed to make light of the situation so nobody would think it had affected her.

"I can't believe she stood in the middle of the café and said Jake had a little prick," Shelly stated with a fake giggle.

"I've seen smaller."

Shelly snapped her head around to stare at Charlene. "What?"

"Um . . . uh, you know what I mean," Charlene said. "It can't be that small, since you've never mentioned it to me all these years. I just—well, it seems like you would mention a thing like that to me. Since I am your best friend." The redhead reached over and patted her friend's hand. "That bitch was only trying to piss you off."

Shelly stared out the window. The bad thing was Angela didn't even have to try to make her mad.

Pulling into Shelly's driveway, Charlene finally spoke. "What are you going to do?"

"I'm gonna have a little talk with Jake. The rest depends on his attitude." Shelly climbed out of the car.

"Are you going to call his cell and bitch him out, or wait until he comes home?" Charlene revved the engine.

"I don't know what I'm going to do yet. I haven't decided."

"I'd wait until he got home, if it was me. That way you can tell if he's lying by his reaction. At least wait until you've calmed down some before you call."

Shelly barely got the car door closed before Charlene tore out of the driveway.

Shelly watched her friend accelerate down the street. She couldn't help feeling like her life was speeding away as well.

# 26

Jake stripped off his muddy jeans and tossed them in the back of his pickup where they landed with a heavy, dull *thwop*. The weather had turned to shit sometime after noon. Working out in the slop made him hate farming all the more, but luckily he kept a pair of ratty sweats and an old T-shirt in the shop for these situations. Jake didn't mind driving the old farm truck soggy and grimy, but he didn't want to dirty up his own truck going home.

It felt good to get out of the wet clothes, but the thought of downing a few cold ones sounded even better to him. Too bad he only had a single bottle of beer left in the fridge at home, unless Shelly had remembered to pick him up a case at the grocery store. He reached for his phone to call and check so he wouldn't have to go out of the way to stop and pay two bucks more for a twelve-pack at the Gulp and Go.

Jake searched for his cell phone among the crumpled pile of fabric on the shop floor and in the drenched jeans he'd just taken off.

"Kiss my ass." The sound of his voice broke the silence and sent the old tabby they kept as a mouser scurrying for cover. Jake hated the cat and had more than once thrown something at it when pissed. His dad claimed to hate it, too, but Jake had caught his old man opening cans of tuna for the damned thing far too often to believe him.

Searching through the junk in the old pickup, he tried to remember when he'd last had his phone so he could remember where he left it.

"Fucking day just keeps getting worse."

If not for the fact he was tired, wet, and filthy, he would swing by the Oasis for a cold draft or three and another gander at Angela, but instead, he opened the small refrigerator his dad kept in the shop. He hated to drink the cheap beer his dad drank, but in a pinch, it would do, and Jake needed something to take the edge off. Relaxed, he might recall where he'd laid his phone.

Even for a Monday, this had been one shitty day. The only good thing about it was the fact his dad was out of town, which meant he'd been able to shirk most of the daily chores.

Jake pulled a can from the unopened thirty-pack and sat down on a tractor tire to mentally retrace his steps. It had drizzled and rained most of the day, so the phone would be ruined if he left it somewhere outside.

This morning the farm truck had a flat, so cracking open a second brew, he checked around the tire machine with no luck. He scanned the tops of the barrels of herbicide he'd been forced to move to get the floor jack. Still no phone.

He opened another can of beer and debated whether or not to drive out to where he'd laid in the mud repairing the irrigation pump that seized up or to that corner where the tumbleweeds had piled up and the cows had trampled the hotwire fence. He didn't debate long.

Fuck getting out in this shit again. If his phone was out there in the rain, it was already ruined anyway.

Hell, he could look for hours and never find the damn thing. Could be anywhere. After repairing the hotwire, he chased three unruly heifers for nearly an hour before he got them penned. More than likely, that's when he lost the phone.

Jake started to feel better after he opened his fifth can. The cheap beer got tastier every swallow. He started to gather the rest of the case and head home, but changed his mind. Why should he? Shelly would only start bitching and ruin the buzz he now had. Better to stay here and rest while he downed a few more, especially given her foul mood these days.

Grabbing another, he turned on the radio. The shop wasn't the most comfortable place to unwind, but it beat listening to Shelly bitch, and the propane heater did an adequate job of chasing out the chill.

Evening gave way to night, and the pile of empty cans at his feet steadily grew. Jake was surprised to learn it was after ten when he finally looked at his watch. Between the beer and the music, he'd lost track of time.

Shelly would be pissed at him for dragging home so late, but he could always tell her he'd been out looking for his phone.

Jake started his truck and opened the shop door to pull out. The damp air had turned much colder in the last few hours. Almost as an afterthought, he grabbed the remaining beers from the refrigerator, just in case he needed them to put up with Shelly.

The beer had improved his mood so much he was able to sing along with Tim McGraw on the radio. He nodded and slapped the steering wheel, thinking how Tim Mc-Graw was one lucky bastard. Getting to nestle between those fine-ass legs of Faith Hill was in itself a hell of a fate, but McGraw had a Major League pitcher for a dad and a slew of number one hits. *Probably had a twelve-inch dick, too,* Jake thought as he pulled into his driveway. Again, Shelly had parked in the middle of the garage, leaving no room for his truck.

"Where the hell have you been?" Her question hit him the second he stepped through the door.

"Hi, honey, it's nice to see you too," he answered with drunken sarcasm.

"Let me guess, you've been to see your girlfriend? And don't try to deny it. She told me all about y'all's escapade."

Jake froze. Shelly grinned that condescending, I-know-fucking-everything grin she used when forced to smile about something that actually pissed her off. Jake hated that fucking grin.

Shelly paused only a beat. "She confessed this morning at the café. How could you do that on my birthday?"

Jake's head reeled. Charlene had sold him out. Now he wished he hadn't drunk all those beers. A clear mind would help him get out of this, but all he could do was stand there like road kill in the headlights of a semi.

"Do you think I'm stupid? That I wouldn't find out?"

"Wasn't my fault," Jake finally answered.

"Oh yeah, who's fault was it?"

"Charlene's."

"Charlene's?"

"Yeah," he said, heartened by the fact his wife had shut up for a second. "You know how she is. I tried to turn her down, but she's been after me for years. I never told you because y'all were friends. I didn't want to ruin that for y'all."

Shelly stared. Her face drained of color. Jake took Shelly's shocked silence as a signal to continue. A new batch of lies hatched in his brain. "She told me if I didn't sleep with her, she would tell you I propositioned her. It was like blackmail," Jake said enthusiastically, taking pride in how well his story developed. "I'm glad you finally know the truth. Now I won't have to do it anymore."

Shelly slumped onto the couch. He thought she might pass out. Her eyes were closed, and she rocked back and forth, running her fingers through her hair.

"Shell?" Jake sat beside her, putting an arm around her shoulders.

Bolting upright at his touch, she shouted, "Get your damn hands off me! Don't ever touch me again."

"Calm down, Shell. You're going to wake the boys."

"Don't 'Shell' me! Don't talk to me at all! The boys aren't even here. I sent them to the Fitzgerald's."

"Oh." Jake stood. His stomach tightened. He was in serious trouble. Without the threat of the boys hearing, Shelly would scream until she lost her voice.

"What exactly did Charlene tell you?" Jake asked tenderly.

"She didn't tell me anything, stupid. I wasn't even talking about her. I was talking about Angela."

It was Jake's turn to sit in stunned silence. Angela? What the hell was Shelly doing with Angela at the café? Like a dumbass, he'd just confessed to something Shelly knew nothing about.

Shelly stood over him with her hands on her hips. "But through your incredible brilliance, I at least know exactly what kind of piece of shit you are."

"Funny. You're real damn funny. You know what? You can sit here and think what you want. You always do anyway." Jake gathered his nearly empty carton of beer.

"Where the hell are you going?" Shelly demanded.

"To the garage. I don't have to sit here and listen to your shit!"

"You've got a lot of nerve. You screw half the town and want to blame me!"

Shelly kept blabbing, but Jake didn't slow down. He crossed through the kitchen and went into the garage, definitely in need of those last four beers.

Chasing those cows didn't seem like a hardship now. All wasn't lost, however. Shelly was pissed and would be for God knew how long, but it could've been worse.

He didn't know how many people knew about him and Angela, but apparently only Shelly was aware of his transgressions with Charlene. That was a good thing. It meant Shelly could protect her valuable reputation. If the whole town was talking about them, there'd be serious trouble.

Jake counted on Shelly's desire to keep dirt under the rug, otherwise she might divorce him. That in itself wouldn't be so bad. Hell, he'd score more pussy as a single man than he did being married to her. But he didn't want her take his boys. And she would too, not because she was mother of the fucking year, but because of how it would look if she signed over custody to him. And then, there was the child support. Shelly was vengeful. She would get Lucas to help her hire a lawyer that would rape him in the courtroom. No, Jake couldn't afford a divorce—not financially, not if he wanted to keep close to his boys.

He probably should get word to Charlene, to let her know he'd screwed up, but until he ran out of beer, Jake lacked motivation to do much of anything but brood. Then slowly, the gravity of the situation began to seep through the alcohol-induced fog and penetrate his brain. He needed to escape the garage before he went crazy. He needed to get some more booze. He needed to warn Charlene. Now more than ever, he wished he hadn't lost his cell.

Easing open the door between the kitchen and garage, he heard Shelly talking. "I can't believe you! You're even worse than Angela!" Shelly shouted into the phone. "We were supposed to be best friends!"

There went his chance to warn Charlene. Taking a step backward, he shut the door as quietly as possible. No way could he go inside now; walking in on Shelly and Charlene's conversation would be entering the eye of the hurricane.

Imprisoned in the garage once again, Jake felt even

worse than before. He eyed the large oil stain spreading out from below her SUV, another damn thing falling apart around here. To compound his other problems, he was now a prisoner in his own house.

House hell—he was penned up in the damn garage.

He could raise the big door and leave, but Shelly might not let him back in. He would be free temporarily, but she would only be that much more pissed he'd escaped. And where would he go if she locked him out?

Suddenly, he remembered the half bottle of whiskey in the cabinet over the refrigerator. He decided to risk another confrontation and sneak in to retrieve the bottle of Jack to help wait out the storm. Grabbing the whiskey from the cabinet, he sniffed at the smell of smoke in the air.

At first he assumed it was the fireplace, then he remembered he hadn't yet cut any wood this year. Besides, the aroma was too strong to be wood smoke. Creeping toward the living room, he peeked to see what Shelly was doing. He heard paper rattling, so he knew she was there.

The floor underneath his feet creaked as he leaned to peer around the corner. Shelly looked up with a devilish grin. Since she'd spotted him, he decided to speak. "What are you doing?" He eyed the flames.

"Just stoking a little fire," Shelly replied innocently. "Since there wasn't any wood, I'm using football cards."

Jake looked at the old wooden box in front of Shelly with panic. "I've had those since I was a kid. Some of 'em are worth a lot of money."

"They're old, but they still burn just fine. See—"she held up a plastic-encased card—"It looks real ancient and says something about this Roger Staubach fellow being a rookie, but it'll still burn. Watch." She flicked the card and its thin plastic case into the flames.

Jake's face contorted into a pained sneer. Shelly wasn't dumb. She knew that was his most prized card, and she knew it hurt him to see it burn. He'd wanted to punch her several times through the years, but this was the first time he actually balled his fists. No, there was a better way to get even. Marching over, he snatched the small wooden crate and stomped off to their bedroom with the remainder of his collection tucked under his arm.

He could play just as dirty. Tossing the whiskey onto the bed, he reached up to the shelves above their headboard and yanked down two porcelain dolls. With a heave, he smashed them against the far wall and grabbed two more just as Shelly ran into the room.

He nodded with satisfaction. "You don't look so damn smart now, do you?"

She pointed to his right hand. "Not that one. My granny gave it to me on my tenth birthday."

"Maybe she can give you a new one. Oh, that's right. She's dead!" He smashed the porcelain figure the same way he had the others.

With a mournful moan, Shelly shrank away from the door. Jake dropped the other doll on his hand and sat on the edge of the bed. Listening to Shelly's sobs in the other room, he understood he was now sequestered in their bedroom, but it beat the garage all to hell, so he didn't mind. And he had whiskey now.

Looking at the alarm clock on the night stand, Jake was surprised to see it was nearly one in the morning. He took a few pulls from the bottle and laid his head back on the pillow.

He woke to the sound of shattering glass, followed closely by the sickening thud of crunching metal. Jake sat up as he heard glass break again, then more metal. Unsure when he'd drifted off, or how long he'd slept, Jake stood and followed the steady noise to the open front door.

There Shelly, with one of the boys' aluminum bats in hand, stood smashing his pickup. She pounded his truck once, twice, three times. Then he exploded.

"Get your ass away from my truck, you crazy bitch!" He ran toward her and ripped the baseball bat from her hand. The force twirled her to the ground. Jake stood over her with the bat raised high, ready to swing down and strike.

"Go ahead, hit me!" Shelly screamed up at him. "Come on, hit me!"

The muscles twitched in his arms. The steady drizzle dripped off his face.

"Hit me," she screeched.

The hairs on his forearms stood on end.

"Come on! Do it! Hit me!"

He badly wanted to unleash the power of his biceps and bring the bat crashing down. She certainly deserved to have her fucking skull cracked wide open.

"Do it!"

He might actually have swung if not for her continuous screams. No way was Shelly going to demand he do anything.

"You're not worth it." He flung the bat as far down the street as he could. The metal clanged and skidded down the pavement.

A light came on at the house next door. Shelly climbed back to her feet and raced back inside the house. Jake had been hemmed in all he cared to be for one night. A check of his watch told him it was ten minutes before two. The Oasis would be closing any minute, but it was the only place in town open at this hour. He couldn't make in time for last call, not with his truck smashed, but he didn't care. He'd go anyway. He could make the walk in ten or fifteen minutes, and Lucas would still be there. Let the bastard refuse to sell him some booze. Jake dared him. He'd wanted to beat the fucker for years.

Jake considered taking Shelly's SUV, but that meant going back into the house for keys, and he had no intention of doing that. Controlling his anger a second time would not be easy.

Walking down the street, his mind raced, but he couldn't see an easy way out of this situation. Shelly would be pissed for months. And his visits with Charlene were most likely gone for good. The rain intensified, hitting Jake in the face.

It rained for a few minutes before the downpour turned to sleet. Jake picked up his pace, pausing only when he reached the front of Angela's. This was all her fault. Why the hell did she have to come back after all these years and stir up trouble? He stood in the street staring at her house. Oblivious to the sleet, he itched to teach the bitch a lesson. And it was the perfect time to have another go at Angela. Shelly was already pissed. He might as well have some fun.

The house was dark, so the slut would still be at the Oasis. He thought about walking to the bar and meeting Angela there, but quickly changed his mind. Lucas would be there running interference, to report every fucking detail back to Shelly. Jake wanted to take his time getting reacquainted without the threat of Shelly showing up to spoil the fun.

It was too fucking cold to wait outside, and he'd rather surprise her in the dark, where it would just be the two of them.

He tried the front door. Locked. Then the windows along the front of the house. All locked. He walked around to the side of the house. Surely he could find a way in from the back. The house sat on the corner, so he wouldn't have to walk far to reach the gate. Entering the narrow alley, he reached for the latch only to find it locked as well.

"Shit!" He didn't want to climb the fence in this slick drizzle. Given his inebriated state and current streak of bad luck, he might hang a nut on the picket and render himself useless for the night.

No one in Grand locked things up, but Old Lady Ross always had been crazy. Fuck it—he'd break a window. There had been one on the side he could slip through easily enough. That wouldn't be all he slipped inside of tonight.

Jake stepped out of the alley too immersed into his fantasies to notice the pickup coming up the street. Only in the last second before impact did he understand he was about to be struck.

The air left his lungs as Chester's pickup slammed into his left side.

# 27

Trying to ignore the whimpering sobs of the small child to her right, Shelly focused her attention on the pallid-green wallpaper. The pattern wasn't interesting or eye-catching, yet she preferred its dullness over the needy and desperate faces surrounding her.

To her left, a bald-headed black man held a bloody rag to his hand. A filthy family sat across from her—the reason for their visit less obvious—but all three of the dirty children had yellow, snot-crusted nostrils and stringy, dull-brown hair. Shelly longed to be away from this bland, sterile room encircled by the injury-prone and ailing misfits of society.

The not knowing plagued her worse than the people. Over an hour had lapsed since she'd gotten any word whatsoever, and if Sheriff Hickman hadn't gone back and talked to the doctors, she wouldn't know anything at all. There'd been no news since his departure.

Despite the lack of information, Shelly breathed easier with the lawman gone. His questions and critical looks made her uneasy. Leaning her head back, she shut her eyes and thought how good it would feel to simply close her eyes and drift to sleep.

After their fight, she had lain down only to be awakened by pounding on the front door. Thinking it was Jake, she ignored the knocks. He could've rotted outside for all she cared. Only when she heard the sheriff calling her name did she go to the door, and then she assumed someone heard them fighting and called the police.

Even now, thinking back, Shelly had a hard time recalling the sheriff's description of the accident. The meaning behind the lawman's words did not sink in until he asked how Jake's truck got damaged. The accusatory tone of Hickman's voice snapped her back to reality, forced her to pay attention.

Her first instinct was to lie about the truck and all the earlier events of the evening, but the serious look on Hickman's face altered her plans. That and a lack of sleep prevented her mind from forming a viable story.

So, with much regret, Shelly relayed the entire account, starting with Angela's confession at the café. She told the officer every last detail, except the part about Jake's football cards. After all, the man was a Cowboys fan—he would look poorly on anyone torching Staubach's rookie card.

She would've preferred to keep the sordid details a secret, but that seemed impossible, and since he was bound to find out the truth anyway, she hoped to win the stern man's sympathy with her version.

It must have worked, too, because the sheriff had driven her the thirty-five miles to the hospital. However, he was still somewhat suspicious and peppered Shelly with questions during the trip. She answered the same inquiries over and over, but still could not answer the one Hickman asked most.

*What was her husband doing in that alley?*

Jake's footprints had been found on the muddy ground behind Angela's house. Chester and L.J.'s stories both confirmed that's where he appeared. Shelly didn't care why he was there; she was caught up on the fact Jake had screwed up both her plan and her life.

The entire town would feel sorry for him. They would blame her. They would gossip about her smashing his truck and tossing him out on such a miserable night. No one would know about Charlene or the doll he'd smashed. The townspeople would see her as the villain. They wouldn't bother to ask why he was behind Angela's house. Shelly feared her reputation would be damaged far worse than Jake's body.

That's why she wanted to hear the exact extent of the injuries. Sheriff Hickman said they'd rushed Jake to surgery the minute he arrived. He also said his leg appeared to be broken and he was unconscious at the scene. But that was all she knew.

One thing Shelly did know. She had to abandon her scheme to get Jake and Angela together. Even if she found a way, the town would sympathize with her husband. Everyone would consider him justified to seek comfort after being thrown out in the street on such a cold, miserable night. Shelly's entire reputation dangled in the balance.

She was glad the sheriff left, but the emergency room felt like the loneliest place on earth. The Fitzgeralds would bring the boys as soon as they woke up. Until then, she would be alone. No way could she call Misty or Charlene after everything that had happened, and Lucas hadn't answered any of her calls.

"Mrs. Sampson?"

Shelly looked at the receptionist and walked over to the desk. "I'm Mrs. Sampson."

The woman shoved a stack of papers across the desk. "Sign these and bring them back when you're finished."

"Can you tell me anything about my husband?"

"A doctor will relay all pertinent medical information as soon as possible. I only handle the paperwork," the receptionist explained without looking away from the monitor.

Shelly returned to her seat. Sifting through the stack of papers only made her angrier. Most of the documents were an unnecessary waste of time. Why did she need to fill out papers on a living will and organ donation? Jake didn't need those. So what if he had a broken leg?

Jake had been knocked unconscious a couple of times playing football, but he always went back in the game, and as far as she knew, he'd never had broken a bone. But he did have surgery on his knee. Surely a broken leg wasn't any worse than that.

"I came as soon as I could."

Shelly looked up at the sound of Misty's voice, shocked to see her after everything that had happened, but she was glad for the company.

Misty hugged her. "I'm so sorry. How is he?"

"I don't know. They told me he was in surgery and they would let me know. I'm sure he's fine though. Sheriff Hickman told me he had a broken leg, but Jake is tough. He'll be okay."

Misty patted Shelly's knee. "I prayed for him all the way here. What else I can do? Call people for you?"

"Thanks. You being here is enough. I'm . . . I don't know what to say. I shouldn't have treated you—"

"Don't even think about any of that." Misty looked around the room. "You have enough to worry about. How are the boys?"

"They're at the Fitzgeralds'. They don't know anything about it yet." She knew Misty would hear everything eventually, so she told her the same version she did the sheriff in the hope Misty would take her side and finally recognize Angela for the conniving bitch she was.

Misty listened as if the story were all old news until the part about Jake and Charlene. Her jaw dropped when

Shelly described their fight. Again, she left out the burning of the football cards.

"Oh, you poor thing," Misty whispered when Shelly finished. "I can't believe Charlene would do that. I wish there was something I could do to ease your pain. I'm sure glad Angela called me. You didn't need to be here alone."

Shelly stared. "Angela called and told you about this?"

Misty nodded. "Yes, she told me about Jake getting hit, but she didn't have any other details. The sheriff was questioning her and Lucas, and he told them he'd brought you here and you were alone. She and Lucas were going to stay and get things sorted out with L.J. and Chester."

Animosity flooded Shelly's mind. What business did Angela have telling people about Jake's accident? And why was Lucas with Angela and those drunks instead of at the hospital comforting her? Shelly started to voice her displeasure to Misty but caught herself. Unless she wanted to be alone, she couldn't afford to offend Misty yet again.

"Sampson family?"

Shelly and Misty stood as a doctor, still dressed in his turquoise surgical scrubs, approached. "I'm Jake's wife," Shelly explained. "And this is my best friend, Misty. Are you his doctor? How is he?"

"Please follow me to one of the private consultation rooms, and I will fill you in on where we're at on your husband's treatment."

Shelly ignored the nervous look Misty shot her and followed the doctor down the hall.

He sat and peered at them over the top of his glasses. "Mr. Sampson has some very serious injuries, but he's out of surgery and stabilized at the current time. However, he is still in critical condition, and subsequent surgeries will be required to repair his injuries."

Shelly frowned. "What exactly are his injuries?"

Clearing his throat, the surgeon referred to a small note

pad in his left hand. "There was some internal bleeding that we believe stemmed from a lacerated kidney. We have repaired that, but there could be other sources of internal trauma as well."

"Oh my gosh." Misty covered her mouth with her hand.

The doctor continued. "Mr. Sampson received blunt force trauma to his skull, resulting in a severe concussion. We will not know the severity of that damage until the swelling subsides. He's on an ICP to monitor the cranial fluid."

Shelly rubbed her temples.

"On the left side, which I believe to be the point of impact, there are several broken ribs that contributed to the collapsing of Mr. Sampson's left lung. We are monitoring that as well, and he may be placed on a ventilator as a precaution. He suffered a compound fracture of his left femur that will require surgery at a later date, once we've stabilized his other injuries." Pausing, the doctor looked up. "Any further questions?"

Shelly shook her head. Jake couldn't be as bad as the doctor indicated. This would take months for the townspeople to forget.

"I will be in and out this morning, but I will make sure one of our family counselors visits you, as they are more attuned to your options and the services available than I am. Feel free to wait in here if you find it more comfortable. Someone will let you know when you can see him."

Lucas stood when Angela walked back into the living room. "How bad is he?"

"They wouldn't tell me since I'm not family. They offered to page the family, but I didn't figure Shelly would want to talk to me. I wish Misty had a cell phone."

Chester rose to his feet and stretched. "Why don't you take me home? I'm old enough to baby-sit myself."

"Okay," Lucas agreed. "Here's my keys. I'll be out in a second."

When the screen door flapped shut behind the old man, Lucas reached for Angela's hand. "What did the hospital really say?"

"Nothing." She lowered her chin.

"Nothing wouldn't give you that horrified expression. Now, what did they say?"

Tears filled her eyes. "Jake's in critical condition. That's all they would say. You don't think he'll die, do you?"

"People like him never die," Lucas said. "They live forever to ruin our lives." He wasn't sure if he was trying to convince Angela or himself.

She leaned her head against his chest. "All of this is my fault."

Lucas pulled her in closer. "You had nothing to do with this, and I don't want to hear you blaming yourself again."

"But I am to blame." Tears spilled from her green eyes. "You heard the sheriff. Jake and Shelly had been fighting. It had to be about me."

"Why would they be fighting about you?" Lucas could think of a lot of reasons, but Angela didn't need to hear that. This entire mess was actually his fault.

He listened while Angela told him about her encounters with Jake since she'd been back. Then she described Misty's trouble with Charlene and Shelly. And finally she told him about yesterday's incident at the café.

Fear, panic, and regret took hold of Lucas as he listened to the trouble he'd created—friendships lost, lives injured, and L.J. in jail.

His feelings confused him. Wasn't this exactly what he'd been waiting for, the end of Shelly and Jake? Not like this, he told himself. He never wanted to see any one get hurt. He only wanted Shelly to be free.

Angela mistook the meaning of Lucas's silence and burst into tears. "See, it is my fault. I am to blame. Jake's in the hospital, and if I'm being honest, that doesn't bother me one damn bit. But L.J. is in jail, and before you know it, you'll be in trouble for allowing drunks to drive. I've ruined everything," she sobbed.

"L.J. did not have a single beer."

Angela continued to cry. "We both know Chester was driving. He always drove. L.J. took the blame, but the police are bound to find out. And either way, they'll think L.J. was drunk. Everyone in this town knows he's an alcoholic."

"Listen to me!" Lucas stated sternly. "We'll get it all straightened out. I'll call this lawyer I know and make sure L.J. takes a blood test. It will work out."

She shook her head. "Nothing ever works out the way it should. Not in my life."

"Don't say that. None of this is your fault." He spoke as sternly as he dared. "I have to go now, but later we need to talk. There are things I need to tell you." He turned and left before Angela could question him.

Right now he needed to drop Chester off at home and swing by the jail to let L.J. know a lawyer was on the way, then he would go to the hospital to check on Shelly. Later, when his mind had cleared and he'd gotten some rest, he would tell Angela everything.


"Is this where I can find the Sampson family?"

Shelly looked up at the pudgy-faced woman peeking into the crowded private waiting area. Taylor, Austin, and Misty now filled the tiny space.

"Yes, it is," Misty answered.

Shelly hated the way her friend acted like everyone was worthy of being nice to. There was something about this woman Shelly instantly did not like.

"I'm in the right place then." The lady stepped into the room to reveal an obese body to match the face. "Let me introduce myself. I'm Priscilla Anderson, one of three patient/family counselors on staff here. It's my job to answer your questions and help you to deal with this trying time."

Shelly could take care of her own problems. She was sick of everyone acting like this was a big deal. The woman spoke to all of them as if they were children with a fake look of concern plastered on her face. And her frumpy appearance didn't help. So, Shelly quit listening. She was only vaguely aware as everyone else in the room asked questions.

Again, she told herself Jake was not as bad as they let on.

Yes, she'd been surprised at his appearance when they finally let her in to see him, but that was because of the swelling. He was unconscious, but that was the medicine. He would be fine before everyone knew it. His broken bones would heal, his lung would be okay over time, and he was too thickheaded to have damaged his brain. Why couldn't everyone else realize this?

"Can we, Mom?"

Taylor's question focused her attention back on the conversation at hand. "Can you what? I wasn't listening." Shelly shot the counselor a look to inform the woman her words were not worth listening to.

"Oh, that's okay." Priscilla patted Shelly's leg. "Your mind must be wandering something terrible. This has to be hard on you. I was just explaining to everyone they could donate blood."

"What? Why would we want to do that?" Shelly asked with a mixture of panic and confusion.

"Let me back up. Some families tend to feel helpless in situations like these."

"Situations like what!"

"Mrs. Sampson, your husband is in very serious condition. He's already received several pints of blood, and with his pending surgeries, he may require more. Sometimes it gives the family a sense of helping in the fight when they donate blood."

"Definitely not," Shelly stated defensively. "You don't even know yourself if he'll need it."

"Please, Mom, I want to," Taylor begged.

"Me too!" Austin shouted.

"I'm afraid you're too small. You have to be older and weigh at least a hundred and fifteen pounds." Priscilla ruffled Austin's hair and turned to Taylor. "You certainly weigh enough and with your Mom's permission—"

"No! I don't see the need." Shelly folded her arms across her chest.

"Mrs. Sampson, I assure you the blood will be put to use, whether it be for your husband or someone else. It will not go to waste. Nobody is saying you have to donate, but if it will make your son feel better—"

"I said no," Shelly said through clenched teeth.

The counselor appeared taken aback. Gathering her nerve, she started in once again. "Perhaps if we went out in the hall, I could explain things a bit better."

"There's no reason to go anywhere. I already gave my answer!"

"Come on, Shelly. I'll go with you," Misty spoke for the first time. "It'll do you some good to get up and stretch your legs."

"Whatever. But I'm not changing my mind. I don't care what she says."

Shelly stood alongside Misty in the hall, listening as Priscilla Anderson explained yet again the psychological benefits of allowing Taylor to donate. Shelly said no. The counselor trumpeted the therapeutic qualities. Shelly again said no. The fat busybody simply smiled and started a new approach.

Shelly argued against Mrs. Anderson's reasoning for a dozen tension-filled minutes. Finally, after Misty took the boys to get something to eat, Shelly had had enough. It was time to put an end to the conversation while the others were away.

"I've told you no a thousand times, but it doesn't seem to sink in!" Shelly raised her voice in frustration. "It's none of your damn business, but Taylor can't donate blood for Jake!"

"Calm down Mrs. Sampson. I don't see why—"

Throwing her hands up in disgust Shelly shouted, "Because Jake isn't Taylor's real father!"

"Oh, that doesn't matter Mrs. Sampson. Lots of children have different blood types from their parents, and even if they are not a match, it's more for Taylor's benefit than Jake's anyway. The blood bank will supply the correct type of blood if your husband needs it," she explained.

Shelly ignored the words. Her eyes were focused on Lucas who had emerged around the corner in the same instant she'd shouted her confession. For a brief moment, Shelly thought he hadn't heard because of his expressionless stare, but slowly his eyes and face contorted into a look of first disbelief, then anger. Shelly opened her mouth but was unable to find words before Lucas turned and walked away.

# 28

Slowly, Lucas became aware of his surroundings. Birds chirped as they fluttered by. A cool fall breeze brushed his cheek. Tires hummed as cars passed by on the highway. He clenched his jaws as one sound and image after another penetrated the emotional coma he'd fallen into. He couldn't remember how he'd gotten here to this roadside park on the outskirts of Grand. His last memory was of Shelly's words echoing down the sterile hallway of the hospital.

***"Jake isn't Taylor's real father!"***

Those words would forever be burned into Lucas's soul. He did not need Shelly to tell him what they meant. *He* was Taylor's real father. *He* had a son. That realization left Lucas confused, terrified, and angry.

How could Shelly keep that from him all these years? Especially when she knew how badly he wanted children? Unanswered questions fueled his resentment.

Why hadn't he stayed and demanded Shelly answer his questions instead of leaving? Lucas was tired of running. He'd run all these years from the fact Shelly did not love him, and in the moment of truth, he should've stopped running and confronted the truth.

Lucas shook his head. He had no idea what the truth was anymore.

Shelly had torn his heart apart. Her cruelty sickened him. She'd lied for years. If only he'd detected the slightest trace of regret or remorse, but there in that hospital, her face had displayed only two emotions—shock and fear. Twenty years of love and affection erased in mere seconds.

Nothing in the world would ever look the same. Not the lone picnic table he was sitting on. Not the trash can riddled with bullet holes next to him. Not the mile of flat prairie separating him from town. His life was as barren as this roadside park, and after having his dream yanked away, he couldn't fathom going a new direction. Lucas wasn't sure how to live without loving Shelly.

There was Taylor to think of, but Lucas didn't have a clue how to approach that issue. Did the boy know? Lucas doubted anybody other than Shelly knew the complete truth. How would Taylor react? Lucas would try to form a relationship, but Jake was the only father the kid had ever known. Lucas stared at the horizon, hoping for answers.

The only thing that came to him was how small he felt sitting out here all alone. This must have been how Angela felt when she came back. "Angela," Lucas whispered. If anybody understood how he felt right now, she did.

His first instinct was to drive straight to her place and tell her everything, but most likely she was asleep. Only a few hours had passed since he left her house, and neither of them had slept after last night's accident. Lucas decided to go anyway. He needed—no, it was time for him to stop thinking that way—he wanted to see Angela.

Angela opened the door to find Lucas standing on the step.

"I didn't expect to see you again so soon."

"I didn't wake you, did I? I can go if—"

"No"—Angela grabbed his arm and led him inside—"Come in. I tried to get some rest, but there was too much on my mind. How about you? Did you get any sleep?"

Lucas shook his head. "I haven't even been home yet."

"You've been at the jail with L.J. all of this time? Is he okay?"

"He's fine. I think he's dealing with this better than the rest of us. I stayed about an hour. Until the lawyer showed. Then I left them alone to talk." Lucas pulled out a kitchen chair and sat before saying more. "I went to the hospital." Lucas rubbed the back of his neck.

Panic gripped Angela. Lucas's pained expression and reluctance to talk told her something was wrong. "Is Jake worse? What is it? You can tell me."

Lucas turned and stared out the window. She waited for him to speak, but the words seemed stuck in his throat. Finally, he stood and paced around. Angela followed him from the kitchen to the living room where he slumped onto the couch.

"What is it?" She sat down beside him. "Jake didn't . . . " She started to ask if he'd died, but her words trailed off.

He shook his head. "Far as I know, Jake's the same. I'm the one who died." Lucas's chest heaved.

"What do you mean?" Angela's heart quickened.

Several long seconds elapsed before he spoke, and then, Lucas told her what happened at the hospital.

In some ways, the news shocked her, but in others it did not. Shelly was the type of conniving woman to lie about such a thing, but how she'd managed to keep such a secret in Grand was a mystery. Angela knew better than most that juicy gossip like that traveled fast. Either Shelly was a lot smarter and more diabolical than she'd given her credit for, or Lucas was the last person in town to know.

"You never suspected?" Angela wondered. "I mean, you must have wondered when she turned up pregnant after y'all . . . " Again, Angela let her words trail off. She didn't want to think about Lucas and Shelly having sex, no matter how long ago it was.

"I left town right after we graduated. I ran away. I didn't want to stay and feel the pain. When I got back, she had two boys. I never doubted her on anything. I guess it's true—love is blind."

"What made you fall in love with her in the first place?"

Lucas shrugged. "I don't know if I can explain. When I looked at her, I saw everything I wasn't, everything I lacked. She seemed perfect. Just being near her made me feel as if there were hope."

Shaking his head, he revealed his affection started in the fifth grade. His mom had just skipped town. Shelly was pretty and seemed to have the perfect life. No one ever pitied her or spoke in hushed whispers when she was around. Her world seemed normal. No, better than normal. It seemed perfect. He began helping her with homework in junior high. They became friends. And before he knew it, he was in love.

Angela began to understand his obsession with Shelly, and when he told her about prom night, Angela realized his story wasn't so different from hers. She felt his pain and could almost feel his heartbreak when he confessed his lifelong love for Shelly. Finally, he fell silent and stared at the ceiling. Angela reached for his hand.

She knew what it was like to grow up in an environment devoid of love and affection. Without a sense of belonging. Without anything to hold onto. Or reach for. She'd searched for those things flat on her back, whereas Lucas had looked to the most perfect girl in town.

"I'm sorry." Lucas clutched her hand.

"Sorry for what?"

"For being an idiot. L.J. was right all along. I deserve this misery. I've been a damn fool."

"You're not a fool. We all make mistakes. Lord knows I have."

"Not as big as mine," Lucas whispered hoarsely.

"Shelly's the one who made the big mistake. She's the one who lied all these years. All you're guilty of is loving the wrong person. Shelly got what she deserved in Jake."

Lucas looked at her. "I'm sorry for hurting you," he whispered.

"You haven't hurt me. Matter of fact, you've given me something I didn't think possible—a reason to hope." She leaned over and pressed her lips to his.

The kiss caught Lucas off guard. The warmth and softness of her lips felt like velvet compared to the iron spike of pain and doubt he'd dealt with today.

Their embrace felt so natural, he was compelled to lean into her and kiss her again. His emotions made the transition from anger and sorrow, to joy. Being this close to Angela felt good. Too good.

He would have loved nothing more than to stay in Angela's embrace, but that was being selfish on his part, and he'd already done too much of that. He had to tell her the truth before he hurt her the same way Shelly had him. He forced himself from her grasp and scooted to the far end of the couch.

"I'm sorry, I didn't mean—" Angela began.

"Don't apologize," he said. "It's me that should say sorry. I've already hurt you enough. I can't do it again."

"You haven't hurt me!"

"You don't know everything. You don't understand everything I've done."

She shook her head. "I don't care about the things you did in the past. All I care about is the present. I'm tired of living for the past. It wasn't fair for me to kiss you like that after everything that's happened, but it was something I needed to do. Just like this is something I need to say."

Angela cleared her throat, stared into Lucas's eyes, and began to reveal her true feelings. "I didn't come back because I wanted to, I came back because I *had* to. I came back hating this town and everybody in it, but you changed my mind. You made me see it wasn't everybody else's hatred destroying me. It was my own. You've given me real hope for the first time in years. I know there's a lot on your mind right now. I'm just saying give us a chance because I care about you, and I think you care about me."

"I do care about you, but—"

"No 'buts.'" Angela placed her fingertip against his lips. "You caring is enough. You're tired and this has been an emotional day. All I ask is you go home and think about giving us a chance. If you want to give it a shot, I'll cook dinner for you tomorrow since the bar is closed. We can start fresh with the past behind us. If not, I'll deal with it and go on."

"But I need to tell you something," Lucas objected.

"No. Not today. Tomorrow you can say what you want, but for now I'm asking you to just think about what I've said."

Angela led him to the front door, and Lucas even managed a smile when she pulled his head down toward hers. She gave him another kiss and whispered in his ear, "A little something to help you make up your mind."

Lucas was more confused than ever as he walked away. Shelly's lies had destroyed the only love he'd ever had, and now Angela offered him the chance to find love once again, but the truth of his actions threatened their happiness before it even got started.

# 29

Shelly stared at the lukewarm coffee and stale chicken salad sandwich. She hated hospital food, but this cafeteria was the one place she could sit alone and think. Since Lucas's hasty departure, she'd wandered the halls of the hospital until her feet ached. She ventured back to the waiting room only once, but the room seemed even smaller than before. Now that the truth was out, the entire world seemed to have shrunk.

Too bad she couldn't hide in the cafeteria forever. What she really wanted to do was go home, but what kind of wife went home and rested while her husband lay in the hospital? At least with him in intensive care, she only had to go in and see him every two hours. The machines and nurses gathered around Jake's bed made Shelly nervous.

He should be awake by now, yet he still had not opened his eyes or said a word. Everybody acted like Jake could die at any time. That wasn't going to happen, but Shelly feared what would happen now that Lucas knew the truth. She wondered where he was, what he was doing. Of course, she'd tried his house and the bar without success.

Taking a bite of the sandwich, she contemplated her next move. Things were going to get worse unless she did some mighty fast thinking. Even then it might be too late. How long would it be before Lucas started telling people

Taylor was his son, not Jake's? If only she'd recovered from her shock quick enough to stop Lucas from leaving, she could have convinced him to keep their secret hidden, at least for a while.

Shelly felt confident she could persuade Lucas of most anything if only she could talk to him.

At least the delay gave her ample time to rehearse a believable story. She had to have all the bugs worked out when she found him. She would seduce him, of course, give him everything he wanted. That excited her on several levels. And it would accomplish two objectives: appease Lucas and payback Jake for screwing Charlene. All of this was Jake's fault anyway—his and that damn hospital counselor.

All these years she'd feared the truth. Never in her wildest dreams did she think she would be the one to let the secret out. How the hell could she've known you couldn't determine paternity by blood type?

To make matters worse, Taylor wasn't even old enough. She'd finally consented to let him give blood after it didn't matter, mostly to get rid of the counselor, but even that hadn't worked.

The people in the lab sent Taylor back after they discovered his age, and the counselor returned to apologize for her error. Because of his height, the woman had mistakenly thought him to be older. The fact this whole situation was unnecessary made her plight all the worse.

Shelly had her stories planned. She knew exactly what to tell Lucas, Jake, and even Taylor if it came to that. However, she still struggled to come up with a suitable explanation to tell the townspeople if word leaked out. She could deny the whole thing. It would be her word against Lucas's, but anyone who truly looked at Taylor could plainly see the truth.

She considered telling everyone Lucas raped her, but

then people would ask why she'd never spoken out. The longer she contemplated, the more determined she became to find Lucas and talk him out of doing something stupid.

Leaving the cafeteria, Shelly understood none of this would have happened if Angela hadn't shown back up. And even worse, Shelly had no idea how to get rid of the tramp now that Jake was laid up. Locating a phone, she dialed Lucas's number again, hoping he would answer a number other than her own. Eleven rings. No answer. She was just about to hang up when she heard his voice.

"Hello."

"Lucas, thank God. I've been trying to reach you all day."

"What do you want?"

"Please Lucas, don't jump to conclusions. Just listen to me."

"No, you listen!"

The harsh tone of his voice cut her like the January wind. This wasn't going to be as easy as she thought.

"Were you ever going to tell me I had a son?"

"Please, Lucas. Let me explain," Shelly stated as sweetly as she could.

"Answer the damn question! Were you?"

Shelly didn't want to respond, but Lucas made it evident he would not listen to until she did. "I wanted to, but—"

"Does he know?" Lucas blurted out, not letting her finish.

"Who?" Shelly asked, still trying the sweet and innocent routine.

"Taylor! Does he know I'm his father?"

"No, of course not. Nobody knows except me and you."

"Tell him. Or I will!" Lucas slammed down the phone.

# 30

Angela promised herself to think before she offered to cook any more meals. She'd been foolish to believe she could fix Lucas a suitable dinner. Her idea of a home-cooked meal consisted of mac and cheese from a box or microwave noodles. Her grandmother had never taught her how to cook, and there'd been little occasion for Angela to learn since.

She'd already phoned Misty half a dozen times for cooking advice, so Angela fought off the urge to dial her friend again. First, she called about the chicken fried steak, then the mashed potatoes and gravy, and finally the bread now baking in the oven.

Misty tried to persuade her into cooking something a little more exotic, but Angela refused. Lucas didn't strike her as the kind of guy who enjoyed casseroles or cream of anything.

On the fourth call, Misty offered to come over, cook the meal, and leave before Lucas got there, but that seemed like cheating to Angela, so she turned down her friend's generosity. A decision she now regretted. The chicken fried steaks resembled giant scabs. The mashed potatoes were lumpy, and the gravy was thinner than her patience at this point. The bread was her last chance to get something right.

Misty would die at the sight of this pathetic meal. Angela wondered if her friend wasn't even more excited about tonight than she was. Misty had actually called the last time to check on her progress and wish her luck. Well, that and to tell her Jake had improved. She explained that the doctors were still keeping him in a medicated coma, but if the swelling in his brain continued to go down, the doctors planned to start bringing him out of it tomorrow morning.

That was good news to Angela. In truth, she had little sympathy for Jake, but if anything bad happened to him, L.J. would be in more trouble. The lawyer had gotten the DUI charges dropped since his alcohol blood level came out clean, but there was still the problem of L.J. not having a valid driver's license in over thirty years.

Angela still had her doubts he'd been behind the wheel when the accident occurred, but both the old men assured her that was the case, and even Lucas seemed to believe their story.

Thinking about Lucas made her close her eyes. She hoped things worked out as well tonight as they did in her daydreams.

The doorbell rang, yanking her back to reality. Panic gripped her as she stared at the clock on the wall. Lucas wasn't supposed to be here for another forty-five minutes, and she hadn't done her hair or makeup, so she peeked through the living room curtains, relieved to see L.J. on the porch.

"What are you doing here?" she asked with a little giggle.

"Brought you something for tonight." L.J. held up what looked like an ancient bottle of wine. "I saved it for years, hoping to share it with your grandmother someday. Maybe you and Lucas can get some use out of it."

Taking the bottle, Angela responded, "Thanks, maybe we can, but how did you know about tonight?"

"Lucas told me when he bailed me out."

"I'm just so glad they let you out. Do you have any idea when they'll set the court date?"

The old man shook his head. "That lawyer said he'd let me know."

"Did Lucas say anything about it? He must know something. He was a lawyer."

"He was too damn nervous about tonight to say much." L.J. winked.

"I'm a little nervous myself."

He nodded. "You know, there's one thing puzzling me and Chester."

Angela eyed the crotchety rascal's smirk. "What's that?"

A smile crept across his whiskered face, and Angela knew she was in trouble. "We thought it awful peculiar for you to cook Lucas dinner since he is only your boss."

"You're horrible." Angela shut the door on him only to open it a few seconds later. "Thanks for the wine!" She hollered to his retreating form.

Lucas would be here before she knew it, so she sat the bottle of wine down on the entryway table and dashed off to the bathroom. She wanted to look her absolute best when he arrived, and she still needed to get ready.

The bell rang just as she finished. With one last look in the mirror and a deep breath, she went to the door.

"I'm not late, am I?" Lucas stood in the doorway in a faded pair of jeans, which fit tight against his thighs, and a dark button-up shirt. For once he didn't have on that baseball cap.

She resisted the urge to reach up and run her fingers through his layers of wavy curls. "No, you're right on time. Come on in." She wiped the sweat from her palms.

He sat on the couch. "You look fantastic." Lucas sniffed the air.

"Thanks. So do—"

"Is something burning?" he interrupted.

"Shit! My bread!" Angela ran from the living room.

Smoke whirled around her face when she opened the oven. Staring at the dark lump that had once been bread, she fought the urge to cry. None of it was fit to eat now. Maybe she could get enough of L.J.'s wine into Lucas before dinner to make him not notice. Then she remembered she'd left the bottle on the table in the entryway. Now they would have a shitty meal and warm wine. Holly Homemaker, she was not.

"Something I can help you with?" Lucas's tall frame leaned in the doorway of the kitchen.

"It's beyond anyone's help. How 'bout we go out to eat instead?"

"Fine by me. Want to go to the Whirlwind or drive into Amarillo and get something decent?"

"I'd rather go to Amarillo, if you don't mind."

Angela stopped dead in her tracks when she walked outside. She looked over at Lucas, who was grinning like the Cheshire cat.

"Like it?" he asked.

Angela walked toward the baby blue Cadillac convertible. She rubbed her hand along the front fender. "It's beautiful. But where?" She turned with a smile. "Did you summon your fairy godmother and have her turn that beat up old truck of yours into this gorgeous carriage? I just need to know, so I can duct tape my shoes in place if need be."

Lucas laughed. "You're way prettier than Cinderella, though I hear she bakes a mean loaf of bread."

Angela slapped him on the shoulder as he opened the passenger door before bowing with a flourish. "You're chariot awaits, oh fairy princess."

She giggled like a schoolgirl and wondered where this night would lead. It had been so long since she went out on a real date.

"I can put the top up if you want," he said after closing her door.

"Don't you dare."

He smiled, but the gesture didn't reach his dark-rimmed eyes. As he walked around the front of the car, she worried that the recent events were all too much. She'd selfishly wanted—almost demanded—this night, but Lucas had so many things clamoring for his attention that Angela felt guilty for adding yet another burden.

"Lucas." She touched his arm just above the wrist when he settled behind the wheel. "We can do this another night if you want. If you just want to go home and rest."

"I'm right where I want to be." He looked her in the eyes. "So, let's get rolling before this sucker turns into a pumpkin." Again, he smiled, but the muscles in his jaw and neck tightened as he fired up the Caddy and backed out of the driveway. Nevertheless, Angela sensed he was on the edge of a cliff perhaps only he could see.

Lucas didn't say a word as they left Grand behind and headed out across the flat rangeland. Crooked cedar fenceposts lined the two-lane highway. Strands of barbed wire contained pastures of cattle and the occasional horse. The two of them had spent hours talking at the Oasis, but now neither spoke. Telephone pole after telephone pole slid by as the Caddy swallowed the white lines painted on the lonely stretch of asphalt. The evening was cool, but the wind felt nice, and Angela recognized the tune on the radio as one he often played on the jukebox at the bar.

"So, tell me about this car."

She was pleased when he grinned again.

"It's a '52 Cadillac. Same exact car Hank Williams died

in the back seat of."

Angela glanced over her shoulder.

Lucas laughed. "No one died in this one. Though my mom did wrap it around a telephone pole when she was pregnant with me. Afterward, it sat behind our house, rusting away. When I moved back, I started restoring it. When I was little, my dad always said the ghost of Hank Williams saved me, and that's why I had the soul of a musician. This car and the guitar I keep at the bar are the only worthwhile things my dad ever gave me."

She reached out and touched the dash. "You're a man of many talents. This car is nearly as impressive as your music."

"My music. You've never heard me play my music, only other people's music."

"I heard you play enough to know you're truly gifted. And Cody Cantu believes in your talent, so you must be good. But I'd love to hear you sing something you wrote."

"I haven't played any of my stuff in front of anyone in a long time."

"And that is a crime," Angela said, "Which needs to be rectified."

He nodded. "I agree. I'm gonna start playing again. I've wasted a lot of time trying to impress the wrong people. I don't care if they think I'm a washout. The guy who couldn't hack it as a lawyer. They can call me a dreamer, a drifter, a wannabe musician all they want from now on. I'll be an underachiever in their eyes, but damn it, I'll be a happy underachiever."

The regret was easy to hear in his words. And while Angela had always used a different, more radical approach by going out of her way to offend rather than impress those same people, she understood how miserable it felt to discover you've become a puppet to expectation.

You had to live your own life. She recognized that

now, and she also realized their conversation was headed places neither of them needed to travel, not in the wake of everything else that had happened. Lucas needed a diversion, an escape from reality, if only for a few hours. And so did she.

"Speaking of a waste," she said to lighten to mood. "I can't believe you've been making me ride to and from work in that ratty pickup when we could've been riding in style." She patted the Cadillac's dash.

"Well from now on, I'm gonna drive this baby around—" he reached for the radio—"with the wind in my hair and the music cranked up." Lucas tilted back his head and began belting out the words alongside the guy on the radio.

That night he sang for her at the bar he'd nearly whispered the words, but now he belted them out in full throat. Angela could picture him up on a stage doing that very thing, his dark curls damp with sweat beneath the lights. His singing voice had enough gravel around the edges to make it interesting. He truly was full of surprises tonight. When the song ended, Lucas turned down the radio.

"I love Townes Van Zandt," he said, pointing at the radio. "He and my dad were friends back in the day. They met in Nashville, but summer of '75 my dad gave up trying to make it as a songwriter and moved back to Texas. Townes came out here and stayed a while not too long before I was born. That Gibson Hummingbird I play at the bar belonged to him. He left the guitar with my dad in exchange for some folding money he needed to get to California. I learned to play watching my dad pluck those strings. Townes is my musical hero, but just like my dad, he drunk himself to an early grave."

Lucas slowed the car and turned into a gravel parking lot in front of a rundown shack on the outskirts of town. The place looked as if it had been constructed from discarded fence pickets.

"Before we go in, I need to tell you something."

Angela read the faded plywood in front of the building: *The Feed Lot, Best Burgers and Steak in Texas and that ain't No Bull.* She hoped they put more into the food than they did the building and sign, but even more than that, she hoped whatever Lucas planned to say wasn't half as bad as the expression on his face.

"When my mom left my dad, she moved up to Chicago. She's still there," he said in a tone that now matched his pained expression. "So is one of my college buddies. We were in law school together."

"Hope they put more into their food than they did this building," Angela said, suddenly terrified of what he would say next.

"Angela, I'm—"

"Don't, Lucas. I don't know exactly what it is you want to say, but the look on your face . . . the tone in your voice tells me I don't want to know. Not now. Not here. Please, let's just go in, have a good time, and eat. I'll listen to whatever you want to say later."

"But—"

"No 'buts.' Let's eat." She flung open the Cadillac's door and hurried toward to the door to keep him from arguing. Lucas caught up to her just as they entered the building.

The place looked even more like a dive on the inside. Rusty old road signs, stuffed armadillos, and various other junk hung from the rafters and wall. Above the small table where they sat, a sickly looking stuffed deer peered down at them with dusty black eyes. One antler was snapped off just above the right ear. Country music echoed in the background. They ordered steaks and a pitcher of beer which seemed like the right thing to do in such a place.

"Did you like living in Chicago?" he asked.

"Lucas, I don't want to talk about Chicago. Or Jake, or L.J., or anything stressful or related to the past. Tell me about you and the guitar. Or rebuilding that car. Or surprise me with some other mysterious secret about your hidden talents. But tonight is supposed to be fun, relaxing, and a time to forget about all that other stuff."

He paused, stared at her a second, and then smiled. "Fine, but I gotta know one thing. Can you two-step? Because if we're going to have fun, it's imperative we catch some good live music."

Time flew by as they ate their rib eyes and talked. Lucas talked about music and various bands and songs with such passion that she found herself getting excited, even though she'd never been all that interested in music beyond the Top 40 stuff on the radio. She'd always been apathetic toward country music as too often it reminded her of Texas.

Angela wasn't sure if it was the steak, the beer, or the company, but her entire outlook shifted. A few weeks back, she would've hated a joint like this. The restaurant typified all the stereotypes about Texas. For years, she despised this image, even while Kenneth was wallowing in all things Lone Star-ish.

Pushing his plate to the center of the table, Lucas leaned forward. His left eyebrow arched like it did whenever he got serious. "What about you? What makes you happy? I want to know what you do to relax and escape when the world presses in."

She thought for a few seconds, but sadly she knew the answer. "Nothing."

Lucas reached across and touched her hand. "Oh, come on. There has to be something. Tell me about the last time you really felt content."

Angela thought. It would have to be from a long time ago. "I found this old picture at my grandma's. It was of my first day of kindergarten. I was sitting on top of my dad's shoulders and my mom was standing beside him, looking up at me. She actually looked proud and loving."

"Mrs. Thurman's class." Lucas nodded. "I sat two seats behind you. Misty had the desk between us."

Angela opened her eyes wide. "How do you remember that?"

He chuckled. "You had those snowy white curls. I'd never seen anyone with hair that blonde before. I spent most of that year staring around Misty, mesmerized by your hair, by you."

Angela grinned. "You did not."

Lucas placed one hand over his heart. "I so solemnly swear."

Angela laughed. "I had no idea. That's when me and Misty first became friends. My school days were all downhill from there on out."

Lucas leaned forward. "I know what you mean. I used to feel good when I made a 100 on a test or aced all my classes. Growing up, report card time was about the only occasion when I felt worthwhile. In high school and college, I had fun sometimes, but at night when I was alone in bed, I never could shake the doubt from my mind. I never knew exactly what, but I always knew there was something out there I was missing. I thought it was her."

Angela did not need him to explain who *her* was.

"But here lately, talking to you, I haven't had those feelings at night. I've gone to bed only looking forward to tomorrow—to you." Lucas lowered his head. "Even before all this other stuff happened. I want you to know that."

Angela swallowed hard. "I feel the same way."

Lucas fell silent. "Here we go again. Getting all serious." He picked up the check from the corner of the table. "Let's get out of here and go find some music that will make us smile."

On the way out the door, he placed his hand on the small of her back. His touch made her feel safe and secure. Emboldened by the beer and the feel of Lucas's hand, Angela slid to the middle of the seat.

They cruised on into Amarillo, even stopped at several small bars on Sixth Street, but based upon the bands scheduled that night, Lucas rejected the idea of staying at any of them.

"Sorry," he finally said as they exited yet another hole-in-the-wall joint. "But I can't in good faith let the first time we dance be to some Garth Brooks wannabe, singing Nashville pop covers. Yes, my name is Lucas Cahill, and I'm a music snob."

Angela laughed, but she wasn't disappointed at all. It had been fun driving around with him in the Caddy, and in truth, she'd just as soon spend the rest of the night snuggled up on the couch beside Lucas as she would in some loud bar surrounded by strangers.

A few miles into the ride back to Grand, Lucas stopped to put the top up after he noticed her shiver. When they started back again, he put his arm around her shoulders and pulled her close. She turned and kissed him on the cheek.

Lucas's skin tingled where Angela's lips touched his cheek. Actually, his skin tingled all over. He'd been apprehensive about tonight, but that was because he'd planned to tell her the truth. He still feared how she would react upon learning he was behind the misleading promises that brought her back, but gone was his regret over manipulating her return. For without that, she would not be nestled against him, sailing along beside him in the Cadillac.

He'd fallen for Angela. He couldn't even pretend to deny that anymore. Fallen, and fallen hard. His only concern was that his attraction was a result of Shelly's deceit, a way to retaliate against Shelly. But as the night progressed, he knew for certain his feelings were more than a result of vengeance. He'd been attracted to Angela long before finding out the truth from Shelly.

Everything about Angela excited him. The way she laughed. The way her nose wrinkled when she smiled. Even the way she chewed her steak mesmerized him. Although scared, he no longer doubted what these feelings meant.

But acknowledging all of this made the job ahead all the more foreboding. He had to tell her the truth. He hoped somehow she would see the silver lining to his treachery. That without him orchestrating her return, they never would have had this second chance to know each other. But would she feel as strongly about that as he did? Would that be enough to overcome the fact he lied and manipulated her future for the sole purpose of winning another's affection?

Lucas prayed so, for he longed to know her better, to learn her dreams, to discover the things that made her happy in the here and now, to take her dancing. He wanted to play his guitar for her, to look into her eyes and sing a song he'd written for her, about her. And yes, he wanted to wake up beside her. He wanted her body beneath his. He wanted his mouth on hers. And having her body so close only increased those desires.

But he couldn't act on those feelings. She'd shared her fears about returning to Grand, her worry that everyone would think she was the same old Angela from high school. He wouldn't risk giving her the impression he was part of that crowd. No, he'd spent his entire adult life not taking any risks. And look where that got him. Pulling into Angela's driveway, Lucas decided for once he would follow his heart instead of his brain. He would gamble, lay his true feelings out there. But it wouldn't be fair if he didn't tell her the truth first. She deserved to know how they'd arrived at this point.

A calm settled over him as Angela unlocked the door. Reaching out, he pulled her closer just as the phone rang. "Don't answer that," he stated, only half kidding.

"I'll only be a second. I'm sure it's Misty wanting to know if we've eloped."

Lucas smiled. Angela had told him how excited Misty was about their date. He also used the opportunity to sneak a peek at her shapely figure as she headed for the phone. He grinned again. Angela's curves inspired him to remain bold.

"Hello? . . . Oh, we decided to go out instead."

Lucas impatiently paced the floor, listening for the call to end. She turned and mouthed the word *Misty* and pointed at the receiver. Angela was even sexy talking on the phone.

"Searching for us all night? Whatever it is, we didn't do it," he heard her joke.

"No!"

Angela's panicked cry stopped his pacing. The happiness drained from her face in an instant. He went to her side.

"But how? I thought . . . Who else knows?"

"What is it?" he asked, concerned.

"Okay. Bye." She finally hung up.

"What is it?" he asked again. The look on her face terrified him.

"We've got to go tell L.J., before the sheriff shows up," she said in a panic.

"The sheriff? What are you talking about?" Lucas grabbed her shoulders. "What's wrong?"

Her eyes filled with tears. "Jake is dead."

# 31

Lucas stared at the phone. Despite himself, he wondered what Shelly was doing right now. They'd always talked on Saturday mornings. She would not call today, and he would not call her. A few short weeks ago he'd waited beside the phone in eager anticipation of their weekly conversations, but the world had turned upside down since that day.

No doubt she had a house full of people. The funeral started in a couple of hours.

He found it hard to forget their years of friendship during a death like this, but even harder to forgive the lie she let live all that time. He hadn't spoken to her since he'd delivered his ultimatum to tell Taylor the truth.

Lucas tried to figure out why he even thought it necessary to attend the funeral. He and Jake were never the best of friends, but Lucas supposed his need to attend the services stemmed from guilt. In a twisted sort of way, his plan had worked. Shelly and Jake's marriage was over. Having accomplished the original goal, his emotional pain had only increased. He certainly hadn't wanted anyone to die for his happiness, and in his mind, he'd all but murdered Jake.

The doorbell rang. Lucas frowned. He rarely had visitors, and none since Abby abandoned her early morning coffee deliveries. He peeked out the curtain.  L.J. stood at the door. He'd half expected to see Shelly since she'd been weighing heavy on his mind.

"Hey, old-timer. What brings you by?"

"Wanted to bring you this." L.J. handed him an envelope stuffed with cash.

"What's this for?"

"To pay back what you gave those lawyers."

"Come on in. Have a seat." Lucas stepped to one side. He didn't want to tread on the old man's pride by out-and-out refusing the money. "You know I only paid the retainers. There's still going to be some fees to represent you."

L.J. nodded. "That new one you hired told me the DA could seek an involuntary manslaughter charge. Whatever that means."

Lucas nodded. He recalled enough from his law school days to know the district attorney could even seek vehicular homicide, but more than likely he would go for a lesser charge since a fair amount of evidence placed the blame on Jake. Regardless, Lucas didn't want to take any chances. That's why he'd hired a new, better, more expensive attorney when Jake died.

The case was winnable, but it would be more so if L.J. had a valid driver's license. Lucas shook his head. All this trouble as a result of his stupid scheme to have Shelly for his own. "Hold onto your money for now," Lucas said. "That way you'll have it if need be. You can always pay me later."

He couldn't reverse the damage he'd caused, but he could do his part.

"I can pay my own way."

"Don't be stubborn, L.J. Let me help. This could run into a lot of money."

"So? Have I ever paid my bar tab late?" The old man tilted his chin in defiance.

"No, but lawyer fees are going to be a good deal higher than that."

"I got money."

"You can't have much. I've known you all my life, and I've never known you to have a job. Except the work you did for Elizabeth," Lucas said.

"She never paid me a cent."

"Then how—"

"That's your damn problem, boy. You only see what you want. You never bother to look at the big picture. I made my fortune as a young man."

Lucas had never given L.J.'s finances much thought, but he couldn't see how a guy who hadn't worked in years, didn't own a vehicle, and lived in a mobile home could have a fortune, regardless of how you defined the term.

"I haven't always lived in Grand. I left once. To get away from seeing Elizabeth Ross tethered to that bastard, Ansel."

Raising one brow, Lucas sat. He'd never heard L.J. say a bad word about Ansel.

"I ended up in Alaska. Went to work on the pipeline. Helped build the line to transport the oil reserves across the state. Wasn't a job for the faint of heart, but they paid top wages to anyone willing. Most men quit or petered out. The days were long. The grizzlies scared some off, but I stayed. Nearly froze my ass off. But I didn't care if I lived or died. Working kept my mind busy."

"How long did you stay?"

"Hell if I know. Never kept track. I worked twenty-hour days for months at a time without a day off. Had no time or place to spend the money, so I saved it. When I got so damn cold that getting warm again was all I could think about, I came back. The minute I stopped shivering, she was the first thing that popped into my mind. That's when I knew all the miles in the world wouldn't be enough. I paid cash for that house I live in and invested the rest." L.J. smiled. "Them damn stocks are still paying off."

Lucas had always heard money was easy to make on the stock market if you left it alone. L.J. was living proof.

"Too bad life doesn't work that way," Lucas whispered. "I've spent my whole life sitting back and waiting on something good to happen."

"That's 'cause you're stupid. You've got to make things happen." L.J. stood. "Deposit that cash. And quit pussyfooting around. Hope doesn't last forever, and once it's gone, there ain't nothing left but regret."

Lucas closed the door behind his friend. He'd tried to take an active role in his future and look where that landed him.

The love of his life was a liar, he had a son who had no idea his real father was not the man about to be laid in the ground, and the one shred of hope for the future could be destroyed by the truth. What he'd done to Angela was no better than what Shelly had done to him, but at least Angela was an adult and used to hard times. Taylor was the one Lucas most worried about.

He ached to tell the boy the truth, but how could he do it now? There simply was no easy way to tell a fifteen-year-old the man he's mourning isn't his biological dad. As much as Lucas longed for a relationship, it would have to wait.

He was doing a lot of waiting lately. He couldn't deny his attraction to Angela, but with all the hardship he'd caused everyone else, he had no right to pursue happiness for himself.

Even with the guilt, Angela dominated his thoughts. To avoid his feelings, he'd steered clear of her as much as possible, but that proved an impossible task as he constantly found himself staring at her as she moved around the bar. He couldn't keep his eyes or mind off of her.

What worried him most about his preoccupation was how different it was from how he'd felt about Shelly. With Shelly, his daydreams had always centered on the house and family they would someday share. His visions for them were about Christmas, teaching the kids how to ride a bike, or family vacations. He never visualized Shelly and him alone. His thoughts were rarely sexual or erotic. He pictured those same family scenes with Angela, but also thought of others. How her bare skin would feel against his. What it would be like to wake up with her naked body snuggled next to his. The sight of her body beneath those clothes.

These thoughts worried him. What did they mean? Were his feelings only about lust? Was he was using Angela to get back at Shelly? How could his feelings toward Angela be genuine if sex and lust were involved? Maybe he'd simply gone too long without a woman's touch.

The questions and doubts in his head were made worse by the realization everything was his fault. He'd tried to change fate by bringing Angela back, and now he was paying the price. He'd gotten exactly what he wished for, except he no longer desired the same thing.

Shelly sat on the edge of the bed. She slid a pair of black panty-hose up her legs. Black depressed her, but she couldn't wear another color, not today. Not to her husband's funeral.

After the services, she could breathe easier. There wouldn't be so many friends, neighbors, and family members lingering about. She did not want their sympathy or their casseroles. She wanted to be alone.

Their presence was only for show, their hugs and condolences for appearances' sake. She knew what they were saying behind her back. She'd seen them whispering and glancing her way. They said sorry, but thought something else. Jake would still be alive if she hadn't smashed his truck, if she hadn't thrown him out in the freezing rain. It would be better if they just came out and said it.

Hypocrites.

The whispers weren't the only thing plaguing Shelly. She was tired of playing the part of grieving widow. Everyone expected her to be sad and confused when she actually felt nothing but anger. Jake's death hadn't caused her to miss him. She was too busy blaming him for dying and leaving her to deal with this mess. How could something as small as a blood clot kill somebody as tough and hardheaded as Jake? Those doctors should've done something to prevent his death.

One good thing came from all of this—Lucas would not speak out about Taylor. He wasn't the kind of guy to bring out the truth in the face of tragedy. With Shelly's reputation and life already dangling in the balance, it was more crucial than ever the truth stay hidden.

Shelly walked to the living room and joined the rest of the family. She'd managed to avoid them most of the morning, but it was time to leave for the church. The funeral home would send a car and the family was expected to arrive together. She hoped things would be easier once everyone left and it was just she and the boys.

At least Jake had sense enough to buy life insurance. Or more likely, his dad had made him, maybe even paid for it. Either way, they would have enough money to pay the bills and still live much as they did now. At least for a while. The money wouldn't last forever, but nothing does. She would concern herself with that when the time came.

Taylor sat quietly in one corner of the room. Shelly

looked the other direction. Her son was a painful reminder that life as she knew it was in jeopardy. Not having to deal with Taylor or Austin was the one beneficial side effect of having family around. Her parents, who'd driven in from Florida, Jake's parents, and other family members had shouldered most of the load in helping the boys cope with the loss of their father. That meant her mother hadn't been afforded the opportunity to mother Shelly the way she normally did—another positive side effect in Shelly's mind.

"Honey, the car is here. Are you ready?"

There was that motherly tone Shelly hated so much. She wished her mom would stop talking to her like she was still twelve. To make matters worse, everyone had started using that tone when speaking to her.

Shelly shuffled outside and sat in the back of the long white car. As they drove through the streets of Grand, she wished everyone would act like themselves around her and stop putting on false fronts.

Staring out the car window, she noticed the church parking lot was completely full. Cars were parked several blocks away as well. How many of these people would be here if they knew the real Jake? If they knew he died drunk? If they knew he smashed her grandmother's doll? If they'd lived with him all these years?

Jake was not worthy of this attention. In truth, he was simply another washed-up loser. Grand was full of them.

Shelly walked into the sanctuary, unable to believe she'd been here with Charlene and Misty for Elizabeth Ross's funeral a mere four weeks ago. So many things had changed that it seemed like a lifetime.

Charlene stood out among the throng of faces. She was as much to blame for Jake's death as anyone, but there she was, decked in black, as if she were the widow. It angered Shelly, but there was no way she would confront her former friend. Charlene wouldn't care they were at a funeral. She would speak her mind anywhere, so Shelly aimed to avoid the redhead at all cost.

She caught sight of Lucas's face at the back of the church, but he averted his gaze as soon as their eyes met. She couldn't believe he wouldn't even look at her. He should be the one comforting her.

It wasn't until Shelly's eyes focused on Misty's tear-streaked face that she finally broke down. Shelly's tears were not a result of Jake's death. They flowed from the realization that Misty was the only person in town that truly cared about her. The rest of the town was fickle and two-faced.

Misty's father spoke to the family in the first row. Flanked by Taylor and Austin, Shelly listened as the preacher extolled Jake's many virtues. He referred to him as a loving father and husband, friend to all, a pillar of the community. It was all Shelly could do not to disagree out loud. He was none of those things, but the eulogy forced her to admit two truths. One, she did not love Jake and never had, and two, things were never going to be the same.

The realization that her entire life with Jake was built on lies hit hard. She tried to remember the last time she'd looked forward to seeing Jake, the last time he'd made her happy, or smile. The only thing about Jake that ever made her feel good was his reputation. She loved the way other women were jealous because he was hers. That's what attracted her to him back in school, and that's what had kept them together.

Sad thing was, nothing had changed since high school. Jake's reputation was built on his football glory days and her lies. Publicly, she'd never said a bad word about him, a fact she now regretted. If she'd told the truth, everyone wouldn't be so quick to blame her for his death. They might even feel sorry for her, for putting up with him.

If Jake's darker side came to light, her reputation just might survive, but she couldn't very well go around town running down his name. A grieving widow couldn't speak poorly of her dearly departed husband, especially not one in her precarious position.

But others could.

Lucas knew plenty about Jake, as Shelly had often vented her frustration to him. And Angela knew things. Misty, Sheriff Hickmann, and Charlene all knew about his infidelity. It would take some personal sacrifice on her part, but Shelly could persuade others to reveal Jake's transgressions.

She spent the rest of the funeral working out the details in her mind. By the time the preacher closed out the eulogy, she could barely contain her blossoming hope for redemption. The opportunity to launch her plan was but a few minutes away. She could plant the first seeds of her future as the mourners filed by the family to pay last respects.

She hugged what seemed like the entire town before catching sight of Lucas in the line. Panic gripped her as Lucas hugged Taylor. After what seemed like hours, Lucas stepped back, stared at the boy, and finally moved toward her. She detected his reluctance as he stepped forward and wrapped his strong arms around her.

"We need to talk," she whispered into his ear as they embraced.

"There's nothing to say."

"Please. We've been friends too long for you not to listen."

She reached for him again, but he pulled away. Afraid of causing a scene, she let him go.

Things hadn't gone as well as she'd hoped with Lucas, but there was still Charlene. Shelly searched for her former friend as the last of the well-wishers filed by, but it was apparent she was gone. Shelly wasn't surprised. Charlene never had been one to abide by proper social etiquette.

Shelly spent the rest of the day listening to the condolences of people who'd already told her how sorry they were hundreds of times. She knew they were saying one thing, but meaning another.

Only the thought of tomorrow made her feel better. She'd already made up her mind to go see Charlene and Lucas right after church. She wasn't going to waste any time getting her life back on track.

# 32

Disappointment shot through Angela when she opened the front door. Not that she didn't want to see Misty, but she'd hoped to find Lucas on her porch.

"Why the long face?"

"Just tired, I guess." Angela stepped aside and waved her friend inside.

"Missed you at church this morning."

"Sorry. I figured you, Shelly, and Charlene would all want to sit together after everything that's happened. I knew they wouldn't want me there."

"Charlene doesn't come to church very often and Shelly would rather sit by you than her."

"What do you mean?" Angela asked confused.

"Nothing," Misty replied. "Just that Shelly and Charlene aren't getting along right now."

"After all that's happened, you would think Charlene could try and get along with Shelly."

"Yeah, I know," Misty replied. "But enough about them. Tell me about you and Lucas."

"Wish I could," Angela answered dully.

"Oh no, what's happened?"

"Nothing. That's the trouble. Everything went great

when we went out last week, but then you called with the news about Jake. Of course that ended our evening, and things have been stagnant ever since."

"I'm sorry."

"Don't be, it's not your fault. It's not anybody's fault. Things have just been crazy since Jake died. We haven't got to talk much because the bar's been full every night with people trying to get the scoop on the accident, and I know there's a lot on Lucas's mind, but he seems reluctant all of a sudden. Instead of hanging around talking, we clean up and he brings me home. I'm not sure he's still interested."

"Oh, don't say that. I'm sure that's not it. Things will settle down, and y'all will pick up where you left off." Misty patted Angela's shoulder.

"Hope you're right, but the thing with Taylor has him pretty messed up, so I'm not sure."

"Taylor? Shelly's son? What thing?" Misty frowned.

"You don't know? I figured you did since you were at the hospital with Shelly. I shouldn't have said anything."

"What are you talking about? I'm confused."

Angela stood and walked across the room. "Taylor is Lucas's son, not Jake's." The thought caused her as much pain as it did Lucas. Sure, he was angry now, but she knew once he calmed down he would see things differently. Shelly was the mother of his son, the woman he'd always loved, and now she was available. It would only be natural for him to want her.

After a few seconds' pause, Misty laughed uncontrollably.

"What's so funny?" Angela asked, harsher than she intended.

"Where on earth did you come up with that?" Misty gained control of her mirth. "Shelly got pregnant with Taylor our senior year. That's why she and Jake got married. Didn't you know?"

"Yeah, and I know a few other things too."

Angela told Misty about Lucas hearing Shelly's confession at the hospital. Then she relayed Lucas's version of prom night.

Misty looked dumbfounded by the end of the story. "Even if all of that's true, Shelly wouldn't have lied."

"She did lie. It's true, Misty. Think about it."

"It can't be true. Shelly would never—"

Angela sighed. "I probably shouldn't have told you any of this, but my head feels like it's going to explode. It's all eating me up inside. But I really believe Lucas and I have a chance. He's been so honest about everything. He even admitted he's been in love with Shelly for years."

"Everyone knows that. That's why I was excited for him and you. Both of you deserve someone in your life, but I never dreamed . . . "

Angela sat back down. "Me either," she whispered.

Silence filled the room for several seconds before a light seemed to click in Misty's mind. "That's why she wouldn't let him give blood."

"What?"

"Shelly refused to let Taylor donate blood for Jake. And Taylor is tall, like Lucas. And dark, but so is Shelly. He's so much thinner than Jake. He looks nothing like Austin. But Shelly couldn't lie about that."

Misty seemed to be talking to herself more than anything, but Angela answered just the same. "I'm telling you, it's true. Everyone isn't as nice as you. Most of us do lots of terrible things."

"But to keep a thing like that secret. Does Taylor know?"

"I don't think so. Lucas said he doesn't want to hurt the boy. Then again, he's hesitant to talk about the situation with me, so I'm not sure what he's decided."

"Oh, poor Lucas. He must feel awful. I'm going talk to

Shelly. She needs to tell Taylor before someone else does. It would be wrong for him to hear it at school or something."

"Don't!" Angela grabbed Misty's arm. "She'll only get mad at you for getting into her business, and then Lucas will find out I told you. No one else knows, so Taylor won't hear."

"He needs to know the truth."

"I know, Misty, but please wait. Give it time. That's what I'm doing with Lucas."

On her fifth trip by Charlene's, Shelly finally mustered the courage to stop. She knew her former friend would make this hard. Years had passed since they'd had a cross word with each other, and now that she needed something from Charlene, Shelly regretted the harsh words she'd spoken over the phone the night of Jake's accident.

A thousand scenarios ran through Shelly's mind as she walked up to the door. Few of them good. Charlene was not the forgive-and-forget kind. She also had a knack for making people pay for favors. Shelly had to make it sound like there was something in it for Charlene, or this plan would never work. Charlene might not even listen. There was a very distinct possibility the redhead would tell Shelly to go to hell and slam the door in her face. Knocking, she stepped backward to wait.

The pounding of her heart thudded louder than the sound of the approaching footsteps.

"What do you want?"

Shelly shifted from foot to foot. "Can we talk?"

"I ain't stopping you. Get to talking."

"Could we go inside?" Shelly glanced around. She didn't want anyone to see them and think anything was wrong.

Charlene stepped aside and let Shelly enter. "Don't mind the mess. Me and Jimmy got a little wild last night. Those cowboys like for everything to buck."

Shelly stared at an upended side table. "Still going strong between y'all, I guess."

"We'll be married before long."

Shelly managed a small laugh. Charlene's audacity amused her. It was nice to talk about something else before bringing up Jake.

"What do you want? You didn't come to talk about Jimmy."

Shelly cleared her throat, choosing her words carefully. "I've been thinking. We both know Jake wasn't the angel everyone else thinks. I know the whole thing between you and him was all his fault."

"And?" Charlene asked impatiently.

"I wouldn't blame you if you wanted to tell everyone about y'alls affair."

"What? You want me to go around telling people I was screwing your dead husband? That'd be radical, even for me."

"It's the least you could do. As my best friend."

"Don't play your guilt shit with me. That was the kind of crap that made Jake come see me in the first place."

Shelly could see a new approach was going to be needed. "This is the type of thing you enjoy, Charlene. Think of the shock on everyone's face. When I don't deny it, everyone will assume it's true. You'll be the ultimate independent woman."

"What's in it for you?" Charlene asked.

"I just want Jake to be known for what he was."

"Bullshit! I know you. You're worried what everyone else is thinking. You don't want to be remembered like Elizabeth Ross, the crazy lady who killed her husband. It's kind of funny. You always talking how strange it was for poor ol' Ansel to die so suddenly after they got in a fight, and then the same thing happens to you. You should've thought about that before you smashed his truck for the world to see."

"It's not like I'm asking you to do something you've never done before."

"I can't believe you are asking me for anything after the way you screamed at me. I don't owe you shit! You're the one who owes me an apology."

Her words infuriated Shelly. Pride would never allow her to apologize to Charlene. "Forget it then. There are plenty of others who know the truth about Jake," Shelly lied. "Lucas knows. And Angela." She hoped the mention of Angela's name would bother Charlene, but it seemed to have the opposite effect.

"Yeah, if you can pry them apart," Charlene said with a sadistic little grin. "Oh, you haven't heard? Maybe if you slept around like me you would find out juicy bits of gossip. Like Lucas and Angela are getting it on."

Charlene's statement took Shelly's breath away. Lucas and Angela? They couldn't be. Lucas would never betray her.

"Don't look so surprised," Charlene said maliciously. "You've strung him along for years. He had to get it somewhere. If you ask me, they deserve each other."

In a wave of panic, Shelly realized Charlene was telling the truth. That explained Lucas's strange behavior, making that demand Taylor know the truth. Angela had to be controlling him, telling him what to say in order to get back at her. Shelly wasn't going to let that whore win.

Not again.

Lucas was hers.

# 33

Lucas tried unsuccessfully not to stare as Angela hurried toward his truck, but that tight sweater and bright smile rendered his efforts futile. He couldn't expect not to notice her womanly charms for the next twelve hours. Especially if customers were again scarce tonight.

The temporary crowd of people vying for the inside scoop on Jake's accident had vanished after the funeral. Yesterday, Lucas found himself alone with Angela half the night. He'd stayed away from her as much as possible by taking inventory in the cooler, but it wouldn't be that easy tonight.

Sundays were always dead, and Lucas feared business would be nonexistent this evening. L.J. hadn't come in with Chester since the accident, but maybe he would to-day. That would at least be one more person to act as a buffer between Angela and himself. With his lustful thoughts, Lucas wasn't sure he could be trusted alone with her.

It wasn't that he did not want to act on those thoughts; he just wanted to make sure he did it for the right reasons. He wanted to be sure hope for the future motivated him, not lust, anger, or revenge. Angela had expressed her pain at never knowing true love. The last thing he wanted was to add another chapter to that book.

A voice in the back of his head told him he was too late for such noble ideas. A lasting and loving relationship built out of the ashes of lies and deceit seemed a long shot, even though Angela claimed she wanted to forget the past.

"It's nice to see you too," Angela commented in reaction to his silence.

"Sorry. I was busy thinking."

"About what?"

"Nothing," Lucas answered. "You ready for another exciting night?"

She sighed. "Won't be all that exciting if you spend all your time in the cooler again."

When he didn't respond, she said, "I know you've been through a lot, but I wish you would at least talk to me. Tell me what you're thinking. Please."

Lucas noted the concern on her face, but putting the myriad of complex thoughts in his mind to a few concise words wasn't something he could easily pull off, so he merely said, "Sorry."

Angela threw up her hands. "I don't want you to apologize. I want you to talk to me. I'm afraid you've given up on us."

The despair behind her words brought home the realization she cared more for him than Shelly ever had. Lucas was glad she felt so strongly, but he wouldn't be able to relax until she knew the truth.

"I promise not to shut you out, but I need to tell you something. I should've told you this from the start but I didn't. I'm sorry."

"Stop apologizing!" Angela shouted. "If you have something to say or do, just do it. Stop being sorry and start living."

"But—"

"No 'buts.' Live for the moment."

"It's not that easy."

"It's not that hard either. Let me show you." Angela leaned over and kissed him. It was the deepest, softest kiss he'd ever felt. The warmth spread throughout his body.

"I'm kinda a slow learner. Think you can show me again?"

He barely got the words from his lips before Angela kissed him again. This time a little harder, raising his heart rate even more. Several minutes and kisses later, he realized they were still parked in front of her house. They were supposed to be at the bar ten minutes ago.

"You seem to be getting the hang of it now," Angela teased.

"I don't know. I might need some private tutoring later." He put the Caddy in drive and headed for the bar. Though what he really wanted was to gather her in his arms and carry her inside.

"We'll have to see about that," she answered with a smile.

Lucas never gave his doubts any thought the rest of the night. He couldn't keep his mind off Angela long enough to worry. All he could think about was how nice she'd felt in his arms. The happiest he'd been in years was the last couple of weeks with Angela. It wasn't lust. He enjoyed the time they spent together doing nothing more than talking too much for his attraction to be purely physical.

Though it was the physical he now craved. He wanted to be alone with Angela more than anything, so much so it annoyed him every time someone entered the bar. He longed to taste her tender lips and yet, time stood still.

Actually, he thought about more than kissing her, and he wasn't the only one having those thoughts. He'd spotted Angela's frustration the last time a customer came in. She wanted them to be alone as badly as he did. However, fate seemed to be playing a cruel trick on them. Just as the one customer would stand to leave, another wandered in. Lucas planned to lock the door the moment the place emptied out, regardless of the time. He was ready to live for the moment.

Unlike Lucas, Angela devised ways to pass the time. She took great delight torturing him. She touched him at every opportunity, enjoying the shudder that passed through his skin. By eleven thirty, there were still several people in the bar, but she sensed Lucas was ready to throw them out. Chester, who had again come in alone, sat quietly nursing his beer. The accident had rendered him quiet and pensive.

Angela took an order for a margarita, checked to make sure neither Chester nor the one table was paying any attention to her, and then proceeded to give Lucas a show by vigorously shaking up the margarita. Leaning over him for the salt, she purred, "Excuse me," into his ear.

He felt the roundness of her breasts as her body pressed against his. The warmth of her breath tickled his ear. He was ready to implode.

Sneaking into the freezer as she delivered the margarita, he tossed a bottle of beer against the wall, hoping she would come running like before. Hiding on the backside of the door, he waited.

"Lucas? Is everything—"

He gripped her waist and spun her around to face him. His lips tenderly brushed hers before he continued downward to her neck. With a nibble on her ear, he drew back and kissed her hard, full on the mouth. Her breath shortened and the heat quickly overcame the chilly air inside the cooler. Having accomplished his goal, he tore himself away and backed out of the freezer.

With a proud smile, he resumed his work. That would teach her to tease him. Or so he thought. As the minutes wore on, he wondered if he hadn't come out the worst. The episode in the freezer only increased his desire. It took all his self-control not to grab her and taste the sweetness of her lips again.

Beyond the lingering, rosy glow of her cheeks, Angela seemed unaffected, but Lucas was proud to have made her blush.

When the next-to-last customer left at one fifteen, Lucas practically dragged Chester to the door.

"Damn, what's the rush? It ain't last call."

Lucas smiled, shot the old-timer a look, and nudged him out the door. Locking it before anyone else could enter, he turned around, his eyes searching out Angela. His stomach tightened in nervous anticipation as he watched her move around the room, wiping tables and preparing the place as if this were any other night. He stepped toward her, and still she didn't look up.

Was she nervous? Scared? Maybe his boldness in the freezer had been too much. He crossed the room. Still she stared down at the rag in her hand. "Angela?"

She dropped the rag and wrapped her arms around him in a tight hug. They stood in the middle of the bar locked in a tight embrace until she said, "I'm scared, Lucas. I've never felt this way. I'm not sure I deserve someone like you, and everything has been so crazy. I'm afraid I'm going to lose you amidst all of the craziness."

Lucas laughed, but stopped when he saw the panicked look on her face. "I'm not laughing at you, it's just I feel the same way."

"What do we do about it?"

"A wise person once told me to live for the moment."

"Sounds more like a scared person to me," Angela chuckled.

Lucas couldn't help thinking how right her laugh sounded to his ears. He wanted to hear that sound the rest of his life.

"Let's close this place up and get out of here."

A few minutes later, they stood in the dark parking lot alone. Lucas opened the Caddy's passenger door and was pleased when Angela slid to the middle. He walked around the front of the vehicle and sat with his thigh pressed to hers. He savored the contact.

Only when he turned on the headlights did he notice a lone car parked in the Whirlwind's lot across the street. As he pulled out into the street, the beam of light highlighted Abby DeWitt's eyes staring back at them.

# 34

"Let's take a drive," Lucas said. "Head out on the highway for a bit."

Something in his voice shook Angela from her trance. She did not raise her head off his shoulder, but she did open her eyes and turn so that she could see his face.

He checked the mirror a few times and then hit the gas, accelerating past the turn to her house.

She liked sitting here next to him in the Cadillac. With his body touching hers, it was easy to imagine a different time, a different scenario. One where the two of them had no strings, no worries, no sordid history to muddy the waters. With her eyes closed and her cheek resting on his shoulder, Angela could pretend they were a real couple embracing both the future and each other—lovers without a care in the world.

Envisioning them as lovers was easy, but a future for them together was harder to grasp. She told herself that was because the concept was more abstract. Even in the beginning, in the best of days with Kenneth, she never looked too far ahead, never counted on their relationship to last. Their bond had always been about the now. A band-aid for the scars of her past. She'd always known they would be ripped apart somehow, and that realization had lessened the blow of his untimely death.

She and Lucas had not even truly begun, and already the fear of it ending left her feeling as dark as the barren landscape flying by the car window. She raised her head and looked at Lucas.

"We headed anywhere in particular?"

He checked the mirror again before answering, "Not really."

Angela glanced at the Caddy's huge speedometer. "Well, are we in a hurry to get there?"

"What? No. I guess not." He lifted his foot and the needle dropped below ninety. Not until the car had settled in at a smooth sixty miles per hour did he speak again. "I just wanted to come out here and blow the dust off a bit. I haven't really had the chance yet, and it seemed like a good night to fly down the asphalt."

"I was starting to worry you were going take me to the roadside park to make out."

He smiled. "What, you don't wanna make out with me?"

"Not at the same roadside park we went to in high school."

Lucas pulled her tighter. "What's this 'we?' We never went anywhere in high school, remember? You don't even remember me."

"What I remember about those days isn't nearly as important as what I'll remember about tonight. So why don't you turn this car around and take me home so we can create spectacular memories?"

"Spectacular?" Lucas smiled. "I like the sound of that."

What he didn't like was Abby stalking them. She hadn't followed them out here on the lonely farm-to-market road, but that didn't mean she wasn't still lurking about, waiting to cause them problems.

He kept a watchful eye, but saw no sign of Abby as they

cruised into town. Maybe she'd gone home to bed since her day at the café started in only a few hours. Pulling into Angela's driveway, he put the car in park and turned to face Angela. There were a lot of things he wanted to say. Too many, in fact, to transform his feelings into words. But he could show her.

He kissed her slow and hard. She slid her hand up his back as they maintained their embrace. When her fingers found his dark curls, she pulled him even closer. Her mouth parted ever so slightly as arousal overtook Lucas. The blood rushed to the lower half of his body. She leaned harder into him, pinning her weight against his hips. He loved the way her body felt against his, and he didn't want to stop, but the full effects of his arousal rendered their current position somewhat uncomfortable.

With one last kiss, he broke their embrace. "I don't think your driveway and spectacular fit together either."

"What, you don't want to give the neighbors a show?"

That look in her eye, hint of a smile on her lips, caused him to swallow hard. God, she was sexy. And the prospect of the show they'd give the neighbors was one that made his heart pound. He leaned in again, forsaking her lips for her ear. "We could give them a show they'd never forget," he whispered. "Except I don't want to share you with anyone."

Angela shivered as his lips tickled her ear. "I could invite you in." His mouth moved down to her neck. "But what kind of girl would that make me?"

His kissed his way lower. "The most spectacular kind."

# 35

Angela liked the way Lucas's bare flesh felt next to hers. This was all new to her. Not the sex; she'd had more experience there than she cared to admit. However, this was her first experience sleeping all night with a man. Her partners had always left after their encounters. Even Kenneth went home to his wife. She was glad Lucas stayed, even if it felt strange to hear his soft, uneven breath beside her.

At least, she thought he was asleep this time. The previous two times she'd assumed he was out, only to be surprised when he resurrected himself. She could tell by his shallow breathing that another rejuvenation was unlikely.

Lying awake, she could not help but wonder what the future might bring. Lucas was more at ease with the lights off than he'd ever been with them on. What would he be like tomorrow? Would he have regrets? She wanted this to be the start of something, not the end. There had been far too many ends in her life already.

She didn't regret having sex with Lucas, but she feared what their intimacy meant for the future. For despite her attraction to Lucas, Angela wasn't sure she could stay in Grand. She wasn't even sure she wanted to stay.

Already, she'd saved nearly nineteen hundred dollars.

In another couple of weeks, she would reach her goal of three thousand, and she'd told herself she would leave once that happened.

There was a definite connection between her and Lucas, but was that enough? The past would always haunt her here—her mom's abandonment, her dad's death, her own mistakes, all the squandered years and opportunities. Could what she felt for Lucas overpower those things? And if not, would Lucas ever leave, especially now that he had a son here?

She lay that way, with her head resting on his chest, listening to the beat of his heart, while a song of doubt danced through her mind. His presence so near contrasted with her fears of losing him, but if geography was their biggest obstacle, Angela had to believe they would find a way. Closing her eyes, she drifted off, confident that this truly was the beginning of something new, and not the end of yet another dream.

Lucas opened his eyes and looked around the room without moving because Angela's head rested upon his chest. Thoughts of last night flooded his brain, bringing to mind two truths: it had been weeks—months, maybe even years—since he'd slept so soundly, and he'd never felt better.

He could have dismissed the second fact as a condition of the first, but Lucas knew his bliss stemmed from more than a few hours of uninterrupted slumber. It was an un-burdening, a freedom, a sense of promise, rather than the lament he'd carried for so long. Of course, the fact Angela had given him far more than spectacular memories last night didn't hurt his mood either.

Matter of fact, this was the first "morning after" of his

life without guilt. Before now, he didn't think it possible to have sex without regret. Starting with his first experience with Shelly, to the second with Charlene, and on through his years at college and back here in Grand, Lucas had always felt a pang of remorse afterward. This morning he felt none of that.

All he could think about was spending every minute with Angela. He loved the way her naked body felt curled against his, but Lucas slowly pulled away to see her face. She let out a soft sigh when he moved, but nothing more. Staring at her sleeping face, he felt fortunate. Angela truly was stunning. Her name fit so well. Not only did she look angelic, but she also gave him hope for the future, making her his guardian angel in an unconventional way. Her natural beauty was even more noticeable as she lay there with her hair slightly out of place and her makeup wiped away. Fighting the urge to rekindle the fire from last night, Lucas slipped from her bed.

Given their pasts and his involvement in bringing her to town, Lucas had doubted they could find a future together. Last night erased those fears. They belonged together. The fire between them was too intense to deny. Fate had thrown them together for a reason, but he wasn't stupid enough to forget the obstacles looming in their path.

The lie he'd let simmer and breathe was perhaps even bigger than the one Shelly hid all these years. But given the fact hers came with a son, a biological bond he had both the obligation and the desire to forge a relationship with, Lucas could not break completely away from the misguided love he'd held all these years. And then there was Abby. Minor in comparison, but after seeing her there in the dark watching them, he knew there would be a reckoning of some sort to come if they were all going to live here in Grand.

And there was that problem — Angela hated Grand. She

couldn't wait to leave it behind.

He kept returning to the biggest of the issues—his involvement in Angela's return, and the fact he was a father. He would tell Angela the truth today. That much he could control, but there were so many factors with Taylor. Jake had only been gone a few days, yet Lucas desperately wanted to talk to his son. Maybe it was too soon to tell the boy the truth, but that did not mean he couldn't begin to lay the foundation of a relationship. Lucas was torn between what he wanted and what was best for his son.

He tried to put himself in Taylor's shoes. Would he want to know? Would there ever be a good time to speak up? Finally, he decided Taylor should know as soon as possible. That way, everyone could begin moving forward.

He wanted nothing to do with Shelly, but Taylor might cope better if they told him together. It seemed the logical thing to do, but if Shelly refused, he would talk to Taylor on his own. There was, of course, the possibility Taylor would resent everyone lying to him all these years and not want a thing to do with his real father. Lucas feared that, but he needed to try.

The longer he thought about it, the more determined he became to get the ball rolling. He hated to leave before Angela woke up, but he was too eager to wait. There was no telling how long he would be at Shelly's, and he wanted to spend time with Angela before work, so he needed to hurry. Lucas found some paper and a pen to leave her a note:

> *Angela,*
>> *Wish I could stay until you wake up, but I need to take care of some thing.*
>
>> *Be back as soon as I can.*

Lucas thought hard about what to write next. He wanted to let her know how much she meant to him, but he couldn't think of the right words. Everything he thought of either sounded corny or didn't convey the message he wanted to say. Finally, he settled on,

> ***I look forward to seeing you later.***
> ***Until then, you will be on my mind.***

He wondered how to sign his name. Was it too soon to write *Love, Lucas?* He didn't want her to think he was the type of guy to throw the word love around. Actually, he'd never said the word to anyone his whole life. Nevertheless, that is how he felt so he wrote *Love, Lucas* and headed out the door, thinking of the future.

He dreamed of a life involving Angela, Taylor, and himself. His dreams didn't always work out, but hope buoyed his spirits. Absorbed in thoughts of the future, he pulled into his driveway and walked to the door.

"Where have you been?"

Lucas jumped at the sound of Shelly's voice. He looked back and forth from her to the SUV parked in front of his house, not believing he hadn't noticed the vehicle, or her presence, on his porch. Seeing her was a shock, but it saved him a trip to her house.

Shelly smiled. "And where pray tell have you been so early this morning?"

Lucas started to lie, but stopped himself. He didn't care what Shelly thought anymore. Besides, she wouldn't like the truth, and he wanted her to feel some of the same pain she'd caused him. "Angela's. I never came home last night."

"I heard she was back to her whoring ways, but I thought you had better taste."

"Angela is not a whore. Or a liar." Lucas stared at Shelly, daring her to contradict.

"I know you're upset, but if you'll let me explain."

"Upset? Upset doesn't come anywhere near describing what I am. Have you told Taylor?"

Shelly looked up and down the block. "Let's go inside."

Lucas studied her. She chewed at the corner of her bottom lip. She was nervous about something. And why was she dressed like that? Tight miniskirts were not her style anytime, but she looked particularly bizarre for a grieving widow on a Monday morning.

"The only thing I want to hear from you is about Taylor. We should tell him together. And the sooner the—"

"Please, Lucas, we've been friends our whole life. More than friends." She reached for his hand. "Don't you at least want to know why I didn't tell you the truth?"

He hated to admit it, but Shelly was right. An explanation might make it easier for him to cope with the lie. Lucas shrugged away her touch, opened the door, and walked to the couch, though he could not imagine mere words curbing his resentment.

Shelly sat, then stood again, and finally walked over to the window and stared out. He waited for her to speak.

"I never meant to hurt you," she said after a bit. "I thought I was helping. I thought I was doing the right thing."

"Helping? You broke my damn heart!"

"You deserved better than being stuck here in Grand, with me and a baby."

Lucas stared. Those were the very things he'd always wanted.

"I didn't want to hold you back. You were headed to Tech. You were smart enough to be anything, do anything. But you would've stayed and found a job here if I told you I was carrying our baby. I wanted more for you. I didn't want to ruin your life."

"You've always known Taylor was my son? Even when

you were pregnant?"

"I didn't lie to you on purpose. I did it because I cared. Jake wasn't going anywhere after he hurt his knee and couldn't play ball. I thought marrying him was best for everyone. I didn't want you to pay for my mistakes."

"So sleeping with me was a mistake! You lied to both Jake and me. You ruined both our lives without asking either of us what we wanted. Sounds to me like you've made a lot of mistakes!"

Shelly's mind reeled from Lucas's harsh words. As long as he was this angry, she wasn't going to convince him of anything. She needed to disarm his hostility.

Closing her eyes, she thought of everything that had gone wrong recently. That was all the inspiration she needed. She opened her eyes wide to let Lucas see the tears. "Do you think this has been easy for me?" she sobbed. "I'm glad the truth is out. I couldn't have handled lying to you much longer. I never loved Jake. You're the one I've always loved."

"But you married him. Stayed with him . . . and did nothing but lie to me."

The anger was gone from his voice. Time was ripe for her to claim what was rightfully hers. "I was young and stupid. But I know what I want now," she whispered in a sultry voice, stepping toward Lucas.

He stared in utter disbelief as she advanced. Shelly claimed to love him, and now she was acting out the opening scene of a porn movie. This was a side of Shelly he'd never seen. It was a side he wasn't ready to accept.

He grabbed her wrist as she advanced on him like a cheap hooker. Her behavior explained the unusual attire. She'd come to his house with this very thing in mind. Holding her off, he asked, "What about Taylor?"

"What about him?" Shelly asked in a throaty whisper.

"Have you told him yet?"

"No." She wiggled her hands free.

"I want to tell him. Today. And I think we should do it together."

"I agree" —her hands caressed his chest— "We should do it together."

Lucas knew she wasn't talking about telling Taylor. Never in a million years did he think she would come on to him like this. Determined not to let her deter his mission, Lucas ducked away and moved to the other side of the room. "Taylor deserves to know the truth."

"You're right, but the time isn't right. My parents are leaving in a couple of days. We should wait until they're gone."

"I've waited sixteen years."

"I know, but we have to think of our son," she said. "The more people involved, the harder it will be on him. When they leave, we can sit down together as a family and tell him. Just you, Taylor, and me."

Maybe Shelly was right. Taylor might handle the truth easier, without others around to ask questions. It was selfish to rush Taylor. Lucas didn't want to, but if waiting a few more days improved his chance to form a relationship with his son, the results would be worth the delay.

"Okay, we can wait. For a few days."

"I knew you would do the right thing," Shelly purred, stalking toward him once again. "And your personal sacrifice deserves to be rewarded."

Lucas stepped back. It would be much easier to form a bond with his son if he and Shelly could be something other than adversaries. Lucas moved back to the couch. He wanted a relationship with Taylor, but at what cost?

"Lucas, you're not the only one tired of waiting. I've waited for years to show you my true feelings. I still remember what it felt like to be in your arms. I've never forgotten. I've always loved you, but I was afraid to act. And after a while, the lies took over."

Lucas understood all too well how that could happen. He held his ground as she approached. That was how he'd felt for weeks. Shelly claimed to love him, but was it true? Was it possible to forget her deceit? She'd lied to him, but Lucas had to admit, he hadn't exactly been truthful either.

She sat on his lap. Her fingers caressed his chest, slid down his stomach. Lucas tensed as her hand settled between his legs. This was not what he wanted. Or was it? He'd worked for this exact moment for so long, and now that it was here, he was paralyzed.

"Relax," Shelly whispered. He felt her tongue slide across his neck as she breathed, "We belong together. We can be together forever."

He tried to argue, but her mouth moved to his and blocked the words. Shelly's lips felt cold and hard. They held none of the spark, the energy, the heat he felt with Angela. More than ever, he knew he'd never truly loved Shelly. He'd been in love only with her persona. All his life he'd longed for the perfect person to love. In his mind, Shelly had been that person, but in reality, she was far from perfect. Angela had shown him true love.

"I love you, and I know you love me," Shelly cooed in his ear.

"You're wrong!" Lucas stood and dumped Shelly onto the floor. "I thought I loved you. For a long time I thought that. But I love Angela in ways I never did you."

Shelly lay on the floor and stared up at Lucas with her mouth hung open.

"I'm going to take a shower. When I get out, I expect you to be gone." Lucas stepped over her body.

"And remember: two days. Then we tell our son the truth."

# 36

Shelly picked herself up from Lucas's floor. Her dignity lay shattered in a thousand pieces around her. Why were all these bad things happening? She attended church, belonged to the PTA, did all of the other things a person was supposed to. And none of it had mattered. Her life was on a fast track to hell. Her destiny in the hands of others.

Even Lucas was beyond her control. Shelly was tired of losing to Angela. Stealing Lucas was the last straw. Without the ability to guide Lucas, she could not keep the truth hidden. Powerless to stop the avalanche of misery, she had until her parents went back to Florida.

Two days.

Then life as she knew it would be over. When her parents left, so would her life and reputation. Shelly wished she were the one leaving town.

Her eyes widened.

Why couldn't she? There was nothing left for her in Grand. The truth would come out, but if she wasn't around to hear the scorn, she'd be unaffected. It was a bold decision, but as she played the idea out in her mind, it made sense. More sense than everything else. Her exodus was the one thing she could control.

She left Lucas's, mesmerized by the possibilities.

Her life would change drastically, but at least there would be an upside. If she stayed, the changes would only be for the worse.

She could go somewhere far away, play the part of the grieving widow. No matter where she went, she would instantly gain admiration as a widowed, single mother. But how could she move from town in two days? If she waited longer, Lucas would tell Taylor, and she would face the repercussions from her lies.

Turning the key, she smiled as the engine fired up.

Once she left Grand, Lucas would discover she was still in control. He would reap the seeds he'd sown. He would mourn losing her. He'd made his bed by threatening her by sharing it with that tramp. Let him lay in it. Shelly was unwilling to share her son with anyone associated with that two-bit slut.

Thinking of him and Angela together infuriated her. Before she left town, she would spoil any chance of them being happy. They'd ruined her life in Grand. She would destroy theirs.

But how could she accomplish all of that in two days? Maybe she could convince her parents to stay longer by pretending she needed help coping with Jake's death. That would be right up her mother's alley, but Shelly didn't know if she could deal with her mother much longer, or hold Lucas at bay.

The wheels turned in her mind as she pulled into her driveway. She could send the boys with her parents. Tell them she needed time alone. Lucas couldn't do anything with Taylor in Florida. Without that threat hanging over her head, taking care of business would be much easier.

Lucas knew her parents lived in Florida, but not the exact location. It would take him several days to track Taylor down, buying her valuable time to get her affairs in order and escape Grand. She needed to hire a mover, transfer her bank accounts, withdraw the boys from school. The trick would be accomplishing all of that without the entire town learning her intentions.

The boys would never want to move, but they wouldn't find out until it was too late. She would tell them they were all going to Disney World. They would simply never come back.

There were tons of holes in Shelly's plan, but blinded by desperation, she refused to seriously consider any of them. Lucas could hunt them down if he tried hard enough, but perhaps he would give up on Taylor before that happened. He'd given up loving her easy enough.

Jarred from her peaceful dream by the ringing telephone, Angela groggily reached for the nightstand. She realized Lucas was not in bed beside her as she answered. "Hello." She coughed to clear the sleep from her voice.

"Angela?"

"Yes, who's this?"

"Shelly, Shelly Sampson. There are a few things you need to know."

Angela sat up in bed, alert for trouble. "What things?"

"I know we haven't exactly been the best of friends in the past, but I'd like that to change. Jake's death has made me realize life is too short for grudges. And Misty is right, we all made mistakes back in school. That doesn't mean we should pay for them now."

Angela didn't buy a word of Shelly's speech, but curiosity kept her on the phone. "It's a shame we don't get along better," Shelly continued. "Grand is such a small town, and we can't avoid each other forever, so I'd like to prove my intentions are good."

"And how do you plan to do that?"

"By being truthful. You were gone for so long, there are lots of things you don't know. Grand might seem like a sleepy little place, but it's actually a small town with some big lies."

"Like Lucas being Taylor's father?"

Shelly inhaled sharply. "Who told you that?"

"Lucas," Angela answered defiantly.

"Did he tell you everything, or just what he wanted you to know?"

"He told me enough."

"Listen, Angela, I've heard you and Lucas have been seeing a lot of each other, and to be honest, that's why I'm calling. If he's what you want, that's your business. I only want to give you all the facts, so you can make a sound decision."

Angela wanted to hang up. "Your warped version doesn't interest me."

"Lucas is not the great guy he portrays in public," Shelly interjected. "Granted, I thought he was until this morning, but now I know the truth about him."

Angela glanced over to the side of the bed where Lucas had slept. "This morning?"

"Lucas called and asked me to come over to his house. He sounded upset, so I drove over fast as I could."

Angela frowned. Why would Lucas leave her house and rush home to call Shelly?

"He didn't answer the bell when I got there, so I went on in. When he called my name, I followed his voice to his bedroom. That's where I found him . . . naked."

Angela's heart thumped madly in her chest. "You expect me to believe that?"

"Believing is entirely up to you. I'm just stating the facts. Lucas said he's been in love with me for years and that he was glad L.J. killed Jake, because now we could be together."

Angela shut her eyes. Shelly's words squeezed the air from her lungs.

"He said we belonged together. He said he would prove his love. In bed. Today and everyday forward. Those were his exact words."

Angela tried to breathe. "How could you make something like this up?"

"I wish I was making it up," Shelly answered. "I was just as horrified as you. Imagine how I felt. First I lose Jake, and then I'm propositioned, forced to shield my eyes from him. All of him. Only a few days after burying my husband. When I told Lucas he was crazy, things turned ugly. He told me he'd spent the night with you, but it hadn't meant anything."

"You're lying!" Angela screamed. The anger in her voice surprised even herself. "If he loves you, why would he admit to being with me?"

"That's what I wanted to know. He told me he hired you, spent time with you, and slept with you, all to make me jealous. I told him he was sick, and then he said it was my loss. On my way out, he shouted he was going back to you until I changed my mind."

Angela wanted to respond, to dispute the lies, but how did Shelly know Lucas spent the night with her? And why had he left without saying goodbye?

"I thought you deserved to know. It makes no difference to me what you believe, but you're smart enough to figure out the truth for yourself."

Angela hung up without responding. She laid her head back on the pillow. Shelly must have seen the Cadillac in front of the house, she reassured herself. Even Misty knew about Lucas's infatuation with Shelly, so her knowledge of that was easily explainable. Angela would feel better after she talked to Lucas. What she needed now was a warm shower to clear her head.

Noticing the note on the dresser, she sat back down to read the message. Her stomach lurched when she read he needed to leave and take care of something.

Her doubt angered her. Lucas was the best thing going in her life. How could she doubt him because of Shelly's words?

The woman had proved to be untrustworthy, but she was the mother of Lucas's child. And he had loved her for years. Angela turned on the shower and waited for the water to warm the ice that had encased her heart.

# 37

Lucas could not shake the morning's bizarre scene from his mind as he drove back to Angela's. Nor could he help but feel embarrassed by both Shelly's behavior and his own. She'd suffered a lot of personal anguish lately, but she quite possibly had a genuine mental problem. However, he considered himself completely sane. So what excuse did he have for allowing that kiss?

He tried to erase the incident from his mind as he arrived at his destination. In half an hour, he and Angela would need to leave for the bar. Lucas wanted to use that time with her for something other than worrying about Shelly. Wanting to hear her voice, he'd tried calling her after his shower, but the phone was busy. More than likely she'd been talking to Misty, and there was no telling how long that conversation would last. Longing to see her, he decided to come back over.

Rapping a tune on her door, Lucas stepped back and waited for Angela's angelic face to appear. A goofy smile spread across his face as footsteps approached.

"Morning!" he stated cheerfully.

"It's more like afternoon," Angela responded.

"Don't go getting all technical on me. You gonna invite me in, or do I have to stand out here on the porch all day?"

He smiled, but she avoided making eye contact.

"Did you find my note?"

"Yes." She paced around her kitchen.

"Good."

After a few minutes of silence, Angela finally asked, "Did you take care of what you needed to?"

"Sort of. Didn't work out exactly how I wanted, but hopefully that will change in a few days."

Angela's eyes misted and her breath escaped in a short gasp.

One look at the pained expression on her face and Lucas knew something was wrong. He guessed she was upset about him leaving this morning. "I'm sorry I left, but I was eager to get things started between Taylor and me. I wanted to talk to Shelly and inform her of my plans," Lucas stated in an apologetic voice.

"So, you did see Shelly this morning?" Angela spoke the words in a breathy whisper.

"Yeah. Why?"

"She called and told me she'd just left your house."

A brick lodged in Lucas's throat. "And?" He hated to guess what she'd told Angela.

"She said some strange things."

"I'll bet. She was acting mighty bizarre at my house, so I can only imagine."

"What did happen at your house?" Angela asked in what sound like both a challenge and an accusation.

"She asked me to wait until her parents left before talking to Taylor. She thought he could deal with the truth easier that way. I wanted to tell him today, but I agreed to wait a few more days. The truth will be hard on him no matter what."

"That's all y'all talked about?"

Lucas wondered what else he should tell her. He wasn't proud he'd kissed Shelly, or felt compelled to test his feelings. He didn't want her to know he'd strayed, even for a few brief moments. But he was sick of the taste of lies.

Angela studied his face. "What? What are you not telling me, Lucas?"

He sighed. "When I got home from your house, Shelly was waiting on my front porch dressed more like a streetwalker than a grieving widow."

"You didn't call her?" Angela asked with a peculiar eagerness.

"No. I was going to get the ball rolling with Taylor, but she was already there."

"Go on."

Lucas's face flushed crimson with shame as he told Angela the rest of the story. He was embarrassed, but with each word, the smile on her face increased. He wrapped up the story by describing the shock on Shelly's face when he dumped her on the floor. He hoped Angela understood he was totally over Shelly.

Angela threw her arms around his neck. "I knew it would be something like that!" She planted a big kiss on him.

"Something like what?" Lucas wondered.

"Shelly's version of this morning was quite a bit different."

"How so?"

He listened while Angela described their phone conversation. The details shocked Lucas and reinforced his belief he'd never known the real Shelly.

"You didn't buy any of that, did you?"

Angela's reluctance to speak gave all the answer he needed.

"How could you believe Shelly after everything she's done?"

"I didn't exactly believe her, but . . . well, it scared me. Not the part about you being naked and wanting to sleep with her. I knew that was a lie; it's not your style. Besides,

I've seen the pain Shelly's caused you this week. I couldn't see you hopping in bed with her."

"So, what did you believe?" Lucas was a hurt by Angela's lack of faith, but it was hypocritical to feel that way. After all, he hadn't even had faith in himself during Shelly's advancement.

"I've been worried you would eventually be attracted to Shelly again. She lied to you, but she is the mother of your son. You will always have that bond with her."

"You're right." He reached for Angela's hand. "There always will be that between Shelly and me, but who knows, Taylor might not want anything to do with me. No matter what, I assure you my feelings for Shelly are a thing of the past. I only thought I loved her." Lucas stopped and considered his words carefully before speaking again.

"Until lately, I never knew what it felt like to be in love," he said. "Before I was in love with an idea, not a person. Then I met you. It's taken me awhile to understand this, and it might sound corny, but when you're around, I know what love actually is."

Angela kissed him on the cheek and choked out, "I love you too."

They sat on the couch holding each other and not saying a word. Lucas had waited for this moment his whole life, and he was afraid too many words would ruin it.

"I'm sorry," Angela finally whispered.

"For what?"

"Allowing Shelly to get to me. I should've known better than to think you were using me to get to her. I'm sure you took a lot of heat from her for hiring me in the first place."

Lucas shrugged. He wanted to get away from talk about Shelly.

"Why did you hire me?"

"Like I said before, it was L.J.'s idea," Lucas answered.

"I have a lot to thank L.J. for." She gave Lucas's hand

a squeeze. "He got me that job, which led me to you, and he gave both of us a little shove toward each other. And I have a sneaky suspicion he was the one who knew where to find me."

"What's wrong?" Angela sensed Lucas's sudden tension.

"L.J. didn't know where you were. I did." He bowed his head.

"What?"

Lucas gripped her tighter and revealed his involvement in bringing her back to town. He watched her emotions take a rollercoaster ride as he described everything from recognizing her in Chicago to hoping she would cause Shelly and Jake to break up.

"Shelly was right—you used me to get to her." Angela stood and strode across the room.

A few minutes ago, she'd been happier than any other time in her life. Finally, she'd heard the words she'd longed for since childhood. She'd heard "I love you" before, but only from drunks with dollar bills clutched tightly in their hands. Now she was hearing she'd been tricked and manipulated. One felt as wretched as the other did blissful.

"Why are you telling me this now?"

"Because I love you, and I don't want to lie to you."

"Then why didn't you tell me before now?"

"I was scared of losing you for one thing, but I did try to tell you—several times. You kept telling me to forget the past and live for the moment."

"When I said the past, I meant when we were kids. Not last week."

"I loved you last week too. I was confused. I've never loved anyone before. I didn't know what it felt like. What I did to bring you back was wrong, but I'm glad I did it."

"Glad?" Angela spun around.

"Yes. I never would've found you otherwise."

She could tell Lucas's words were genuine, but that didn't alleviate her confusion. He loved her, and she'd thought she loved him, but that was before this revelation. She wasn't even sure she knew the true Lucas anymore. The scheming, the manipulation, the actions he described were vastly different from the Lucas she'd fallen for. What else did she not know?

Lucas broke the silence. "Tell me what you are thinking."

"I don't know."

"Please, Angela, don't let this consume you. I screwed up. I lied. But I'm not one bit sorry. My stupidity gave me the chance to fall in love with you." He dropped off the couch onto one knee. "You asked me not to give up on us. Now I'm asking the same."

She didn't want to give up on Lucas, but things were not as simple as before. The total and complete trust she'd placed in him were gone. Could she ever get it back? Did she want to try? A myriad of feelings coursed through her. Anger. Sadness. Doubt. Affection. She felt all of those things, plus some.

"I'm not giving up, but I need time. Right now, I don't know what to say or do."

"I understand." Lucas checked his watch. "It's almost three. Do you want to take the night off, so you can think things through?"

She started to say no, but caught herself. Staying home was a good idea. Working alongside Lucas at the Oasis and sorting out her emotions at the same time would be impossible. She nodded.

"Oh. Well, okay. I guess I'll go on then." Disappointment dripped from his voice. He stood and walked out the door.

Angela watched him go.

He wasn't the only one disappointed. She was disappointed—disappointed he'd lied to her, disappointed in herself for believing in him too much when she'd been around enough men to know none were as good as Lucas appeared. Feeling her old bitterness and resentment rising, Angela grabbed the phone and dialed Misty. She needed to talk to someone before her thoughts began to eat away at the peace she'd only recently found.

Ten minutes later, Angela waited for Misty's reaction. She'd told her every detail about last night and this morning, both Lucas's visit with Shelly and her own. The silence emitting from Misty's end of the phone was more than Angela could take.

"Aren't you going to say anything?"

"I don't know what to say." Misty sounded defeated. "I thought I knew these people, but you've found out things about them I never would've dreamed possible. Has the whole world gone crazy, or just Grand?"

Sighing, Angela answered, "Maybe it's me."

"You're not the one doing all the lying. I can't believe they could do these kinds of things. We all grew up together. We're supposed to be friends."

"You're too nice, Misty. Just because you try to do the right thing doesn't mean everyone else does."

"Shelly says the same thing. So, what are you going to do now?"

"I was hoping you had some advice." Angela plopped down in the kitchen chair.

"Wish I did, but I'm at a loss for words. I am going to have that talk with Shelly."

"Don't. It won't help. All it will do is get you involved in this mess."

"I'm already involved. I can't sit around and watch everyone destroy each other's lives. What kind of person would that make me?"

"A smart one," Angela replied sarcastically.

"Things are out of control. No one realizes what they're doing anymore. Shelly's a reasonable person. When I point out the fact she's only hurting Taylor, she'll stop this nonsense."

"I doubt it. Besides, Lucas is just as guilty."

"Maybe, but if she hadn't lied and strung him along for years, none of this would've happened. Lucas is confused. At least he told you the truth willingly. You didn't have to overhear it in some hall. He's shown remorse, which is more than Shelly."

Angela still felt bad, but Misty's words made sense. "What are you going to say to her?"

"I don't know, but I'll think of something," Misty said. "The girls have a program at school tonight, and it's time to pick them up now, so I'll have to wait until I drop them off in the morning."

Angela hung up, feeling no better. Misty was right—Lucas was sorry for his actions, but did that matter? He'd proven he was a user, and she did not need to be getting involved with another one of those.

Bad thing was, she'd already gotten involved. And Angela wasn't sure she wanted to get uninvolved.

# 38

Shelly stared at the cloud bank building on the northern horizon with the hunger of a lover's eyes. Finally, she'd caught a lucky break. The forecast called for freezing temperatures and two to four inches of snow by tomorrow morning. That, along with the fact her dad absolutely hated cold weather, made today perfect.

Her dad had moved to Florida solely to escape the cold Northers that barreled across the Texas Panhandle four or five times a year. Upon hearing the forecast, he'd decided to head home a day early—excellent news to Shelly. The quicker they left, taking Taylor with them, the better.

It hadn't been easy talking her parents into going along with her plan. At least as much of it as she dared share. Her mother was all for taking the boys, but she wanted Shelly to come as well. The woman could not see what was so important it couldn't wait until they came back. Of course, her mother didn't know Shelly wasn't planning to come back.

Austin was eager to leave for Florida, but Taylor was a much harder sell. He wanted to wait and come when she did. Keeping the boys home and secluded from their friends had been difficult, but Shelly could breathe easier once the car was loaded and they were gone. Tossing the last suitcase into her parent's trunk, she turned toward the house with a smile on her face. Another fifteen minutes and she could relax.

The sound of a car pulling to a stop erased her smile. She cursed at the sight of Misty's minivan. Shelly needed to get rid of Misty. She could not let her friend discover her parents were leaving today, not with the boys anyway. She wasn't about to let her plan go awry this close to success. Walking toward the minivan, she hoped to send Misty on her way before anyone else came outside.

"Morning, Misty," Shelly stated as cheerfully as she could.

"Hi," Misty answered, sounding tired and weary.

"What brings you around so early?" She hoped getting straight to the point would keep Misty from tarrying.

"Can we talk?"

"About what?"

"All the stuff going on." Misty's chin jutted forward.

Shelly's eyes narrowed. She didn't like where this was going, and she didn't like this tone of voice. She was about to let Misty know her opinion of people meddling in her business when she changed her mind. Misty was easy enough to manipulate. Besides, if things worked out, Shelly could use little Miss Gullible as an accomplice, even if she didn't know she was helping.

"Sure, but I'm kind of busy right now. How about I swing by your house in an hour or so?"

"We should talk now."

Shelly gave Misty a long look. It wasn't like her to be so assertive. Shelly gave a panicked glance at the house. Someone could emerge any second and put her entire plan in jeopardy.

"Okay, fine. Where do you want to go?"

"We don't have to go anywhere," Misty answered.

"Yes we do!" Shelly tried to calm herself. "My dad is

still asleep on the couch," she lied. "You remember how grouchy he can be. I don't want to wake him up. Let me run in and get my purse. Then we can go somewhere and talk."

Shelly hurried toward the house without giving Misty time to reply. She raced around inside, quickly saying goodbye to her parents and boys. Of course, her mother wanted to know what the emergency was, so Shelly rapidly explained Misty needed someone to drive her back to the doctor up in Amarillo. Her mother said something else, but already halfway out the door, Shelly didn't hear.

She ran to the car and hopped in. "Let's go!" she shouted.

"Where?"

"I don't care. Just drive." Shooting backward glances at the house, Shelly felt like a criminal fleeing the scene of a crime.

Satisfaction and relief gripped her when they pulled away. If she could keep Misty away long enough, no one would know Taylor was gone for at least another day.

Misty twisted slightly in her seat as they drove. "Do you want to tell me your side of things?"

"My side of what?" Shelly answered sweetly. She'd learned her lesson at the hospital. She wasn't about to say anything until it was clear exactly how much Misty knew.

"The story between you, Lucas, Angela, and Taylor."

Shelly wasn't surprised Misty knew about Taylor. If Angela knew, it stood to reason Misty did too. That slut had no business gossiping about her, but the knowledge reinforced Shelly's need to get Taylor out of town. Misty's knowing was unfortunate, but Shelly could use it to her advantage.

"I don't have a story to tell. All I know is the truth."

"What is the truth, Shelly? Because some of the things I've been hearing are unbelievable."

Shelly realized they were traveling in a circle. If she didn't do something fast, they would be going right back by her house.

"Why don't we drive out to the old roadside park? It's quiet. We can talk there without any interruptions." It also happened to be north of town, rather than south, the direction her parents would travel.

This was exactly the type of situation Shelly had feared all these years, but now that it was here, she was surprised by her calmness and proud of how clearly and quickly she thought on the fly.

"Okay. I haven't been to that park since high school," Misty commented as she turned the van around. "Why didn't you tell anyone Taylor was Lucas's son?"

Where had Misty found all this newfound boldness? It wasn't like her to just come out and speak her mind.

"Because I didn't know myself until recently."

"Didn't you at least wonder?"

"No," Shelly answered as calmly as she could.

"How could you not?" Misty sounded confused.

"Until Lucas asked me if Taylor was his son. I never even considered the idea Jake wasn't his father."

"Why not?"

Shelly tried not to smile. Manipulating Misty was even easier than she thought. With her most serious look, she turned and stared at Misty. "Because I didn't know me and Lucas ever slept together."

"How could you not know a thing like that?"

Shelly forced tears down her cheeks as they pulled into the roadside park. Crying on demand was getting easier all the time, and her sobs would make her story easier to sell.

"I was drunk," she wept. "You remember how upset I was when Jake dumped me for Angela. When I got to prom and saw them together, the sight was more than I could take. I left, but you and Charlene were still there, and I didn't want to go home and explain everything to my mom. So, I went to Lucas. I needed to talk to somebody."

Pausing to work up some more tears, she gave Misty time to accept what she'd said. Of course, Misty had witnessed all of that herself.

"I remember telling Lucas how bad I felt. Then he made us some drinks to make me feel better. Whatever he mixed must have been strong because I don't remember much after that. Then a few months back, Lucas confessed he took advantage of me when I passed out."

"Lucas told you that?" Misty asked.

"He didn't choose those words, but that's what he did."

"Didn't you realize something happened, after you found out you were pregnant?"

"No. I told y'all about me and Jake making up the day after prom. I assumed that's when it happened."

"How do you know for sure it wasn't? Maybe Taylor is Jake's."

"Come on, Misty. It's obvious. I never suspected a thing until Lucas told me the truth, but then it became painfully clear. Taylor looks and acts too much like Lucas to be Jake's son. You only have to look at Austin to see that. Don't you think?"

Shelly hoped getting Misty to agree about Taylor would make her agree with everything else.

"Yeah, it is kind of obvious once you know the truth. I didn't believe it at first, but then I started to think of how much Lucas and Taylor look alike. I was shocked when I realized it had to be true."

"*You* were shocked? How do you think I felt?"

Misty shook her head. "I can't believe all of this is happening here in Grand."

"It's hard to learn people you care about aren't what

they seem." Shelly tried to sound sad and pitiful. She could tell Misty was trying to decide what to believe.

"Why didn't you tell anyone the truth after you found out?"

"How could I? I was afraid of hurting Jake and Taylor. I guess I should have, but it's hard to tell the people you love something like that. And despite what Lucas did, I was willing to forgive him. After all, we were just kids when it happened. I was hurt, but we'd shared too many good times over the years for me to abandon our friendship."

"If Lucas already knew, why did he get so upset at the hospital?"

"What are you talking about?" Shelly was perfectly aware what Misty was talking about, but she didn't have an answer, so playing dumb seemed the best recourse.

"Lucas told Angela he found out about Taylor at the hospital. He said he overheard you saying Taylor wasn't Jake's son."

"What? Lucas was never at the hospital. You were there all day. Did you see him?"

"No, but you didn't want Taylor to donate blood, so I thought . . . "

"I'll admit I was afraid somebody would learn the truth if I let him give blood, but I gave in. I signed the permission form. You were there. Remember? I don't know how Lucas's name got involved with any of that."

Misty shook her head. She stared across the empty fields. "I don't understand why he would lie to Angela about that."

"I'll tell you why," Shelly answered confidently. "He wanted her to feel sorry for him. He's been trying to get on her good side, hoping to make me jealous. He told me that himself. I guess Angela didn't tell you about him practically raping me either."

"Yeah, she told me what you said about him being naked when you got to his house, but Lucas doesn't seem like the type of guy to do a thing like that."

"He didn't seem like the type to get me drunk and have his way with me, either, but he did. Some people just aren't what they seem. That's why I called Angela."

"Why did you call her?"

"I just told you. I wanted to warn her about Lucas. She deserves to know the truth."

"But why would you warn her?" Misty cocked her head like a curious puppy. "You don't even like her. You've never liked her."

Shelly did not like the doubt in Misty's voice. Worse, she was running out of answers for the questions. Why couldn't Misty accept this as fact the way she did everything else?

"I don't understand any of this." Misty frowned and shook her head.

Shelly sighed. She couldn't endure much more of Misty's badgering without losing control. Her parents surely were gone, and maybe Misty would still have some doubt about the truth if they went back now.

"I don't think you brought me out here to talk at all. Seems more like you brought me out here to accuse me. I can't believe you doubt me after we've been best friends for so long." She folded her arms across her chest. "Take me home. The boys need me, and I don't want to sit here and listen to the last friend I have accuse me of things I did not do."

"I'm not accusing anyone. I just want everyone to do what's right," Misty explained as she pulled out of the roadside park.

"That's exactly what I'm trying to do." Staring out the window at the passing countryside, Shelly tried not to smile.

"Are you?" Misty sounded skeptical.

"Yes. But since you don't believe me, let me ask you this, whose husband was run down in cold blood? Who was gotten drunk and raped by one of their best friends? Who has to raise two fatherless boys? Answer those questions and tell me who the victim is in all of this!"

"You've been through a lot these past few days, but no matter what the truth is, Taylor needs to know who his real father is." Misty turned down Shelly's street. "You can't hide this forever. What if he hears it at school, or around town?"

Spying her now empty driveway Shelly smiled and replied, "I promise you, that won't happen."

Staring at her empty driveway, Angela sat on the front porch swing. She shivered at the cool air coming off the approaching storm. In a few hours, it would be too cold to sit outside, then she would be locked in the house with doubt and worry as her only companions. She hadn't felt this lonely and hopeless since her arrival in town. She thought about calling Lucas, but couldn't quite bring herself to dial his number.

He'd called from the bar last night and his house this morning, but she'd ignored his requests to come over. Angela wasn't ready to be close to him again, mostly because she was afraid her resistance would crumble in his presence, and she still wasn't ready to forgive his manipulation.

She was just about to walk over and see how L.J. was when Misty's minivan turned the corner. Angela was eager to hear how things went with Shelly.

"Did you make her see the light?" she asked, as Misty walked up to the porch.

"Not exactly." Misty shook her head.

"Hate to say I told you so, but I told you so."

Angela was dying to know what was said, but she didn't voice the questions in her head.

They sat on the swing in silence for several minutes.

"You patch things up with Lucas yet?"

"Not exactly. He called a couple of times and we talked, but I'm still trying to decipher my emotions. My trust is gone, but my feelings for him aren't, if that makes any sense."

"Yeah, I know what you mean. That's how I felt listening to Shelly. Some of what she said made sense, but other things were clearly lies. I'm disappointed in her, but still view her as a friend."

"Everybody is your friend, Misty. Don't get me wrong, that's a good thing, but sometimes you're going to get disappointed in them. Like I am in Lucas."

"You might be more disappointed when I tell you what she told me."

Angela gave a hollow chuckle. "I'm not sure I'd believe anything she has to say about me or Lucas at this point."

"I was doubtful, too, at first."

"Okay, I'll bite. What did she say?"

Misty retold Shelly's version of prom night. It sounded plausible enough, but Angela knew it for a lie. She'd seen the hurt in Lucas's eyes the day he learned the truth. If he'd known, or even suspected beforehand, he wouldn't have been so crushed.

"If he was bold enough to get her drunk and have sex, don't you think he'd be bold enough to reveal his feelings these last sixteen years?"

"Maybe, but . . . "

"There are no 'buts!' Shelly was trying to cover her own ass!" Angela hadn't meant to yell at Misty, but the combination of Shelly's audacity and lies annoyed her. "I'm sorry. It's not your fault, but I know Lucas. He is the nicest, most compassionate man I've ever met. I don't think he could do something like that to anyone, much less someone he loves. He's not a liar either. If he was, he wouldn't have told me the truth."

Misty said, "Sounds to me like you've made up your mind about him, whether you want to admit it or not."

Misty was right.

Angela did love him, and it was obvious he loved her. He'd made a mistake, but who was she to say it was worse than the dozens she'd committed in her own life?

"You're right, I have. I'd be a fool to drive him away."

# 39

Wednesday morning dawned with Lucas as distraught as he'd ever been. The last forty-eight hours had been the longest of his life. He hadn't eaten, slept, or done anything other than worry. He couldn't focus to play the guitar, and last night, he didn't even open the bar. What was the point? Monday it had pretty much been him and Chester. Charlene's idiot hadn't come back to apologize, so the feedlot guys were still avoiding the place, and gossip over Jake's death had fallen off, so damn few stragglers wandered in.

Instead of running the bar, he spent the afternoon and evening driving around on the dirt roads in the country-side surrounding Grand, listening to music and thinking about Taylor and Angela. Lucas was desperate to sit and talk to both.

So desperate in fact that he regretted letting Shelly convince him to wait before talking to Taylor. Seemed like a good idea at the time, but that was before he knew the full depth of Shelly's crazy. Angry as she was over his rejection, there was no telling what she'd told Taylor by now. Lucas had no doubt she would do everything in her power to sabotage his relationship with Taylor, just as she'd tried with Angela.

Of course, Shelly's efforts hadn't poisoned Angela's faith in him nearly as much as his own confession—actually, his stupidity, for it was clear that's what his scheme had been born of.

He'd talked to Angela only twice since revealing the truth, and she'd been distant both occasions. Nevertheless, Lucas was glad he'd told her. There had been far too many lies left to fester.

Angela asked for time, so even though it pained him to give her distance, Lucas decided he'd focus solely on Taylor for the moment. Lucas had always wanted a son of his own, but he'd never guessed he would start with a teenager.

What if Taylor genuinely didn't like him? It might be better to not have a son than to have one who hated you. Under the best of circumstances, finding out the truth would be hard on Taylor, and this certainly was not the best of circumstances.

What if he failed live up to Jake in Taylor's mind? Jake might not have been father of the year, but he was a man's man—a star athlete in his day, an outdoorsman, an all-around hell-of-a-guy by Grand's standards. Lucas could see through all of that, but Taylor might not. Those were things that impressed teenage boys.

Despite these doubts, Lucas itched to make that first step, but he was unsure when Shelly's parents were scheduled to leave. Today, but what time?

Lucas again decided the walls of his house were too confining. Leaving meant he could drive by Shelly's to see if her parents were gone. Even if they had left, Taylor was probably back in school by now.

It didn't really matter if her parents were still there or Taylor was at school, Lucas needed to get out of the house. Maybe the wide-open spaces of the countryside would open up his mind to ideas on how to talk with Taylor.

Grand looked rejuvenated this morning under the covering of white powder that fell overnight. The white flakes concealed years of windblown deterioration and general decay. It cheered Lucas to think a place as plain as Grand could be made to look better by only a few inches of snow, and if the town could be made to look cleaner and brighter so easily, maybe his life could as well.

He embraced the metaphor until it dawned on him his every action left a lasting mark on the pristine snow, much in the same manner his actions had. He didn't want his words and decisions to scar Taylor the way his footsteps and tires marked the snow.

Pulling to a stop in front of Shelly's, several things leapt out at Lucas. First, there were no strange cars in the driveway. Second, there was still virgin powder on the pavement. Nobody had come or gone since the snow had fallen.

Lucas knocked on the door.

"Oh, it's you," Shelly answered and walked back inside, leaving the door wide open.

Not the greeting he'd envisioned. He certainly hadn't expected her to welcome him with open arms, though he'd hoped for less hostility. This was yet another side of Shelly he'd never seen. Standing in the doorway, it felt almost as if she were setting a trap for him.

Lucas called out, "Is Taylor here?"

"No."

He waited for her to say more, but she didn't seem inclined to. He took a few steps inside. "When will he get home from school?"

"He's gone."

"Gone?" Lucas rounded the corner of the living room. "What do you mean 'gone?' Gone where?"

Shelly stared out the window to the plowed fields back beyond the house. "You don't seem to care about his feelings, so you don't deserve to know."

"You damn well better tell me! As his father, I have the right—"

"You don't have any rights!" She turned and glared. "He's my son, not yours! If you want a son, have your tramp Angela spread her legs and give you one, because you're not taking mine!"

Her words tore into him like a jagged saw blade. Underestimating her bitterness, he hadn't considered the possibility she would keep Taylor away from him altogether.

"Look, Shelly, I don't want to play these games. I don't want to take Taylor from you. I want to share in his life. That's it. You will always be his mother." By remaining calm and reassuring, he hoped she would be reasonable.

"Damn right, I'm his mother! That's why I sent him away. I had to. Your whore was spreading the news all around town! I didn't want Taylor to hear it from the wrong person."

"Angela is not a whore! And she is not spreading anything around town."

"She's already told Misty, Charlene, and God knows who else you are Taylor's father."

Lucas shook his head. Angela might tell Misty, but there was no way she would tell Charlene anything. "Why didn't you just bring Taylor over so we could tell him together? What good is sending him away going to do? He has to come back sometime."

"I'm not gonna sit by and let you and that bitch see my son! As long as you are screwing her, you can forget seeing Taylor!"

"You can't keep him from me. I'll track him down if I have to."

"Over my dead body!"

"Whatever it takes." Lucas turned and stormed from the house.

Shelly was beyond reason. Crazy is what she was. How

had he been so blind?

Back in the truck, he slapped the steering wheel. He should have known Shelly would keep Taylor from him. After all, she'd hidden their son from him for years.

But he wasn't going to let her keep Taylor from him. Not anymore. If she refused to be reasonable, he would track Taylor down just as he threatened.

Lucas couldn't bear the thought of being alone again all day, and he didn't want to push Angela away by pressuring her, so he decided to swing by L.J.'s. Then again, Angela might spot the Caddy sitting across the street and assume he was checking up on her, so Lucas briefly considered driving out to Chester's instead. But trying to have a serious conversation with the old-timer could be trying. Everything was a joke to Chester. He wasn't even particularly concerned about the pending court case of his best friend. Chester's advice would simply be to get a stiff drink and not worry about it. Lucas wasn't up to that brand of wisdom today. He needed real advice.

Who did that leave? He could call Cody, but his advice would be to leave it all behind and join him on the road. That had always been his advice, and truth be told, it made more sense to Lucas now than ever before. Lucas had no other friends in town he could really talk to, so he was about to throw caution to the wind and go see Angela anyway when a better idea sprang to mind. Misty was friends with both Angela and Shelly. She could give him some insight into what each was thinking.

Despite having grown up with her, he'd never been particularly close to Misty. He didn't dislike her, they simply did not see much of each other. She rarely visited the Oasis, and he went out of his way to avoid the family-oriented functions she attended with Shelly.

He'd never been to her house, but this being Grand, Lucas knew exactly where she lived.

"Hello, Lucas," Misty said, answering the door. She didn't seem all that surprised to find him on her porch.

"Hi, Misty. I was wondering if I could talk to you."

"Sure, come in. The house is a mess, but you know how kids are."

"No, but I wish I did."

He surveyed his surroundings. The living room was far from messy, but it possessed a lived-in, homey aura. "Have you talked to Angela lately?"

"Yesterday. Why, haven't you?"

He shook his head. "Not in the last two days. I know y'all are friends and talk often, so I was wondering if you had any idea what's going through her head. The good. The bad. Anything." Lucas stared at Misty. "I don't know how much Angela has told you, but I messed up. I hurt her, but that was before I knew her. I sort of regret what I did, and I sort of don't. I wouldn't have had the chance to fall in love with her otherwise. That's why I came to see you."

Misty met his gaze. Her eyes studied him, almost as if she were sizing him up.

"What are your intentions?" she asked pointedly.

"What do you mean?"

"I don't want to speak until I know your plans. Angela is my friend, and she's been hurt enough. The last thing she needs is you using her to make Shelly jealous."

"I love Angela. And I've already hurt her once, but I'll spend the rest of my life making up for that fact if only she'll give me that chance." Lucas stared straight into Misty's face.

"Okay, but answer me one question."

"Fire away," he stated, eager to erase her doubts.

"Did you get Shelly drunk and take advantage of her prom night?"

He was stunned by her question. He felt like a thief

caught red-handed with the goods. He hadn't anticipated this line of questioning. "Those aren't the exact words I would choose to describe that night, but I guess you could make that argument."

The look of disappointment on Misty's face forced him to explain. Telling the secrets, which he'd been harboring for the last decade and a half, was much easier the second time. Or maybe it was the fact he was telling Misty this time and not Angela that made the retelling less stressful. He started with prom night and finished by describing his confrontation earlier that morning with Shelly.

Misty's expression softened as he shared his story and personal feelings. She transitioned from mistrust and worry to relief and joy. The indecision drained from her eyes. For the most part she listened quietly, but occasionally reacted to his words with statements of surprise or empathy.

He wrapped up his story by professing his love for Angela a second time.

"She loves you too," Misty replied sweetly to his words.

"How do you know?"

This time it was his turn to listen. She told him everything about her conversation with Shelly and Angela the day before.

He felt betrayed to learn Angela had indeed told Misty the truth about Taylor. Shelly wasn't lying. It was Angela's fault Taylor was gone.

"What's wrong?" Misty asked.

"Nothing!" he answered bitterly.

"Something's wrong. Those lines in your forehead are about to give me a headache. What is it?"

"Shelly wasn't lying. She did send Taylor away because Angela told you. She probably told Charlene too."

"You're wrong, Lucas. Angela would never tell something like that to Charlene, and Shelly wouldn't know if she did. Shelly was only using that as an excuse."

"You don't know that!" he snapped. He didn't mean to be angry with Misty, but he couldn't help it.

"Yes, I do. I'm getting tired of listening to you and Angela find excuses not to be happy."

Lucas stood and paced around the room. Everywhere he turned, a member of Misty's family smiled back from a framed picture.

Misty sighed. "Shelly's not even talking to Charlene. She wouldn't have any idea if Angela told her anything."

"They're best friends. Why wouldn't Charlene tell her?"

"Charlene was sleeping with Jake."

"What?"

Misty told him about Charlene and Jake's affair. She repeated exactly what Shelly told her about both Charlene and Jake's confessions. He listened to every last detail, paying special attention to the part about their fight just before Jake's accident. Jake and Shelly's fateful fight wasn't solely the result of his misdeed. Despite his dislike of Jake, and his growing resentment toward Shelly, Lucas had struggled with guilt over the accident, over the belief he'd all but murdered Jake by triggering Angela's return to Grand. Misty's story made it clear there was plenty of blame to go around. And it gave him an idea how to change Shelly's mind and make her bring Taylor back.

# 40

Jake and Shelly were meant for each other. Lucas could see that plain as day now. Both were arrogant, selfish, and insolent. Her acting like an innocent, naive farm girl when underneath she was nothing more than a cold, calculating bitch.

A month ago he never would have, or could have, thought of her in those terms. Matter of fact, he would have violently defended her had anyone else spoken those words. Staring in the eye of his old delusions left Lucas both humbled and ashamed. Turns out he was the naive one.

He'd wasted far too many years mourning his dull life and coveting Shelly's—the perfect woman, living the perfect existence.

Staring up at her house, he was surprised to discover the anger and resentment had seeped away only to be replaced by resolve and the desire to make up for lost time.

Patches of grass were now visible in her yard as the early afternoon sun continued to melt away the snow. In a few hours, all traces of the early winter storm would be gone, but he no longer needed a buffer to make the town appear brighter.

In his heart he believed Angela would find the forgiveness to once again accept him, and he would force Shelly to accept his demands. She wouldn't like being backed into a corner.

He'd never actually been in love with Shelly, only her image. His inability to separate one from the other made him a fool, but now he could use that very same image to force her hand because Shelly also loved her image. And at this point, she had little else to cling to. He knocked at her door a new man.

Shelly swung the heavy oak door open. "What do you want now?" The surprised look on her face told Lucas she hadn't expected to see him again so soon.

"Let's talk." He calmly pushed the door all the way open and slid past her.

"You can't just traipse into my house anytime you want!"

He plopped down on the couch without turning around to reply. He heard her shove something in the coat closet him, but when he turned around, she quickly closed the door.

"What do you want?" She joined him in the living room.

"Have a little temper tantrum, did you?" He pointed at the mass of papers and clutter scattered around.

"Something like that," she responded coldly. "I don't know what you're doing here. Unless you've come to your senses and sent that whore packing, nothing has changed. You still can't, and won't, see Taylor!"

"You're wrong. You're going to have Taylor back tomorrow."

"The hell I am! Why would I possibly do that?"

"Because that's your only option. Keeping him away will make things worse on you. Bring Taylor back, or I'll make your life here a living hell."

"Oh, big, tough Lucas. You're so scary." She extended a hand toward his face and pretended to shake.

"You know, Shelly, I've listened to you gossip about and demoralize nearly everyone in this town. I've heard you talk about how pathetic and poor Misty is. You've made fun of Charlene for being divorced and sleeping around. And they were your friends."

Lucas stood and walked toward her. She backpedaled until her torso rested against the far wall. Lucas leaned down close to her face. "You've talked about how ignorant the rest of this town is, how ugly their kids are, what shitty jobs they have. You sat up on your high horse looking down on everybody. You claimed to be better than everyone else. What's even worse, I believed you. I agreed you were perfect and so was your life. But you know what? I was wrong. You call Angela a whore, but you're the biggest whore of all."

She slapped him in the face. "I've been married to the same man since high school."

Lucas grabbed her wrist before she could strike again. "I'm not talking about that kind of whore. You're a whore to your own pathetic standards. Your life isn't perfect. Never has been. Everything about you is built on lies. Now you're a slave to your own reputation."

"Oh, aren't you the smart one all of a sudden. Did Angela give you that line? You and her are just jealous like everyone else around here. Jealous! Jealous of me!"

"The only thing I'm jealous of is the fact you've been part of Taylor's life, and I haven't. I don't give a damn about you!" He let go of her and backed away.

"The hell you don't! You've been in love with me your whole life. Now you're mad because you can't have me!"

"I love Angela, not you. I was crazy to ever think you were anything but a self-righteous bitch. Which is why I'm going to start telling the world about your lies if Taylor isn't back tomorrow. I'll make sure everyone in this county knows the truth."

He expected to be met by Shelly's ire, but instead her laughter smothered him like a wet towel. Her amusement irritated him. "What's so damn funny?"

"You. Do you really think anyone cares what you say? If not for me, no one in this town would even know you exist. Nobody cares what the motherless son of a dead drunk thinks. It'll be the bartender's word against mine, Shelly Sampson. Who do you think everyone will believe?"

"You think the town loves you, but they love a good story more. I'm sure Jake's parents will be interested to know you've sent their grandsons away, or at least grandson. And oh, won't the gossip queens enjoy the gory details of Jake and Charlene's fling."

"That's about Jake, not me. Go ahead, tell them. I don't care. It'll only make everyone see I'm the real victim in all of this."

"Keep believing that. But when you walk down the street, try not to pay attention to the stares and whispers," he said. "And stick to that story about me getting you drunk on prom night. It's almost believable. Of course, they'll wonder why you were with me on prom night in the first place."

"You've talked to Misty and now you think you have all the answers. She's as stupid as you are. Nobody cares what either of you say."

"I also talked to Charlene and Jake's parents," he bluffed. If Shelly could toss names out, so could he. "None of them are on your side. What's the rest of the town going to think when all your friends turn against you?"

Lucas barely had time to duck the flying lamp Shelly sent streaking at his head. "Get out!" she screamed. Her primal shriek echoed through the room.

He could not help but smile at her sudden, animal-like transformation. He'd not only touched a nerve, he'd scarred her inner psyche. The rage on her face erased the last hint of her beauty. Standing before him now, she was as ugly as humanly possible.

"Remember, if Taylor's not back by tomorrow, I'm gonna start talking." He calmly strolled out the door.

"Don't turn your back on me!"

He shut the door as another loud crash punctuated his departure. Knowing he'd accomplished his goal, he could concentrate on setting things right with Angela.

If Misty was correct and Angela truly did love him, that was all the motivation he needed. He would do whatever it took to win back her trust and her heart. For the first time in his life, Lucas felt confident he could express his true feelings and desires. He was ready to completely give himself over to love, happiness, and Angela.

# 41

Apprehension gripped Angela as she hung up the phone. She'd done her share of worrying over the years—about money, the past catching up to her, about what to do, where to go next—but she was not use to worrying about other people. Life was much easier when she only cared about herself. This hopeless, almost desperate need of reassurance was crippling. If only she could talk to Lucas to know he was okay.

With each unanswered call, her concern grew. She'd tried to reach him all afternoon yesterday, and now this morning. He wasn't at this house. He wasn't at the Oasis. Where could he be? There weren't that many places to go in Grand. The pessimistic side of her formulated dozens of horrible scenarios.

She should have gotten her car fixed, that way she could search for him. She should have been more forgiving. She should have kept him close instead of sending him away.

Something terrible might have happened to him. Stress from the recent events could have caused him to have a heart attack. For all she knew, he was laid out unconscious or dead in his house right now. The thought of suicide lingered in the back of her mind. Lucas had been through a lot lately, but she knew he was stronger than that. She also worried for herself. It would be just her luck to finally find and accept happiness only to have fate snatch it away.

The uncertainty tormented her. Maybe Misty could her drive around and look for him. But what if her worries were for nothing? Lucas would think she was crazy.

Maybe he'd finally been able to talk to Taylor and they were spending some quality time together, Angela's optimistic side reasoned.

But then she heard the sirens.


Lucas had just left Shelly's when he saw the smoke. Not much at first, but thickening and turning blacker every second. His heart quickened. Something smack in the middle of Grand was on fire.

His first fear was for Angela.

He mashed the Caddy's accelerator, but Angela's street was calm and quiet when he turned onto her block. He slowed, but the smoke continued to rise. Like a beacon, the rising cloud drew him to it. He drove on past Angela's house and turned onto Main. He noticed the onlookers first, standing in the street and in the Whirlwind parking lot, all staring over at the Oasis.

Several pickups blocked the street so Lucas pulled up behind them and got out of the car. Only then did he notice the smoke billowing from his bar.

A siren began to wail. Lucas stared at the rising smoke, his eyes not really comprehending its meaning. A finger of flame flicked upward, licking at the roof.

The bar was on fire.

His bar.

Lucas looked around at the faces. Everyone was just standing.

Doing nothing. But what was there to do?

His guitar.

The one his dad left him.

The one Townes Van Zandt gave his dad.

It was inside the burning building.

Lucas sprinted toward the building. The black smoke was thick in the air above, and while he'd seen flames from farther back, up close the structure seemed just fine.

"Lucas! Don't go in there!"

First, it was a lone man's voice, then came a chorus of others.

"The fire department is on the way!"

"Stay out!"

"Lucas! Lucas! Lucas!"

He ignored them. Fumbled with his keys. The door-knob wasn't hot. He pushed in the key.

"Lucas! Lucas!"

"No!" A woman's voice pierced the air, shrieking above the others, calling his name. "LUCAS!"

The smoke was thick inside, so he crouched down and scurried toward the bar, knocking over tables and chairs as he felt his way through. There were no flames, at least not that he could see, but he felt the heat. Sirens wailed and so did that now lone, piercing voice calling his name.

The far wall growled like an angry beast and burst into flames, cutting out all other sounds.

Smoke burned his eyes and clawed his throat. The heat made him wince, but then he was there, touching the bar. Feeling his way. Grabbing the guitar case.

Coughing, gagging, he straightened his back and fo-cused on the feeble light framed by the front door. Pulling his Cowboy Junkies cap down over his mouth and nose, he loped that direction but tripped and fell on an over-turned chair.

The guitar case slipped from his grip.

He found it again after a few seconds and began crawling toward the door.

But the smoke was too thick. He could no longer see light streaming in. The flames hissed, popped, roiled all around him.

Shelly loaded the last of the boxes into the back of her SUV. The movers would pack everything else when they came on Friday, but she would be in Florida by then. The sirens continued to wail, but they no longer made her heart skitter the way they had when she first heard them. Her fear they were coming for her was ridiculous anyway. She'd committed no crime.

With her vehicle loaded with all the important stuff she'd need right away, Shelly opened the garage door. She smelled the smoke and wondered what was on fire while at the same time counting her blessings. The whole town would be focused on the fire. No one would notice her escape.

Backing out of the driveway, she stared at the smoke rising over near the grain elevator. She was dying to know what was burning, but she couldn't risk being spotted, so Shelly headed the other direction. Later, once she traveled a few miles away on the farm-to-market roads, she would cut back over to the highway that sliced through town.

Relief and a sadistic smile engulfed her. She was leaving, and there wasn't a damn thing Lucas or anybody else could do to stop her. It felt good to be in control again.

Lucas's threats echoed in her head as she took one last look back at Grand. It wasn't that his words scared her or even altered her plans. What shook her was the fact he'd had the nerve to challenge her. He'd never doubted or questioned anything she told him before Angela came back to town.

Lucas and that whore.

Shelly couldn't believe she'd lost him to her of all people. Her only regret was she would not be around to see his face when he discovered his threats were meaningless. Away from Grand, nothing he could say or do would ever affect her.

Angela tilted her chin up.

She was leaving.

She had won.

They wouldn't have the satisfaction of looking down their noses at her. The rising smoke in her rearview mirror only added to her sense of triumph.

Let the whole damn town burn. It served them right.

# 42

Angela stepped outside. She smelled the smoke before she saw it. One set of sirens had already arrived. Now she could hear more coming.

Then she heard the fire.

The crackle and snap. A dull roar.

Angela took off running, pulled along by worry and an irrational fear that the flames were the reason she could not reach Lucas.

Lucas drug the guitar case along, but he'd lost the cap and now his lungs burned from holding his breath. He dropped his face low to the floor hoping for a clear sight of the door, but it was so dark and smoky. He crawled on, using his free forearm and elbows as well as his feet to propel himself forward or at least away from the heat at his back. The door, the exit, the only way out couldn't be more than ten or fifteen yards, but damned if he could see it through his watery eyes.

The roar and crackle of the fire was loud, but through it he heard that voice.

"LUCAS! LUCAS! LUCAS!"

To the right. He angled toward the voice.

"LET ME GO!"

"GOD, NO!"

"LUCAS!"

The screeching was frantic and it pulled him—guided him.

Until there it was. The door. And hands. And bodies. Suddenly, he was being yanked forward, out of the smoke. The guitar case fell from his hands. He flailed for its handle, but they kept pulling him farther away.

"My guitar." He tried to say, but his voice was so hoarse and scratchy. Did anyone understand? They had to get his guitar.

And still that voice screeched. "Lucas! Lucas!" she gasped.

Abby. It was Abby's voice, but his eyes were still so watery he couldn't focus.

Coughing, he turned his head to look for her. But he didn't have to look hard because the next thing he knew, her arms were around him. Hugging him tight. But then she was gone. Pulled away. And they were still dragging him.

"No! Let me go! Lucas! Please be okay. Lucas!"

He tried again to speak. To thank her. It was her voice that led him to the door. To safety.

He coughed again. His head spun. And then everything went black.


Angela knew a block into her frantic run that it was the Oasis burning. She knew without seeing the flames, by where the smoke was rising and by the flash of red lights reflecting off the walls of the grain elevator. It was early. Lucas had no reason to be there, she told herself, but why couldn't she reach him?

The street was crowded with people and cars. There was the Cadillac, parked in the middle of the road. The driver's door hung open. Angela felt better at the sight. He hadn't been here. He just arrived. She slowed and greedily sucked air into her lungs. The run had left her exhausted. She searched the crowd of onlookers while she caught her breath.

Lucas was tall, so she searched for his head among the throng.

Black smoke hung over the block, partially blotting out the sun. The fire still roared despite the water being poured onto the flames, and there were people all around. Fireman rushing about, onlookers standing with their mouths hung open, a lady screaming, "LET ME GO!"

Angela began to cut her way through the crowd.

Still searching.

Then she saw it. The stretcher in the back of the ambulance. A body was laid out on it, but all she could see were feet, and then the door closed. She reached the ambulance in a few strides, but when she grabbed for the door, a man latched onto her wrist.

She turned toward him. It was a paramedic. "Who's in there? Please no, tell me it's not Lucas."

The paramedic grimaced. Then nodded and said, "But he's breathing and there are no burns."

"I want to see him." She wrenched her arm free and again reached for the door.

"Miss you can't. Frank is treating him. We—"

His words were cut off by a screeching woman. "Let me go! God damn you, Charlie! Let me go, right fucking now!"

Angela was jostled in the ruckus of bodies suddenly pressed in on her.

"Johnny, you and Frank get him up the road. Otherwise I'm gonna have to arrest Abby."

"Angela! Angela!" Abby DeWitt began yelling her name. "Lucas is in there. He ran inside and the smoke was so thick."

Angela turned back around, but the paramedic was gone. She reached for the back door yet again, but the vehicle moved forward, out of her reach. It was leaving. With Lucas. She moved forward, but then another hand grabbed her.

"Let it go. Let them take care of him."

Angela stared at the sheriff's deputy who'd spoken. "What happened?"

"We don't know yet."

"Oh my God, Angela. It was horrible. He ran in there and I didn't think he was going to make it out." Tears streamed down Abby's face.

Angela turned back to the cop. "Where are they taking him?"

"Amarillo," the man answered. "He sucked in a lot of smoke."

"Which hospital?" Angela looked frantically around. She had to get to Amarillo.

"Northwest, I reckon."

She spied the Cadillac. The door was open, but were the keys in it?

She ran to the car. The keys were gone.

Angela broke down. Sobs racked her body. She was going to vomit.

"Get in." Angela looked up. Abby DeWitt stared back at her from behind the wheel of a car. A running car. "Hurry up. We have an ambulance to catch."

# 43

Shelly drove all night to get as far from Grand as she possible. But instead of feeling better, each passing mile brought more tension. She tried to shake her foreboding doom. She told herself it was the darkness that she would feel better when the sun broke over the horizon. But as the stars faded and the sky turned from purple, to gray, to blue, what she felt was more akin to terror than victory.

Or even relief.

Fleeing Grand wasn't the end of her trouble, nor would it be a new beginning. More likely, it was the beginning of real trouble. By the time she crossed over the Mississippi River, Shelly was trembling. Hands shaking, she pulled over at a visitor center welcoming her to the river's namesake state. That stupid song taunted her.

M, I—*crooked letter, crooked letter*—I—*crooked letter, crooked letter*—I—*humpback, humpback*, I.

Lucas had taught her that song while tutoring her for a social studies test. He'd made her sing it over and over until she now sang it every time she saw the word *Mississippi*. She didn't want to think about Lucas, but how could she not? He wasn't going to sit back and let her take Taylor away. She'd seen the determination in his eyes when he threatened her. He would do everything in his power to track them down.

She stared over at the interstate, resenting the semi's humming along I-20. She also resented the water flowing in the nearby river and the clouds drifting overhead. The world continued to move, yet she was frozen with fear.

Lucas would eventually be successful in his pursuit. It would be impossible to hide herself and two kids. The boys would have to attend school. That would create a paper trail. No matter how far from Grand she ran, nothing would change. Every single day she would wake scared the truth had tracked her down.

Shelly walked toward the banks of the Mississippi. The interstate bridge was on her left, an older bridge spanned the river to her right. The new and the old. The past and the future. They were meant to be separate, but she was caught between them and left to wondering not if, but when, it would all collapse yet again.

She could not cope with that same old fear gnawing at her, day in and day out.

She couldn't go to Florida. She couldn't let anyone know the lies she'd told.

Staring at the water, Shelly made a grim decision. She wouldn't go back. Not now. Not ever.

She'd seen a movie once, a really weird movie about a woman fascinated with an old English writer that drowned herself by filling her pockets with rocks and walking into a river. Shelly wondered what it would be like to drown, but even more, she wondered what Lucas would say afterward. Would he admit his mistake then? Would he shed a tear? Would he regret driving her away?

She walked to the edge of a dirt road where she could see the water through the trees.

How many rocks would it take?

She didn't have very big pockets.

# 44

*Mid-November, Grand, Texas*

The Caddy was loaded, but Lucas wasn't ready to back it out of the garage just yet. He had one more thing to do first.

Most everyone in town knew he was leaving this morning, so he hoped she would come say goodbye. She hadn't stopped by in the four weeks since the fire, and he'd only talked to her the once at the hospital. But still, his gut told him Abby would come see him this morning.

There in the hospital they'd said a lot, although they spoke very few actual words. He'd thanked her for calling to him, for saving his life. She'd told him not to. She'd apologized. He'd told her not to.

That was it. After that brief exchange, she'd slipped away and left Angela and him to be alone. Apparently, Abby and Angela came to an understanding, even formed a bond, during their hasty trip to the hospital, because for the last month Angela had eaten lunch over at the Whirlwind almost every day. Lucas knew she'd urged Abby to come see him, but Abby said she couldn't, not yet.

Now time was running out before he and Angela left. For how long was anyone's guess. Lucas knew they would be back to visit if nothing else, but exactly what the future held was still up in the air.

Lucas could have crossed the distance between his house and Abby's, and if it came to that, he would go see her. But he still hoped she would come. What he wanted to do, to say, would be so much better here in the garage. Sort of full circle back to the days before everything changed.

The gate creaked. Lucas smiled.

She stopped in the doorway and stared at him. Steam rose from the mug in her hand.

"I was waiting, hoping you'd stop by."

"How could I not?" She walked over and handed him the mug. "Hot and steamy," she said. "Just how you like it."

"Yeah." He took note that her blouse was buttoned all the way up. "I got something for you too." He reached behind him and grabbed his guitar, the one he'd saved from the bar, from where it sat in the passenger seat.

He began playing and said, "This one's for you, Abby . . ."

*Dreams it seems are funny little things*
*Born in the dark, lit by a spark*
*Passion, and fire, unrequited desire*
*No, they don't all come true,*
*Still you listen, when that voice calls to you.*

*Spent many a day, chasing what I couldn't catch*
*Yeah, I struck—match after match*
*She came to me offering a whole lot more*
*Don't know why, but I tossed her gift out the door.*

*Dreams it seems are funny little things*
*Born in the dark, lit by a spark.*
*Passion, and fire, unrequited desire*
*No, they don't all come true,*
*Still, you listen, when that voice calls to you.*

*I rolled them bones just a hopin' for a winner*
*Shouted like a preacher at a sinner*
*Doubled down for a shiny, two-bit prize*
*But found nothing 'cept those ol' snake eyes*

*Dreams it seems are funny little things*
*Born in the dark, lit by a spark.*
*Passion, and fire, unrequited desire*
*No, they don't all come true,*
*Still, you listen, when that voice calls to you*

*She didn't care I'd let her down so damn hard*
*Kept me alive when I shoulda been charred*
*Dreams it seems are funny little things.*
*Born in the dark, and lit by a spark.*

Continuing to play, he said, "A work in progress since I'm still tinkering with the chord progression, but I thought you should be the first to hear that one." Stilling his fingers, he looked at her and said, "I never meant to hurt you, Abby. I never meant to fall in love with Angela. I'm the reason she came back. I tricked her into coming, hoping she would break up Shelly and Jake."

She nodded. "I know. Angela told me."

"I was a damn fool."

Abby shrugged. "We all do stupid stuff in the name of love."

"Thanks for coming to see me off this morning," Lucas said.

"Thanks for making sure I could. For keeping me out of trouble."

"Trouble?"

"Come on, Lucas. Don't play dumb. You're the smartest guy in town. We both know I went a little crazy there for a while. And we both know Shelly didn't start that fire."

He shrugged. "She disappeared right about the time the place went up in flames. And that note they found with her car in Mississippi said she she'd made too many mistakes to go on living. Sure sounded like a confession to me."

He plucked a few chords on his guitar before adding, "Sure makes her look guilty, and how things look is all that seems to matter."

Abby shook her head. "I hope not. I hope there's more truth to the world than that."

Lucas put the guitar back in the case and stowed it in the backseat of the Caddy so Townes's Hummingbird could make the ride south alongside Hank's ghost. "The world needs more truth," he said. "I'll grant you that. But too much truth, and we'd all be in trouble."

"Tell Cody hi for me," Abby said.

Lucas nodded. "When we play a show up this way, you better be there."

She grinned. "I wouldn't dare miss it."

They stared at each other for a few seconds before she said, "Can I have one kiss for the road?"

He walked over and kissed her on the forehead. "Thanks for being the spark, Abby. This is one dream I wouldn't be chasing otherwise."

# 45

The two of them sat on the swing, not saying a word. She would miss many things about Grand when she left this time, but the cadence of this squeaky swing, and the reassuring presence of L.J. nearby were tops on the list. She'd been out here for several hours, long enough to see the moon fall and the eastern sky lighten. Her bags were already packed and stowed in the Caddy's trunk. All that remained was saying goodbye, and now that he'd joined her, neither she nor L.J. were in a hurry to rush that.

"I'm sure glad you came back," he said after a few more minutes.

"Me too," she answered.

"Don't stay gone so long this time."

"I won't."

L.J. dug out the makings for a smoke. He licked the paper, rolled the cigarette and said, "Don't let Lucas get blinded by the lights. He's a good man, but nobody ever said the same about Cody Cantu."

"Cody's okay. A bit too talented and too pretty for his own good is all. But don't worry, I'm not letting Lucas go. I nearly lost him in that fire, and we wasted too many years getting here. Lucas and I were meant to be together. That's the only way to explain the twisted road we traveled to find each other."

Lucas pulled up at the curb as L.J. lit his smoke. Taking a puff, he spoke around the cigarette. "Twisted roads are the only ones worth driving."

Both Angela and L.J. stood and hugged. "Your grandmother would be proud of you," he said. "And so am I."

Angela nodded, but it was too damn early to cry, so she didn't chance any words of her own. She'd vowed not to leave town in tears. Not this time.

But she broke that promise. Not there on the curb with L.J., but a few minutes later when they turned down Main street.

The smoke-stained foundation of the Oasis sat directly across the highway from the concrete structure of the grain elevator where her dad had drawn his last breath, and the combination of the two brought on the tears she'd fought so hard to hold back. Her dad was gone, and wondering why or how all these years had done nothing but add to her pain. Nearly losing Lucas to that fire had taught her the why or how doesn't really matter.

She loved him. He loved her.

That was enough for today, for tomorrow.

# Acknowledgments

Twisted Roads was not the original title of this book, but it is an apt name. Not only for the characters, but the story itself. You see, I completed the original draft of this book many years ago, and much like the crooked path Lucas and Angela traveled to find each other, this novel took its time finding its way home. Because of the novel's extensive journey the list of people I need to thank is far too long to mention everyone deserving of a shout-out, but there are some I am compelled to name.

I wish to thank Jodi Thomas, for it was an assignment in one of her writing classes way back when that I first began to write this tale. From there, Hilary Sares took up the story's cause and guided me to improve upon it. Thank you Hilary for believing in my talents when few did. Vicky Schoen, we have indeed traveled a twisted road together in the pursuit of literary success. You have cheered me on, corrected my mistakes, and collaborated on just about everything I've ever written. I owe you a great debt for making me a better writer.

And of course, I want pledge much gratitude to the gang at this novel's original publisher, TAG Publishing for their unwavering faith in me and my writing. Special thanks to Jessika Carrier, and Andy Reyna for your unique contributions to the original cover and to Jere "Loudmouth" Tooley and Jostlynn Plums for this edition's cover. Kathy Lundberg, Albert and Karen Tanner, Arlene Tellman, Aaron and Kim Sage, Steve Austin and Joanne Brothwell, many thanks for reading early drafts, and letting me pick your brains. Sarah Stone did an amazing job of copy editing this edition and I assure you any lingering mistakes are either of my own choosing, or my undoing post edit. Contact Sarah at sastone83@gmail.com

Much like Lucas, I'm an avid fan of Texas/Alt-Country music, and I have been blessed to become friends with a few of these talented artists. My friend AJ Swope fielded a million questions while I was writing this book. He helped me get inside the head of a Texas singer songwriter and I will forever be indebted to him. Sadly, AJ was killed in a tragic car accident before I finished the final draft. It pains me he never got to read the complete story and it grieves me even more the world has been denied years of great, AJ Swope & The Last Train Home music. AJ you were a hell of a songwriter, a generous soul, and an inspiration. I will miss you my friend.

**www.makeajsmusicmatter.com**

I came to know the talented Zac Wilkerson via AJ. Zac, too, is a talented singer/songwriter and his songs never fail to spark my muse. Zac, I appreciate you answering my eleventh hour questions about music. More info about Zac, and his music can be found at ZacWilkersonmusic.com. Do yourself a favor and check out this talented musician.

Tarek and Zalen y'all will always been the best things I ever had a hand in creating.

And most of all, thanks to my loyal readers.

*PLEASE READ THE OPENING CHAPTER OF TRAVIS'S UPCOMING NOVEL*

...

**WAITING ON THE RIVER**

*FOUND AT THE BACK OF THIS BOOK.*

# About the Author

A native Texan, Travis lives in the Texas Panhandle. Travis writes both Women's Fiction and Humor. Travis is best known for his comedic coming-of-age memoir, THE FEEDSTORE CHRONICLES, and his long running blog where he pontificates, about both writing and life -- which for him means bacon, beer, and books.

### To learn more about Travis visit:
Amazon -- amazon.com/author/traviserwin
Twitter -- @traviserwin
Facebook -- facebook.com/TexasTravis
Blog -- traviserwin.com/blog

## Other Works Available

*The Feedstore Chronicles* available in print, ebook, and audio.

*Waiting On The River* coming May 2017 in print and ebook

*Whispers* available now exclusively on Kindle

# Waiting On The River

*Darkness fell early this time of year, and with it came both relief and a resolute comfort. For her it was not unlike the feeling of being tucked carefully into bed after a long, hard day. The cover of darkness meant this, her little corner of earth, was hidden away. Out of the spotlight. Logic told her Eagle's Rest, Idaho, was about as far from the spotlight as she could get, be it day or night, but Lindsay Parker struggled to relax no matter where she called home this month.*

*Each day she scrutinized not only the faces that stopped in at the Talon Cafe for a bite to eat, but also the license-plates of every strange car passing through. The latter being a new habit, picked up after coming here. Back in Seattle she would've gone crazy trying to maintain such a vigil, butthe remoteness here in Eastern Idaho held advantages. Still, she couldn't get too careless. Because here, there was no way to fade into the busy throng of city-life if someone came nosing around. Here, she was vulnerable in ways she'd never been. But here, she also felt a burgeoning hope, long absent in her travels becaseu in this out of the way place she was an actual part of something, not just another nameless faceless person in the crowd.*

*In Eagle's Rest she was not a stranger, and neither was anyone else. That combination made for all kinds of terrifying possibilities.*

*Her perch in the passenger seat of Cody's Jeep, afforded her a view of a good portion of the town as it lay along five or six blocks of Idaho State Highway 32, highway in name only. Ray Everham's blue heeler loped across the road, disappearing into the shadows beyond the glow of the town's sparse streetlights. The dog was only one of several that regulalry had the run of the town soon this Wednesday evening, there didn't appear to be a person, a vehicle, so much as a stray pooch out of place.*

*The plastic windows on Cody's CJ-7 did a poor job holding out the November chill, but Lindsay didn't mind. She liked the cold and was glad fall had given way to winter. Yet another thing that came early here, in the shadow of the Tetons, where dates on calendars didn't matter nearly as much as the arctic winds.*

*Outside the Jeep, Cody rubbed his gloved hands together and cupped them over his ears as he waited for his tank to fill. Unlike her, he often complained about the cold. Peculiar, given he was born and raised here in the Rockies, and had spent his winters outside working the ski lifts.*

*Where Lindsay grew up, they were lucky if it snowed once or twice a year.*

*Gassed and ready to get going, Cody cranked both the ignition and the heater before he even pulled the Jeep's door closed. "Swear to God I'm moving to California before next season."*

*Lindsay said nothing. She'd tried California. Southern, Northern and in-between without finding much of anything that made her want to go back.*

*Cody turned left out of Ray's Service Station. The wrong direction.*

*"I thought we were going to the movies?"*

*He shook his head. "Want to show you something first."*

*"What?"*

*Cody shook his head again.*

*A few minutes later he turned off the pavement and into the National Forest. They'd come out to this area often back in the summer, to hike or mountain bike, but this time of year snow covered the ground most places. The twin beams of his headlights provided the only light for as far as the eye could see.*

*"Unless we turn around we won't make it over to Driggs in time to catch the movie."*

*He mumbled something but kept driving down the dark gravel and increasingly snow-packed, road until he had to slow down after fishtailing around an icy, uphill bend.*

*"Where are we going?"*

*"I want to show you something," he repeated before adding, "but I might have to stop and lock in my hubs. Snow's deeper up here than I counted on."*

*"Just tell me where we're going."*

*"No. It's a surprise." He leaned forward to stare intently where his headlights stabbed through the darkness. He'd slowed way down, but still the Jeep slipped its way along, losing traction in the ever-increasing powder.*

*"Cody, this is stupid. We're going to get stuck out here." She gripped the sissy bar, dividing her attention between his tense face and the narrow, dark road. "And I'm not dressed to dig or push."*

*He grinned, but only for a second. "I've never been stuck in my life, but at least we'd have a good story to tell."*

*Cody was a horrible storyteller. He left out vital facts, rambled on getting off track often as not, and generally finished with broad assumptions based on the belief the rest of the world thought exactly as he did. Finding the point, or even the punchline, in his stories was like hunting a pine cone after a blizzard. Sure it was buried there somewhere, but never worth the effort it took to dig the thing up.*

*Just the fact he thought getting stuck in the snow -- on a pitch black night -- in the middle of nowhere, was anything but an exhibit of stupidity proved the point.*

*She could hear the old men now. Gathered at the counter of the Talon Cafe in the morning while she refilled their coffee mugs. Yeah Joe, I reckon down there in Tulsa there ain't no snow to get stuck in. She wasn't from Tulsa, but Lindsay was perfectly happy to let them be wrong on that front. But up here in God's country, He chooses to weed out the tourists and tree-huggers by making life a bit more challenging.*

*Joe, or Ray, or Stuart ... whoever happened to be within earshot would chime in, Yep, ain't everybody cut out to be an Ida-*

*hoan.*

*They'd say it all with a smile and in a very poor imitation of her Oklahoma twang, but Lindsay wasn't dumb. The verdict on her was still out with most everybody except Cody and Janine. The Talon's regulars liked her well enough, but not enough to overlook the fact she was a foreigner in their world. Never mind the fact it was a Cody, a lifelong resident and true-blue Idahoan, driving them straight to Stupidville.*

*"Stop!"*

*Cody hit the brakes. The CJ-7 angled sharp right. They slid a solid twenty yards, but stopped three feet shy of a massive pine.*

*"What the hell?" He looked at her like she'd lost her mind.*

*In a way she had, but Lindsay couldn't go along with this journey not one more second.*

*"I'm freaked out, confused, and just a little pissed off  you brought me out here this time of night when I thought we were going to the movie."*

*Cody was back to grinning, but she wasn't through. "It's not funny. When we get stuck.  Not if, but when. Because if you keep barreling blind down this stupid, dark-ass road we certainly will get stuck. It won't be you forced to listen to every old man in town say, 'Damn Janine, these eggs are slimier this morning than a Targhee road come November.' They won't even mention your damn name. It will be mine, the tree-hugging, vegan, Southern girl that hears all about it."*

*He laughed. "Ahh hell, Linds, everybody is over that tree hugging, vegan stuff. We all figured out quick enough you weren't like that idiot you came here. He --"*

*Jabbing her finger at Cody she cut him off. "And if they do mention your name it will be Ray Everham saying something like, 'You and Cody shoulda gotta room at the Kozy-Inn. Hell, I'll set you up a cot in the g'rage of the Fill'n Station if you need a place that bad. Got a barrel of lube there and everything.'" Even though she was trying to be funny, Lindsay still didn't like the fact Cody just kept grinning that stupid smile of his that displayed the small chip in his right front tooth. It made him look even younger than the twenty-five he'd just turned last week. Still four years and a few months younger than she.*

*"Quit staring at me, and turn this damn thing around."*

*He shook his head. "Can't. You're too gorgeous for me to even look away."*

*She rolled her eyes.*

*"I like when you get all stoked up and your cheeks turn red."*

*"It's too dark in here for you to see my cheeks."*

*"It's not that dark."*

*He was right. What with his radio display, and the Jeep's headlights reflecting off the pine's large trunk, and the snow all around it wasn't near as dark inside the Jeep as it was down the stretch of road and surrounding forest. Still his flattery wasn't going to lead her where she didn't want to go.*

*"Wipe that look off your face, because if you think for a second I'm going to give Ray Everham's innuendos credence out here in the middle of this frozen damn forest, you're even crazier than he is."*

*Cody shrugged and dropped his voice a few octaves to say, "I'm here. You're here. There's not another soul around for miles."*

*"Turn the Jeep around."*

*"Your loss," he grinned and shifted in reverse. But the grin faded when the back wheel spun without grabbing hold. He tried a few more times. The CJ-7 rocked but didn't move.*

*He put his hands up at her pained expression. "Relax. I just have to lock in the hubs. We'll be out of here in minute." A wave of frigid air rushed in when he stepped out into the dark roadway.*

*Folding her arms across her chest, Lindsay stared beyond the pine tree right in front of her, out into the forest. Snow crystals glimmered under the headlights giving the scene the look of a fancy Christmas card.*

*Cody crossed in front of the Jeep, blocking the light for a sec-*

ond, thereby spoiling her respite from reality. If they got stuck out here all night, he dang sure wouldn't be singing "Winter Wonderland."

He crouched down by the front wheel for a minute before coming around to her side and opening her door. "Take the wheel for a second. I just wanna give a little push to make sure we get out." He stood back to let her get out of the Jeep. Using his teeth he pulled the glove off of his right hand as he stepped into the glow of the headlights.

Only in that half-a-heartbeat it took for him to drop to one knee, did Lindsay realize getting stuck in the snow was the least of her problems tonight.

Past experience should have made it easier for her to react. But no, she stood there -- helpless, hopeless, heartless -- and silently watched Cody pull that small velvet box from his pocket.